TINY LITTLE TROUBLES

Also by Marc Lecard

Vinnie's Head

TINY LITTLE TROUBLES

Marc Lecard

ST. MARTIN'S MINOTAUR ✄ NEW YORK

TINY LITTLE TROUBLES. Copyright © 2008 by Marc Lecard. All rights reserved. Printed in the United States of America. For information, address St. Martin's Press, 175 Fifth Avenue, New York, N.Y. 10010.

www.minotaurbooks.com
www.stmartins.com

Library of Congress Cataloging-in-Publication Data

Lecard, Marc.
    Tiny little troubles / Marc Lecard.—1st ed.
        p.   cm.
    ISBN-13: 978-0-312-36022-1
    ISBN-10: 0-312-36022-3
    1. Adultery—Fiction.   2. Scientists—Fiction.   3. San Francisco (Calif.)—Fiction.
I. Title.
    PS3612.E334T56   2008
    813'.6—dc22

                                         2008013628

First Edition: August 2008

10 9 8 7 6 5 4 3 2 1

To Jane, for putting up with it all

ACKNOWLEDGMENTS

Thanks to Michael Homler, editor extraordinaire, and to copy editor Art Gatti for putting me on my mettle, making me defend my choices, and saving me from innumerable potentially humiliating boneheaded mistakes. And thanks once again to managing editor Amelie Littell, designer David Rotstein, publisher Andrew Martin, and all the production folk at St. Martin's for making me look good, which is not an easy job. Especial thanks to cover artist Philip Pascuzzo for pimping out the bots.

Readers who want to know more about nanotechnology can start with *Engines of Creation* by K. Eric Drexler (Anchor Books, 1990). And to make yourself nostalgic for the good old days when nanotechnology merely threatened all life on the planet, read the remarkable tome *The Singularity is Near* by Ray Kurzweil (Penguin Books, 2005).

Any errors, misinterpretations, mystifications, or misunderstandings are, of course, all my own doing.

TINY LITTLE TROUBLES

1

The Edge

Pablo Clench was bored.

His shift over, Clench leaned on the bar at the Honeybuzzard in North Beach, sucking down a few tequilas before heading home. The alcohol seemed to be having zero effect on his downer mood.

Being night shift floor manager in one of Jimmy Cacapoulos's San Francisco strip clubs was a pretty good gig, he supposed. Plenty of people would think so; he used to think so himself. Seeing dozens of women bare-ass naked every day had its plusses. He got to bust heads now and then—not as much as when he worked as a bouncer, but enough to keep his hand in. And there were plenty of opportunities to make a little extra cash, what with the girls, who usually had personal problems that could be exploited, and the lust-crazed clientele, their never very outstanding judgment further clouded by waving tits and booty.

But it was getting old.

Clench's experience had been, if you've seen one bare butt you've seen 'em all. After being around constantly naked women a while, the thrill wore off. It got to be like herding cattle.

Electric cattle prod, that's what I need. Clench's flagging interest level revived briefly. *Show 'em who's boss.*

But it wouldn't work. The girls'd complain, go to Jimmy, who protected his strippers—within limits—the way he'd protect any other investment. Jimmy wouldn't want them shocked and tasered, maybe flopping around the floor in some kind of seizure, or having heart attacks.

So that was no good. Fuck the cattle prod.

But there had to be something he could do that would bring back the old savor, the edgy sense that he was in charge and making things happen, the feeling that the world was a big piggy bank stuffed with change and he was the hammer, about to break it open and get paid.

There was a quarter-size puddle of tequila in the bottom of his glass. Clench killed it, licked the inside of the glass, thought about getting another shot. Nah. It was shit tequila anyway, the same stuff they served the customers. Nothing behind the bar was worth a can of robot piss.

Clench levered himself off the bar and walked toward the door. The bartender, busy adding up the night's receipts and calculating how much he could safely skim, didn't even look up. Two of the strippers, winding down after their shift, watched him warily from the end of the bar, but Clench ignored them.

Outside the club it was dark and cold, the bone-chilling cold of sea wind blowing through a fog bank. No traffic on Broadway, only a few losers straggling along on the dirty sidewalks. The neon signs of the other strip clubs—but not Cacapoulos clubs, Jimmy was very careful about his electricity bill—flashed and glowed further down the street toward Columbus.

Another shitty night. Clench wasn't sleepy. In fact he felt like beating the crap out of someone, just for fun, but the bars were closed already and it was just too much trouble to go looking for an after-hours place.

Maybe it was time, Clench thought, to go see some people he

hadn't seen in a while, catch up on the news, find out what was going on. You never knew; might be something he could take advantage of.

He thought about some of his old girlfriends. Most of them had left town without telling him where they were going. A few were in jail, or dead.

But there was always Aphrodite.

Aphrodite Anderson had never been his girl, really. She was Jimmy Cacapoulos's mistress; Clench had only fucked her to even things up between him and his boss.

Then he remembered: Tonight was one of Jimmy's nights at Aphrodite's. Whew, close call. The thought of accidentally seeing his boss's naked buttocks—or any other body part—was enough to put Clench off sex for a month, or longer. Forever.

Plus, Jimmy would be pissed if he caught Clench sniffing around, and it was never a good idea to get Jimmy pissed off.

So fuck it, Clench thought. *I'll just go home, smoke some weed, get a couple hours shut-eye.*

Tomorrow, though, tomorrow he would try to scare up something new and profitable.

For sure.

2

Better Living
Through Robots

Aaron Rogell looked out over the shabby figures scattered around the unfinished cafeteria of the start-up. Maybe it hadn't been a good idea to have the first press conference in such a big room. The half-dozen or so media people seemed lost in it. With a twinge of disappointment, Rogell saw that there wasn't a single television news crew present.

"Who do we have, Sasha?"

Sasha Goode, the PR liaison, was sweating and hesitant. He knew it was a bad turnout.

"The SF Daily Mockery is here," he said, leading with his best shot. Unfortunately it was his only shot. "A couple alt weeklies from the East Bay, *Good News*—"

"*Good News*, Sasha?" Rogell interrupted. "*Good News*?"

The sweat ran faster down Goode's spine. *Good News* was a Christian bimonthly from somewhere in far Contra Costa County, probably there under the impression that nanotechnology had something to do with abortion.

Goode didn't reveal that two of the cafeteria chairs were occupied by bloggers.

"A radio station," he said brightly, failing to mention that it was a college station with a broadcast radius measurable in city blocks. "They asked to interview you afterward."

Rogell sighed. In a way this was good, he thought. No sense in attracting too much interest right away. He reminded himself that all this was preparation, seeding, a softening up of public opinion. When he was ready for the real thing, he'd get everyone's attention, no doubt about it.

Rogell had planned the emergence of his invention carefully. Genetically Modified Organisms had had a rough time of it, he knew, because, one, the developers hadn't done the research to show people the technology was safe; and two, they had tried to keep people from finding that out. Naturally, people were suspicious: What were these guys hiding?

His guys, of course, were potentially very scary. He knew this. He knew that tiny little robots you couldn't even see, moving atoms around in molecules like crates in a warehouse, would scare the shit out of people once they understood the implications. There had already been plenty of sensationalist fiction and cheesy made-for-TV movies about nanotech.

He sighed again, causing shivers of job-loss fear to run up Sasha Goode's legs and back.

"All right," Rogell said. "Let's get started."

Rogell had no fear at all of public speaking. He liked the multiplication of his personality by many listeners—not that many this time, of course, but still . . .

"The problem with nanotechnology is a simple one, in a way," Rogell was saying. The press had settled back in its chairs, prepared for a long and incomprehensible explanation.

"Making molecule-scale robots is relatively easy now. But to be effective there have to be a lot of them."

"How many?" asked the reporter from the Daily Mockery. He alone of the assembled press was wearing a tie.

"Billions," Rogell said. "Trillions, even. Now, you might ask yourself, how do you make trillions of robots, each one smaller than the point of a pin?"

The reporters were silent, frozen, staring back at him like a crate of hypnotized gerbils.

"Okay, how?" the Daily Mockery asked finally.

Rogell paused and smiled. This was as close to his big secret as he would allow the masses to approach.

"They make themselves," he said. "Unlike living things, which are subject to random mutation, my creations are responsible for their own evolution." Rogell tried not to look too godlike. "Utilizing a process of directed evolution, each generation creates the one that follows, each generation lasting only minutes, seconds. Until at last, the penultimate generation builds my working nanorobot horde. The workers of the future."

"What stops the process?" the reporter wanted to know. "Why don't they keep on evolving and replicating?"

A reasonable, even intelligent question. "As I said, this process is not true evolution, not, that is, random mutation selected by adaptive advantage. I guide the process. And I design a limit—the end of history, as it were—into it. The final generation does its job—and dies.

"I've given my robots memory—like the memory chip in your computer, but much, much smaller. The robots are walking memory chips. This allows them to be programmed for simple functions. And I've given them the ability to use heat as a fuel source—thermal actuators."

"How much heat?" the reporter from the Mockery asked.

"Not much. The heat of an incandescent bulb. The heat of the sun on an unusually hot day."

"Body heat?"

Rogell smiled dismissively. "In the unlikely event of my nanorobots being introduced into the human body, yes, body heat would allow them to function."

"How do you do all this?" the reporter asked. "What's the mechanism, I mean?"

Rogell smiled smugly.

"Trade secret, I'm afraid."

After the press conference Rogell strode rapidly through the vast empty spaces of the main—and so far only—Rogeletek building. The reek of wallboard, Spackle, and drying paint filled his nostrils. Gray office partitions stood like rows of dominos, waiting to be moved into position. Cables snaked across the bland gray industrial carpet.

He had the building and the backing, Rogell thought. Now all he needed was the people.

The core guys, of course, were in place, or nearly. Commitments had been made; many of his colleagues had been eager to leave academia and sign on to his start-up (even though their compensation leaned heavily on stock options). No one had forgotten the brief, glorious summer of the tech boom. Everyone knew at least one person who had "gotten out in time," and whose time was now his or her own, unanswerable to imbecile bosses, to committees or interfering administrations. Everyone knew in their hearts that the boom would come again, and this time they planned to be ready.

Other personnel—support staff—would be easy enough to hire, Rogell thought. After all, wasn't the twin-bladed scythe of downturn and outsourcing still slicing through the Bay Area? There would be plenty of people glad to work for whatever he decided to pay them.

The press conference and the prep leading up to it had left Rogell feverish and keyed up. He realized he hadn't had sex for a week, the longest dry spell since he had gotten out of high school. No wonder he'd been beating off so much lately.

Guilt washed over him. Amanda—his wife—was waiting at the house. She loved him—he knew that. But since the baby, he had developed a problem there.

It wasn't that he didn't find her attractive, though some of the body changes brought about by pregnancy had appalled him at the time. But the thought of making love to her, putting his thing in the same place his daughter had come from, suddenly wasn't a possibility anymore. It was like taking his equipment out in a daycare center and waving it around. It just felt wrong. He couldn't do it.

At least not often.

Rogell quickened his pace, pushed through an exit door, and jogged across the parking lot to a red Mercedes convertible. He hopped in the Mercedes and peeled off of the nearly empty parking lot, managing to beat several members of the press to the freeway.

The massive green shoulder of San Bruno Mountain loomed over the packed, bustling cars. Up on the side of the mountain, on a sub-peak that stuck out toward Oakland, Rogell could see his new house, all alone, the first and last one on its street. (The costly permit stretching and extensive bribery that had allowed the house to be built in that particular spot would surely never be repeated.) The money from his patent sales had paid for it, with some left over.

He hadn't used any of his own money for the start-up, of course. Backers put up the capital. And there was a sizeable bank loan.

He was in hock, he knew, up to his chin—well past it, really. But aside from an occasional twinge of anxiety, his faith in the future was absolute.

All he needed was to get laid.

3

Blowing Off Steam

Through the long windows in the big main room of the Rogell mini-mansion, Amanda Rogell, née McClanahan, looked out over San Francisco Bay toward the East Bay hills, Mount Diablo looming behind them. It was really an ugly view, she thought, a shapeless litter of freeways, cars, and housing, strewn over the rolling hills like the clutter in a teen bedroom.

Somewhere down there in the twisting intestines of the highway system, she knew Aaron was making his way back to her. It still surprised her that this made her glad. Amanda had spent most of her life since she was twelve freeing herself from any kind of dependence on other people, but now one of her constant thoughts concerned someone else. Where was Aaron? How was he doing? Was he happy? When will he be coming home? Amanda found this hard to get used to.

A slight vocal sound, unrecognizable as human by anyone but a mother, drifted out of a white plastic speaker on a nearby table. Amanda tilted her head toward the crib monitor and listened intently. Rustling and faint cooing noises let her know that her daughter, Delia, was awake now and talking to herself.

Having a child was something else she hadn't counted on. The worst part was that she had wanted to become pregnant. That hadn't ever been part of her plan, but suddenly, unexpectedly, she had wanted to, and just as suddenly it was reality.

Aaron had seemed to expect her to want an abortion—he didn't push it, but after all, it was what anyone who knew her would have expected, what she would have expected herself. She had her career—she was making a name for herself as a brilliant, unstoppable defense attorney, the kind that inevitably gets described as "high-powered." And Amanda had never been someone who put up with being tied down. "Don't fence me in" had been her motto for as long as she could remember.

But all her plans had changed in an instant when she got pregnant and decided that she wanted the baby. In the back of her mind resentments and frustrations lurked, like monsters hiding behind the new, as-yet-unused playset. A whole lifetime of planning and aspiring knocked aside in an instant by cellular division; sandbagged by biology—things were not working out as she had thought they would.

But that didn't seem to matter anymore. Amanda just hoped she could surf ahead of all the bad stuff and hold on to what she wanted. And right now what she wanted was to be a mother.

Aaron was another surprise. When she had first met him in college, she thought he was good-looking, smart, just a little full of himself—but she'd had no use for these qualities, or any others, at that point in her life. She lost sight of him for a while—in the vortex of law school, other human beings had become distant, annoying presences, and she had had no time for relationships. But some years later, when a friend reintroduced them at a party, the feeling between them clicked into place.

When they first got together they made love three or four times a day. It was basically all they did for a while. The first week was a blur of body parts and rolling; in memory, it seemed like one long screw. Now of course, with the baby and his job pressures, they were lucky if they made love three or four times a month. If that.

The Mercedes buzzed up to the front of the house. Within seconds Aaron was in the house, nervous, jumpy, as if dancing on hot rocks.

He bounced over to her, kissed her on the cheeks, her neck, on the lips with a little thrust of tongue.

"Mmm," she said, pushing him away gently. "Did it go all right?"

Aaron's eyes were momentarily blank; clearly he wasn't tracking. She saw the split second he recovered himself, one PowerPoint slide replacing another.

"Great!" he said. "It went great. Not much coverage, but it's early in the campaign. It'll pick up."

"Did you make the points you wanted to? About it being safe?"

Aaron's lust fell back far enough for him to look smug.

"Yeah," he said, grinning tightly, "I made them. I actually think they understood me this time. I put it in terms a child of seven could have understood."

Amanda smiled and put her arms around his neck.

"Sure that isn't too advanced for them?"

Encouraged by her embrace—although he never needed much encouragement—Aaron nuzzled her neck and put his hands around her waist. Amanda permitted this, though she wasn't feeling sexy and doubted she could be made to. But when she felt a tongue in her ear, she moved away from him.

"Amanda . . . ," Aaron began hoarsely, moving after her.

The white plastic crib monitor added itself to the negotiations at this point. A loud wail of hunger or discomfort came through the small speaker, distorted and amplified until it sounded like wind keening in barren, rocky peaks. Amanda's head turned toward the sound. Then without a look or a word to Aaron she rushed out of the room.

"You have to go out again?" Disappointment surged through Amanda like a kind of seasickness.

"Sorry. A dinner meeting with Vitek." Vitek was one of the angels whose backing made Rogeletek possible. A vegan, career hypochondriac, deep adept of the hidden-germ theory, and something of a recluse, Vitek hated eating with anyone else present. He had dined alone for fifty years.

Amanda had no idea of this. As far as she knew, Vitek was intensely convivial, a rollicking bon vivant who had dinner with her husband at least once a week.

"Well, be careful coming home, Aaron. You know how much you always drink at these dinners. Take a cab if you have to."

"Don't worry," Rogell answered, shrugging his coat back on. "I'll be fine."

Rogell knew he shouldn't be doing this. For one thing: Amanda. If she found out it would devastate her. Rogell hated the thought of that. He did truly love Amanda and would have done anything not to hurt her.

Almost anything.

But he had to. Had to do this. He needed to. He wanted to. His dick had a mind of its own. Sex thoughts filled his head, got in the way of his real thinking, gummed up his planning. Rogell worried that the pornographic visions reeling across his mental screen nearly constantly would suddenly become visible to other people, that wires would cross and he would suddenly find himself in a meeting with staff—or worse, with moneymen—babbling and drooling about nates and bubbas, cunts and tongues and multiple penetrations. Even thinking about worrying about it made him hot. It was hopeless and endlessly involving.

He had to.

Besides, Rogell recited his litany of excuses to himself as he drove, *it's not like it really meant anything*. There was no emotional content; it was mere physical relief. Blowing off steam.

And he would never be caught, anyway.

Just driving toward San Francisco gave him a hard-on. Rogell wondered if he could get away with a quick pull, but it was still much too light out for that, with the top down.

He wondered if there was enough time to stop off in the Tenderloin for a blow job, just to settle him down before the serious business of the night.

But it was way too late for that. He'd promised Aphrodite—his regular go-to girl, his (though he hesitated to call her this) mistress—that he'd be at her place by seven. He'd even made dinner reservations.

Vitek would have to dine without him one more time. Rogell had more urgent issues on his plate.

4

Taking Care of Business

Aphrodite Anderson's condo was in a gorgeous thirties building, an art deco masterpiece stuck in the high side of Russian Hill like a four-story sugar cube. Rogell wondered how she managed to pay for it. An inheritance, maybe.

Aphrodite answered the doorbell and buzzed him in. The entry stairs swooped around in a Hollywood fantasia of elegance and speed-lined futurity. Rogell always expected hordes of Busby Berkeley maidens to descend the staircase in swimsuits, smiling brightly, flowing around him as he climbed to Aphrodite's apartment. But only art deco ghosts breathed past him in the gold-flecked mirrors that lined the stairwell.

Aphrodite was waiting in the open door of the condo for him, leaning lasciviously against the door frame. She had the subtle body language of an ex-pole dancer, which she was.

Rogell could smell her from halfway down the stairs, an overpowering aroma of musk, woman, and expensive designer fabrics.

A new note had been added to the symphony of smells, a sort of barnyard, dunghill reek. Rogell sniffed appreciatively.

"Something new?"

Aphrodite beamed. She loved it when Aaron noticed her latest purchases. She swirled, model-like. A thin leather coat floated out around her, broadcasting the barnyard smell.

"Do you like it? I bought it just today! A real leather wrapper, made of genuine goatskin, signed by Sebastien Manichea!"

"Lovely," Rogell said, fingering the thin, smelly garment. "It doesn't have any buttons, though."

"Oh, Aaron!" Aphrodite laughed at his geeky scientist cluelessness. "It's not supposed to have buttons. Now come on in and sit down while I finish getting ready. I can't wait to eat; I'm starving!"

Rogell was starving also, though in a different way. He sat down and made himself be patient.

"Where are we going, anyway?" Aphrodite called from her bedroom, wrestling on earrings as large and complicated as chandeliers.

"I made reservations at Caveat's, down on the waterfront," Rogell yelled back. "It's a new place, very hip. You'll like it."

Aphrodite didn't answer; she was frowning into the mirror as she struggled with the heavy earring. "Down on the waterfront" probably meant a fish place: squid heads, whole anchovies, dead things in shells. Aphrodite hated fish. She hoped they had something she could eat. Maybe a salad.

"Oh, okay," she said dubiously. "Did you call a cab?"

"I have the Mercedes," Rogell said. "There's valet parking. We could walk, though. It's only five or six blocks."

Since Aphrodite had been promoted from strip club dancer to rich man's plaything, she had tried to avoid leaving her apartment except to shop, and then she always took cabs. Asking her to walk six blocks (and then back—uphill!) was like asking her to climb Mount Everest on her hands and knees, in the buff. Not going to happen.

"Let's take the car, Aaron."

Rogell had hoped to walk behind her and watch her ass muscles moving under her clingy dress, but there was a lot to be said for speed and efficiency. They would get back to her bedroom that much faster.

"Sure thing. Top up or down?"

What a question: *Her hair!*

"Up, please."

"Whatever your little heart desires," Rogell said.

There were plenty of meat things on the menu at Caveat's, so Aphrodite was happy.

"What are prairie oysters?"

"You'd like them. Why don't you order some?"

Aphrodite shuddered delicately. "I hate seafood. I think I'll get a steak."

Rogell watched, fascinated as Aphrodite tore into her filet mignon with the energy and finesse of a wolverine dispatching an elk carcass.

As did so many things for Rogell, Aphrodite's table manners had strong erotic overtones. He was glad now that they had come in the Mercedes; walking back would have taken much too long, and he might have had to screw her in an apartment vestibule. He could hardly concentrate on his dinner, good—and expensive—as it was.

A white-coated valet ran off to fetch Rogell's car from its illegal sidewalk parking spot. Aphrodite and Rogell lingered outside the restaurant, savoring the chilly, foggy dampness after the overheated dining room.

Rogell noticed a broad-shouldered man in the shadows who seemed to be staring at them. Periodically the man took a drag on his cigarette and the glowing tip lit up a pair of eyes squinting in their direction.

"Know that guy? Over there?" Rogell dipped his head toward the man in the shadows.

Aphrodite smiled blankly and looked the other way, then gave a quick, glance at the man.

"Who? The parking valet? No, I never saw him before. Why, do you know him?"

"I thought he was looking at us."

"Probably angling for a tip," Aphrodite theorized. She stared fixedly in front of her, smiling at a telephone pole.

Rogell looked back cautiously. The man was still staring at them. He had moved, so that one shoulder and part of his head were lit up by one of the pink lights flanking the restaurant entrance. Rogell got a quick glimpse of a squinting eye framed by long hair, lit by the red glare of the cigarette. Then the man moved into the shadow again and Rogell lost sight of him.

"Well, he won't get one from me," Rogell said. "Where the hell is my car, anyway?"

Climbing the stairs to Aphrodite's apartment, watching her magnificent musculature shift and ripple under her expensive clothes, Rogell felt his cock stiffen and strain against his trousers. Guilty thoughts of Amanda blew over him like wisps of fog.

Then at the top of the stairs Aphrodite turned around and smiled at him invitingly. His mind went obligingly blank. He followed her into the apartment.

After a long, athletic session of lovemaking and a brief recovery period, Rogell and Aphrodite lounged around in her living room. The lights of North Beach and Telegraph Hill spread out below them.

Suddenly smacking himself on the forehead, Rogell lept up from the sofa and trotted back into the bedroom, where most of his belongings were lying. He reappeared holding a slim box, expensively gift-wrapped.

"I almost forgot," Rogell said. "These are for you." He handed Aphrodite the box. She accepted it demurely, thinking, too light for jewelry. She resisted a strong urge to shake the box. Opening it, she lifted out several pieces of fabric.

"Thank you, Aaron!" she breathed. "Thongs!" *Underwear?* she thought. *What are you, my mother?* Not that her mother had ever given her thongs, but still . . .

"You look good in a thong," Rogell said. Thinking of the back string of a thong bisecting her ass cheeks, disappearing into the smooth cleft, he felt himself getting hard again. "But it's not just the thongs. It's how I made them. Would you like to see?"

"You made these?"

Rogell nodded.

"Well, okay, yeah," Aphrodite said uncertainly. "I'd like to see."

"I can take you on a tour of the lab tonight."

"What, right now?" Aphrodite was naked under her filmy dressing gown, and, well, smelly. She was much too lazy to even think of showering and getting dressed at this time of night.

Rogell grinned, swept up by his own impulsiveness. "That's right, now. Come as you are. It'll be fun."

"Like this? I'll catch cold! Someone will see us!"

"Throw on a coat. No one will see us. Come on!"

Whoopee, Aphrodite thought, *die of pneumonia touring an underwear factory.* But she wanted very much to humor Aaron; she had a big purchase coming up, and her other friends were poor-mouthing her to death. She hoped to catch him in one of his expansive, generous moods.

"Okay Aaron. If you say so," she said. A strange shiver of exhibition-ism ran through her as she thought of going out in public naked. She had never minded dancing in public; but that was different, that was performance. This was personal, and a little kinky.

"Maybe it'll be fun!"

"I'll see to that," Rogell leered.

The lab was the only part of Rogeletek that was truly completed, but it was the most important part, the beating heart of his business. Enor-mous stainless steel tanks loomed in temperature-controlled rooms be-hind thick Plexiglas. Long tables filled immense hangarlike spaces, covered with computers and arcane laboratory equipment. Mysterious control panels and flat-screen monitors covered one wall.

Rogell beamed, thinking how overwhelming all this would be to someone seeing it for the first time.

"What do you think? This is my laboratory."

Aphrodite was dimly impressed, but mostly cold. Her feet were bare, and the dressing gown barely existed. If it weren't for the floor-length fur coat she had thrown on at the last minute she would have frozen to death in the lab's aggressively air-conditioned microclimate.

"It's nice," she said. "Is it always this cold?"

"Well, it has to be for the bots to be quiescent, and the equipment to work properly," Rogell explained.

"This floor is really cold," Aphrodite complained.

Rogell glanced down at her bare feet.

"Here, let me carry you." He regretted his offer once Aphrodite was in his arms; there was little fat on her frame, but six feet of well-conditioned dancer muscle took Rogell to the limit of his physical strength. He felt strange things happening in the small of his back.

The minifactory of nanobots he was about to show Aphrodite was his secret pride and joy, built for one purpose and one purpose only. It was his own personal science project, the first proof his theory would work in practice, the first demonstration model of the nanorobot assembler horde.

Thong city.

Barely out of graduate school, he had programmed those first bots to make themselves, then make thong underwear. The bots had provided him with a last-minute Valentine's Day gift, avoiding relationship difficulties and advancing materials science at the same time. He'd tinkered with the bots, improved the program, developed their capabilities, but left thongs as the ultimate product. The first financial backers had been a bit surprised when Rogell had demonstrated his bot horde, but had put it down to the mild eccentricity of a creative type.

The start-up, of course, would not be making thong underwear. The main product would be a new kind of cloth, its molecules precisely ordered, water resistant, feather light, so tough it could only be made into garments by other nanobot hordes (which Rogell would supply). Afterward, once more capital was found and a new facility built, the hydrogen-cracking bots would get to work.

The beauty of all this was that none of the actual manufacturing would be done by Rogeletek. The bots would be made there; the application would happen somewhere else. Rogell would show manufacturers how to get set up, supply them with bot workers, and sit back as the market expanded—a market ultimately dependent on his creations.

But Rogell would always have a soft spot in his heart for the original, lingerie-generating horde.

Rogell carried Aphrodite through the lab—it was as cold as a meat locker—and put her down by the door to a small room off to one side of the steel tanks. This was Rogell's private, personal lab. The security lock on the door opened only to his voice command.

"Honeypot," he whispered into the plastic grill. Aphrodite was a few feet away, looking bored. He didn't think she could hear him.

Except for its size, Rogell's lab looked exactly like the rooms outside to Aphrodite. She was beginning to really shiver now and wondering why on earth she had agreed to come.

"What is this?"

Rogell smiled and swept out his arms to encompass the sterile, brightly lit room.

"My personal laboratory. My chamber of miracles. Would you like to see how I made your thongs?"

"Sure," Aphrodite said miserably. She just wanted to get this over with.

"Come over here."

He led her by the arm to a long, low table on the other side of the room. A case of some sort, made of metal, plastic, and Plexiglas, took up the entire tabletop. The device looked something like a very long steel attaché case with windows in it.

"Et voilà!"

Aphrodite frowned. She had come all the way here to see this?

"Voilà what?"

"This is the thong factory. This"—he put a hand on a portion of the device—"is where my assemblers stay when they're not working. A kind of barracks for robots."

"Robots?" She couldn't see any fucking robots. Aphrodite was beginning to suspect this was some kind of stupid trick, a practical joke. And if that's what it turned out to be, then look out.

"Robots too tiny to see with the naked eye. But smart enough to move atoms around in molecules, and put them where I tell them to."

"If they're too tiny to see," Aphrodite asked reasonably, "how do I know they're there?"

"By what they make. Watch." Rogell flipped up a panel at one end of the device and activated several switches. Soft whishing noises came from within. "All I have to do is release the bots into the fabrication chamber," he flipped another set of switches, "introduce a supply of silicon—the basic feedstock—and then—it's so simple, really—warm them up and turn them loose!"

Through the Plexiglas panels Aphrodite could see several coils of wire begin to glow red. A pile of something that looked like gray sand lay in the middle of the thing. She couldn't see any robots, no matter how much she squinted up close to the Plexiglas.

She noticed that the sand stuff was beginning to swirl around, as if hidden air jets were blowing it. The sand rose up into the air in a cloud that seemed to swim into itself. Then it settled down, and she saw a thong lying there, where no thong had been before.

"Wow!" she said, forgetting to shiver. "That was cool!"

Rogell basked.

"You made them do that?"

He nodded. "A simple program, or series of programs, actually, for the different categories of bot. Miners, assemblers, finishers. It begins in biology and ends in engineering. Simple rules, simple programs, limited functions. Controlled interactions, *yes/no, if/then.* The result is something of far more complexity than you would imagine, from the inputs."

Aphrodite smiled as prettily as she could. He had lost her at "program."

Rogell saw the blank look on Aphrodite's face and tried another tack. Thinking ahead to more media interviews (they would come), he was trying to come up with a radically simplified, nonthreatening explanation of what he was doing, something anyone, even the president, could understand.

"Do you remember those Walt Disney cartoons? Those mice, with pants on, and little gloves?"

Aphrodite nodded. Now she was on solid ground.

"Remember the little white gloves they wore? You do? What was peculiar about those gloves?"

Aphrodite shrugged.

"They only had three fingers. Right? Well, my robots have three fingers on each hand, like a Mickey Mouse glove: a positive finger, a negative finger, and a neutral finger. By programming them to exchange the charges as the situation requires, I can make them pick atoms up and put them down. Do you understand now?"

"Like a flea circus!" Aphrodite enthused. She wasn't really tracking with the mice.

Rogell deflated slightly. He popped open another panel on the side of the factory and turned a small knob. The thong moved along as if carried by a cortege of fleas, and was deposited in a chamber at the far end. A small panel came down and hid the thong from view.

"Chill it to deactivate any stray nanobots." Rogell thumbed another button, resulting in interior hissing sounds. "Blow off the workers—an important step. You don't want any of these guys hanging around afterwards."

Another button, then another, and a small panel slid open. Rogell reached inside, pulled out the thong, and handed it to Aphrodite.

"Whoa!" she said, fumbling it. "It's cold as ice!"

"It'll warm up. Try it on," Rogell urged.

But Aphrodite's mind had moved to other possibilities.

"If you can make underwear out of a pile of sand, what else can you make?"

Rogell smirked and shrugged modestly.

"I can make anything. What did you have in mind?"

"What about diamonds? Can you make diamonds?"

Rogell nodded. "In theory. Yes, of course I can. I can make anything, given the proper materials." He smiled and shook his head. "The ancient alchemists were right, after all. You can change matter. You can change lead into gold."

Aphrodite didn't know or particularly give a shit about the ancient alchemists. But she liked diamonds.

Wedged into the sofa like a throw pillow, Amanda jerked up from deep, warm sleep and began staggering toward the baby's room until she realized, in midstagger, that it was the cell phone ringing on the coffee table that had woken her up, not the crib monitor.

"Hello?" she said, eyes half closed, voice full of sleep.

"Amanda!"

It was Aaron. "Aaron, where are you?"

"In San Francisco. Look, the dinner broke up late. I had a little too much to drink, I guess—you know how Vitek is. Anyway, I'm going to stay at Jimmy's place in North Beach. I don't want to drive home in this condition. Okay?"

"Of course. Aaron, please be careful. Promise me you'll take a cab?"

"I promise. See you tomorrow. Love you."

"Love you too," she whispered to a dead phone.

"You called your wife?" Aphrodite asked.

Aaron ducked his head. "Yeh."

He seemed a little embarrassed, which amused her. Like she would care.

"Good boy," she said ambiguously.

At that moment they were speeding in the Mercedes down 101 just a little past and about three hundred feet beneath Amanda. The lights of his house above him had reminded Rogell that his wife and his baby were up there, Amanda probably waiting for him to call. Waves of guilt washed over him briefly. But having called and lied her back into a sense of security, he felt better.

When they got back to Aphrodite's place they were both starving. Even though it was late, Aaron stopped in an all-night Safeway and bought a bag of delicatessen stuff: olives, cheeses, and breads. And little bottles of bubbly. They spread the tablecloth on the floor in front of the fireplace and had a nice little picnic. Aaron kept looking at her bare legs and feet sticking out from under the fur coat—Aphrodite had been chilled to the bone by the lab climate, and kept the coat on—until she thought he was going to lean over and bite pieces out of them.

He didn't though. The whole thing was kind of nice, Aphrodite thought. It didn't matter that Aaron had invited himself over for the night; she didn't have anyone coming in the morning. She could just relax and enjoy herself.

Aaron smiled greasily, a dot of potato salad in the corner of his mustache.

"Well, Aphrodite, here's to the beginning of a new era: abundance, universal prosperity, a really remunerative IPO. A time when our invisible servants will bring us the whole world at our command, tied up in nanotech ribbons!" He raised his plastic Champagne glass to her.

Aphrodite smiled uneasily. She liked Aaron, he was generous and everything. But he was weird. A lot of the time she just didn't get where he was coming from.

"Well, cheers," she said, toasting him with her Champagne.

Rogell smiled, staring back at her with hot, hungry eyes.

"Cheers," he said.

"May all your troubles be little ones," Aphrodite Anderson said.

5

Just Something
About Pablo

Aphrodite slept late the next morning, even later than usual. She had awoken briefly as Aaron was leaving, then sunk back into warm sleep before the door closed behind him.

She wouldn't have gotten up until after one if the phone hadn't started ringing at noon.

"Oh, fuck!" She must have forgotten to turn the answering machine on.

Aphrodite pulled a pillow around her head, blocking the sound a little. But whoever it was wouldn't give up. And it was hot with the pillow over her face, and she couldn't breathe.

She got up and stumbled to the phone.

"Who's your new boyfriend?" Pablo Clench's taunting voice jumped out of the phone at her the second she picked it up. A spasm of fear went through her, as it always did when she heard his voice.

"Pablo! What are you talking about?"

"I saw you!" Clench said playfully. "Outside Caveat's last night. Some dude with a mustache, looked like a high school science teacher."

Aaron would have hated that description.

"He's not a teacher. He's a real scientist."

"A scientist! He must be rich."

"How would you know?"

"You wouldn't be fucking him if he wasn't."

Sudden anger gave Aphrodite courage.

"Just leave me alone, Pablo! What are you hanging around for? You're going to screw things up for me. He is a nice guy, a scientist. He's not going to want to know people like you. Just stay away!"

"Guys like me, huh?" Clench didn't sound genuinely offended. "Well, I just happened to be there, chillin' with my good friend Rob, watching him park cars, moving some product to the restaurant customers. But don't worry. The next time I see you with a date, I'll put a bag over my head."

Aphrodite wanted to hang up, but was afraid of making him mad for real. Clench was serious bad news; she hated to think of him pissed off, especially at her.

"Pablo, please," she sighed. "Let me live my life, huh?"

"What do his scientist buds think of him porking a stripper?"

"I don't dance anymore, Pablo, you know that. My past is my own business."

Clench chortled. "That means they don't know. Maybe the guy doesn't even know. It would be too bad if anybody found out. Might take the gloss off a new romance."

"Aaron trusts me," Aphrodite said angrily. She was instantly sorry she had told Clench even as much as his first name.

"Aaron. Aaron," Clench repeated thoughtfully. "That's a nice name. Aaron."

"Pablo, just leave me alone. What do you want out of me?"

"I'll come over and tell you in person," Clench said. "You know it's been a while since I visited. You must be missing me."

This time Aphrodite slammed down the phone. But there was no avoiding Pablo Clench.

Back when she was dancing she had gone out with Pablo for a while. He was the manager of the strip club she was dancing at, and it had seemed like a good move, career-wise. Plus he seemed pretty cool, a laid-back, mellow guy with nice clothes, good drugs, and an expensive car.

That was before she got to know him well. And by then it was too late.

At first it had been kind of fun. Pablo liked to enjoy himself, which meant a lot of drinking and doping. It was a wild ride for a while.

Nothing seemed to affect Clench, no amount of whiskey or chemicals moved him off his center. He always looked the same, no staggering, slurring, no manic behavior. He was always just sitting there, watching everybody with a little smile, his eyelids at half-mast.

The only thing was, sometimes he would get incredibly mean, a focused, relentless meanness, like some kind of invasive surgery. Fortunately, these fits of cruelty were usually followed by sudden unconsciousness.

Once—Aphrodite forgot what they were taking—she had seen Pablo turn into this enormous, alien insect thing, a ten-foot praying-mantis-like creature with human eyes that got bigger and bigger until it was the biggest thing in the room, waving its insectoid, dagger-coated arms like a symphony conductor. The people she was with had to hold her down for a while and help her out of the club afterward.

Well, that was just the drugs, right? But even with all the mind-altering substances she had ingested over the years, no one else had ever turned into a monster bug. There was just something about Pablo.

And Pablo never let go of you. Ever. Not really. Once you let him into your life he was like a bad case of herpes. He kept showing up, usually at the very worst possible time.

Like now.

Aphrodite knew Pablo was curious about Aaron, knew he was wondering how he could get something out of the situation—money, leverage, fun. She knew he would keep coming around, pestering her, bullying her until he got what he was after.

And she knew she would give it to him

The problem was, he owned her. It wasn't just the money she owed, the gambling debt, or the drug money he fronted her, though that was a big one. She could probably pay that off if she coordinated donations from her boyfriends in the right way, so that nobody freaked out or got too big for his britches.

It was what he knew about her. Not so much her past—she didn't really try to hide that, wasn't ashamed of it. No one really gave a shit that she used to be a stripper; some of her guys even thought it was cool.

Her present was the problem. She usually tried to balance a couple boyfriends at a time, to help keep expenses down. It was three right now: Carl, the Montgomery Street guy; Aaron—he was her special sweetie; and Jimmy Cacapoulos, her ex-boss.

Cacapoulos was her least favorite, but in a way her easiest-to-maintain relationship. She didn't even have to screw him much; just feed him until he fell asleep, like a fat, greasy baby. And he was generous, like Aaron, unlike the cheap, fuckwad banker, whose days, now that she thought about it, were numbered anyway.

Aphrodite realized that neither Cacapoulos nor Pablo fucked her all that much. Carl either. Her boyfriends each wanted something else from her: Jimmy to be pampered and fussed over and fed; Carl, that she fawn over him and admire his big-swinging dick, executive macho; Pablo—well, it was never clear exactly what Pablo wanted. You only knew it was going to hurt.

Aaron made up for the lack of cocksmanship the other men displayed.

Aaron, her special little love machine. He was all about fucking. He was like the Energizer bunny with a nine-inch dick.

But none of these guys knew about the others. They all thought they were her one and only—well, except for Pablo, of course. And none of the others seemed like the type to handle it well if they found out they were part of a string.

And Pablo could tell them. Could and would. He would enjoy it.

The front door buzzed. She knew it was Pablo, but got up to let him in anyway. May as well get it over with, she thought.

Almost instantly there was a knock at her apartment door. How did he do that? He must take the stairs three at a time.

Pablo Clench was standing there, outside her door, a little, lopsided, close-mouthed grin, not breathing heavy or anything. As if punching the buzzer button had made him materialize on her doorstep.

"Pablo!" She gave it her best shot, putting her arms around him and kissing the air six inches from his head. "How are you?"

Terminal, she hoped.

Clench put his arms around her and backed her into the apartment, giving her a little peck on the cheek—his breath could shave a goat— and a vicious pinch on the ass.

"Hey babe," he grinned. "How's tricks?" His gaze roamed her apartment as if he were seeing it for the first time. Aphrodite knew he was looking for some difference, something new he could interrogate her about, something he could pry open into usable information.

The sight of Clench eyeballing her stuff filled Aphrodite with a spirit of rebellion.

"Pablo," she said, "why don't you just tell me what you want and then get the fuck out of my apartment?"

"Now, that's not a very nice thing to say," Clench said. "I haven't been to see you in—how long? A month? And you're ready to kick me out after two minutes."

"Pablo, I have things to do today," Aphrodite said, wondering what they were. "I hope this isn't going to take too long."

But Clench had resumed his tour of her apartment, examining it like a curious first-time home buyer. He wandered toward her bedroom door, and Aphrodite made the mistake of saying:

"Don't go in there!" He had given her so little time, she hadn't cleaned up after last night, or even cracked a window, and her bedroom was strewn with clothes and, well, a funky smell: sex, feet, night farts.

And Pablo Clench, just walking into her bedroom like that, was like a kind of brain rape.

But that was exactly the point. Clench looked over at her, hands in his pockets, grinned his little grin, and pushed the door open with his foot. He disappeared into her bedroom.

"Whoa!" his amused voice came from inside. "Partying last night, huh?" She could hear him in there, opening the closet door, pulling back sheets, moving things around.

He emerged holding up one of the thongs Aaron had given her, stretching it out in front of him like a rubber band.

"This a present from one of your boyfriends?"

Aphrodite hated to see him touching her stuff, but she said, as if helpless, "Yeah. Aaron made them for me."

Clench's eyes rounded in mock surprise. "Made them? I thought he was some kind of scientist, not a lingerie designer."

"He is a scientist," she defended him. "I mean, he didn't actually make them, his little robots did."

This stopped Clench in his tracks.

"His little . . . *what?*"

"Robots. You can't see them, though. But he can tell them to make things, and they do it."

"Invisible robots making underwear? Aphrodite, what the fuck are you talking about?"

Aphrodite told him.

Pablo Clench sat down slowly, the thong crumpled in his hand.

"How do they work, these robots?" he wanted to know.

Aphrodite frowned. She wasn't that clear on all the science stuff. Rogell's carefully crafted explanations had been wasted; she hadn't understood a single thing he had said.

"He puts gloves on them, or something," she said bitterly.

"Whatever. But they're like, tiny?"

"You can't see them at all," Aphrodite agreed. "They go inside things and change them. Aaron said they can change anything into anything else."

Clench was intrigued.

"These things can make anything? Why aren't they making diamonds, or something useful, like heroin? Why thong underwear?"

"He wanted to surprise me," Aphrodite said. "I would have liked diamonds better, too. But he said he could do that, that diamonds would be next."

Now Clench smiled fully, and she realized why he seldom did that. Clench's teeth, riddled with caries, were a greenish color, like algae-stained rocks. The teeth were strangely fused together, as if melted in some hideous dental experiment, and protuberant. His slightly buck-toothed choppers didn't look human, more like a kind of beak, something hidden deep in a nest of writhing tentacles.

"You have such interesting friends," he said.

Pablo Clench's takeaway from his meeting with Aphrodite was that this Aaron guy was someone he wanted to meet.

Aphrodite's friends were not always so interesting. He'd had some success in the past, it was true, following them and digging up their daytime lives. He thought of it as market research. Often the home life of Aphrodite's loverboys was wildly at variance with the night side, and they were not eager to have the two brought together. Clench helped out here, explaining to them what might happen if, say, their wives or rich in-laws or boards of directors found out the kind of lowlifes they were hanging with in their off hours, and what they were really up to that night when the meeting ran late.

Some of the lover boys simply disappeared when Clench laid out his proposals, but others would agree to pay. They didn't last long; between Clench and Aphrodite they were bled out in short order.

But it was good while it lasted.

One dude, though, had held out on him. That was annoying. Clench had been forced to tell Jimmy Cacapoulos that some yuppie was putting moves on his girlfriend. This was a waste; the dude would find it hard to open a checkbook now that his index fingers had been taken off with pruning shears. Being allowed to watch the finger removal session was a slight and temporary consolation.

But "Aaron" seemed like a hot prospect; all of Clench's senses were tingling. The guy smelled and felt like real money, not gram-a-coke money, not brand-new-Cadillac money, but real, honest-to-Jesus, serious, big-time buckolas.

Some people he knew didn't think much of the white-lab-coat boys, except maybe as potential crank lab personnel, but these were ignorant fuckheads. Clench knew better. He read the papers. Clench knew that scientist guys could cash in large and free when their discoveries had commercial potential. The lessons of the dot-com boom were not lost on Pablo Clench. And nanotech, everybody said, was the next big thing.

There was always the possibility, of course, that this stuff about little robots was pure bullshit, something the guy made up just to impress his girlfriend. Aphrodite was not the sharpest knife in the drawer. It would be easy to fool her about many things.

But, nothing ventured, nothing gained. Aaron could stand some looking into, some time spent on research.

At a minimum, he could sell the guy some drugs, or maybe blackmail him if it turned out he was married or otherwise in a place where he wouldn't want it spread around that he was keeping an ex-pole dancer as a mistress in a multi-million-dollar Russian Hill fuckpad. There had to be something he could get out of this guy.

He could just feel it.

6

Dirty Little Secrets

They went to Caveat's again; Aaron really liked it there. The waitstaff, getting a read off his self-image, sussed that he was probably somebody important, some behind-the-scenes guy you would never recognize on the street, but connected to Hollywood or the music business, maybe even (taking a certain geekiness into consideration) Silicon Valley. They treated him accordingly.

Aaron had glowed and swelled like a well-stroked penis.

Aphrodite was glad enough to hang out at Caveat's. She knew a lot of the people there, as it turned out, and the food was good. Aphrodite liked to eat.

But she almost lost her breakfast when they got out of the car at Caveat's front entrance and the parking valet came up to them.

It was Pablo Clench.

He smiled at Aaron, bent over in an exaggerated, stoop-shouldered crouch of deference, like a lawn jockey, holding out one hand for the car keys. But Aaron barely looked at him.

"Here," he said, folding a twenty around the keys. "Try not to park it so far away this time."

"Yes, boss." Clench grinned and bobbed his head like a wind-up monkey. When Rogell turned to go into the restaurant, Clench gave Aphrodite a big wink. She tried not to look at him and hurried after Aaron.

Clench didn't take Rogell's Mercedes very far, just around the corner, where he drove into a parking garage, taking the car up on the roof where he was less likely to be disturbed.

There were hardly any cars up there, and Clench was able to spend a leisurely half hour going through the glove compartment and searching every square centimeter of the ride for clues to Rogell's life.

He carefully copied Rogell's address from the registration he found in the glove compartment, the name of his insurance company, the names on a few business cards he found jammed in the cup holder.

Even Clench, jaded by a lifetime of cashing in on other people's failings, addictions, and obsessions, was surprised by the number of condoms he turned up, in the glove compartment, under the mat on the back shelf, in the map pocket of the driver-side door, behind the sun visors.

What did anyone need so many scumbags for, Clench wondered. Was he collecting them? Was there some kind of premium offered by the condom company, and he was saving up wrappers for it?

Rogell seemed to have an active lifestyle.

The bag of gearshift knobs he found under the driver's seat was intriguing, and Clench resisted the urge to take it. The guy would notice that, Clench thought, obviously he had a use for them. Maybe he put them up his ass, and rode around like that, feeling that trademarked sensation.

The trunk was less informative, though he found more prophylactics there, and a set of towels apparently taken from a local hotel.

Satisfied he had learned all there was to be learned, Clench drove back down the parking garage, driving a little too fast, making the tires squeal as he negotiated the turns on the ramp.

He gave the twenty to the guy at the exit gate. "Keep the change," Clench told him with a casual, devil-may-care wave.

Plenty more where that came from.

He put the car right around the corner from the restaurant, bouncing it at speed up a steep curb onto the sidewalk, straining the suspension, hearing the undercarriage pancake with quiet satisfaction. The ride would not be molested there, thanks to the grease liberally applied to the traffic cops by the restaurant management. Clench would have a short walk to retrieve it.

Whistling, tossing Rogell's car keys high in the air, catching them first in one hand, then the other, then behind his back, Pablo Clench jogged back to Caveat's.

Clench was a natural researcher, curious and relentless, and the Internet was a blessing to him. It was easy enough to go to the public library, cross off the next name on the waiting list for Internet access, write down his own, and then Google up a storm.

It was amazing what you could find out on the Web, Clench thought. Who would ever guess that Aaron Rogell and he had gone to the same high school down in Santa Monica? Not that Clench had attended many classes. That was probably why they didn't recognize each other.

There was some interesting shit about nanotechnology online, really freaky, some of it, like cloth that healed its own rips, and window glass that grew to fit the frame.

But none of the pages he found talked about making little robots, except in a joky way, like it was something so uncool and out of it that no one did it anymore, even though they'd never done it in the first place.

Maybe my man Aaron is on to something here, Clench thought. *He's out there by himself.*

A start-up. What Aaron had was a start-up. Pablo Clench knew all about them; some of his best clients had been guys in start-ups during the dot-com thing. They had a lot of needs, and a lot of disposable. Clench had positioned himself where these things met. He had liked it there.

Apparently Aaron had all he needed, from the sale of some patents on things he came up with while he was still in college. The guy could have just stayed at home, punished the monkey, and gotten stoned, but instead he was out there, inventing little robots and putting them to work. Clench approved of this. It showed initiative, gumption. *Those that can, make,* he thought philosophically. *Those that can't, take.*

Well, I wish him luck, Clench thought. *Here's hoping he makes lots of money quickly, so I can get my hands on some of it.* He wasn't sure how to do that exactly, but Clench had faith. He knew that when large sums of money are just sitting around begging to be taken, there was always a way.

Then he had this genius idea.

The first thing Clench thought of was to kidnap the guy and his little robots and keep them in a basement somewhere, making shit. Piles of diamonds. But there were problems with this scheme. For one thing, it would be like keeping a hamster. (Clench had kept hamsters when he was a little kid, but they hadn't lasted long. Small, furry animals have no stamina and can seldom withstand being used for a handball, or crucified.) You would have to feed it, and take care of it, and it would probably die. The guy would try to get away, the cops would come after him.

No. Bad plan. The human element was too uncertain. The real deal would be to steal the guy's idea, the process itself, and sell *that* to the highest bidder.

That would work, Clench thought.

But who would he sell it to? Rogell's competition, maybe. There seemed to be plenty of new companies out there mining the nanotech field, but no one had exactly Rogell's deal, as far as he could tell. No one else had the robots. So maybe he could get the plans, the blueprints, whatever you used to put tiny little robots you couldn't even see together. The secret. Secrets were always saleable.

Clench thumbed through the stack of downloads he had printed out at the library. He was getting sick of reading this shit; he hadn't done so much reading since high school, reading and copying all the term papers he stole or extorted. And he still didn't have the name of a single contact.

He needed help. And the more he thought about it, the more he realized: a lot of help. He would have to convince Aaron to give up his precious secret, after all. He couldn't do that by himself. He would at least need someone to hold him down.

And he would need someone to deal with the scientific end of it, someone who could tell a page of robot specs from a porno novel written in code.

He would need guys, more than one. He would need a team.

7

The Operation

The barker at the Honeybuzzard Lounge was a longhaired guy with a droopy mustache. He leaned toward a trio of approaching business types. The suits were walking three abreast, grinning at their own coolness and daring.

"Hello, gentlemen," the barker said. "Through this door is just what you're looking for. Beautiful women, beautiful girls, completely naked on stage for your viewing pleasure. These girls love their work, and so will you."

As Clench approached the barker wove him effortlessly into his spiel.

". . . this gentleman knows what he wants. He knows where he's going. He's going inside to see fabulous naked beauties shake their woo-woo in his face. He's smart, he's happy—follow this guy."

Pablo Clench nodded to the barker, patting him on the shoulder as he went by. Clench had started out as a barker for a Cacapoulos strip joint and still took a professional interest in the various personalities that lined Broadway on weekends.

Clench dove through the curtained doorway and into the club's black-lighted interior. It was early yet, still light out in fact, and only one older, chunky babe was up on stage strutting her stuff. Later on there would be crowds of them: pole dancers, cage dancers, table dancers, lap dancers.

Led Zeppelin's "Stairway to Heaven" belted out of cheap but enormous speakers on either side of the stage. The chunky babe thrust out her body more or less in time with the music. Flab rolled; cellulite rippled. It was as erotic as watching a cement mixer pour a sidewalk.

Clench paused to watch a moment, leaning on a chair back. A scientist might have been interested in his thought processes as he looked at the woman gyrating on the low stage, be fascinated by how precisely it resembled the mental pattern of a lizard watching a crippled insect move through its field of vision.

But now was no time for fun. It was one of his nights on at the Buzzard, and he had a shitload of actual work to do. And at the end of the day he hoped to talk his boss, Jimmy Cacapoulos, into bankrolling him for what Clench had come to think of as "the operation."

Reluctantly, he pulled himself away and got down to work.

Later that night, actually about two A.M., Pablo headed up the backstage stairs for Jimmy Cacapoulos's office. Knots had been untied, crises calmed, fires put out. Clench's right hand still tingled from putting out the last fire, a very drunken Filipino dude who felt oppressed because they wouldn't let him light the waitress's costume on fire with his shitty little cigarette lighter. With the help of a bouncer and Alonzo from the kitchen, Pablo had convinced the guy that he didn't really want to do that.

No blood had gotten on his suit jacket, but he had sweated through it at the armpits.

That little pyromaniac son of a bitch should pay my dry cleaning, Clench thought.

Clench knocked on a metal door at the head of the stairs, thought he heard a grunt of some kind, and went in.

Jimmy Cacapoulos was a powerful man, and had once looked the part. Power brought perks, however, chief among them eating and drinking as much as you wanted to without anybody giving you shit of any kind about it. As a result Cacapoulos was now shaped like a heavy-duty Hefty bag completely filled with raw suet. People who still clung to the stereotype of fat men as jolly had never met Jimmy Cacapoulos.

Sex, the foundation of his power, no longer meant much to Jimmy. He could have girls whenever he wanted, but would rather have a good meal and a nap. Maybe he was getting old.

No maybe about getting fat. His belly had become so pendulous he could no longer see his dick without a mirror and a flashlight. Sex urges blew over him like minor rain squalls, quickly evaporating. Surrounded constantly by naked babes, as the job demanded, this was probably a good thing.

For someone who wasn't especially into sex, Jimmy Cacapoulos had made a lot of money from it, before branching out into illicit drugs, extortion, and commercial real estate. He had started his career in the Tenderloin, and still owned a string of adult bookstores, porno movie houses, and massage parlors there, but most of Cacapoulos's strip clubs now lined Broadway in North Beach. He had carefully positioned his clubs to be next to or even between more well-known and successful clubs. You saved money on the signs that way, he would explain to anyone who had to listen.

Clench knew his idea would be a hard sell. Jimmy Cacapoulos loved making money, but he was always hesitant to lay any out.

"Robots? What are you going to do with fucking robots?" Cacapoulos wanted to know.

"These robots represent cutting-edge technology," Clench said. "They can make anything out of anything. No one else has them."

"But do they want them?"

"They'll want them," Clench said. "They can make anything. Like magic. Out of nothing."

"*Anything*. Can they make a hundred-dollar bill out of a pile of dogshit? That's what I'd like to see. Then I might be impressed."

"They can make diamonds, Jimmy. Diamonds. These things can make diamonds out of sand. And the guy who invented them, the scientist, says that's just the first course. Give them the right stuff to work with, these robots can make gold, diamonds, any drug you want. Crack, smack, whatever your pleasure."

Grudgingly, Cacapoulos came around to Clench's way of thinking.

"Okay, so these robots might be worth something. But you're not a scientist. How are you gonna know you got the right ones? This guy, this scientist, could tell you anything, you'd have to believe him. Because you don't know. You don't know shit about robots."

"Jimmy, that's a good point. A very good point. And I already thought of that. That is why we will have to convince the scientist guy—his name's Rogell, Aaron Rogell—to help us."

Cacapoulos's little eyes gleamed derisively out of rolls of fat.

"*Help* you? How you gonna convince him to do that?"

"We'll just have to explain the situation very thoroughly," Clench said. "I'm sure he'll come around in the end."

Cacapoulos grunted and farted, frowning as he ran this info through the shit detector/calculator that passed for his brain. He had spotted another flaw.

" 'We', you keep saying 'we'," he pointed out. "You don't mean me, I know that. But who is this 'we' you keep talking about?"

"I do mean you, Jimmy. I'll need some guys for this operation. Guys that will require payment. That's where you come in."

"Guys, how many guys?"

"A few. Maybe ten. Maybe more."

"What do you need so many guys for?" Jimmy Cacapoulos complained.

What a cheap bastard he is, Clench thought.

"I want to keep an eye on the guy," Clench explained. "The scientist. Box him in. Make sure nobody else gets between him and me and interferes with my plans. Make sure he doesn't do a book."

"Can't you do that by yourself?" Cacapoulos whined. "With maybe just a couple of guys?"

"I need to lull him," Clench explained. "To make him think everything's normal, everything's going fine, while we complete our research and nail down a buyer. Then, when he's good and relaxed, not expecting any bad shit," Clench karate-chopped the air in front of him.

"Then, whammo-zammo."

Jimmy Cacapoulos was still massively disgruntled.

"It's a lot of fucking money for some cockamamie scheme about robots you can't even see," he moaned.

Almost there, Clench thought. When the fat bastard begins whining, you know you've got him.

"Think of it as an investment," Clench told him. "Think: What is it you want most? Out of anything. What is it?"

Food, Jimmy Cacapoulos thought. *Sleep.* "Money," he said.

"Lots of money."

"How much is lots?"

"Millions," Clench said. "Enough for everybody."

8

The Cutting Edge

There was something wrong with the Mercedes, Rogell noticed, a tendency to pull to the left, as if another hand had laid itself on the steering wheel and tried to tug him into the curb. Maybe the tires just needed rotating? But he had only had the thing a few months.

Get another car next time, he thought with annoyance as he caromed down the winding road from his big house to the freeway. Maybe another Mercedes, but one of the old gull-wing coupes from when German engineering still meant something. Or a Ferrari. Maserati, whatever. After the company got going, really going, he'd be able to afford anything he wanted. Get a car made just for him, from scratch, a bespoke automobile.

Just the thought that he could get whatever car he wanted soothed away his irritation at the Mercedes's handling. By the time he jumped on the freeway entrance to zoom the scant mile to Rogeletek, the slight stain on his good mood had been expunged, flicked off like lint from a suit collar.

The Rogeletek building, when it came into view, was only a slight setback. Concrete-slab prefab, the former vitamin warehouse utilized the same engineering principles as a house of cards. In even a moderate earthquake, the results would not be pretty.

But it was only temporary, and in his mind Rogell inhabited the new complex, built not in South City but out in the fringe suburbs where land was cheaper and you could really stretch out. He envisioned something like the campus of a small, well-appointed university, discreetly landscaped, long, low buildings clustered around an administration building, parking lots hidden underground or behind grassy berms.

It would all come to him, in time. And not very much time, now that he was almost ready to really roll with the robots. He tooled the Mercedes around to the executive parking lot—a pad of asphalt in back by the loading dock, cut off on one side by a set of rusting abandoned railroad tracks—and crunched over a litter of eucalyptus nuts and sand to the parking space with his name stenciled on it. Only Tom Prouty, Phil Melaleuca the fulfillment VP, and Dan Funk, the CFO, had been similarly honored so far. Their spots were still empty. Aleister MacBlister, the lab head, was here already, though; Rogell recognized his prim fifteen-year-old Toyota Corolla, carefully washed, waxed, and vacuumed. Maybe he should ask MacBlister to do his car. But that would probably offend him in some way. MacBlister was oddly touchy about many things.

As Rogell had hoped, the lab had a new, hidden sensuality after his midnight visit with Aphrodite. He could almost see her, naked, grinning, crouched in the kneehole of his desk. His penis stiffened uncomfortably at the thought. Similar distracting porno phantoms were scattered around the room like hunting trophies hanging on the walls of a basement den.

Although his fellow administrators had not shown up yet, the lab was already filled with industrious scientist-peons, overseeing the manufacture of new bots for the bot horde, fine-tuning the manufacturing process, adjusting, refining, innovating for the future.

Rogell didn't need to go through the lab to get to his office; in fact, this route took him out of his way. But he made sure to do his walk-through every morning, suiting up in the dressing room, waiting patiently while the air jets blew the dust of the parking lot out of his suit cuffs, passing behind the workers in lab coats, all scientists together, working for the common good. Rogell had a smile and a nod for everyone, an extra-appreciative glance-and-a-twinkle for the young women.

The lab workers raised their heads as Rogell strode by, smiling back. Some waved. Many of them had been gored by the recent downturn, and were not eager to return to food service work or big-box retail.

Visions of naked Aphrodite grinned down from the walls.

Aleister MacBlister, the lab director, saw Rogell from across the room and began scuttling toward him. Rogell smiled, waved, and nodded, but MacBlister kept coming. Rogell increased his pace, hoping to reach the lab door unmolested, but MacBlister got there first.

"Dr. Rogell," MacBlister said, "may I speak to you for a moment?"

Frantically Rogell searched his mind for an excuse, but came up empty.

"Certainly, Aleister. What's on your mind?"

"It's these new techs," MacBlister said. "They're not working out."

Rogell saw daylight and flew toward it.

"You should take any personnel problems to Tom Prouty," he said with visible relief. "I don't want to get involved in the day-to-day running of the lab. That's your job. Whatever you need, take it to Tom."

MacBlister hovered in frustration. Shimmying back and forth between cowardice and rage. He seemed about to dematerialize.

"Tom," he said, "is precisely the problem. If Tom hadn't tried to foist off a crew of brainless incompetents with zero-relevant experience on me, the lab's productivity ratings wouldn't be falling off the bottom of the chart. I can't meet my assigned goals like this."

MacBlister had lots more whining in storage, but Rogell cut him off.

"Take it to Tom," he said, allowing his briefcase to lead him toward the door like a big dog on a leash. "He'll fix you up. See you at the ten o'clock meeting." The heavy door opened and Rogell slipped through.

It was after hours in the Naked Love Act Cabaret. The round white plastic tables decorated with tiny red hearts were empty. Plastic glasses rolled on the floor, sticking here and there in nameless substances. Red plastic drink stirrers lay around like broadcast seed pods from some alien tree.

A large curved bar covered in quilted white leatherette ran along one side of the room. It bulged oddly in unexpected places, as if tumors grew under the covering. Seated at the bar, balancing on a red-and-white barstool, was a solitary figure.

Clench had come to the Love Act, one of Cacapoulos's lesser clubs, to get away from the craziness of the Buzzard and give himself space to think. Frowning and hunched over, he studied the personnel files of Rogeletek he had bribed out of one of the personnel girls there.

The girl would always remember her night out with Pablo as the strangest date she had ever had. She never knew how lucky she had been. Pablo had only wanted information from her, so she was able to get through the experience without any of the discomforts, psychological and physical, that Clench usually visited on his love objects.

Clench had never applied for a job in his life, but he was going to now. The position he had in mind was vice president of human resources, essentially, the personnel director for all of Rogeletek Enterprises. From what he had been able to find out, personnel directing was part of his gig at Cacapoulos's various clubs: He had to audition dancers, find out what each could do — and what they *would* do, for the right enducement.

The job at Rogeletek didn't seem that much different. He could handle it, no problem.

And vice president for human resources seemed to be exactly the right place on the organizational chart, to put his plan into operation.

Clench's method of applying for the position had some unusual features. For one thing, he planned to apply to the man already holding down the job, some guy named Thomas Prouty.

Prouty and I should talk this over, Clench thought. *Maybe I could convince him I'm the better man for the job.*

Clench had great confidence in his powers of persuasion, but in a crucial case like this, he thought he might need some help. Someone to put his point across. Someone who could add those little touches to his argument that made the difference between a successful negotiation and a trip to the police station.

Clench thought he knew just the men for the job.

Billy and Earl, the Colley brothers, were twins—fraternal twins, not identical twins, as Earl would quickly point out to keep people from thinking he was anything like his brother, Billy. In fact, Billy did resemble Earl; it was as if someone had beaten out Earl's face with a hammer and stretched it over Billy's much larger head.

"It sounds like a pretty big job," Billy Colley frowned as he tried to work his mind around the description of Rogeletek Clench had given him. It was like trying to slip a sandwich bag over a ten-pound watermelon.

The Colley boys were not swift, and Clench had often wondered which of the two was slower on the uptake. It was a hard choice. But each of them had good points, too, not the least of which was a willingness to do almost anything he asked. They were usually bright enough to carry out his instructions, too, if only just.

"This *is* a big job," Clench said, "that's why I came to you. I'm going to need a couple things. One, Billy, I need you to work with me inside. And I need more guys, guys who do what you tell them, who don't mind a little wet work. Two, Earl, I need you to follow someone for me, find out everything you can about him. Think you can handle that?"

"No problem," Earl said. He was a head or two shorter and a hundred pounds lighter than his brother, and hyperactive, whereas Billy was slow-moving and deliberate.

"You need some help, that's easy," Billy said, still frowning. "We know some good people. Tell us what you want them for and we can get them. But following somebody, I don't know."

"I do," Earl butted in. "I can do that. I'm good at that."

Billy Colley turned his frown on his brother. "Bullshit. When did you ever follow anybody?"

"I followed you," Earl said. "Yesterday."

"You did, huh? Where did I go then, smart-ass?"

"You went down to the club," Earl said.

"I do that every day. You didn't have to tail me to know that."

"Then at 10:30 you went out again, down to the Walgreens. You bought some hemorrhoid cream, vaseline, and a box of rubber gloves." Earl paused and stared squint-eyed at his brother. "What did you need that shit for?"

Billy Colley's head seemed a half-size larger; his face was getting red.

"None of your goddamn business," he said. "What are you following me for, anyway?"

"Just to see if I could."

Earl turned triumphantly to Pablo Clench.

"See? I'm so good, even my own brother didn't make me."

"That's great, really great," Pablo Clench said. He hoped he was doing the right thing, using these whackjobs. "You can apply your talents on this guy Rogell. Once you get his daily routine down, I want you to follow his every move. If he pisses in a mailbox, or shoplifts a stroke book, or kicks a cripple in the ass, I want you to get it on tape."

Clench produced a fair-size cardboard box and forced it into Earl Colley's unwilling hands.

"What's this?" Earl asked.

"You ever use a video camera before?"

Earl looked down at the box as if he were waiting for it to explode. "Nope."

"It's easy. You just point it at what you want to take a picture of, press the button. That's it. Just make sure you take the lens cap off. Don't drop it."

Earl looked down at the cardboard box with growing comprehension. "This's like a TV camera? I can film shit and show it on TV?"

"More or less."

"Cool!" Earl said.

"You simple piece a shit," his brother said. "Didn't you ever use one of those before?"

Earl shook his head. He had never once in his life thought about taking a photograph, much less making a video. His only personal contact with photography had been at the DMV and the police station.

"Hey Billy," Earl said, possibilities beginning to cascade through his brain. "We could make porno films!"

"That's a great idea," Clench told them. "So long as they're starring Aaron Rogell and his scientific dick."

"Tom Prouty called," Mercedes said as Rogell strode into his office.

Rogell pulled up short. MacBlister would never follow him into his office uninvited; he was safe for now.

"Did you talk to him?" Rogell asked. "He must be really sick, he hasn't been in for days."

"He sounded really funny," Mercedes agreed. "His voice was all weird. He didn't sound like himself." She pawed slowly through the pile of crumpled paper slips that took up most of her desktop; several slips fluttered to the floor. Mercedes didn't care or even notice. This was her first secretarial job, and she was still learning.

Rogell frowned. The VP for human resources was an important position. Prouty had been in the top slot for only a month, and already he had failed to show up for two days in a row.

This was annoying, but not as annoying as the possibility of being bothered with personnel matters himself.

"Well, can he work from home?" Rogell asked. "We don't want to fall behind. This is a crucial time for the company."

"He said his phone doesn't work," Mercedes explained.

This stopped Rogell.

"Mercedes," he said with great patience—Mercedes was really attractive, and he didn't want to upset her—"he called you up to tell you his phone didn't work?"

"I know, it's weird, right? But I called him back right after and it just kept ringing, no one picked up. Maybe he was calling from somebody else's phone."

"Do we have his cell number?"

"No."

"Well, send him an e-mail, text message, whatever," Rogell said over his shoulder as he fled into his private office. "And Mercedes, I'll be really busy this morning. Hold my calls, will you?"

Aaron Rogell didn't enjoy dealing with the personnel side of the start-up. He felt that the people he hired should just get down to work and do the jobs he had assigned to them and leave him alone to continue the essential work of planning the company's future. He put in a lot of time on it, after all. His staff should be willing to do the same, even for the relatively small amounts of money he paid them. The company's future was their future, too. The big payoff would lift all boats, even the half-inflated life rafts, air mattresses, and horsey rings of the lab staff. People should just stop complaining and get to work. The nearly constant difficulties and minicrises that were becoming a regular feature of life at Rogeletek were beginning to stress him out.

Rogell's standard response to stress was always the same: more sex. It was getting hard to schedule it in, though, and he knew that Amanda was getting restless, to say nothing of the people at Rogeletek, who would eventually start to wonder where he went on his three-hour lunches every day.

But there was really no choice. Now more than ever he needed to get laid at least several times a day, if not more. And Aphrodite, though lovely and fuckable, wasn't always available.

Fortunately, he had some alternates to fill in the gaps.

Time to go see Chickie again, Rogell thought.

9

Chickie Baby

San Francisco's Tenderloin district was soft, damp, and corrupt, like a large, rotting sponge someone had used to wipe up vomit and forgotten to wring out. Parts of it were actively dangerous, especially if you were an elderly person with an uncashed Social Security check, or a clueless tourist wandered up from the hotel district.

Rogell steered the Mercedes slowly through the crowded streets as the night came on. Street-side loungers were prone to suddenly hurl themselves into the traffic stream, he knew, as if to physically challenge the slow-moving autos and delivery trucks. Perhaps they were trying to kill themselves, Rogell thought. He could understand that.

It wasn't a joyful district. The furtive, hurrying figures were intent and focused. Desperation ruled. No one seemed to be having any fun. Ragged, dirty men and women gathered around the entrances to certain buildings, or leaned against parked cars, black holes of pure need, waiting to be filled.

Chickie's friends were a little more festive: Black women in gold lamé hot pants and high blonde wigs; tough-looking Mexican girls with eye makeup put on with a putty knife, and pale white women smoking, screeching, and gesticulating, as tall as men (which was not surprising, since they were men) all clustered near the entrance to a featureless, green-painted concrete-block building. Bold white letters on the tattered awning in front identified it as "The Green Neon Lovehole." Loud rap music pulsed and rattled out of invisible speakers.

As Rogell slowly drove by, one of the girls sitting on the back shelf of a parked convertible with the top down swiveled her head, as if she recognized the sound of his car. Her eyes widened with delight.

"Bernie! Hey, Bernie baby! Good to see you, lover! Get your ass over here and party!"

Rogell smiled wanly and began looking for a parking spot. In his early encounters with Tenderloin paid sex he had used a pseudonym, a *nom de rut*, feeling a little cowardly but thoroughly justified. To Chickie and her friends, he was Bernie Bernstein, a certified public accountant. It was the best he could come up with on the spur of the moment.

Rogell parked the Mercedes half on the sidewalk, up an alley. Back in the shadows, several heads lifted attentively and watched him walk out to the street and turn left.

Chickie hopped down from the convertible when she saw Rogell, scurried over, and attached herself to his arm. Even in high-heeled sandals, she barely came up to his shoulder.

"Hey Bernie, I missed you," she cooed at him as the rest of her set looked on with blank indifference.

Everything about Chickie was ambiguous. Young or old? Male or female? Her blonde curly hair was very obviously a wig. She was thin past anorexia, frankly terrifying to most would-be customers. Rogell didn't mind.

Rogell was pretty sure Chickie was a girl, but he had never tried to fuck her. Blow jobs were Chickie's specialty. The fact that all her teeth had been hosed away by drug use and terrible hygiene was a net positive.

They stumbled back to Rogell's car together. Several shadowy forms melted away from the Mercedes as they approached, like roaches leaving a dirty plate when the kitchen light comes on.

Rogell got in first. There was a disposable hypodermic on the passenger seat, and the gearshift knob was missing. It was a good thing he hadn't been gone longer.

Rogell picked up the syringe gingerly and flung it into the street. Chickie hopped in and smiled broadly.

"Same thing as always?" she grinned toothlessly.

Rogell smiled tightly and began taking off his trousers. This was more than was strictly necessary, but he liked to feel his naked ass on the leather of the car seat, liked to feel the cool night air on his bare skin, liked the increased danger of discovery.

Chickie liked it too.

"You know, Bernie, I really like the shape of your dick. I really do. Not just sayin that."

Soon it became difficult for her to say anything. Rogell vocalized for both of them; he had always been a noisy lay. His moans and yelps echoed off the brick walls of the alley like the cries of a tortured sea lion, but no one came to investigate. No one gave a shit. That was the true beauty of the Tenderloin.

Then it was over. Rogell emerged from his come trance to see Chickie fixing her makeup in the rearview mirror, a dab of shiny semen in the corner of her mouth. She wiped it away with the back of her hand and repaired the shape of her lipstick.

A casual proffer of currency concluded the session. Chickie jumped out of the Mercedes, turned, and leaned back in.

"You know, Bernie honey, you should really spend some time with me, all right? I could do for you real good, like you never knew. It won't cost you too much, either. We could have hella fun together."

Rogell smiled politely, but this of course was out of the question. Chickie had her role to play, like everyone else, and this was it.

"See you around, babe," he said with a playboy wave.

"Okay, honey, come back soon." Chickie staggered off on ridiculous platform sandals, twisting and lurching on the uneven pavement of the alley.

Rogell checked the upholstery for suspicious stains and replaced the gearshift knob from the bag of spare knobs he kept under the driver's seat. He checked his grooming in the rearview mirror, fired up the Mercedes, and headed up the alley toward Russian Hill and Aphrodite.

Pablo Clench's cell phone shivered and hummed discreetly. He picked it up, saw the Colley brothers' number.

"What's up?" he asked. "You get something on him?"

"Did we ever," Earl Colley said. "This's going to be easy."

Clench didn't like it when things were easy. Easy was usually wrong. "Why is that?"

"The dude hangs out at the Lovehole! Well, not inside. But he goes to one of the girls hangs out on the street there, in front of the place."

"One of yours?"

"You bet." The Colleys didn't sully their hands with actual pimping; they subcontracted it. But they kept close tabs on their business interests.

"I know her, anyway. She'll do whatever we ask her to do, so long as we pay her up front."

Aaron certainly seemed to be giving up lots of useful material. The Tenderloin stopover surprised even Clench.

"Just do whatever it takes," he said. "We have a budget for this thing.

Just get me something on this guy, something he won't want to see on the six o'clock news."

"That's not going to be a problem," Earl Colley said.

"The men from the security company were here today, Aaron," Amanda called out to Rogell from the kitchen.

Rogell had just walked in after an absorbing day at the company, and his mind was stretched between the new business plan he was hammering out with Dan Funk and the evening of perverse fornication he was planning for Aphrodite. He was distracted.

"What security?" he called back.

"The security company for this house," Amanda yelled patiently. "The alarm people. They said there were here to install an upgrade."

Rogell walked into the kitchen, picked Amanda up around the waist, and lifted her off the ground. Popping and grinding came from the lower back area strained by Aphrodite, but he was able to kiss her several times before half-dropping her.

"I didn't order any upgrade."

"They said it was in the original contract, and it wouldn't cost us anything," Amanda said. "I looked over their paperwork and it looked okay."

"Well, let's keep an eye on the next bill. I'll look into it," Rogell said, forgetting about it immediately.

10

Burning the Black Dress

Amanda had been born and raised in San Francisco, and although she had been many places since, in some recess of her brain she still thought of the City as the center of the universe, the place you would come back to to validate your existence. Finding herself in a small cafe in Menlo Park with a baby in a front carrier was something of a shock then, as quietly disturbing as the fact that she now lived in South City. Berkeley or Marin, yes, she could see that, maybe even Oakland at a stretch. But South San Francisco?

Mindy Valentine, her friend from Stanford, had arranged this meeting, "to get you out of the house," Mindy had explained. Amanda wasn't sure she needed to get out of the house. She liked it there, inside the domestic bubble with her baby and her husband. Well, sometimes with her husband.

But Mindy was insistent. It was obvious that she was going to keep on trying to help Amanda until Amanda gave in and let herself be helped.

Mindy came back from the counter with two tall lattes, putting them assertively on the round, metal table and climbing into her chair like a fighter pilot climbing into the cockpit.

"So how are you doing, Amanda?" Mindy said over the rim of her latte. "How is the life of the young mother?"

Amanda was bending over the sleeping Delia, making sure she wasn't suffocating or otherwise in peril.

"It's different," she said. "I never expected to be doing this. But it's wonderful."

"You're happy?"

Amanda nodded carefully so as not to disturb Delia. "Completely happy."

"That's great," Mindy said. "I'm so glad for you." It was clear that she regarded the whole kid scenario as a deep betrayal.

"What about your practice? Are you cutting back?"

"I gave it up. You know, I couldn't possibly, while I was pregnant. Not just the physical difficulty, I mean, but the theater of it."

Mindy considered this. "It could help, sometimes," she said.

They sipped their lattes in silence for a while. Delia slept on.

"How is Aaron?" Mindy asked. "How is he adjusting to fatherhood?"

As Mindy asked the question Amanda realized she had been dreading it.

"I hardly see him anymore," she said. "He's so busy with the start-up, he's almost never home while I'm awake."

"You mean he doesn't spend time with Delia? Doesn't he, I don't know, take the baby some nights? Doesn't he spell you?"

Amanda shook her head. It was inconceivable that Aaron would do this.

"When he's not at the lab, he's out meeting with people, venture capital, public relations, other businessmen. Getting a new business going is not just about science, you know. You have to bring the world in." She could hear Aaron's voice as she said this.

So, apparently, could Mindy.

"Is that what he tells you? What an asshole."

Amanda found herself unable to leap to his defense.

"You shouldn't have to give up everything just to give him his daddy fantasy," Mindy said. "What about *your* needs? What about *your* world?"

Amanda recognized Mindy's arguments; they were the same ones she used against herself.

"My world has changed, Mindy," she said. She couldn't help but steal a downward glance at Delia.

Mindy didn't say anything out loud to this, but her body language clearly said "Jesus fucking Christ."

Amanda expected this response.

"This is what I want, Mindy," she said. "For now. This is my choice, not Aaron's. He wanted to wait until the start-up was in the black. I made this happen."

"Well, the least he could do is help you out. If he's too self-involved to do it himself, he could hire some help, a nanny for you, or something."

"Oh, I wouldn't want a nanny. I don't want to miss a second of Delia's development."

Amanda's madonna-like smile further enraged Mindy.

"Aren't you worried that, with the baby and everything, your weight gain, Aaron might lose interest in you?"

This was cruel, and Mindy knew it. Amanda was young and fit, and her shape hadn't changed that much, considering. But she *had* changed, softened, broadened, her tits big and swollen. When her attention shifted from Delia to herself, Amanda felt baglike, not very fetching.

Amanda said nothing. Mindy applied herself to scooping up the last of the latte foam from the bottom of the glass, appalled at herself but still angry.

There was a long silence while they both recuperated from Mindy's remark.

Mindy was still poking at the remnants of foam in the bottom of her latte. There wasn't much left.

She's going to scrape through the sides of the cup if she keeps that up, Amanda thought.

Finally Mindy pushed the well-scraped latte aside and leaned forward.

"Look, Amanda, I didn't know how to tell you this. So I'm just going to say it straight out. I saw Aaron."

This didn't immediately compute for Amanda.

"Saw him? When? He never mentioned that he ran into you."

"He never saw me. He was too busy to notice. Amanda, I saw him down in the Tenderloin, hanging out with a bunch of hookers. In the middle of the day."

"Aaron would have been at the company in the middle of the day," Amanda pointed out.

"How do you know? Do you ever see him during the day? Does he ever come home for lunch? See the baby? Check in?"

Amanda shook her head after each question.

"No, he's much too busy. He would never have the time to go up to the city. Why, even after work, he never stays very long at home. He works so hard, and then he has to go out to dinner with the people who put up the money for Rogeletek. And with other businessmen." Amanda trailed off, hearing the echo of other possibilities in what she was saying.

Mindy heard them too. Her expression clearly said, "I rest my case."

"I had the cabdriver go around the block and come back," Mindy said. "I wanted to be sure it was really him."

"And?"

"It was Aaron all right. When we came around again I saw him walking arm in arm with some skinny little prostitute. They looked like they were heading straight to the hotel room. I got a good look at him, full profile. I had the driver slow down so I could be sure. Aaron was maybe six feet away. If he had looked up he would have been looking straight into my face. But he was too absorbed with his little hooker to notice me."

This was someone else's story, not mine, Amanda thought.

"When was this?"

"A couple weeks ago. I was going to call you up and talk to you, but I couldn't bring myself to tell you all this over the phone. Then I thought I should just leave it alone, that it was none of my business how you two lived your life."

"What changed your mind?"

Mindy frowned down at the table.

"Amanda," she said, "Prostitutes, in the Tenderloin? What if he brings home a disease, syphilis, gonorrhea, AIDS? It's a dangerous situation. I had to let you know."

"Aaron wouldn't do that," Amanda said. "See prostitutes, I mean. It's just not like him."

"Honey, wake up," Mindy said. "You don't know everything about him."

It couldn't be true. It just couldn't.

As she drove the Cherokee back up the Peninsula, Amanda tried to digest this new budget of information. Aaron seeing prostitutes? It just didn't add up.

Or did it?

And if it was true, what would she do about it?

Mindy had had an idea about that.

"What do you see in him, anyway?" Mindy had wanted to know. "He is such a prick. You should just leave him."

"What about Delia? What would we do? Where would we go?"

"Well, what good is Aaron to you now? If you never see him? Besides," Mindy had said, "this is a community property state."

Aaron as heartless prick: She wondered how many of her friends thought that about him. All of them, probably. She knew Aaron could be a dickhead, an arrogant bastard at times. She was glad she didn't have to work for him.

But she also knew that she saw a side of him no one else did. He could be boyish, and charming, and playful with her. Their sex life was hot—at least, it used to be, before she had the baby. And Aaron was always fun to be around. Except maybe lately, but that was mostly her fault. And he was nearly as smart as he thought he was.

She could no longer imagine life without Aaron. Strange and annoying as that was, she knew she had to deal with it.

But the question of the moment was, could he imagine life without her? Was he busy practicing for such a life? What if all those meetings he went to weren't really about business? What if it really had been Aaron that Mindy saw?

What the hell was he up to, anyway?

Aaron Rogell parked the Mercedes—still pulling like a fractious mule—jumped out, and jogged into the house. He had allowed himself a forty-five-minute pit stop at home before his dinner meeting in the City—a legitimate one this time.

Amanda pulled the door open before he reached it. Rogell stopped dead, the massive force field of his self-absorption penetrated by Amanda's surprise attack.

She stood in the open door, smiling shyly. Her dress—more like a gown—swept down to the floor, strategically revealing expanses of white décolletage and leg. Her hair was arranged around her face to maximum effect. A simple string of pearls matched the whiteness of her neck and stood out against the black velvet of the gown. She looked stunning.

Rogell was stunned.

"Amanda!" he stuttered. "You look beautiful!"

Amanda looked down. "I didn't want you to forget. Come on in." She stepped back and Rogell cautiously followed her into the house. Something was definitely up.

He swept Amanda into his arms and kissed her, feeling her body warm through the expensive fabric, catching a fleeting glimpse of her breasts.

"What's the occasion?" he asked, nuzzling her white neck. "Forget what?"

"Us, Aaron," Amanda whispered. "I didn't want you to forget us."

"I would never do that." And in fact Rogell was overwhelmed with all the reasons he had been attracted to Amanda in the first place.

Amanda fired him up. She shared this ability with most living creatures and several inanimate objects, it was true—but she had always had a special purchase on his erotic imagination. Silently, Rogell calculated how many sex acts could be performed in the few minutes he had available. Perhaps a quick phone call could buy him some more time.

"Let's go out, Aaron," Amanda smiled. "I made reservations at the Villa Alba, remember that place? We haven't been there in ages. We deserve a night out."

Rogell pulled back.

"What about the baby? Where's Delia?"

"Mom's driving down from the City," Amanda said. "She said she'll babysit, she doesn't mind. She's glad to. We can stay out as late as we want!"

"But Amanda . . . I can't."

Amanda froze.

"What? *Can't?* Why not?"

"You should have called me," Rogell said. "I've already made plans, business plans. I have a real . . ." he caught himself just in time. "A real, real important meeting tonight. With the money. I can't get out of it."

"I'm sorry," Amanda said. She hung on his lapels as if drowning. "I wanted to be spontaneous. The way we used to be. Remember?" She looked at him pleadingly.

Amanda wondered what was wrong with her. Of course he had a meeting. Of course he was busy. He was always busy. He never had time to just be with her anymore. It was what you had to expect in business. It was up to her to be adaptable and understanding.

The fucking son of a bitch.

"But I'll come home as soon as I can, afterwards," Rogell improvised desperately. "We'll have, we can . . . I know! I'll stop at Lucca's and get some food, we can have a picnic! Just us, on the floor, like we used to."

But Amanda would not be bought off by a little pasta salad and white wine.

"No, no, that's all right," she said. "We'll do it some other time. I'll call you next time, first, and make sure you have room in your schedule."

Amanda pulled away from him and swept out of the room.

The torn and shredded gown wouldn't stay lit at first. Perhaps she had wadded it too tightly under the grill of the large brick barbecue behind the house. Perhaps it was because the shaking of her hands made most of the matches go out before the fabric caught properly. It wasn't until she had soaked it down good with about a gallon of firestarter that it began to burn really well.

By the time her mother rang the front door bell it had been reduced to ashes not quite as black as the dress itself had been.

The meeting with the money went well. The food was good, the service attentive and invisible. The astronomical bill was discreetly covered by

Rogell without a whisper of protest from the assembled venture capitalists. Conversation had flowed easily, segueing from sports to Hollywood
celebrities to science to Rogeletek with scarcely a nudge from Rogell.
Before he knew it he was in full presentation mode, laying out the financial potential of his invention, painting a picture of a new world of
high productivity, near-zero labor costs, and epic profit margins.

The part about labor costs had gone over especially well, he
thought. Nanobots didn't have unions—one more attractive feature.
And he had dismissed any concerns about potential environmental
damage as so much whining from fatally marginalized eco-maniacs
and clueless luddites.

His audience had lapped it up like a rare vintage wine.

Using his fork as a pointer had probably been a little gauche, but
scientists, like artists, were forgiven a certain awkwardness in advance.

Amanda was probably hurt, Rogell thought as he got behind the
wheel of the Mercedes, hurt and even a little angry. But he would make
it up to her. Not tonight. She was probably still a little miffed. Best to let
her cool down a couple days. Then he would surprise her—take her
out to the expensive place he had just wined and dined the venture
capitalists. Well, maybe not that expensive. But a place just like it, just
as good. Someplace romantic.

Rogell frowned, sensing a problem. Until she cooled off, he knew, it
would be hard to start something sexually. It was hard enough anyway,
what with the kid always crying and Amanda being worn out and depressed about everything.

And his needs were ramping, fed by the praise and attention of the
money guys, watered by good food and wine. A little sex to top off the
night would be just the thing.

Unfortunately, Aphrodite was out. Literally. She had warned him
that Wednesday was not a good night for her. "I need my space," she
told him. He knew better than to intrude.

But there was always Chickie.

Rogell turned hard to the right, cut down Harrison, and sent the Mercedes up Van Ness past City Hall and the Opera, heading for the Tenderloin.

But Chickie and her friends weren't at their usual station. The only whore in the usual spot was an aging drag queen with a baritone voice and a heavy beard that no amount of foundation makeup could disguise.

"Hey baby," the drag queen boomed. "No—Chickie and them got rousted. They're all down at the Hall of Justice, signing in. They'll be back soon. Wanna party while we wait?"

Rogell's robust sex drive didn't stretch that far, however, and he didn't feel able to wait. He cruised the Tenderloin aimlessly for a while, but the streets seemed deserted. A dead night.

But the upside of this lack of activity was that he was able to park the Mercedes directly in front of his favorite adult book store—surely a sign of some kind from the porno gods—and make a quick stopover.

Time to take the matter in hand.

After a couple days of not hearing anything, Clench gave the Colleys a call.

"You guys getting what we need?" Clench asked.

The nasal voice of Earl Colley came over the cell phone.

"Yeah, are we ever. This guy, Clench, I'm telling you."

Even with poor reception Clench could tell that Colley was impressed.

"What are you telling me?" he asked.

"He's something else. You won't believe the shit we got. He just . . . it's like he can't stop."

.   .   .

On Rogell's next visit to the Tenderloin, Chickie had a proposal to make.

"Hey lover," she said, "You know how I always say we should spend some more time together?" She clung to Rogell's arm and smiled toothlessly, looking up at him.

"I've heard you say that, yes."

"Well, I got a room now, not my own room where I sleep," she hastened to explain. Chickie didn't look as if she ever slept. "A room I rent. From this guy. That I can use to bring my lovers to. You interested? We could have a nice time."

Rogell shook his head. "What's wrong with the time we have now?"

"Oh, nothing, nothing, honey. But we could have something special. You know what I mean? We could do stuff we can't get into in the car. We could do anything you wanted." She clung to him, nearly tripping them both.

Rogell stopped, intrigued.

"Anything?"

Chickie nodded vigorously. "Anything you want, baby. Anything at all."

"Well," Rogell said thoughtfully, "there was something I always wanted to try. I've thought about it a lot. But it would take a lot of work to put it all together."

"I'll take care of it, lover," said Chickie, the confident administrator. "Whatever you want. You just tell me."

Things were going pretty smooth, Clench thought, in spite of his worries about the Colley boys. But it was too much to expect perfection.

"You really started something, you know, with that fucking video camera," Billy Colley said.

Even over the phone Clench could tell that Billy was exasperated to the point of homicide.

"What's going on?" Clench said. "Your brother figure out how to use it yet?"

"Use it? The goddamn son of a bitch won't put it down! He films everything in the house. The little fucker filmed me brushing my teeth. If I didn't lock the door, he'd film me taking a shit. Then, like that's not bad enough, he watches everything he shoots on the television. He tries to get me to watch it! I got better things to do than watch myself sleeping on the couch. I tell you, Clench, my brother's losing his goddamn mind. I'm sorry you ever gave him that thing."

"Just so long as you do what I told you."

"Well, you're not gonna have a problem there. We got lots of stuff on Rogell. You should have everything you need real soon."

"I'm glad to hear it."

"But when we're done with this, that's it, all right?" To Billy Colley this was the essential point, and he wanted to make sure it was understood. "No more Mr. Video Camera. You'll take it away from him, right?"

"Sure Billy," Clench said. He didn't really give a shit one way or the other, but he wanted the big musclehead to be calm and focus on the job at hand. "Then I'll take it away from him."

11

Lifting the Rock

"Hel-lo. Tony Baloot Investigations."

Amanda didn't say anything right away, poised like a diver above deep water.

"Hello?" The voice on the phone sounded weary and defeated, as if it expected most of the people who called to just breathe into the phone and say nothing.

Quick. Before he hangs up, she thought.

"Hello. Can I speak to Tony Baloot?"

"Speaking."

"Mr. Baloot? I'd like to talk to you about an investigation, something confidential and private."

"Confidential and private investigations are my specialty," Baloot said. "Talk away."

"I'd rather not discuss it over the phone."

"This is a secure line."

"I'm sure it is. But I'd rather explain it to you in person."

Baloot sighed heavily into the phone. "All right. When would you like to come in?"

Like a dentist, she thought. But Baloot's appointment calendar had more openings than most dentists. Far more.

"Could I come by today?"

"Sure."

"In about a half hour?"

"Come right over," Tony Baloot said.

Baloot's detective agency was just off South San Francisco's main street, in an office up over a florist's shop (his mother's). There was just the one room; even the toilet was down the hall, past a storage room filled to bursting with cardboard vases and sun-faded artificial flowers. There was nothing in Baloot's room but a big square desk, a folding chair, a curious smell, and Baloot himself.

"Come on in," he said unnecessarily when Amanda opened the door and stepped inside.

Tony Baloot was a soft middle-aged man with a taste for cheap tropical shirts and canvas fedoras. He looked like the kind of man who would smoke foul-smelling little cigars, and he did. A scanty mustache sketched itself across his upper lip like a small collection of insect leg parts.

Baloot got out from behind his desk and bustled around to offer Amanda the folding chair. She was his first customer in weeks, and his other sidelines—betting on high-school ball games and fencing stolen groceries—hadn't been doing too good lately.

Do this right, he told himself. *Don't fucking blow it.*

Back behind the desk Baloot folded his hands and tried to look friendly and reliable.

"Now, Mrs. Rogell? What can I do for you?"

.   .   .

Amanda was not overwhelmed by Baloot's office, or by Tony Baloot himself. Perhaps it would have been better after all to use someone in the City, she thought, someone reputable. But she couldn't bring herself to talk to anyone she knew about her marriage difficulties. And the thought of anyone she knew—or who knew people she knew, or had even heard of her—rummaging around in her private life was unbearable. Tony Baloot at least had the virtue of obscurity.

Amanda sniffed and frowned. The dry, dusty air had a curious undertone, a faint smell she couldn't quite put a name to. Was it coming from Baloot? She stared at him; he summoned up a hopeful grin. No. A fug of stale cigar smoke and BO wafted off him every time he moved, but this smell was more pungent and meaty. Did he have a dead body under the desk? There didn't seem to be anyplace else in the office to hide it.

Amanda couldn't know it, but fifty pounds of stolen linguisa sat in the kneehole of Baloot's desk warming toward corruption. One of his grocery store contacts had dropped it off that morning. Baloot had planned to hide it in his mother's floral cooler, behind a funeral arrangement, as he had often done successfully in the past, but his mother had come in early, before he could hump the bulky package downstairs. His desk was the only available hiding place.

"Mr. Baloot, I have a problem," Amanda began.

"Most people who come see me here have a problem," Baloot said encouragingly.

"I don't know how to say this," Amanda said, feeling unexpectedly confused. "I have . . . suspicions." Now that she had almost said them out loud, her fears seemed ridiculous, disloyal.

Baloot, on the other hand, felt a surge of confidence. When Amanda walked into his office he had been intimidated. This lady was not the kind of client he usually dealt with, when he had a client at all. She seemed too smart, pretty, and well-to-do to need his services.

But suspicions were Baloot's meat and potatoes.

"Your husband?" he asked gently.

Amanda nodded.

"You think maybe he's seeing somebody else?"

"Well, I don't know. And that's just it. Something about him is different, something has changed. And I just don't know what it is." Amanda, horrified, felt a storm of tears backing up. She fought it down. It was like suppressing the urge to vomit when drunk. But she didn't want to fall apart in front of Tony Baloot if she could help it.

"There, there," Tony Baloot said.

Amanda looked up, astonished. Did he actually say that? She was afraid he was going to step around the desk and hug her.

But Baloot stayed put.

"Many people come to me with similar problems," he said. "It's better to know the truth, whatever it is. So you don't have to worry about it."

"I want to know what he's doing, Mr. Baloot," she said. "I want to know, and then I'll know what to do about it."

"Trust me," Tony Baloot said.

Amanda stared at him. This seemed an absurd proposition. But wasn't that what she was about to do?

"I do this all the time," Baloot elaborated. "Nothing you can tell me is going to be a surprise, believe me." He looked down and fussed around in his desk drawers, finally pulling out a small spiral notebook and a stubby pencil.

"Now why don't you tell me about your problem? Start from the first time you noticed anything funny."

Once Amanda began to talk about her fears, all the little dissonances, the passing suspicions that had been rationalized away, the stories that didn't quite add up, all came together in a convincing narrative of guilt. It was a purely circumstantial case, true, but if she were a prosecutor putting this before a jury, it would be Aaron's ass.

At the same time, a counternarrative was forming itself, one that explained away every circumstance, downgraded every appearance of guilt. She was simultaneously both prosecutor and defense counsel, making her case before a judge.

From the bulging of his eyes and the thin film of sweat on his forehead, Judge Baloot was having a hard time keeping up.

Tony Baloot put down his pencil. The pages of the spiral notebook were covered with his broad childish scrawl almost to the end.

He suppressed a sigh. He had heard all this before, so many times. It was so fucking obvious what was going on. At first he had been a little intimidated; the guy being some big deal scientist had made him feel out of his depth. But after all, the guy was the same as all the guys his female clientele sicced him on: horny, selfish, fucking anything that moved, then trying to hide it.

But one thing stood out from the sordid story. The guy had money. Baloot smiled weakly at Mrs. Rogell, his fee rising as he inventoried her clothes. He would have to lean over the desk to see her shoes, but better not. She would think he was looking at her legs and get mad. Still, he bet they were worth a lot, like everything else she wore.

"Well, Mrs. Rogell, I'll take your case." Like he could afford to do anything else. "I charge seventy-five an hour, plus expenses." He paused to see if she would say anything to that, but the lady didn't flinch. "I normally report once a week, but you can have more frequent reports if you want."

"Once a week would be fine." Mrs. Rogell leaned toward him. "But what do you think about what I've just told you? Does it sound like my husband is having an affair?"

"Well, it's too soon to say," Baloot said. "The evidence isn't in yet. I'll know more when I've had a chance to watch his movements for a while."

And build up some billable hours before I bust his cheating ass.

. . .

So now it was done, Amanda told herself, walking carefully down the ladder-steep stairs from Tony Baloot's office. She had put machinery in motion that would tell her, objectively, whether her fears had any foundation.

As she passed the florist's at the bottom of the stairs she noticed the woman behind the counter staring at her angrily. When the woman saw Amanda looking at her, she whacked the bouquet she was putting together down on the counter like a pro wrestler body-slamming an opponent, staring back at Amanda with bulging eyes.

What is her problem? Amanda thought. *Does she know why I'm here? Does she know about Aaron?*

Just paranoia, she thought. Get a grip. She dismissed the angry florist from her mind and climbed back into the Cherokee.

12

Baloot on the Case

Watching Rogell would be harder than he thought—Baloot saw that right away.

Once he got rid of the linguisa and borrowed some money from his ma, Baloot had gone down to the pawn shop on Grand and got some of his surveillance equipment out of hock. Then he had driven down to Rogeletek and parked up the block, waiting for Aaron Rogell to appear.

It was easy to spot him. The red Mercedes roared out of the parking lot and zipped up the street before Baloot could jolt himself into action and get the car started. Luckily, he was pretty sure where Rogell was going.

Baloot caught glimpses of the Mercedes up ahead, and got a good look at it as it jumped onto 101 North. Baloot's '79 Buick smoked and farted onto the freeway, nearly getting rear-ended by a pickup when Baloot forced his way into the traffic stream. He was just in time to see the red Mercedes, a half mile ahead, getting off at the last South City exit.

Baloot didn't bother following Rogell all the way up to his house. There wasn't any other way down from that hill. He'd get spotted up there anyway, without any other houses around. Instead he waited at the foot of the hill, biding his time.

Sure enough, right around sunset, the red Mercedes blasted by him, heading for the freeway north.

This time Baloot was ready for him. He got on the Mercedes like stink on shit and followed it into the city.

The real problems started once Rogell stuck the Mercedes in a Tenderloin alley and got out walking. It wasn't that it was hard to tail him on foot; Tony Baloot was actually good at shadowing people, curiously invisible, like a soft, tubby ghost.

No. The problem was that he was not the only one keeping an eye on Mr. Rogell.

Baloot put his Buick up the alley from the red Mercedes, locked it up, and left it, praying that it would still be there when he got back. He didn't have to worry. The shadowy forms that converged on the Mercedes while Baloot was still scurrying out of the alley had less than no interest in older model Buicks covered liberally with rust and primer. The Mercedes drew them like a big red magnet. Baloot heard breaking glass behind him, put his head down, and walked faster.

Rogell seemed to have a lot of friends in the neighborhood. People—mostly women—sitting on car fenders and stoops waved and smiled as Rogell strode by. One bandy-legged, sandy-haired guy got up and walked after him. At first Baloot thought the guy was going to catch Rogell up, maybe borrow money from him, or mug him. But the bandy-legged guy kept back of Rogell, didn't even try to come up with him. From time to time Baloot saw him take something from his coat pocket and fiddle with it. The guy pointed it at Rogell—was he going to shoot him?

Holy shit, Tony Baloot thought, *the guy is* videotaping *him*.

Rogell was on his way somewhere, that was for sure. He cut across the street in the middle of the block and zipped along toward the corner. Baloot was pretty sure now where he was heading. A big, neon-green, windowless building stood on the corner with a tattered marquee announcing "The Green Neon Lovehole." Sure enough, Rogell walked up to the Lovehole. But instead of turning under the marquee, he walked toward the rear of the building and disappeared up the alley.

The guy with the camera followed him, hurrying a little to catch up. Baloot followed the guy with the video camera.

Turning the corner into the alley, Baloot nearly walked into the guy.

Bandy-legs gave him a look like the back of a shovel.

"Entrance around front, buddy," the guy said.

Baloot grinned as harmlessly as he could.

"Just looking for a place to piss, that's all."

Bandy-legs was not mollified.

"Well, don't piss on the building. I catch you doing that I'll tie a knot in your dick."

Baloot snuck a glance up the alley, couldn't see Rogell at all, and began to back away.

"Guess I'll find somewhere else. Sorry."

"You do that," the bandy-legged guy said.

He stood with his hands on his hips and watched as Baloot hurried back to his car to think things out.

Lost a side mirror and a vent window, Rogell noted as he climbed back into the Mercedes. Why would someone break glass to get into a convertible? It didn't make sense. At least his top hadn't been slit. Anyway, he always left the doors unlocked, just so that kind of thing wouldn't happen.

The gearshift knob was gone again, too. Rogell sighed, replaced it.

It was just a cost of doing business in San Francisco, after all. A kind of luxury tax.

He jammed the Mercedes up the narrow alley, not noticing the rusty Buick that got in behind him and followed him up the alley, its lights off.

Amanda meant to wait calmly for Baloot's weekly report, but after five days she called to check in.

"Have you found anything yet, Mr. Baloot?" she asked.

"Are you a prostitute?" a voice croaked.

"Get off the line, Ma," Tony Baloot said.

"No," Amanda said. "I'm not a prostitute."

"He calls prostitutes, they come to my store looking for him," Mrs. Baloot continued. "I don't like it, Tony. I don't want you to do that no more."

"I won't, Ma, I promise," Baloot said. "Please get off the phone."

There was a click as the extension hung up, and Baloot said nervously,

"You still there, Mrs. Rogell?"

"Yes. What did you find out?"

"Well . . ." Tony Baloot tried to marshall his thoughts. He had found lots, but it would be wasteful to tell Mrs. Rogell everything all at once.

"He's certainly up to something," Baloot said. "You'll see in my report. He patronizes pornography theaters, is familiar with street prostitutes, and visits a condo on Russian Hill."

Not necessarily criminal, Amanda thought. Vitek, probably, or some other venture capitalist. Vitek lived on Russian Hill.

"Whose condo?"

"The deed's in the name of James Cacapoulos. I know him. Strip joint owner. Not a nice guy. But the name on the mailbox is Aphrodite Anderson."

That name didn't sound like any venture capitalist Amanda had ever heard of, though she supposed it was remotely possible.

"She used to be an exotic dancer. Worked for Cacapoulos, in fact," Baloot went on.

All right, not a venture capitalist, then.

"Are you sure she was the one Aaron was going to see?" Amanda asked.

"Well, yes, I traced him to the building, saw which bell he rang. Definitely," Baloot said.

"You saw him go in?"

"I saw him go in. I saw him come out."

"But you never saw them together."

"No," Baloot admitted. "Not together."

Amanda frowned. The faintest chance she was wrong, the remotest possibility—a wisp, a phantom.

Kill it, she thought. *Know the pain.*

"I want you to get a picture of them together," she instructed Baloot.

"How together?" Baloot asked. It might be hard to get a shot of them fucking.

"Just together," Amanda said.

"That should be possible," Baloot said.

Baloot spent a studious morning going over the documentation that came with his electronic surveillance equipment, and made a few phone calls to people who actually knew how to use it. He thought he remembered enough.

The main problem was that he would have to get into the building in order to install it. But Baloot thought he could handle that all right.

Aphrodite Anderson froze when the door buzzer went off. She was sure it was Pablo Clench.

The door buzzed again. She tried to feel back along the wires to whoever was ringing it. Maybe not Pablo, after all. It didn't have that urgent, nasty, invasive thing that Pablo gave it. So maybe it was someone else.

The buzzer went off a third time. Aphrodite jumped up and pressed the intercom.

"Hello?" she breathed into it, trying to sound alluring and intimidating at the same time to cover all possibilities. "Who is it?"

"Building maintenance," the intercom fuzzed back at her. "Miss Anderson, we need to get into your apartment."

"What for? It's very inconvenient right now," she whined into the grille. Inconvenient? She would have to put on some clothes or a robe or something to let them in. Plus, she looked like shit. Plus, she was at the beginning of a serious bad mood and needed a drink or two.

"That's okay, we can come back later," the maintenance guy said. He sounded nice, gentle and a little pleady. "Just let us know what time would be good. We can come back anytime. It's just about the toilets. But it can wait."

"The toilets? What about the toilets?"

"Well, some people have been complaining, they say their toilet is backing up. You haven't had any problems like that, have you?"

"No," Aphrodite said doubtfully, thinking about it, trying to remember the last time she used the john. "Everything seemed to be working okay."

"Well, that's good," the building guy said. "Because some people, you know, they've had regular geysers coming out of their toilets. Got stuff all over the place, a big mess to clean up. Smelled terrible, too. But if yours is working so far, that's okay. I just need to check later."

Aphrodite suddenly visualized a river of turds flowing across her bedroom carpet.

"Later? Can't you come up right now?"

"Well, I guess I can, if it's all right with you. Sure."

"Just wait a minute while I put something on."

"Take your time," said Tony Baloot into the intercom. "I'm in no hurry."

Tony Baloot came out of Aphrodite Anderson's bathroom smiling reassuringly.

"Everything looks fine in there. You're good to go."

"You're sure?" Aphrodite said nervously.

"Oh yeah, no problem," Baloot said, trying not to look directly at her. Aphrodite's idea of "putting something on" involved considerably less material than many women would have thought appropriate.

"You don't have a lot of tools, do you?" Aphrodite asked him. "Plumbing stuff, I mean."

Baloot hefted the small gym bag he was carrying in his left hand and turned up the wattage on his smile.

"Just a few. I'm only inspecting right now. If anything was wrong, I'd have to call up the crew, so they could come up with their sewer snakes and monkey wrenches and porcelain hammers and everything."

"Porcelain hammers?"

"Yeah, you know, to break up the toilet, in case we have to take it right out. Sometime the bathtub has to come out too. Depends on how bad the problem is. Say, can I use your phone?"

"What for?"

"Tell the plumbing crew they don't have to come up after all," Baloot smiled. "They'll be relieved, they don't have to drag all that equipment up all these stairs."

"Sure, go ahead," Aphrodite said. "The phone's in there, in the living room."

Baloot put the gym bag on the floor and picked up the receiver. Aphrodite had retreated into her kitchen for some orange juice and vodka. Baloot dialed his own number and talked to his answering machine while he attached the small magnetic bug he had palmed in the bathroom to the bottom of the phone.

(Actually tapping the phone line would have required more work than Baloot was willing to put into the gig; plus, he thought he was missing a few of the parts. He settled for sticky-backed microphone transmitters. At least he'd be able to hear half of the phone conversations.)

Aphrodite came back in, sipping from a big glass of OJ and Absolut.

"Oh, I'm sorry, would you like something to drink?" she asked Baloot, suddenly remembering her responsibilities as a hostess. Well, sort of a hostess.

"No, that's all right." Regretfully Baloot turned her down. "I have a lot of toilets to inspect today."

He didn't trust himself alone with alcoholic beverages and Aphrodite Anderson's long, strong dancer's legs. God only could tell how that would go, but it would probably end up in some kind of trouble. Maybe the police would get involved again. Or worse. The last time he had had drinks with a client, he had ended up asking her to marry him.

13

Looking Up

Aaron Rogell's days were nearly as full as his nights.

Rogeletek continued to simmer. With a full complement of staff on board now—in spite of some carping from Melaleuca and MacBlister—the company began to look and feel like the real thing, and not some fly-by-night performance art event in an abandoned warehouse.

The acquisition of Mercedes Hernandez as his personal secretary had been the cherry on the sundae. Mercedes was a really good-looking young woman. It had required every fragment of Rogell's limited self-control to keep from trying to fuck her on the desktop during the job interview.

You don't want to cause a scandal, Rogell kept reminding himself. In the enclosed, biospherelike atmosphere of the start-up, such shenanigans might ricochet out of control and cause unforeseeable damage. Plus, there was always the threat of legal action. And, too, Amanda might find out. Much better to wait until cash flow allowed him to rent or buy a second home, a pied-à-terre, maybe something up in Tahoe, for the odd business trip. It would be natural that his personal secretary would accompany him on such trips. And there was no need to tell anyone else about the place.

Especially Amanda. *Amanda.* Guilt thoughts began to gnaw at the periphery of Rogell's fantasy, like a school of hungry piranha. To distract them, Rogell deliberately induced another fantasy: He and Amanda would have their own little getaway, somewhere else entirely, he decided. A cabin in the Gold Country, or someplace even more spectacular, like Big Sur. Someplace special. Someplace so deluxe it would make up for his serial infidelities without her even knowing it.

Rogell grinned to himself, making plans for the future. He felt a warm, self-satisfied glow. He felt nearly monogamous.

Things were definitely looking up.

Thomas Prouty came into his office unannounced. His clothes were rumpled and oddly pulled out of shape. One button on his button-down collar had come undone, and his jacket buttons were in the wrong holes. He was sweating and wild-eyed. Rogell wondered if he was drunk. On Prouty's forehead there was a large, shiny red mark that seemed to be smeared with oil.

"Tom? Are you all right?"

Prouty flung himself in a chair. He stared at Rogell for an embarrassingly long time without saying anything, so long that Rogell considered calling security. It might have been one way of getting the conversation started.

"I'm resigning," Prouty said suddenly. He seemed to be listening to himself with disbelief. "Effective immediately. As of today."

This was bad news.

"Tom, something is wrong here. I can tell. Let's talk about this, work it out. Is it another offer? You're very important to this project, and I recognize that. I can match almost any conceivable offer. Tell me what we're dealing with here."

Prouty clung on to the chair arms as if the furniture were flying through the air at supersonic speed. He stared at Rogell, panting slightly. Rogell thought they were about to sink into a minutes-long, excruciating silence again, when at last Prouty spoke.

"It's not that. It's not the money. I'm very grateful to you for how you've treated me. It's not that."

"Then what is it? A more engaging project?" Though what could be more interesting than the Rogeletek robots, Rogell was unable to imagine.

But Prouty shook his head again.

"No. I just have to get out, that's all. I'm going back to Cincinnati."

"What will you do there?"

Prouty looked even sicker, if possible, but he said, "I don't know. Start over. Live in my mother's basement. I don't know." He stood up suddenly, his legs shaky. "I just have to get out of this place."

Rogell was disappointed. He had thought Prouty was doing an excellent job. But he had burned out, apparently, in the fierce pressure cooker of the start-up.

Rogell had a deep belief in rolling with the punches. He had accepted Prouty's resignation before the man had stopped talking, and was already moving over possible replacements in his head.

He could have saved himself the trouble. Prouty, leaning on the edge of the desk as if to keep from falling over, said, "But I don't want to leave you in the lurch, Aaron. I found somebody to replace me."

A little knot of anxiety untied itself in Rogell. This was the kind of problem he liked, the kind that solved itself.

"That's great, excellent. Anyone we know?"

Prouty shook his head; this seemed to cause him pain, because he winced, and paused before he spoke.

"No, no one you know, I think. I hope not. Someone from outside. A Mr. Murray. Arthur Murray. He's very well qualified. He worked as a personnel director in the entertainment industry for some years, he tells me."

"Entertainment? That's not really relevant to what we're doing here, is it?"

"Oh, he's done other things as well. He's been everywhere, really, done just about everything. A most impressive résumé." Prouty was looking worse by the minute, and no longer seemed to care how he looked. As Rogell watched silently, a long, clear stream of nasal mucus reached the corner of Prouty's mouth before he brushed it away with the back of his wrist.

"Well, I'm really sorry to hear you have to leave us," Rogell said, standing up and offering his hand to end the interview, making a mental note to wash it immediately afterwards. "When do I meet your replacement?"

"He'll be here tomorrow. Nine sharp," Prouty said, shaking hands limply. "I told him to come straight to your office."

"Well, we're sorry to lose you, Tom. I guess you can do your own exit interview, though, can't you?" Rogell smiled at his own little joke; Prouty seemed less amused.

Rogell walked Prouty to the door. Up close, the red mark on Prouty's forehead was even more apparent. It was bright red, shiny, and shaped something like the prow of a rowboat.

Rogell had made a similar mark the last time he had tried to iron one of his own shirts.

"What happened to your head, Tom?" Rogell said, genuinely concerned. "That looks painful."

Prouty put a tentative hand to the red mark, jerked it away, and winced.

"Nothing," he said. "It's nothing. Just an accident, that's all."

Prouty staggered from the office.

. . .

Arthur Murray was waiting outside his office when Rogell arrived the next morning.

Murray stood up and smiled as Rogell walked in. He was dressed carefully, though oddly, in a pale linen suit, a lime green shirt, and a yellow tie. *Hair could use a wash*, Rogell thought, *and a little trim.* But he could put up with some sartorial eccentricity as long as the man could perform. This was San Francisco, after all. At least there were no visible piercings or tattoos.

"Dr. Rogell!" Murray stuck out his hand and Rogell shook it briefly.

"Mr. Murray. I'm glad to see you're an early riser like me. Come on in, please."

Arthur Murray had a curiously flattened face, as if he had been hit at birth with a shovel. Fairly greasy light brown hair arced back from a low forehead and hung down to his collar. A wispy, faint Chinese sage mustache and a small soul patch completed the unappetizing picture.

Where have I seen this guy before? Rogell thought. *He looks so familiar.* He ran various possible locations through his mind without a match. He had met so many people since the start-up, and he was beginning to lose track. Rogell had never been particularly good with faces.

Seated in Rogell's office, Murray looked around with curiosity and satisfaction, as if he were planning on buying the place, not applying for a job.

Rogell hated this part, talking to strangers, asking probing questions, trying to foresee problems. It was right outside his comfort zone. The queries that occurred to him always seemed wildly off topic: Where did you buy a jacket like that? Was your nose broken at birth, or was that a later accident? He would forget what job they were supposed to be talking about, ask scientists about typing speed, receptionists about gene transfer techniques.

But that was precisely why he was hiring Arthur Murray, to do this for him. The hire was a foregone conclusion, unless Murray began to act out in a radical way, attacked him, or fell to the floor in spasms. All that remained was to navigate through the next few minutes without embarrassing himself.

Rogell picked up the résumé Prouty had left on his desk and read through it quickly. Everything seemed in order, impressive even.

He looked up. Murray was staring at him with a strange, knowing expression, pulling on a corner of his mustache. The look vanished in a second; Rogell couldn't be sure it had ever existed.

"Well, Mr. Murray," Rogell said. "I see that you have broad experience."

"You might say that," Murray agreed modestly.

"Most of it, however, has been in other industries, entertainment, security. Tell me how you'd apply that experience to our special needs here at Rogeletek."

Arthur Murray leaned forward across the desk.

"I don't pretend to know as much about science as you do, Dr. Rogell," Murray said. "But according to what Tom told me, your needs in that department are well taken care of." Prouty had been very forthcoming after the head-ironing. Clench had learned a lot. He had even taken notes.

"I usually oversee those hires myself," Rogell admitted.

"Okay. But what I do know, and where my experience can be really valuable to this company, is in the security area. Now, from talking to Tom, and by my own observation, you seem to be very vulnerable in the security area."

"We have a good alarm system," Rogell objected. "Impenetrable firewall, password protections, encryption. Our network is safe as we can make it."

Murray dismissed this with an angry, erasing motion.

"No you're not. You're safe from the kind of attack you expect.

You're safe from industrial espionage. You're safe from yourself, from how you would go about getting in here. But you haven't protected yourself against the unforeseen."

"Give me an example."

Arthur Murray leaned back and smirked.

"An armed assault. Kidnapping. The physical removal of valuable scientific property."

Rogell was shocked.

"Surely not, Mr. Murray. Are you talking about gangsters invading Rogeletek?"

Murray shrugged. "Why not?"

"I just don't think gangsters would be very interested in our product," Rogell said. "Even if they could understand what it is."

"But they could be hired by someone who understands. Who wants what you've discovered. And it's not just gangsters you have to worry about. What you've done here will be very interesting to foreign governments. Unscrupulous foreign governments with limitless resources. If we baffle them, turn away their espionage attempts, they may decide on a frontal assault."

Rogell was terrified and bewildered. These things had never occurred to him, but Arthur Murray's hypnotic personality and vivid presentation was making them real. He supposed that Rogeletek was more important than even he realized.

"What would you do to forestall this?"

Murray smiled thinly. He radiated confidence.

"I know security, Dr. Rogell. I know people. I have access to resources. I could make this place as secure as the tenth level of the Pentagon."

"I didn't know the Pentagon had ten levels."

"There, you see?" Murray said. "How secure is *that?!*"

Rogell felt himself drifting into unknown waters. He imagined tanks breaking down the walls of the laboratory, ski-masked fighters with AK-47s rapelling down from the skylights.

Murray watched him, head a little to one side. When he judged that Rogell was ripe for it, he straightened up and leaned forward.

"Take me on a tour of your facilities, Dr. Rogell," he suggested. "Let me look things over, point out your vulnerabilities. Then let me call my people. I could have a new, effective security cadre in place in twenty-four hours."

Rogell nodded, got shakily to his feet. He felt grateful to Tom Prouty for introducing him to Murray. He would never have thought of these things by himself.

"All right. Come with me. I suppose we should start with the laboratory. That seems like the most important area."

"Sounds good."

Rogell paused at the door and put a hand on Murray's shoulder.

"The job is yours, by the way." He hesitated; his prepared questions seemed trivial and irrelevant now. "What about the business group?" he half-whispered.

"Another one of my specialties," Pablo Clench said confidently. "Just leave it to me."

Clench was pleased with his performance. *Baffle them with bullshit,* he thought. *Keep 'em spinning.* But in the avalanche of horseshit he had just unloaded on Rogell, there had been a few nuggets worth keeping, ideas worth a second look, even a third.

The shit about foreign governments, for instance. That had just been meant to put the fear of God in Rogell, shake up his thought process. But maybe it was an area worth investigating for real.

Sometimes I amaze myself, Clench thought.

Rogell gave Arthur Murray a free hand to implement his cutting-edge ideas. Rogell believed that the best managers found good people and let them do their jobs. If that sometimes meant destroying the financial security of a few other employees, possibly ruining their lives forever, well, you can't make an omelette without breaking eggs.

True, the scene with William Hendricks, head of Rogeletek security until that morning, had not been a pretty one. When Clench had let Hendricks and all of his department go, Hendricks had come straight to Rogell's office.

"I've done a good job for you," Hendricks said. "Why are you letting me go?"

Rogell shrugged, embarrassed, and tried to slide down in his chair. But there was no sliding room left.

"Rogeletek needs new ideas," he said to Hendricks. "I wasn't seeing them from your department. I'm sorry. But to meet the new security challenges of the post-9/11 era, we need fresh thinking, far more so-phistication than the older security thinking, such as yours, can pro-vide." Rogell heard the voice of Arthur Murray echoing in his head.

"My daughter is just starting college," Hendricks said. It seemed to Rogell like a change in topic.

"Well, you have to make sure she gets a good education," he told Hendricks. "Our economy is changing rapidly, and if you don't keep up with the changes, you'll be left behind."

Rogell didn't say, "like you" out loud, but it echoed in the room be-tween them.

"I have my mortgage payments to make," Hendricks said, now more to himself than to Rogell. "Payments on my car. I'm overextended on the credit cards already. I need this job! I can make any changes you want, just tell me. Tell me what you want me to do."

Rogell clasped his hands in front of him, then abruptly opened them, palm up, miming disappearance.

"I'm sorry, Mr. Hendricks. I've already made my decision. What I want is for you to leave this office."

"You can't do this to me!" Hendricks said. He stood up suddenly, leaning over Rogell's desk, his fists clenched.

In response Rogell pushed a button on his telephone pad.

"Mr. Murray?" he said into the mouthpiece, "could you come into my office, please?"

The new security team was in place as quickly as Murray had promised, so quickly that they appeared to have been waiting in the parking lot.

They were certainly a rough bunch, Rogell thought, but he supposed that was a good thing. That was the point, after all.

The security personnel—"Don't call them security guards, they hate that," Murray had warned him—looked good in the uniforms Murray had designed for them, a military gray with black trim. They looked like the bad guys in a James Bond film, very intimidating.

The weaponry added to the effect. It had seemed like overkill to Rogell—did anyone, even street gangs, really need automatic weapons in South City? But the new director of security operations had insisted.

"You never know when you're gonna need that kind of firepower," Mr. George Patton said.

The full complement of Rogeletek's executive staff turned out to welcome Arthur Murray and the new security director on board. Aside from Murray and Aaron Rogell, there were just three people seated around the vast oval table.

Rogell squinted at the meager assembly. "Where's Dan?"

"Not in his office when I went by just now," a sandy-haired guy in a white lab coat offered.

Heads turned as the conference room door opened and a slight, well-dressed man slipped into the room.

"Sorry I'm late, everybody," Dan Funk said. "I was deep in the latest expense figures and I guess I lost track of the time."

"Dan Funk is our CFO, Mr. Murray," Rogell explained. "The financial brains of this operation. We wouldn't be where we are today without him." He smiled at the Rogeletek executive cadre gathered around the table. "Well, gentlemen, we should probably get started. I'm sure you all have a lot on your plates. Let me put on one more item before you go back to your tables."

Strained smiles greeted this attempt at wit.

"Let me introduce you to our new Vice President for Personnel Relations, Arthur Murray," Aaron Rogell, president and CEO said. His voice rose into its lecture range in volume and resonance. "Murray will be climbing into Tom Prouty's big chair. He brings vast experience to this company, especially in the security realm. When any of you have personnel needs, bring them to Mr. Murray. He'll see that you get the people you need."

Rogell introduced Clench individually around the table. Clench shook Dan Funk's narrow hand, noting the slight widening of the eyes, followed by a sudden narrowing as he took Clench in. *Watch this guy,* he thought.

The sandy-haired guy in the lab coat—he had a pocket protector, too, Clench saw—turned out to be Aleister MacBlister, Chief of Laboratory Services. *Why am I not surprised?* Clench thought.

The little weasel-faced guy with the Clark Gable mustache was Philip Melaleuca, vice president in charge of preparation and fulfillment—the shipping department. He looked sharp, too. Could be trouble.

Last but not least was Mr. George Patton, the new head of security.

"Of course, you two know each other," Rogell said.

"Pleased to see you again, sir," Clench said, shaking Billy Colley's big paw.

Dan Funk stared across the conference table at Arthur Murray, eyes narrowed, lips pursed. He didn't seem completely sold.

"Mr. Murray," Funk said.

"Art. Call me Art."

"*Art.* Where did you say you worked previously?"

"Well, I worked most recently in the entertainment industry,"

Murray said. "Before that, in security. That's my field, what I know best."

"Security, as in security guards? Banks, malls, hotel lobbies, that kind of thing?"

Murray grinned at him. "Higher level than that, Mr. Funk. Private security. Escorts. Interventions. Government work."

"Impressive." Funk did not sound impressed. "Where in the government?"

"If I told you that, I'd have to kill you," Murray grinned. Next to him Rogell laughed hard, as if he'd never heard that one before. And maybe he hadn't, Clench thought. Aaron was pretty sheltered in some ways.

Clench/Murray leaned back in his chair and plucked at his mustache. This had been almost too easy, up to now. But just to make it interesting, this Funk fucker was going to break his balls. He just couldn't warm up to the guy: sitting there in his neat little suit, looking at him like Clench had just wiped dogshit on his freshly polished shoes.

The skinny one with the little mustache, Melaleuca, leaned over and put his two cents in.

"What I wondered," Melaleuca said, "have you ever worked in a scientific establishment before? What are your contacts at Cal, at Stanford, MIT?"

"Exactly what I was wondering myself," Funk put in.

Clench was glad that he had already scheduled Funk's appointment with the Colleys. It was going to be a real pleasure to discuss his future career with him.

"I have extensive contacts in the scientific world," Clench said, thinking back to his crank lab days and trying to come up with a name or two to throw at them, "chemistry, biology . . ."

"What about genetics?" Melaleuca wanted to know.

MacBlister, who up to now had said nothing at all, piped up too.

"That's right," he said. "What about genetics? That's central to what we do here."

Clench began to feel it a little. These assholes were cramping his style. He shot a look at Rogell.

"I admit I'm not up to speed in every area," Clench said. "but I intend to consult with Dr. Rogell about the science-side hires." He grinned. "You have to admit, his experience trumps all of ours."

Rogell lapped this up.

"I have complete faith in Mr. Murray," he announced to the table. "He and I will be working closely together on personnel matters. But please, bring your needs and problems to him, not me."

Funk and Melaleuca sat back, not appeased, but willing to save it for the second act.

Too bad, assholes, Clench thought. There wasn't going to be any second act.

Daniel Funk was an important part of Clench's operation, too, though he hadn't explained this to Funk yet. Just an accountant, Clench thought, just a fucking accountant with a corner office. But Funk oversaw the tidal surges of money that flowed in and out of Rogeletek. It would be important to get to know everything about him.

It had been a mistake not starting the exit interviews with Dan Funk, Clench decided. Prouty was easy, soft, malleable. He could have been saved for last. It had been like eating dessert first, to start with the guy.

But Funk, on the other hand . . . Funk was trouble, he could see that. The guy was just too quick. Funk had seen that there was something bogus about Arthur Murray the second he laid eyes on him.

It was time for an emergency intervention, before the guy had a chance to think about it, to compare notes, to make phone calls.

Clench reached for his—formerly Tom Prouty's—desk phone and dialed up an in-house line.

"Hello, Mr. Patton, sir," he said. "We need to meet."

. . .

Dan Funk was not at the next executive meeting.

"I'm sorry Dan Funk can't be here," Rogell apologized. "He's not usually late for things. I hope everything's all right."

"I'm sure everything is just dandy," Arthur Murray assured him.

The night before he had introduced Funk to the Colley brothers. Brother Earl—along with several of the Rogeletek security guards in their snazzy new uniforms—was babysitting him at the moment. Clench hoped to interview him later. He was sure by the time they got together that he and Dan would be seeing eye to eye.

Pablo Clench sat in Tom Prouty's former office, soaking in the sun. Floor-to-ceiling windows made up one wall, a big desk, nearly the size of Clench's hotel room, took pride of place. A smaller desk along one wall held not one but two computers.

In the wastebasket were two framed pictures of Tom Prouty and some sort of certificate that Prouty had left behind. The guy had not bothered to clean out his desk, either, and Clench looked forward to excavating the midden of Post-it notes, business cards, and memo-randa. You never knew what you might come across.

Clench was rapidly discovering that he had a real talent for person-nel work, at least for certain aspects of it. The amount of information Rogeletek had compiled about its employees, for instance, was truly impressive. One of the two computers was devoted solely to a powerful database that, if asked nicely, would spit out comprehensive histories of anyone in the building. It made fascinating reading.

But it was just a beginning. Clench knew that you couldn't know too much about the people that worked for you, what with all the impostors and scam artists out there. Anyone could fake a job history, stuff a resume with impressive but bogus credentials, leave out inconvenient facts and felony convictions. You had to dig deeper, he knew that.

Happily, he typed in "MacBlister," and after several false starts—scientist types apparently called their résumés "CVs"—accumulated a fair amount of data. Clench scribbled down a list of people to call—just to verify everything. No matter how slick computers were, Clench knew that if you really wanted to find the down-and-dirty on someone you had to talk to their friends.

You couldn't beat the personal touch.

The Colley brothers had their own version of the personal touch. Clench didn't get a chance to check in with the brothers until the next day, but he had hoped that all problems would be solved, and that he would only have to pitch a few cleanup innings. Work pressure had kept him from overseeing the interview personally, though, as he had originally planned.

That had apparently been a mistake. Things were not going to be that simple.

"You did what?"

"We dropped him," Billy Colley explained. "We didn't mean to drop the guy. His pants came off. You know, his legs didn't have any hair on them, any hair at all. I think he waxed them."

"Billy, the fuck are you talking about? Wax? What has that got to do with anything?"

"Well, they were real slippery, that's all," Colley said. "That's why we couldn't hold him."

"So where is he now?"

There was a fairly long pause on the Colley end of the call.

"Well, they can't find him," Billy Colley said after a while.

"They? Who is they?"

"The rescue guys. I think they're coast guard, or maybe like a marine division of the local cops and fire department. I'm not sure. I didn't want to be too nosy."

Visions of catastrophe rolled over Clench.

"Billy, when you say you dropped him, where exactly did you drop him?"

"Devil's Slide," Colley said. "We were just holding him over the edge, you know, to soften him up a little. To make him, like you said, more amenable to discussion. But it was real wet down there, fucking foggy, and Earl's foot slipped, then the guy's pants came off. So we dropped him. It's about three hundred feet down, big rocks and shit. They think the tide washed him out to sea."

"I was counting on this guy," Clench complained to Jimmy Cacapoulos later that night. "I needed him. Not for shark bait, not floating around in the fucking ocean. I needed him to work the financial side of things."

Cacapoulos seemed unmoved.

"Some people are hard to convince. It was me, I would have agreed to anything soon's I saw the Colleys. But then, I know those guys." Cacapoulos was looking for a toothpick. He opened his desk drawers, rummaged through them, came up with a slightly used one.

"I may know a guy you could use, come to think of it." Cacapoulos turned the toothpick in the light, examining the stain on one end, then jammed it between his teeth.

"Who?"

"That guy, Trick Fitzpatrick, used to do the books for Joe Maloney's clubs."

"Fitzpatrick? I thought he was inside, for ripping off Maloney."

Cacapoulos smiled happily at the memory. "Yeh. He was. But he got out six months ago. More than you can say for Joe Maloney."

Joe Maloney had been a rival club owner. Cacapoulos had arranged for Trick to come and work for Joe. When Trick went down for embezzlement, the DA's investigation had turned up more fishy transactions in Maloney's operation, enough to force Joe to join Trick inside. Maloney had been into some nasty shit, and a lot of it. The few anonymous phone calls Cacapoulos had made had probably been unnecessary.

But you can never be too careful.

"What kind of guy is this Fitzpatrick?"

"Real smart," Cacapoulos said. "Knows all about computers. Good with numbers. Bit of a lush, but not too bad."

"A drunk and a computer geek. Doesn't sound real useful to me."

"Maybe," Jimmy Cacapoulos said, "maybe not. One thing I forgot, shows you what kind of guy Fitzpatrick is. The guy who ratted him out?"

"Yeah?"

"His roommate. Another computer guy. Didn't approve of the kind of shit Fitzpatrick did, and Trick was dumb enough, or drunk enough, to tell the guy one time. So the guy goes to the cops, and that starts the whole ball rolling."

"Drunk and stupid. You've convinced me, Jimmy. Sounds like just the guy I need."

"Wait, I'm not finished. When Trick gets out of the joint, he goes back to the same apartment, to see his roommate. They go out together. Trick comes back alone."

"He took the guy out?" Now Clench was impressed.

Cacapoulos nodded, his neck wattles quivering. "They found the guy in the Richmond the next day, his head squashed flat. They never tied it to Trick, though you can bet they tried. It was pretty obvious what happened. But he walked."

Clench was thoughtful.

"Maybe you're right. I should talk to this guy."

"You know I'm right. I'm always right. I'll give you his number."

14

Lab Rat

MacBlister turned out to be easier to deal with than Clench had expected. Scientist types, in his experience, frequently had a rod up their ass when it came to ethical questions. But in the end, MacBlister had been very accommodating.

When Clench had approached him with the suggestion that he might want to retire so that more qualified people could take over, MacBlister's response was immediate.

"Like Tom Prouty? I don't think so."

That was interesting, Clench thought. The pencil-necked scientist wanted to push back. But he hadn't reached for the phone to call security, or spill the beans to Rogell. So maybe he just wanted to play.

"Tom Prouty made a wise decision," Clench pointed out. "Cincinnati is lovely this time of year, and Prouty is still in a condition to appreciate it."

"Are you suggesting that Prouty's injuries were not accidental?" MacBlister asked.

"You might want to consider a career change yourself," Clench went on. "You're still young. You could retrain, retrench, while you still have your health."

"You might want to do the same thing," MacBlister said. "While you still have your liberty."

Clench tried a new approach.

"By the way, that shit you made up, back in college, all that science stuff you faked, do you still have copies?" Clench asked. "I need them for my files. Prouty didn't seem to know anything about that."

That got inside MacBlister. Clench watched, fascinated, as the geek's entire head turned a deep red, even the shiny scalp that peeked through thin strands of sandy comb-over.

"That was a setup," MacBlister said. "I don't know who you've been talking to, but ask them. They'll tell you."

"Yeah, that's what my sources said, too," Clench said, stroking his chin. "They said everyone knew you copied other people's notes, so they salted some and left them out for you. Which is worse, with like, scientists? Making shit up or stealing it? I'm just curious."

MacBlister was still red in the face, but he recovered gracefully.

"All that is in the past," he said. "It doesn't mean a thing. Even if you told all this to Dr. Rogell, even if he believed you, it wouldn't stack up against the things I'm doing for this company."

"Don't be so sure," Clench said, just to keep MacBlister off balance. The school stuff had just been an extra ladle of gravy; Clench was relying on an extended interview with the Colley boys to help the creepy scientist decide on a new career.

"I'm not so sure Dr. Rogell would appreciate this conversation," MacBlister said. "If you think you've got something, why don't you bring it to him? Let's see what he says."

Clench looked thoughtful.

"That's right, you guys go way back, don't you?" he said. "I guess I was forgetting that. You went to school with him, and everything. I guess you were pretty close."

"That's right," MacBlister said. "We were pretty close." Well, he had shared a lab table with Rogell. For one semester. But that was pretty close.

"That's great," Clench said. "I like to see people get to know each other. I guess it was being so close and everything that let Rogell steal all your ideas, wasn't it? I mean, isn't that what you went around telling people? That he took your ideas and got all the credit? I bet Aaron would like to hear that. He probably feels guilty about it. I bet if you remind him he'll feel so bad he'll just hand the whole company over to you."

The red flush was creeping back across MacBlister's scalp.

"Look, Murray, what is it you want from me?"

"Big changes are coming here at Rogeletek," Clench told him. "Big changes. You can be part of them. Or you can get out of the way. Your choice."

"And if I don't feel like 'getting out of the way'?"

Clench shrugged. "Well, then you can discuss it with my associates in more detail—more excruciating, painful, permanently damaging detail."

"I don't know what you're planning," MacBlister said. He didn't seem to be worried by Clench's suggestion of personal violence. "But I'm sure it must be worth a great deal to you to not have your plans interfered with."

Clench leaned back, crossing his legs, arms behind his head, bouncing one foot as he contemplated Aleister MacBlister. Though a scientist and a dickhead, they had something in common after all.

"A lot, for sure," Clench agreed. "My question is, what would you consider a great deal?"

MacBlister named a sum Clench thought was reasonable. Very reasonable. He had a hard time keeping the grin off his face.

Not only a dickhead, he thought, but a bargain basement one.

"Every month," MacBlister added, very serious.

"We can do that," Clench said. "No problem. Monthly payments in that amount can be made to your personal account."

"I'd like that," MacBlister agreed.

"If there were any hint of a leak, however," Clench warned, "any sign that you've been talking out of turn, we'd have to take up this discussion where we left off."

"Talk is cheap," MacBlister said.

So are you, asshole, Clench thought happily.

After all, they could always kill him later.

"A hundred bucks a month. Can you believe it?"

Jimmy Cacapoulos couldn't. That someone, in a position to make real trouble, would be bought off so cheaply was inconceivable.

"He must be up to something," Cacapoulos theorized. "You better keep your eye on the guy."

"Oh, I trust him," Pablo Clench said. "You know why? Because he wants to put it to Rogell. I can just feel it. He wants Rogell to fuck up so he can feel better about himself. I know guys like him. They only feel good when someone else is blowing it. That's why we were able to get him so cheap."

"Well, cheap," Cacapoulos said. "There's nothing wrong with that."

The more he thought about it, the more Clench thought that there might be more MacBlister could do for him. He was glad now he hadn't just turned the guy's skinny ass over to the Colleys. He could use a scientist to help him make sure Rogell was coughing up the real stuff, someone who knew what was what. And who would know that better than the head of Rogeletek's own laboratory?

Beautiful, Clench thought, *truly beautiful; and it just goes to show: if you have a good plan and follow it, all the details fall in place by themselves.*

It might not even be necessary to cut MacBlister in fully on the deal. The monthly payments—MacBlister had insisted on the first payoff right away—gave leverage far beyond their slight fiscal heft. They were delightfully incriminating. Can you say coconspirator? Clench thought happily. Plus, the IRS always liked to know about any unreported income. Clench was sure MacBlister would be cooperative when the time came.

There had been moments early in the operation when Clench had had his doubts about its viability. The Colleys, while dependable in their way, were not smart, and seemed determined to rip Clench's plans to shreds and piss on the pieces.

But he understood MacBlister. Jealousy, envy, grudging, grinding resentment—these were feelings he could use. Clench had been worried about the science part, too, though he would never have admitted it to Cacapoulos. It would have been easy for these smart scientist types to fake him out; what did he know about fucking robots? Cacapoulos was right for a change.

But with dickhead at his right hand, checking things out, giving him the scoop, he would be all right.

When Clench thought of MacBlister now, he felt a faint glow, like a cheap, fragile incandescent bulb lighting up near his duodenum. You had to like a guy, after all, who would trash his friend's career, business, and family life for a small amount of money and a heaping plateload of petty vengeance.

Philip Melaleuca was a tougher nut to crack. Some people, as Jimmy Cacapoulos had pointed out, were very difficult to convince.

"He kept coming up on us," Billy Colley complained. "Tough little geezer, I'll say that for him. No matter how many times we hit him, he kept getting back up. He spit in my goddamn face!"

Earl's opinion was much the same.

"The guy wasn't being reasonable," Earl said. "Instead of like, agreeing with us, telling us some bullshit to get us to stop hurting him, he kept saying he was going to the cops, that we'd get arrested and thrown in jail. Now tactically, that was a dumb move. He should have just done what we wanted, and gone to the cops later."

"Yeah, well, it's his own fault if we went too far," Billy said.

"You got him to agree to go away, didn't you?" Clench asked.

"Well, no, not agree," Billy admitted. "We got him to go away, though. He won't be back for a while."

In the end they had had to force Melaleuca through the narrow mouth of a steel carboy. This required some modification of Mr. Melaleuca, but even then, the Colleys had had a hard time fitting the pieces through. The carboy, polished up and sealed, with a return address for SF General Hospital, was shipped to a warehouse in the North Mariana Islands, to be left until called for.

It was too bad, really, Clench thought ruefully, and must of been a bitch to clean up afterward. This routine slaughtering was starting to make Clench nervous. The bodies were beginning to pile up, and soon questions would be asked.

And nothing was accomplished by killing everybody off. Clench needed personnel in place to keep things running until he was ready to move, not ripening toward explosion in a quonset hut somewhere.

Though Clench didn't understand the full, horrific implications of fucking up a shipment of nanobots, he was dimly aware that the Cacapoulos musclehead he'd assigned to cover it was not the right man for the job. But what choice did he have? Chopping up Melaleuca had not been on his storyboard. He could only hope that Melaleuca's underlings knew what they were doing, even if their new boss didn't—that's the way it usually worked, anyway—and would fend off pure catastrophe long enough for Clench to put his ultimate scheme in motion.

But he would have to move fast.

15

Big Trouble

Rogell couldn't understand the storm of attrition that seemed to have come down on his employees. First Prouty, then Dan Funk's suicide, now Melaleuca's disappearance. Everything in distribution seemed to be accounted for. Melaleuca's apartment—he had lived alone—was stripped bare. His car was gone from the parking garage. Evidently he had been planning his disappearance for some time. *You can never tell, can you?* Rogell asked himself sagely. Melaleuca had seemed the least likely of his employees to do a book. At least he hadn't stolen anything.

Unlike, apparently, Dan Funk.

Rogell and Murray had discussed Funk extensively after his suicide.

"Often in a case like this, where the employee takes his own life," Murray had told him, "you find some kind of financial fraud is at the bottom of it. Cooked books, embezzled funds, checks to personal accounts, like that."

"Poor Dan," Rogell said, shaking his head. "I hope it was nothing like that. Have they found the body yet?"

"Part of it." Legs had washed up on the nude beach below Devil's Slide. The assumption was that they belonged to Dan Funk. The rest was thought to be wedged in a cliff face somewhere, or else eaten by crabs."

Well, thank god he still had Arthur Murray. Or did he? A sudden wave of panic swept over Rogell; he hoped Murray wasn't planning to go away suddenly. Talk to him, feel him out, offer him more money, he thought. Rogell began to sweat. He reached for the phone.

Murray answered on the second ring.

"Arthur Murray Enterprises. How can I help you?"

"Mr. Murray, Rogell here. I think we need to talk about these sudden vacancies, these personnel issues we've been having lately."

"Dr. Rogell, I'm glad you called, and I totally agree. In fact, I've been giving these problems my closest attention. As you know, we've already hired a replacement for Melaleuca."

"Yes, I've met him," Rogell said doubtfully. "He didn't seem very suitable."

"Glotz is just a temporary, a stopgap," Murray said, "just to hold down the fort until we can find someone better. Meanwhile, he's a strong manager."

"Well, I'll trust your judgment on him," Rogell said. "But I'm more concerned with finding someone to take over for Dan Funk. I brought Dan on board myself, you know. He was key to getting the company under way. We can't let the financial side go dark for a single minute."

"Dr. Rogell, I totally agree. And I want to assure you that I'm on it. In fact, I'm nearly ready to make a hire."

A wave of pure relief washed over Rogell, and with it a feeling of warm gratitude to Arthur Murray. *I still know how to find the best*, he thought. "I'm glad to hear it. Can we meet then, in a couple hours, to go over the candidates?"

"Candidate," Arthur Murray corrected. "And you can do better than that. You can meet the man himself."

. . .

"There seems to be someone in Dan Funk's old office," Rogell said when Murray sauntered in to see him a few hours after their phone conference.

"The new guy," Murray said. "I want you to meet him."

"Yes, I want to talk to him. But, the *new* guy? You've *hired* him? Without discussing it with me?"

"Of course not," Murray said. "I would never do such a thing. I just wanted to give him a trial run, a sort of audition before the interview. To see if he can do the job."

Rogell was perplexed. "Trial run? Audition? I never heard of such a thing before."

"I always work that way," Murray said.

"What is he doing in there? It seems insecure, to have him pawing through Dan's stuff like that."

"Don't worry," Murray reassured him. "I'm having him look through Funk's books, just to see that everything is on the up-and-up. I'll have the results to show you soon."

In the middle of a thirty-foot-long table in the vast, empty conference room, Pablo Clench laid Trick's inventive, back-dated accounting before the boss.

"These are very serious accusations, Mr. Murray," Rogell said. "I just can't bring myself to believe that Dan Funk would engage in wholesale fraud."

Clench/Murray was unruffled.

"I know just how you feel," he said. "It's a terrible feeling when you find out that trusted employees have been stealing you blind. But the proof's right here, in black and white. It's a good thing I brought in Abbott to go over the books, or we might not have found out what was going on until it was too late."

The file of spreadsheets that Clench had printed out showed pretty clearly that an increasing portion of the expense streams for the lab, for labor, and for materials acquisition were being diverted to vendors that had no previous history with the company, and sported bland, uninformative names like "Nova Management Acquisitions, LLC" and "Paymenow, Inc."

The payroll showed a number of checks disbursed to employees that Rogell had never heard of before. Surely he would have remembered names like "Betty Bonanza," "Krystal Bright," and "Rebecca Rockets."

Rogell read through the spreadsheets with mounting horror. It didn't take much financial sophistication to see what had been done. Phantom workers, fake companies, and bogus subsidiaries were fastening onto the Rogeletek revenue stream like starving lampreys, multiplying like E. coli in a warm tuna fish sandwich.

Nor did it take much imagination to guess where the money was going after it left Rogeletek.

"Dan Funk was doing this?" he asked.

"No one else."

"No wonder he killed himself. He must have realized he couldn't get away with this much longer."

"Well, I think Mr. Abbott passed his audition with flying colors, don't you?" Murray asked.

"Oh yes, yes indeed." The thought of what he had just narrowly escaped made Rogell break out in a thin sweat. He looked up gratefully at Pablo Clench.

"And I want to thank you for bringing him on board, Mr. Murray," he said.

"*De nada,*" Mr. Murray said. "It's the very least I can do for the company."

.   .   .

Patrick Fitzpatrick, when Rogell finally met him, was a pleasant surprise. Bud Abbott, as he was known at Rogeletek, dressed more conventionally than either Arthur Murray or Mr. Patton, and seemed quite intelligent. His light brown hair was cropped short; he wore gold-framed eyeglasses, a striped shirt, and a charcoal sport coat.

But though impeccably dressed and well groomed, Mr. Abbott gave off a peculiar smell. Rogell couldn't quite place it. A disinfectant of some kind, maybe, as if the man used Lysol instead of deodorant.

"Well, I'm pleased to meet you, at long last," Rogell told him. "Mr. Murray speaks very highly of you, and I was favorably impressed by the detective work you did on the late Mr. Funk."

"My pleasure," Trick said. "I'm looking forward to helping this company in any way I can."

"Well, for a man of your evident ability, that should be easy," Rogell said.

Trick smiled. "I really think I can help lighten your load."

"Good, we need to be light, light and agile, to insert our product in an everchanging market. I'd like to sit down with you and hear your ideas for taking this company forward. Can you be in my office in, say, thirty minutes?"

Trick didn't answer immediately; he seemed lost in thought. But Arthur Murray, who had faded into the background while his candidate took center stage, broke in.

"Can we do this tomorrow? I have a lot to go over with Mr. Abbott, personnelwise."

Rogell looked at his watch. It *was* late in the day. He *did* have a lot he wanted to do. And he *had* planned on leaving early enough to swing by the Tenderloin before going home to South City.

"All right," Rogell said. "Tomorrow then, at, say, eleven?"

"We'll be there," said Pablo Clench. "With bells on."

16

Whammo-Zammo

Aaron Rogell was feeling productive. The morning had started out normally enough—though at Rogeletek in recent weeks the bar for abnormality had been raised quite a bit. But no major crises had occurred, no one else had gone missing, no strange, new employee had been dragged in for him to meet. He was in his office, working on a presentation he planned to deliver at the Next Level New Technology Conference in Los Angeles next month. Many important people would be there, including many manufacturers looking for a competitive edge in the global marketplace—an edge Rogell and his nanobots would be glad to supply.

Rogell was deeply absorbed in his work, and didn't look up when he heard his office door open.

"What is it, Mercedes?" he said. "Can it wait?" He was a little surprised his secretary would just walk in on him and, now that he thought about it, a little pissed. Finally he looked up, trying to think of a forceful but still elegant reproof, then stopped, mouth half open, stunned into silence.

Arthur Murray was standing there, smirking at him.

"Morning, Dr. Rogell," Murray said, very casual. He pulled up a chair and fell into it. "Busy?"

"Well, as a matter of fact, I am," Rogell said. "Arthur, you shouldn't just walk in on me like that. I don't like it. Where is Mercedes? I'm surprised she didn't stop you."

"Oh, I sent her home."

"Home? Why did you do that? Was she sick?"

"In the pink of health," Murray said. "I just didn't want anything to interrupt our little talk."

"Talk? Arthur, what is this? I'm busy now, I don't have time for a talk. We're scheduled for later this morning, aren't we? Is this so important it can't wait?"

Arthur Murray crossed his legs, hooked his folded hands over his knee, and leaned back, rocking slightly.

"Important? I'd say it was important," Murray said. "Yeah. Pretty fucking important, if you ask me. It's not every day that an important scientist and inventor turns over his proprietary secrets to his employees to avoid an ugly scandal."

"Scandal? Employees? What on earth are you talking about?" Rogell asked.

"I'm talking about us, about you and me," Murray said. "I'm talking about the future of this company. I'm talking about your bizarre after-work habits, your little hobbies. Your little friends. Know what I mean, Bernie?"

It took a moment for Rogell to recognize his own *nom de fuck*, but when he did the earth moved beneath him.

"I don't understand," he said, shakily.

"Oh, yes you do. I think you do," Murray said. "But I was afraid a simple man-to-man talk wouldn't be enough to convince you. So I arranged a little audiovisual presentation. I think you'll really get a kick out of it."

"Mr. Murray, you'll really have to explain yourself a little better,"

Rogell said. Was the man drunk or conked out on exotic drugs? Had he flipped completely? What the hell was going on with personnel? Was there something in the pipes making everyone at Rogeletek run away or go insane? Were rogue nanobots eating their brains?

"That's exactly what I'm going to do," Murray said. Without taking his eyes off Rogell, he slipped a cell phone out of his jacket pocket.

"Lou?" he said after a pause. "You can bring in the monitor now."

Rogell and Arthur Murray sat in tense silence, Murray smirking, Rogell desperately trying to find the right attitude to adopt. He had just about settled on outrage and forthright anger when his office door opened and a shorter version of his security director, George Patton, backed in, pulling a cart with a large television set on it. The man winked and smiled at Rogell.

Helping the shorter Patton were two large men Rogell had never seen before. They looked at him with intolerable, knowing grins.

"Hey Bernie, how's it hangin'?" one said. The other large man choked back a laugh.

This has gone far enough, Rogell thought. *Too far*. He pushed himself back in his chair, put a finger under his collar as if to loosen it, and glared at Murray.

"I think this meeting is no longer productive," Rogell said. "Patton, send some security to my office, will you? I'd like you to escort Mr. Murray and his associates off campus."

This apparent non sequitur was directed at his security chief, and spoken into a collar mike Rogell had activated by finger pressure as he loosened his collar.

"Yes boss," the tiny receptor in his ear canal responded. A slight uneasiness blew over Rogell. Boss? Yes, *boss?* He would have to remind Patton to stick to protocol.

Across the vast desktop, Arthur Murray seemed unruffled. He leaned back in a fairly casual pose for someone who was about to be escorted off the premises by heavily armed and muscled guards.

The office door opened and Rogell's office quickly filled with large men carrying weapons. The disturbing thing about this, for Rogell, was that the large men were not in the paramilitary uniforms he had gotten used to seeing around Rogeletek, but in cheap suits and casual clothes.

"I don't think you really understand the situation, Dr. Rogell," Pablo Clench said, standing up.

The video monitor flickered and hummed. The heavily armed men leaned against the wall and sat on chairs and office furniture that they had moved around in a semicircle in front of the television set.

It was like in high school, Clench thought, when the regular teacher was out sick, and the substitute showed movies to keep everybody quiet.

"Ready, Lou?" he called out. "Let's get started."

"Who are you supposed to be?" Rogell whispered venomously to Earl Colley.

Earl extended a hand in friendship.

"Lou," he said. "Lou Costello."

"You are *not* Lou Costello."

Earl shrugged, turned back to the video monitor, and pressed the Input button on the remote.

"This first one's a little rough," he apologized. "We got better as we went along."

The video suddenly cracked into an image: Aphrodite Anderson's face, looking both annoyed and depressed, filled the screen.

"All right, come on in and get it over with," she said.

Aphrodite walked ahead of the camera, occasionally looking over her shoulder. She seemed miffed, but compliant.

"In here," she said. "Try not to make a mess of everything." Abruptly she walked out of the frame.

The camera roamed the room like a hungry animal, picking out objects, examining them, and putting them down uneaten. You could almost hear it panting.

"What's the point of view in this one?" Clench asked.

"I hid the camera in the clock above the door," Earl said. "The teddy bear clock."

Mysterious scraping and breaking sounds. Then a rapid pan and the vidcam was looking down over the top of Earl Colley's head onto an expanse of bedsheets and pillowcases, like aerial photography of snow-covered mountains.

"How did you fit that camera I gave you in the teddy bear clock?" Clench asked, genuinely curious.

"Didn't," Earl explained. "Got another one. Really small. Made for this kind of thing. It's really cool, no bigger than a lipstick. Look." He began to dig in his pockets, but Clench held up his hand.

"Later, Earl. Show me later." Turning to Rogell, he said apologetically, "I hate people who talk through the whole movie, don't you?"

Rogell said nothing, glowering at the screen.

The frame went blank. Then Aphrodite's bedroom suddenly jumped back into existence, this time with new additions. A hairy backside was lunging and rolling on the bed, bare legs and feet thrashed and tore at the sheets. Perhaps it was the camera angle, perhaps the abundance of body hair, but the writhing figures on the bed were surprisingly unerotic.

"Let's fast-forward through this, Earl," Clench said. "I think we've established that Aaron's friendship with Aphrodite is more than platonic. Let's get to the good stuff."

17

The Good Stuff

A new sequence filled the screen—coarse, fuzzy black-and-white footage. "We didn't shoot this," Earl Colley hastened to explain. "I used the security camera shots instead. It was easier. We lost some more quality when we digitized it, but we were lucky to get this at all. Who knew the guy was going to show up at the all-night porn store?"

A steady shot from a high angle—apparently a surveillance camera—showed an empty aisle in a shop of some kind. A bookstore, maybe, though the titles on the magazines that lined the aisle weren't readable. At the far end of the store was a cash register, a clerk looming grayly behind it.

A head and shoulders came into the picture, striding from under the camera and down the aisle. Though the face could be seen only partially, it was clearly Aaron Rogell.

Oh, dear God! Rogell thought, as he recognized the adult bookstore in the Tenderloin where he spent most of his money. *Not the doll. Dear God, don't let them show the doll.*

But they showed the doll.

The security cam patiently watched the back of Rogell's head as he negotiated something with the register clerk, paid his money, and received a package.

The video cut abruptly to a different viewpoint, once again from overhead, but now in color, with better focus: a small room furnished with a metal stool, small shelf, and something that looked like a slot machine with a viewfinder.

"Shot through a two-way mirror," Earl explained. "The lighting wasn't all that great."

"Sshh!" Clench warned, finger to his lips.

There was no need to be quiet. The images spilling across the screen were silent. A door opened; Aaron Rogell entered the little room with something under his arm, which he proceeded to lay on the shelf. In his other hand he carried a small paper bag.

"What's he got in the bag?" an audience member asked.

"Our boy plans to stay awhile," Clench explained. "He brought a lunch."

"What's that other thing he's carrying?"

"Ssshhh!" Clench shushed again. "Watch. You'll see."

Rogell ripped into the larger package with practiced movements. Soon he had disentangled what looked like a Halloween mask of a woman's face from its wrappings. He brought the mask up to his face, put his lips to it and puffed his cheeks. A form unfolded, a woman, mouth round, as if with surprise, lifesize—or nearly—buck naked, blonde.

"Whoa!" someone commented. "Blow job doll!"

What happened next took most of the audience by surprise. Rogell began to slap the inflated blow-job doll, forehand and backhand, to punch it and kick it; the doll bounced around the little room, always coming back for more.

"Yeah! Smack that bitch!"

Rogell lowered his head into his arms. He couldn't bear to watch the rest. He could follow the action clearly enough without watching, both from his memory and from the laughter and running commentary from his audience.

"What's that? What is he putting in her mouth?"

"We found out after, it was *bifteck tartar*," Clench pronounced expertly. His stint as a busboy in a French restaurant had not been wasted. "Raw meat."

"Look at that guy! What is he doing? What's that runny stuff?"

"That's a soft-center French cheese, probably a Camembert, maybe a brie," Clench said.

"Look, he's smearing it on her. Oh, man, he's fuckin' eating it! Wha!" The doll suddenly went limp, collapsing in Rogell's hands. "He must a bit into it! He fuckin' popped her!"

Clench leaned over and patted Rogell on the shoulder.

"Chin up, Aaron. It's almost over."

The doll sequence ended abruptly, with no resolution. The audience stayed put, watching the screen expectantly.

"Next one's my favorite," Clench said happily.

The opening sequence of the next video was a kind of backstage introduction. It showed a bare, dirty little room with a single bed. A young woman sat on the bed, looking up at the camera, waiting.

Uh-oh, Rogell thought. He knew that girl.

Chickie looked sadly at the camera. She was hard to recognize at first without her wig on; her natural hair was reddish, scanty, and cropped close to her skull. She held the blonde wig in her lap like a toy poodle.

"I see him, like, once a week," Chickie told the camera. "Usually it's just, like, I suck him off in his car. He told me his name was Bernie." Chickie paused; seconds of humming silence ticked off on the digital clock in the upper right of the frame.

"He pays good," Chickie said after a while.

"Mr. Big Tipper," Clench said.

"The rest of this sequence," Earl explained, "I shot from a surveillance cam bracket. There was a cam there already, but I took it down and used one of mine. The bracket was motorized; I could track pretty good with it. The cam was right out in the open, but they never noticed."

"Too busy," Clench posited.

On-screen Rogell entered the little room, grinning.

"Hi, Chickie," on-screen Rogell said. "Everything set up?"

"I got everything, just like you asked," Chickie said. Her wig was back in place.

"Everything?"

"Everything."

Rogell was disrobing as they talked and was soon mother-naked. His body was pale and somewhat hairy, but, though a little soft in spots, he had stayed in pretty decent condition. Nevertheless, his striptease was greeted by hoots and shouted commentary from the audience.

"Don't turn around! Don't turn around! Aaahh!"

The watchers were treated to a full crack shot as Rogell clambered onto the little cot with Chickie.

Without further preliminaries, they got down to business.

Rogell sweated as he watching Chickie's bobbing, swiveling head on the video. Fortunately her head filled most of the screen, leaving his male parts in the background, but the sound track featured his moans and exhortations clearly.

"Oh Chickie! Oh Chickie baby! Yes! That's right! Suck me, baby, suck me!"

Just the thing to liven up a budget meeting.

"Enter the goat," Clench announced. He was enjoying himself.

The door to the little room opened. Human figures, dimly seen, were active in the darkened corridor outside. Then a large billy goat was shoved into the room and the door slammed shut.

The goat trotted in, a fine, bearded specimen. It seemed mildly confused, perhaps tranquillized or otherwise drugged up.

Rogell was sweating profusely; he knew what came next.

"What is really disgusting is, this is a male goat," Clench pointed out.

"Fuck," one of the muscle guys said, outraged. "A male goat?"

"Watch."

They watched. The sex of the goat was not in doubt.

"Whoa! How did they get it to do that? Did they, like, train it or something?"

"Just doing what comes naturally," Clench said.

Rogell, in silent misery, nevertheless made excuses. This was nasty, okay, but nothing the fringier films from Tijuana hadn't shown a thousand times. A goat was smaller and somehow less disgusting than a burro, wasn't it? Wasn't it?

The audience was riveted.

"Aahh! What is he doing to the goat? What if it kicks him there? What a pile-up! The whole fuckin' bed's gonna come down!"

"Some people just need to be the center of attention," Clench said.

"Man!" said one of the thugs, "that is sick!"

18

Dick in the Wringer

The monitor went blue. The audience, with one exception, was satisfied. It had been a good show.

"Pretty absorbing, huh, Dr. Rogell?" Pablo Clench asked. "Did you enjoy that?"

Rogell was silent.

"No? Well, it's always a shock seeing yourself on screen the first time. Not quite what you expected, is it? But I thought you came across pretty well. The camera loves you, Aaron."

The haggard scientist stared back at Clench.

"What is it you want, Murray? Money? This is blackmail, isn't it?"

He's so quick, Clench thought.

"Not necessarily," Clench said. "This could just be a test screening, before the videos get distributed more widely. I think your backers would enjoy them, don't you? Vitek, and New Capital Funding Services, Benner and Halfleck, the whole money crew? To say nothing of your friends and relatives. Don't you think Aunt Cecily will like the goat video? She likes animals. I bet your wife likes them, too. Maybe she can share them with your kid, when Delia gets old enough."

Anger shot Rogell to his feet, hands flat on the desk.

"You wouldn't dare. Leave my wife out of this. And my child. Delia has nothing to do with this."

Clench grinned happily. "Nothing? What if Daddy brought home a case of hoof-and-mouth disease? Shouldn't your family at least know where it came from?"

Slowly, Rogell sat back down. As the complex ramifications the potential video viewing might set in motion began to unfold in his brain, he felt his anger dwindle and fade away, replaced by cold, stark, staring panic.

Rogeletek was like a newborn, after all. Sudden shocks to the system could harm it, even kill it. So much depended on public perception at this early stage, especially that portion of the public that lent him large sums of money. The video documentation of his sexual experiments might distort that perception.

Might big time.

And Amanda—she might not be open to whatever explanation of the videos Rogell came up with. At the moment nothing was occurring to him. He doubted anything could stop Amanda from seriously freaking out. It would not be pretty, and it would not be cheap.

"What do you want?" he whispered hoarsely.

Clench leaned forward, hand behind one ear.

"I'm sorry, did you say something? 'Cunt'? Did you say 'cunt'?"

"Want," Rogell repeated, a little louder. His throat seemed to have been reamed out with a wire brush. "What do you want? How much?"

"How much? You mean, how much to make the videos go away forever? To not show them to everyone you love and treasure and borrow money from?"

Rogell nodded weakly.

"That much, huh?" Clench rubbed his chin thoughtfully. "I don't know. We have a lot invested in those videos, a lot of time and money. There were training issues, liability, a lot went into the production. I would hate to see them just be destroyed. I don't think anything less than the specifications for your robots could reconcile me to that."

Rogell's eyes widened. "Specifications? You want me to give you the very thing my business is built on, my future?"

Clench nodded. "Your future? I'd say you have a great future in film, Dr. Rogell. If robot manufacturing dries up, I mean. I know some people down in the San Fernando Valley, filmmakers, I could introduce you. Let me know."

"What would you do with my discovery, anyway?" Rogell asked. "You're no scientist. What good would it be to you?"

"Oh, nothing, probably," Clench said. "Though I bet your competition would be glad to get their hands on the plans."

"You overestimate their value. Eventually my competitors will reverse-engineer the bots. No one is going to pay for information they eventually could get some other way."

Clench shrugged. "People pay for an edge, a leg up. I already have some feelers from a potential buyer. You just don't realize how valuable you are, Dr. Rogell!"

Rogell chewed on his lip. Sell the bots? It was out of the question.

"What if I pay you? How much will it take to make you go away?" he asked. "I have some money in the bank. Just name a figure."

Clench stared back, smiling.

"You know, Dr. Rogell, if you give a man a fish," he said, "he'll eat for a day. But if you teach him how to make little robots you can't even see, and make diamonds out of dirt, he'll be able to retire to a Caribbean island for the rest of his life."

"I can pay you a hundred thousand."

"A hundred thousand! Wow!" Clench said. "That's . . . that's so fucking cheap. You have that much in your household accounts, from the patents and shit, I mean. Your old lady probably goes through that much in a couple months. You know"—Clench's eyes widened as a sudden thought came to him—"you could probably reassign the patents as well! That would be nice. In case we burn through the robot money too quick. A little something to tide us over."

Rogell stared sideways at the desktop. His hands writhed and twisted over one another like a fornicating couple.

He turned over his options desperately. They seemed somewhat limited. His entire life's work was poised to vanish, to be whisked out from underneath him like a tablecloth in some magician's act.

Maybe Amanda would forgive him. Maybe she would understand.

Maybe she would lawyer up with high-powered attorneys and institute divorce proceedings. No: certainly. Maybe the courts would award her the house, the cars, even the business. But at least there would be an estate to divide.

He would lose Delia, true.

But maybe now was the best time, before the kid grew up and began to develop individual, likeable characteristics.

"It's a big decision, huh?" Clench said sympathetically.

Sweat dripped down Rogell's forehead.

"Can't you give me a little more time to think this through?"

Clench stared back, unreadable.

"No time."

Pablo Clench was beginning to run through his patience. *The guy is stuck*, he thought. *We'll be here all fucking day at this rate.*

"Look, it's easy and simple," he explained helpfully. "Give us the process. We give you the tapes, the originals."

Behind him Earl Colley frowned, but wisely kept his mouth shut. Earl had no intention of surrendering his original files.

They aren't tapes anyway, fuckface, Earl thought. *I got it all on DVD.*

Rogell stared at Clench in terror, bathed in sweat, his eyes wide.

"No," he said quietly.

Clench couldn't process this.

"No what?"

"No, I won't give you the secret of my invention."

Clench stared at him, taking this in. It had never occurred to Clench that the guy would hold out, would let his whole life be ruined for a few pages of some kind of science shit.

This stuff must be worth more than he had thought.

"The videos should play well on the six o'clock news," Clench reminded Rogell. As a threat, maybe that was too much, too unrealistic. The six o'clock news would not give a shit, and even an insulated geek like Aaron Rogell would probably realize that.

"They'd be a big hit at the company office party," Clench fell back on the tried and true. "Your backers will like them too, not to mention your wife."

Rogell was green and shaky now; he seemed to have shrunk a size. But he shook his head.

"Still no," he said.

Even if I lose everything, he thought, *I'll still have my discovery. I can start over again, rebuild from scratch.*

Maybe Amanda will come back when she sees what I've done.

Motherfucker, Clench thought, *he means it. The guy means it.*

This was bad. There was no plan B. Clench had to come up with something quick. He could feel all the muscle guys staring at him.

He stood up.

"All right, let's take it to go," Clench said. "Pack all this shit up, bring Mr. Goatfucker, and we'll start over again in the morning."

Maybe by then he would think of something.

It was nearly five o'clock. Most of the lab workers had already gone home. The stragglers heading for the door eyed the strange parade curiously: their boss, flanked by Arthur Murray and George Patton, followed by a half-dozen security guards, automatic weapons at port arms, marching briskly across the lab. The whole thing looked peculiar; something was obviously up, something funky and weird. Several of the lab workers would give their impressions later to the police and the news cameras. They had been sure something really funny was going on. One of them had almost said something.

But in the moment, it was none of their business. The last lab guy left; the heavy metal door to the clean room swung shut.

At the far end of the lab they ran into MacBlister, coming out of the men's room. He stopped dead when he saw them, goggling as he wiped at the tips of his fingers with a wad of toilet paper.

"This is it, huh?" he said.

"Totally," Clench agreed. "Why don't you come with us? I need somebody to keep the science shit straight."

MacBlister fell in step.

Rogell couldn't quite take this in.

"MacBlister! You? You're with them? But I went to school with you! We worked together! I've known you for years!"

MacBlister eyed Rogell coolly.

"Time to share the wealth, Aaron." He hadn't called Rogell by his first name since they shared a table in sophomore chem lab. "You've had it all your way for a long time. Now it's my turn."

Clench picked up on the animosity and grinned.

"Everyone wants a piece of you, Aaron," he said.

. . .

The bizarre assembly halted in front of Rogell's personal laboratory. Seeing his private workshop about to be invaded and violated by a bunch of gangsters stunned Rogell.

I won't let them in, he thought. *I don't care. Let them hurt me, so what? I'm not going to be part of my own destruction.*

But he never got a chance to test his pain tolerance. No one asked him for the password. Instead, "Lou Costello" leaned over and opened the front of the security controls, poked in code like a teen girl dialing up her cell phone, then took out a small tape recorder, pressed a switch, and held it up to the grille. Rogell heard a voice saying "honeypot." He barely recognized it as his own, but the security system was way ahead of him. The digital readout flashed to "access granted."

Costello glanced sideways at Rogell and winked.

"Miked it," he explained. "Picked it up in my office. Recorded it. Simple."

Lou Costello pushed the door open.

The thugs shouldered in.

"All right, let's clean this place out," Clench instructed. "I'll keep an eye on the doctor here."

Rogell watched hopelessly as the security guards began to rip open doors and filing cabinets, piling papers and lab equipment randomly into white folding-file boxes. A lifetime's work, soon to be loaded into the back of a stolen minivan.

Trick Fitzpatrick appeared as if by magic and seated himself in front of Rogell's personal computer. Earl Colley came over to help him through the elaborate maze of passwords Rogell had guarded his secrets with.

Writing them down had been a bad idea, Rogell knew that. But his memory for passwords was like his memory for faces—nonexistent.

. . .

The bank of stainless-steel refrigerators gave up their contents last. There wasn't much inside, a few plastic boxes with snap lids, a handful of small glass bottles and pipettes holding a clear solution.

Clench's interest perked up at the bottles, which reminded him of the painkillers he had stolen from the hospital once. Better be careful though, he realized. Probably not Dilaudid in there.

"Better get some coolers in here," Clench ordered. "No telling what would happen if this shit thawed out."

"Careful. Don't open that," Rogell warned a thug who was fiddling with a small plastic container that looked something like a piece of Tupperware. "You might spill it."

"What would happen if he did?" Clench was curious.

"You wouldn't like what would happen."

Clench reached over and took the Tupperware box away from the thug.

"This shit is dangerous—is that what you're saying?" Clench asked doubtfully. "I mean, if I open this container, it isn't going to go off or something, is it?"

"It isn't going to *go off*," Rogell said, trying to shade the contempt out of his voice. "That container holds my first successful, fully operative nanobots. No, it's not Tupperware. It's a kind of plastic, but made up of nanoparticles, precisely aligned, then layered in sequence, so the bots won't find their way through. Don't open it, you might spill it. But even if you did, you'd have to inhale it on purpose to do yourself any damage."

"Damage, what kind of damage?" Clench asked.

Here we go again, Rogell thought. *Even these half-witted thugs have the same questions.*

"Look," he said patiently, "would you drink a cup of gasoline?"

"No way."

"Would you pour it over your head and put a match to it?"

"Not unless someone was forcing me to," Clench said.

"You interact with highly dangerous substances every day," Rogell was getting into his lecture voice. "Gasoline. Natural gas, propane. Chlorine. Weed killers, oven cleaners. The average household has enough poisons in it to kill off a small town, to fight trench warfare."

Clench was intrigued. "I never thought of that," he admitted.

"You just have to be careful," Rogell said. "That's all. You have to use commonsense."

Clench stared at Rogell. He sensed something off, a line of horseshit he was being asked to swallow. *Don't shit a shitter*, he thought.

"Billy," Clench said. "Open it."

Billy stared at the little box, then shoved it over to Clench.

"No way. You open it."

Clench took the container out of Billy's enormous hand, set it down on the lab table, and levered the top off. When nothing bad happened, the crew of muscleheads gathered around, still at a discreet distance, and craned their necks to see what was inside.

It didn't look like much. The container appeared to be full of laundry detergent.

"That white shit, that's the robots?" Billy Colley wanted to know.

"Just a medium. A packing material. So you know where they are, since they're invisible," Rogell explained. He seemed a little embarrassed. "This was my first attempt to create functioning nanobots. Since then, of course, we've become much more sophisticated. Now we use a liquid medium to carry the bots."

All this meant little to Billy Colley.

"So they're just walking around in there? Suppose they get out?"

Rogell nearly smiled. "They're dormant. It takes heat to wake them up and make them do their job. Anyway, they don't walk, they roll. On wheels made of atoms. Through intermolecular space."

Intermolecular space. *Fuck this guy*, Billy Colley thought, *thinks he's so fucking smart*.

Clench was getting impatient. He still had a sense that Rogell was trying to put something over on him, but he wasn't sure what. He snapped the lid back on the square container and handed it back to Billy.

"Okay, let's keep moving," he said. "We'll just take this with us, if you don't mind, Doctor. We can deal with it later. Put it in a cooler with some dry ice or something."

"Where are you taking it?" Rogell asked anxiously. "You want to be careful with it. It's not that you might be harmed in some way. Everyone is frightened by my robots, but they don't realize how fragile they are. If you take them off campus, you might not have the capacity to store them properly. The bots could be damaged."

"It's not a campus, fuckhead," Billy Colley interrupted.

Rogell looked up, startled.

"You called it a campus. It's only one fucking building," Billy elaborated. "A campus is lots of buildings, and trees, and grass. This shithole is not a campus."

While the offloading of Aaron Rogell's private laboratory went on around him, Aleister MacBlister was carefully poring over the documentation of the bot manufacturing process. He had been wanting to get his hands on this material ever since he had come to work for Rogell, but had only been given just enough data to do his job and grow hordes of exponentially self-reproducing nano-scale robots. But the root idea, the seed, the concept that made the whole process work, the initial catalyst, had been kept from him. This was a source of resentment: Didn't Rogell trust him?

As far as he could see, it was still being kept from him. There was nothing in Rogell's papers to indicate how the bot growth process began.

He thumbed through the pile of documents again, then lifted his head.

"There's something missing."

Across the lab, Clench froze.

"Missing? What's missing?"

"Well, the mechanism that would allow the bots to begin reproducing," MacBlister explained. He would have gladly launched into a long, excessively detailed explanation, but Clench held up a hand, palm outward, like a traffic cop.

"Aleister. Wait. So these things won't work without this 'mechanism'?"

"Well, yes, the nanobots will work, that is, the ones we have will work. But we won't be able to make any more."

Everyone in the little room turned to look at Rogell.

Though still green and shaky, Rogell allowed himself a smug little smile. It very nearly made Clench kill him on the spot.

"It's all there," Rogell said. "All right in front of you."

Clench came over and stood directly in front of Rogell. He put his hands on Rogell's shoulders and shook him slightly.

"Aaron. Tell us where."

Rogell shook his head.

"You won't tell us?"

Rogell shook his head again. The smug little smile reappeared.

Clench stared into Aaron's eyes. Then he dropped his hands and stepped away, looking defeated.

"Well, if you won't tell us, you won't tell us," he said. Clench pivoted suddenly. His left hand looped out and caught Rogell on the chin, snapping his head back. Then his right hand connected solidly and drove the head back again.

Rogell dropped to the floor like a deflated blow job doll.

"Wrap this piece of shit up and let's get out of here," Pablo Clench said.

19

The Scientist in the Basement

Aaron Rogell lay quiet and still in the back of the van. He had little choice: His head was wrapped in duct tape, with very small holes poked for his nose and mouth. His hands and ankles were bound firmly with computer cable.

Being blinded by duct tape didn't signify at the moment, since he was hidden under a blanket or tarp of some kind. It was hot and smelly under it. The holes in the duct tape didn't let in much air, and Rogell had to concentrate on his breathing. This was good, as it kept his mind occupied and distracted him from the very grim reality of his situation.

After a long, jolting ride, the van stopped moving. Pablo Clench lifted up a corner of the tarp.

"How we doing in there, Doctor? Everything copacetic?" Clench let the tarp fall back. Rogell could hear him giving orders, presumably to Rogell's former security personnel.

"Wrap him up in the tarp and carry him into the house. Don't worry about the neighbors. Pretend he's a fucking rug."

Rogell felt himself rolled, wrapped, and lifted. After a short carry he was dumped roughly on the floor, uncovered, and stood on his feet.

"Take that shit off his legs so he can walk," someone said, "I'm not carrying him no more. Dr. Rogell, you hear me in there? You gotta go on a diet, man."

"Welcome to your new home, doctor." Rogell recognized Clench's raspy, sardonic voice. "This is where you'll be staying until you tell us all about your little secrets."

Rogell felt himself grabbed by many hands. He was upended and hoisted in the air like a piece of furniture being loaded into a moving van.

"Take him down the basement."

Downstairs, Rogell was deposited in a chair and the duct tape ripped off his head. It hurt like fuck.

Pablo Clench and another man were standing in front of him. Clench was leaning forward, hands on his knees, like a doctor about to examine a patient.

"Feeling better, Dr. Rogell?" Clench asked.

Rogell saw that the other man in the room was the employee he knew as Bud Abbott. Now Rogell began to doubt that that was his real name.

Faux Abbott nodded and smiled, a wry, self-deprecating little smile, as if to dissociate himself from the whole mess.

"This is your new host, doctor," Clench said. "You two know each other already, so I'll spare the introductions. But I just want to warn you, so you don't get any ideas from his meek and mild manner. Don't fuck with him. He is a killer. Isn't that right, Trick? Beat his partner's head in when the guy ratted him out. He may look like a nice guy, but don't test him. Okay?"

"Okay," Rogell said. It was strange to hear his own voice again.

Trick smiled grimly.

"I think we better take that cable off his hands," he said to Clench. "I can see his fingers turning blue. Your guys put it on too tight."

"He'll look better in nice new chains anyway," Pablo Clench said.

. . .

The chains weren't as bad as they had sounded, Rogell thought. Trick—Abbott's true name seemed to be Trick—had put wristbands under the chains so that they didn't rub. The shiny metal links didn't weigh that much, either.

But they were still chains.

The chains themselves were attached to a longer chain, locked in turn to a massive steel staple set in the concrete floor. Rogell had some freedom of movement, but the chains didn't let him reach as far as the door.

Aside from the chains, the small, windowless room was furnished with a single chair. Not an armchair or even an office chair, it looked like a kitchen chair from the fifties, ripped Naugahyde and little brass rods. It was not comfortable.

Rogell spent his first hours of captivity announcing his presence at the top of his lungs. He was sure someone would hear him and call the police. This was America, after all. Bellowing men in basements were investigated. Weren't they?

After a while Trick looked in on him.

"Look, I'm sorry, I want you to stop that yelling. The neighbors are starting to complain."

"Good. I want them to complain."

"No you don't. Because if you don't stop yelling I will take steps."

"Oh bullshit. You can't scare me. If you were going to kill me you would have done it already."

"Who said anything about killing? What I'll do, I'll tape your mouth shut with duct tape again. You'll be eating your dinner through a fucking straw. Is that what you want? Then just keep it up."

20

Gone Missing

Well, Amanda thought, *that was interesting.*

She shut the door behind the departing police and leaned heavily against it. She hadn't slept in forty-eight hours. She'd been sitting by the phone ever since 6:33 that morning, when, after a second long, sleepless night, she had finally called in a missing-persons report for her husband.

For twenty-four hours before that, she had been frantically calling everyone she or Aaron knew even slightly, even people they couldn't stand. No one had heard or seen anything. Aaron had dropped off the face of the earth.

Hospitals and police stations had been next, without results. Both a radio in the kitchen and the six-foot-screen TV in the main room were blaring news channels she monitored with half an ear. There was no news of Aaron Rogell anywhere.

Words like "industrial accident," "kidnapped," and "disappeared" tumbled through her brain. Abducted by aliens. Eaten by robots. No one could tell her a thing.

"Absconded" was another word that occurred to her. "Fled," as from responsibilities. Done a book. Run for it. Ducked out.

Then the police had called her back.

Aaron, they told her, had vanished into thin air, along with about a third of his staff. His office, and several other offices at Rogeletek, had been ransacked. The Mercedes was still in the parking lot, but there was no sign of Aaron anywhere.

The police were looking into it.

The detective who came out to talk to her had looked hopelessly young to Amanda. *The least they could do is send a fully grown adult,* she thought.

"Usually, if there's a kidnapping—whether it's terrorists or criminals—the kidnappers make some sort of ransom demand," the detective had said. "Money, usually, sometimes a prisoner release, or some other political demands. But in this case there has been nothing like that. Not a word."

"But what do you think happened?" Amanda asked.

"We're still gathering the facts," the young detective said. "If it's a kidnapping, we can expect the kidnappers to contact us soon. If it's something else, that will turn up in the course of our investigations."

"Something else?" Amanda asked. "What would 'something else' be?"

The detective looked embarrassed.

"You'll be the first to know, Mrs. Rogell, I can promise you that. We'll be in close contact. I'll call you right away as soon as we know anything."

But it was Amanda who called him, every day, sometimes several times a day. Nothing, she realized, could move forward until Aaron was back, for good or bad. Nothing.

She couldn't leave him, after all, if he wasn't even there.

. . .

While the police seemed very low-key about the whole thing, the newspapers, magazines, and especially the cable news shows were all over the story. Aaron, from being an obscure businessman who couldn't get coverage in the local classifieds giveaway, was now the center of a media storm: ROBOT SCIENTIST DISAPPEARS.

Soon the narrow road up to their house on San Bruno Mountain was lined day and night by the vans of TV crews. Reporters wandered over the lawn and fell into the ravine behind the house. Rogell's isolated minimansion took on a beleaguered, crowded atmosphere, like the last twenty minutes of a zombie movie. It got so bad that Amanda took Delia and moved in with her mother. The TV crews didn't seem to realize she was gone, and remained camped out on lawn, freezing in the cold, foggy winds of summer.

A week after Aaron had disappeared, driving back to the South City house to pick up some clothes, Amanda noticed that something had changed. She wasn't sure what it was at first. Then, slowly, she figured out what was missing.

The media was gone.

The TV vans that had lined the road like vendors at a flea market had disappeared. Even the print journalists had vanished.

Aaron's disappearance had fallen off the news cycle.

21

Moves

Life in the basement room quickly settled into a regular routine. Every day Trick brought down some food for Rogell. It was actually pretty good food: Thai takeout, mostly, sometimes Chinese or Italian.

His days were measured in piled-up takeout boxes and empty coffee cups. Mealtimes were his only way of keeping track of the time. Trick seemed to be gone a lot, and midday meals came irregularly, but breakfast (coffee) and dinner (takeout) happened like clockwork.

"How long are you going to keep me here?" he said to Trick's retreating back one day.

Trick paused in the doorway, looking over his shoulder.

"As long as I need to." *Until Pablo tells me to let him go,* he thought. If *Pablo lets him go.*

Rogell glared at him, pad thai noodles bristling from the corner of his mouth.

"Look, I'm bored to death down here, day after day, nothing to do but stare at the wall. How about bringing me a pencil and paper, at least."

"So you could try and communicate with the outside world."

This exasperated Rogell.

"How am I going to do that? There are no fucking windows in this place! What am I going to do, tie a note to a mouse and let him go?"

Trick thought it over.

"How about a TV? There's no cable down here, and I don't know about the reception. But I could bring you one."

Rogell didn't answer this, angrily shoving food into his mouth straight from the container. In just a few days of captivity, his table manners and social skills had deteriorated considerably.

"Sure. Okay. Whatever you want."

"Are you a chess player?" Trick asked, out of the blue.

Rogell looked up, surprised.

"I play some," he said. Rogell actually thought of himself as a superb player.

"Well, so do I. Maybe we could play a game or two."

"It's your loss," Rogell said.

To Rogell's consternation, Trick turned out to be a more than fair player. In fact, he beat Rogell easily in the first few games. *I was taken by surprise,* Rogell excused himself. *I underestimated him, wasn't ready for his use of strategy. Time to concentrate.*

The next few games were excruciating, humiliating losses, too, but at least they took a little longer to play out. *I've been away from my game too long,* Rogell thought. He spent the long, empty days alone going over their games in his head, identifying his weaknesses, missed opportunities, moves he should have made, building strategies for the future. It passed the time.

And a dim plan was beginning to form in Rogell's brain, a plan that might enable him to escape from the basement, get back to the real world and find out what was happening to Amanda and to his company.

Trick drank a lot, Rogell noticed. He always brought a full bottle to their now daily chess games. It was usually empty by the time they finished.

But if he could keep Trick drinking beyond the game, Rogell thought, eventually he would pass out. And when he did, then Rogell could go through his pockets, maybe find the key to his chains and make his escape.

But first he would have to relearn to drink, to keep up with Trick, and spur him on. Not shot for shot of course—that was obviously a losing strategy. But just enough to keep Trick going, hitting the bottle, pouring it down.

It was worth a shot, anyway.

The next time Trick came downstairs and set up the chess board, Rogell was ready for him.

The game, as usual, didn't go well for Rogell.

"Mate in three moves," Trick announced. He topped up his highball glass with Maker's Mark.

"Bullshit," Rogell said testily. "I don't see it."

"I know you don't." Trick glugged down several fingers of bourbon.

"What's that you're drinking?" Rogell asked.

"Bourbon. Want some?"

"Sure. I'll take a glass."

Trick handed over his highball glass.

"Here, take it. I can get another."

"Thanks. Cheers." Rogell poured bourbon down his throat. It burned all the way down.

"Maybe it'll improve your game," Trick said.

. . .

Rogell had never been a heavy drinker, but he had put away a few in his time, especially when he was in college. Well, that was more wine and beer, not hard liquor. But he had always thought of himself as having a pretty good head for booze.

But he could see he needed more practice. After the game wrapped up—mate in three moves, just as Trick had predicted—Rogell put down the remains of his drink in a single swallow.

"Kills the pain of loss," Trick said, leaning forward to replenish Rogell's highball glass. He filled it to the brim, killing the bottle.

Rogell closed his eyes. The bourbon was burning through his body like a column of fire. His brain was spinning like a cyclotron. He forced his eyes open again before the centrifugal force threw it right out of his skull.

Trick smiled. "Feels good, don't it?"

Rogell nodded, not trusting himself to speak. He watched in amazement as Trick drained his glass in a gulp and stood up. Rogell doubted very much that he could stand up; he had no intention of trying.

"Need some more whiskey," Trick said. Was that a little slur, a little thickening in his voice?

"Be right back."

As soon as Trick was out the door Rogell looked around desperately for somewhere to dump out his bourbon. No good place presented itself; there was nothing in the little concrete block chamber except for the television, two chairs, and the empty whiskey bottle.

Pour it in the TV. But it would just leak out. Or else catch fire and burn the TV to a cinder, filling the room with poisonous black smoke and destroying Rogell's only link with the outside world.

Okay, not the TV then. But where?

Trick came back before he could think of anything.

"Ready for another one? I am." Trick filled his glass and settled down in the folding chair. He looked ready to talk. At least part of Rogell's idea was going as planned.

"I'm good, thanks," Rogell said. He sipped cautiously at the bourbon.

"So tell me, Trick," Rogell said after a decent interval. "How did you get into all this? Kidnapping, I mean, and embezzling. Was it a lifelong dream, something you always wanted to do? Or just something you fell into?"

Trick was thoughtful and quiet for a while, taking big slugs out of his glass.

"I was never any good with money," he said finally. "No matter how much I brought in, I always needed more. The people I worked for seemed to have plenty of money. I knew they could always get more. So I helped myself to some of it."

"Did you get caught?"

Trick nodded. "Oh yeah. Right away. But I did restitution, and the owner didn't sic the cops on me. Bad for business. But it helped me, in a way, since that little problem brought me to the attention of Jimmy Cacapoulos."

This was a new name to Rogell.

"Who? I never heard of him."

"I guess you don't hang around North Beach much. He owns half of Broadway, big chunks of the Tenderloin, strip clubs, massage parlors, escorts, and legit businesses, too. He was looking for someone to do the books at a friend's place. That's what he said, anyway. So I went to work for Joe Maloney. But Jimmy threw a lot of things my way as well, some of it not so legitimate. I didn't care; I needed the disposable. But then I got caught again."

Rogell remembered what Clench had said.

"Your roommate?"

Trick nodded. "Yeah, he found out what I was doing—shit, I told him myself—and took it to the cops. They had a hard-on for Maloney for years and took it from there. I ended up doing some time. Just as well the roomie stuck his nose in, though; if Maloney had caught me and not the cops, I would have gone to the bottom of the bay, not to prison."

It was a touching story. Rogell discovered that he had drained his glass while listening to it. Trick saw the empty glass and quietly filled it up.

"Well, cheers," Trick said, raising his glass. "Here's to better luck for everybody."

Rogell let a burning tide of bourbon roll down his throat, savored it, and made a strange gasping noise, half satisfaction, half suffering.

"Cheers. I need a little luck to beat you at chess."

Trick smirked, drank.

"Aaron, there isn't that much luck in all the whiskey in the world."

Bourbon became the standard accompaniment to their ongoing chess tournament. And in fact, it did help Rogell's game a little, loosening him up and making him more willing to take chances. He actually won a few games.

But his plan to drink Trick under the table and get his hands on the keys went nowhere. If Trick did any passing out, he did it elsewhere. In Rogell's little dungeon, Trick, though slurred of speech and with a tendency to knock things over, never checked out.

Instead it was Rogell who always gave in first, sagging in his chains. Once he had come to sprawled out across the chessboard, pieces scattered across the floor, his eye swollen nearly shut from where Trick's queen had poked it.

"One way to get out of a game," Trick had commented.

.   .   .

As the days of his captivity lengthened into weeks, Rogell's drinking became a regular feature of his existence (such as it was). Trick kept him supplied, and monitored his progress from social drinker to lush with the proud, appraising eye of a teacher for a star pupil.

Rogell found some advantages to being a drunk. He didn't really like the numb nowhere of chronic alcohol poisoning, and he never got used to the constant puking. But he found that his sexual obsession was much diminished; he hardly beat off at all anymore, sometimes falling asleep in midwank. As for picking someone up, his drastically challenged personal hygiene would have made that difficult, even if he were no longer chained up in a San Bruno basement. Rogell smelled like a urine-soaked mattress; his clothes were crusted with dried puke and pickled in old sweat. Even the crack whores would think twice about servicing him in his current state.

This was the true purpose of addiction, he thought, to substitute itself for all your other problems.

People can get used to anything. Rogell's days quickly settled into routine: watch TV, masturbate, drink, eat, get beaten at chess. The only variable was that several times a week Pablo Clench and his minions would appear and kick the living shit out of him.

22

A Visitor

Of all the weird and unaccountable things that had happened in the weeks after Aaron's disappearance, the weirdest was the morning Amanda found Aleister MacBlister on her doorstep.

She had spoken with MacBlister briefly on the phone—he had wanted her permission to keep the lab going—not, he explained, to manufacture nanobots, but merely to maintain the protein vats where the assemblers were grown. She had no idea what he was talking about; it was all beyond her, and she wasn't sure she had any authority over the business, anyway. But she had said yes, keep it going. She was sure Aaron would want that. When he got back he would straighten things out.

When the doorbell rang early on a Saturday morning she was sure it was something important. Maybe even Aaron, escaped from whatever circumstance—kidnappers, memory loss, alien abduction—that had kept him away. She raced to the door and flung it open.

MacBlister was standing on the doorstep, blinking and smirking.

"Mrs. Rogell?" he said, in an oddly meaningful way.

Who does he think I am? Amanda wondered. *The au pair?* She had met MacBlister, briefly, at some company function not long after

Aaron had hired him, but he had left—typically for MacBlister—little trace in her memory.

"That's right," she said, choking back her disappointment. "What is this about? Is this about Aaron's company?"

MacBlister seemed nonplussed at this directness.

"Well, yes, it is, in a way. I'm Dr. MacBlister, the head of labs at Rogeletek. We spoke recently on the phone. May I come in?"

A tidal wave of resistance swept over Amanda; she did not want to let this guy in her house. But she couldn't think of any good, rational reason why not, so after a pause long enough to be insulting, she stepped back and held the door open.

"Sure. Come on in, Mr. MacBlister."

"Doctor."

"Doctor. Dr. MacBlister."

Dr. MacBlister looked around approvingly as she walked him through the house to the living room, with its big windows overlooking the bay. He settled into one of the big leather chairs facing the window before Amanda had even asked him to sit down.

There was something about Dr. MacBlister, Amanda thought, some indefinable quality, that filled you with the overwhelming urge to kick him in the ass. Maybe it was the satisfied way he visibly inventoried every object in the room, like an insurance adjuster.

Comfy now? she thought, but said, "Can I get you something, Doctor? A cup of coffee? I just made a pot."

"No, thank you, I don't drink coffee," MacBlister said. It was clear what he thought of those who did.

Amanda actually would have liked a cup herself, but decided to wait and drink in MacBlisterless solitude. She sat down across from the skinny scientist and leaned forward.

"Now, Dr. MacBlister, what have you come to see me about?"

MacBlister smirked.

"Mrs. Rogell, I realize that the sudden—disappearance—of your husband must have been a great shock to you."

Amanda nodded. "Shock"—that was the word, all right.

"And I don't want you to think I'm rushing things." Another significant look—almost a leer. *What was with this guy?*

"But this is a critical time for Rogeletek," MacBlister continued, "a make-or-break moment. We're weeks away from rolling out our first product. It is essential that this schedule be met."

"What is it you want me to do?" Amanda asked. "I've already given you permission to maintain the labs until Aaron gets back."

The smirk widened. "But suppose he doesn't get back? I know that's a hard thing to accept, right now. But just suppose, as a contingency, that he never comes back."

He knows something, she thought. *The miserable, bony little son of a bitch knows something.*

"Well?" Amanda wasn't sure she had enough breath to say more.

"I'd like to propose to you that you delegate full authority to me to run Rogeletek in Dr. Rogell's absence," MacBlister said. "And to do this properly, I'll need access to his personal papers, his files, and complete documentation of the manufacturing process."

Complete documentation? He didn't want much.

"Why do you need to see Aaron's files?" Amanda asked. "Don't you have everything you need to run the lab already?"

MacBlister blushed. "Yes, but Dr. Rogell retained . . . portions . . . of the process in his own hands. There are aspects of manufacturing that he oversaw personally. Now, with Dr. Rogell absent, someone needs to step in to keep the project on schedule. If he returns . . ."

"*When* he returns," Amanda said.

MacBlister nodded. "*When* he returns—he can take the reins. But there have to be reins to take, an operating, productive company to return to."

"Of course."

Amanda stood up suddenly, forcing MacBlister, after brief, squirming confusion, to stand up as well.

"*Doctor*, I'll think over everything you've said, believe me," Amanda told him. She took MacBlister by the elbow—he had leather patches on his tweed sports coat—and steered him toward the front door. "But I'm sure you can understand, in an important matter like this, that I have to give the matter careful consideration before I commit anything to writing."

MacBlister was obviously unprepared for her resistance. *Did he think I was just going to sign over everything to him without a whimper?* she thought.

"Well, yes, of course, I understand," MacBlister blithered. "But I hope *you* understand the time-sensitive nature of all this. The process at Rogeletek begins in biology . . ."

But ends in engineering. Aaron's voice echoed in Amanda's head.

". . . but ends in engineering," MacBlister blundered forward. "An interruption to the process at this point would put us seriously behind our scheduled rollout. And if we miss those dates, there will be serious financial consequences."

"What sort of consequences?"

MacBlister swallowed audibly. *You'd think it was his money*, Amanda thought. *And maybe he thinks it is.*

"Our continued funding depends on meeting the schedules we've laid out," he said. "If nothing else, we want to preserve investor confidence."

They had reached the big double doors to the Rogell residence. Amanda opened one door, briefly considered flinging MacBlister down the steps—it was a matter of leverage, after all, not brute strength—but decided against it. Her intuition was screaming that the creepy little scientist knew a lot more than he was letting on. It would be harder to find out his secrets if she put him in the hospital.

"My concern is with Rogeletek—not for myself, but for what the company can do to advance nanotechnology in the marketplace," MacBlister said. "I'm sure that's a concern we both have in common." MacBlister smiled and squinted at her. He batted his eyelashes like a geisha.

Christ almighty, Amanda thought, *he's trying to flirt with me.*

"I'll call you as soon as I've made my decision. Depend on it," she said. "Thank you for coming in person to tell me all this, Dr. MacBlister."

"Oh, no, Mrs. Rogell," MacBlister smirked, "thank *you.*"

It took a great deal of self control to not slam the door shut and catch MacBlister in the ass with it, but Amanda closed it as slowly and carefully as a tai chi master setting down a brimful cup of tea.

The cops should look into this MacBlister character, Amanda thought, instead of sitting around waiting for the kidnappers to call. MacBlister knew something about Aaron's disappearance, she was sure of it. If the police were to question him at length—say, for forty-eight hours in the station house—the tweedy little creep might cough up something useful.

Amanda knew that the local police no longer engaged in rough stuff while questioning suspects, at least not for white-collar crime. And during her career as a defense attorney she had been very vigilant against any suspicion of suspect abuse. But she couldn't help but wonder if a one-time exception might be made for Aleister MacBlister.

The police, as it turned out, had already had some very useful talks with Aleister.

The little TV only pulled in three channels, one of them in Spanish, but it was Rogell's lifeline to the outer world, and he watched it every waking moment when he wasn't playing chess or masturbating.

It had taken him a moment to recognize his own face when it swam up on the tiny screen.

"That's me!"

Trick looked up from his Szechuan bean curd. "You look great."

"Where did they get that photo?" Rogell wondered. (Supplying the press with Rogell materials had been Sasha Goode's last official act before he moved back to his parents' house in Chula Vista.) In the picture he was grinning, his eyes gleaming with intelligence, looking slightly upwards, as if at a monumental achievement.

Distracted by his own image, Rogell didn't at first follow what the anchorperson was saying about him. But as the story slowly soaked in, he stopped eating and paid full attention.

"Holy shit!" he said. "They're saying the police think I kidnapped myself! That it was all a scam to loot Rogeletek!"

"Well, that's what it was," Trick pointed out, using a pair of greasy chopsticks for emphasis.

"But I had nothing to do with it!" Rogell's voice had risen a full octave and a half with rage and exasperation. "It was all you, you murdering, thieving bastards! You stole my ideas, my business, ruined my marriage, alienated me from my child, and now everyone is saying I did it myself!"

Trick shook his head, chasing the last chunks of tofu around the bottom of the cardboard container with his chopsticks.

"You need some civility lessons, Aaron," he said. "No wonder all your employees hated you."

Amanda thought the new police theory of Aaron's disappearance was horseshit, too, especially when Detective Koch appeared on her doorstep.

"Search our house? Why would you need to search our house? You're supposed to be out there finding Aaron!"

Koch looked slightly embarrassed.

"We have reason to believe that Dr. Rogell engineered his own disappearance," he told Amanda. "If you know anything about this, it would be better for yourself, and for Aaron, if you told us now."

"MacBlister put this idea in your head, didn't he?" Amanda raged. "That little creep. Can't you see that he knows more about this than he's telling?"

"Mrs. Rogell, you can let us in of your own free will, or I will come back with a search warrant. Either way I'm going to search the house."

Amanda stared at the imbecile policeman, fighting down her own first impulses. It would be a bad idea, of course, to actually hurt him. They would just throw her in jail, and then who would be left to find Aaron?

"Are you going to let us in?" Koch asked.

She swung the door wide.

"Knock yourselves out."

The police were thorough, but didn't come up with much, and Detective Koch seemed pretty sheepish as his men carried boxes of paperback books and six-year-old income tax forms out to the patrol cars. The most interesting material they turned up was an extensive pornography collection, stashed in a false-bottom drawer in Aaron's desk. *Funny, I never knew about that,* Amanda mused as a uniform walked by with a well-thumbed stack of stroke books. *Chalk up another thing I never knew about Aaron.*

Which reminded her of something. And of someone.

"I want you to find him," Amanda said to Tony Baloot. "You're supposed to be a private detective, aren't you?"

Baloot smiled ruefully, willing to overlook Amanda's prickly manner. She was under a lot of strain, after all.

"I can do that, Mrs. Rogell," he said. "I have his routines pretty well mapped out. I'm good at this kind of thing. I should be able to locate him."

"Good," Amanda said. "That's more than the cops have been able to do." She stared resentfully at Baloot, who looked as if he were waiting to be kicked.

"And whatever the circumstances," she told Baloot, "I mean, even if the cops are right, and Aaron's running some scam on his own company, even if he's holed up with some bimbo somewhere, just let him know one thing for me, will you?"

Baloot smiled brightly. His clients were often pretty intense, but this was the worst he had ever seen it.

"What's that, Mrs. Rogell?"

"Tell him, wherever he goes, I'm coming with him," Amanda said.

23

Getting to Know You

Trick unlocked the door to Rogell's dungeon and stepped back out of the way. Pablo Clench and Earl Colley walked into the little room, smiling and nodding.

"Good morning, Doctor," Clench said. "How are we feeling today?"

Rogell felt a sick wave of fear wash over him. What were they going to do to him this time? Would he be able to stand it? He wasn't sure how much more pain he could take.

Earl Colley began taking some kind of electronics out of a bag. Electroshock? Some kind of hi-tech cattle prod? But on closer inspection, the objects turned out to be a DVD player and a small video camera.

Rogell felt a surge of full-body relief, though mixed with a fair amount of confusion. Were they going to show him the sex tapes again? What would be the point?

Earl gave the room's tiny black and white television a look of complete contempt.

"I can't use this piece of shit," he complained. "Trick! Is this all you've got?" He scurried out of the room.

Clench lounged in the other chair, hands in pockets. He smiled at Rogell.

"More show and tell," he said. "Just like last time. That was fun, wasn't it? This time'll be even better."

Rogell said nothing. They stared at each other, Clench's hungry, undersea eyes fixed on Rogell's.

Rogell looked away first.

Trick and Earl Colley came back into the room carrying a big, new TV set. They set it up on the card table, and Earl fiddled with the DVD player briefly.

"All set?" Clench asked, and when Earl nodded: "Okay. Lights, camera, action!"

Earl turned out the overhead light, then leaned over and pressed the Play button on the DVD player. A rooftop, somehow familiar, filled the screen; beyond it the blue water of San Francisco Bay and a gray-green smudge of distant hills.

With a prickle of anxiety, Rogell recognized his own house.

"This's the house in South City," Earl explained. "I was uphill, behind a bush at first. Then, when they came outside, I got up to the fence. I cut a hole in it the night before," he said proudly.

An abrupt cut to a woman seated in a white metal lawn chair, a brunette, her abundant hair pulled on top of her head and held in place by rubber bands and a headband. The shot was from behind; the woman appeared to be reading. A small cradle stood next to her; from time to time she leaned over and fussed with the gauzy cloth covering it.

"Amanda," Rogell whispered hoarsely.

"That's her all right," Earl said brightly. "In a minute I zoom in so you can see her better."

Sure enough, the shot suddenly leaped forward so that the woman's head and shoulders filled the entire screen.

"No sound, Earl," Clench pointed out.

Earl shrugged. "Mike's off," he said. "Nothing to hear, except the wind—it's windy as fuck up there."

The video went on, Amanda reading, the wind occasionally disarranging the cover on the cradle, forcing her to readjust it. The wind ruffled the pages of her magazine as she leaned over and interacted with her invisible child.

Pablo Clench was visibly impatient.

"Earl, give me a preview: Is anything going to happen here? Because if not, let's move on."

"Yeah, you're right, nothing's happening." Earl thumbed the remote and the scene disappeared. "It made me realize, though, it's pretty boring being a housewife. You sit around all day doing nothing, all by yourself. Seems like a shitty deal." He shot Rogell a significant look.

"Now, these next scenes," Earl went on, "these're from the spy cams we installed last month. Not a lot happening here either." He opened file after file from the menu, staying with each only a few seconds. A lot of the videos showed empty rooms through which Amanda occasionally passed, usually holding the baby. A few showed some domestic activity, Amanda cooking dinner for herself, the housecleaner vacuuming, Amanda eating dinner by herself; Amanda breast-feeding the baby. (Earl stayed with that one a little longer than the others.)

"Not a lot of footage of Aaron," Clench pointed out.

Earl shook his head. "Nah, he's not there a lot, he's like, in and out, 'Hi, honey, I'm home,' 'Bye, honey, I'm gone' kind of thing."

"Well, he's a busy man," Clench said. "We know that."

Rogell hunched forward in his kitchen chair, eyes fixed on the screen, grinding his teeth audibly.

"Now this footage," Earl announced, "this is the money shot. This is with a different camera, in low light conditions, up close and personal."

The scene was a wash of green and black, the camera advancing slowly through the darkened hall of Rogell's house.

"You got inside?" Rogell croaked. "What about the alarms? How did you turn off the alarms?"

Earl looked at him with pity.

"We *installed* the alarms, Aaron."

A weird green light filled the TV screen, with green slashes across it. As the camera slowly came closer, Rogell saw Amanda lying in bed; the green slashes were turned-down sheets.

The camera continued to move slowly in until her head and shoulders filled the screen. Her face was turned away from the camera.

The shot came even closer, and moved directly above the sleeper's face. She was lying on her side, clutching a pillow to her. Her mouth hung open and a small, damp spot was apparent on the pillow. Her beauty and vulnerability came through the bizarre optics of the night-sight video, and stunned Rogell into speech.

"Bastards," he said. "You fucking fucking, bastards."

Clench grinned happily.

The camera slowly moved back until all of Amanda was in the frame. Then the shot tracked slowly down her body, like a lascivious hand, and then back up. One bare foot stuck out of the covers.

After one more, slow, loving pan, the camera tracked away from Amanda and across the room—toward the crib.

Delia was sleeping restlessly, making little stifled cries, but didn't wake up, even when the cameraman—Rogell assumed it was Earl Colley—reached over and put his hand above Delia's head, thumb and forefinger apart, as if measuring her skull.

The hand disappeared. Slowly, whoever held the camera backed out of the room. A last, lingering shot showed both his wife and his daughter asleep, unaware they were being filmed.

The video ended. Earl snapped off the set and turned the lights back on.

"Well!" Pablo Clench said, "What did you think of that? Really sensitive camera work, I thought. I especially liked the part where he tracked down your wife's helpless, sleeping body. It's like anyone could have come in and done anything they wanted with her. And the baby . . ."

"All right, all right. I get it," Rogell said disgustedly. "You made your point. You can have the specs."

The first emotion Pablo Clench felt was disappointment. He realized he was enjoying torturing Rogell, and looked forward to their little sessions.

"You mean it?" Clench said. "You really, really mean it?"

Rogell nodded. He wouldn't look at Clench, but stared at the knee of his trousers. It was worn through and paint-stained—an old pair of Trick's.

"In that stuff you took from my private lab there was a notebook, one of those old composition books with the marbled covers."

"I remember those," Earl Colley put in.

"There's a date on the cover, August 30, 2006. No other identification."

"That's it?" asked Clench. "That's the one?"

Rogell nodded. "That's it. Everything you want is in there. If you can understand it."

"This is brilliant," MacBlister said. *I could have done this*, he thought, *given time*. "He's taken a single, simple program and applied it in a way no one ever thought of before. He makes the bots manufacture the basis for their own evolution. Each generation passes along the information for the next, augmented. Soon you have multiple generations, each one capable of a single action, but programmed to work with the others. Billions of others." Respectfully, he turned over the pages of the notebook, which were covered in close, dense scrawl, in different softnesses of pencil and different colored inks. The pages were so heavily overwritten they had a kind of sculptural quality.

"But you could have thought of it, right, Aleister?" Clench said. "I mean, you understand this stuff as well as Rogell does, right? So he just got there first. But does that give him the right to make all the money from it?"

"Well, legally it does," MacBlister demurred.

"Possession is nine-tenths of the law," Clench said. This was a maxim Clench had lived his life by. Personally, he thought that having your hands on something was ten-tenths of keeping it for yourself.

"And, for sure, we possess it now."

"Now are you going to let me go?" Rogell asked.

"Not yet," Clench said.

"Why not?"

"We have to make sure the specs work," Clench explained. "That they're all there. That you're not feeding us a line of horseshit, like we were your wife or something."

He smiled widely at Rogell. His microlayer of geniality was completely stripped away now.

"And, let me tell you, if you are fucking with us, if this is not complete, I can guarantee that you will suffer."

Rogell nodded, a quick study. "I understand that."

"Suffer slow. And for a long time," Clench went on. His eyes bulged slightly and his lips were parted, showing green, carious teeth. "And not just you, Doctor. Your wife will suffer, your daughter will suffer. Got any living relatives?"

Though he could think of a few of his cousins who might be better for a visit from Pablo Clench, Rogell shook his head again.

Clench watched him in silence awhile, as if waiting for Rogell's body language to betray something. But Rogell's body had forgotten how to speak.

"No relatives? No old aunts and uncles we can toast, old grandmas we can dissolve in battery acid? No? Well, maybe some friends and colleagues then. Bound to be someone in your life besides Tenderloin crack whores."

Clench stared at Rogell. Rogell stared back for a while, fascinated, then went back to looking at his folded hands. He wished he could put his head down and go to sleep, but doubted that this would be permitted.

"You think that we can't tell if the information here is complete," Clench went on after a while. "And you're right. We can't tell. But the people helping us with this, they can tell. And believe me, they will let us know if it is not all here, if it doesn't work right."

Clench paused again, impressively. Rogell was impressed.

"Then we'll have to do this again," Clench said. "Only, next time it won't be so much fun."

24

Around the World

Vin Nguyen looked like a Vietnamese Roy Orbison. He wore a generically retro sharkskin suit sharp enough to cut sheet metal, a black pomp like a breaking wave, and shades.

Vin was Clench's pipeline to the wider world outside the Tenderloin and North Beach. He claimed to be extensively connected in the Asian underworld, with close friends and useful acquaintances in Hong Kong, Tokyo, and Singapore.

The Tenderloin club Vin had met him in looked like an abandoned grocery store from the street. Inside it was dark, glittery, sophisticated, like a nightclub in a Hollywood movie from the thirties. Everyone in the club was Vietnamese. All the men were killer handsome, all the women knock-down gorgeous. Men and women alike were decked out in a brittle, perfect high style that made Clench, who liked to dress up, feel like he had spent the night in a dumpster.

The club habitues stared at Clench with a sullen, disbelieving hostility, then proceeded to ignore him completely. Even Clench's normally impervious chutzpah was dented. He was glad when Vin led him to a small back room and closed the door.

Vin's shades reflected back the dim overhead light. Clench wondered if he could see anything at all.

"I guess I didn't understand you when you called," Vin said, folding his hands and leaning forward. "You said, 'invisible robots'? What is that, like a code or something?"

"It's just what it is," Clench said. He explained Rogell's invention as best he could.

"They can make anything, any fucking thing at all, heroin, diamonds, you name it." he finished. "It's a real opportunity for the right customer. I thought with your connections, it was something you could handle. Maybe something the Chinese would be interested in."

Vin frowned. "I don't know. This is something new to me. But maybe I know a guy who would be interested. Let me talk to some people, and I'll call you. No promises, though. This is weird stuff."

"You're telling me," Clench grinned. "Way weirder than you know."

"The Chinese are not interested in this," Vin said over the phone.

"Too weird for them, huh?" Clench said.

"No, not weird. They already got 'em," Vin said. "I thought you said nobody else had this shit."

"Nobody stateside, that's for sure. I didn't know about the Chinese."

"They laughed at me. I should charge you extra for that. But still, there's somebody interested. Nobody I deal with before, kind of freaky people. They make me nervous. But for real, you know? You better watch your step."

"Don't worry about me," Clench said.

"Hey, I don't give a shit about you," Vin said. "I just want my commission safe."

"You'll get it," Clench said. "Now who have you got lined up?"

"Well, this is nothing I want to talk about on the phone, all right? You better come see me. I'll tell you in person."

"Vin, what is this spy story shit?" Clench said, exasperated.

"I think I'll take a walk down Broadway tonight at ten thirty," Vin went on as if Clench hadn't spoken. "I should pass Enrico's right around then. Maybe I see you there, huh?"

Sure, man, that'll fool the CIA, Clench thought.

"I'll be there," he said.

Vin was already in Enrico's when Clench got there, sitting at an inside table tucked in the back by the restrooms.

"Nice table," Clench said, seating himself. "They must know you here."

Vin said nothing. He barely looked at Clench, but slid a cell phone over the marble tabletop. Clench's hand closed over it.

It was like passing notes in high school, he thought. More spy shit. But if Vin thought it was necessary he'd play along.

"Call the number on speed dial," Vin said. He paused to deal with his shirred eggs, which took careful management. "They tell you where to get the next message. When you finish with the call, erase the speed dial. Then get rid of the phone. Throw it in the bay."

"Wow," Clench said, impressed in spite of himself. "These guys are serious, huh?"

"You better be serious too, you don't want to follow the phone. You still want to do this? 'Cause once you make this call, there's no going back on the deal."

"Hey, let's do it," Clench said. "I like serious people."

Clench slid the phone into his jacket pocket and stood up. Vin went back to juggling egg yolk. The interview seemed to be over.

"You comin' along on this?"

Vin shook his head so violently that a hair or two came loose from his pomp and stood straight up.

"No way. You on your own with this one."

The cell phone was just the beginning of a long, annoying trail leading to the rendevous. There were two pay phones and a cab ride with a stranger who gave him yet another goddamn cell phone before, finally, a dishwasher in a Chinese restaurant, not Chinese himself, gave him the meet. Clench had tried to get the guy to cough up more info, but the guy's English, fine at first, disappeared entirely under Clench's questioning.

Who cares anyway? Clench thought, scribbling down the meet info before he forgot it, against the dishwasher guy's explicit instructions. *So long as I get paid.*

He stared at what he had written on the back of a booze invoice from the Buzzard. It didn't make much sense, but that was par for the course these days.

Kalimaha? he wondered. *Where the fuck is Kalimaha?*

25

Bot Sale in Kalimaha

Aleister MacBlister took his time answering the door. Probably some kid selling magazine subscriptions, he told himself, or his next-door neighbor complaining about something again.

But deep under all these thoughts he was expecting a visit from Pablo Clench, whom he still knew as Arthur Murray. For the past month, every time he had opened the door he expected to see Murray standing there, blond, baleful, calling in his chips. It was not a sight MacBlister looked forward to.

This time it actually was Clench. He seemed pleased to be there.

"Aleister, hey!"

"Arthur," MacBlister acknowledged with a nod. Cold fear gripped his colon.

"Going to invite me in?"

"Please." MacBlister stepped back; Clench followed him in like a tango partner.

Once inside Clench looked around mockingly.

"All that money we paid you, you still live in a dump like this.

In fucking Belmont. Belmont!" Clench shook his head.

"Arthur, look . . . ," MacBlister began.

Clench waggled his eyebrows interrogatively.

"Arthur, I hope you're not worried about me, about me saying any-thing. Because I wouldn't do that."

"Saying anything? Why would I think that? You weren't planning on saying anything, were you?"

"No—I—of course not," MacBlister choked.

"Well, there you go." Clench was touring the condo; he seemed to be making a mental inventory of the furnishings. "Now, brush your teeth, throw some things in an overnight bag, and let's get out of here."

"Why? Where are we going?" MacBlister was sweating with terror now. He was sure this was just a routine to keep him calm and pliable until the thugs that had kidnapped Aaron Rogell beat him to death in some dark alley. Or worse.

Clench suddenly wheeled around and put a hand on MacBlister's shoulder. MacBlister noticed that his thumbnail was long, broad, and yellow. It looked like a shoehorn.

"Aleister, look, I need your help. In your capacity as a scientist. I found a buyer for our product—you recall our transaction."

"Vividly," MacBlister agreed.

"I need someone who understands the science, in case the buyer asks me questions I can't answer. I don't want to fuck this up. I need you, Aleister. Will you help me?"

It was clear that refusal was not an option.

"I . . . sure, I guess. Yes, of course."

"Attaboy." Clench shook MacBlister briefly by the shoulder. "Now get some clothes and we'll boogie."

"Where are we going?"

"Nowheresville," Clench said. "Somewhere between not there yet and gone."

. . .

Nowhere turned out to be in Los Angeles, in a quonset hut somewhere just off the runway at LAX. The hut was occupied by perhaps twenty menacing Asian men in black suits and sunglasses, and one small, wrinkled man in a khaki military uniform. This was General Geng, one of three depraved generals who ran the Democratic Republic of Kalimaha, a vicious, backward dictatorship wedged in between Burma, Malaysia, and the South China Sea.

The general, too, was wearing sunglasses. Clench wondered if the man's thick, black mustache was for real or from a costume shop.

The general stood up. Somehow the sunglasses guys were already standing up all around him. Clench hadn't seen them move, yet there they were. Scary guys.

MacBlister was bent over what looked like a deformed attaché case, fiddling with switches. The plan was to show the general how the bots worked, even if the end product was not exactly what the Kalima-hanese had in mind. MacBlister was wearing a white lab coat over his usual pocket protector–geek ensemble. Clench had insisted. Nothing said "expert scientist guy" like a lab coat, he thought.

The bots went in—neat how that happened, Clench thought. He had envisioned just pouring the shit in through a funnel or something, but this was better: An intricate tube-and-valve arrangement fed the bots from the Tupperware to the attaché case. *Otherwise, the shit would get all over,* Clench thought approvingly, *and then where would we be?*

MacBlister straightened up, and the Kalimahanese bent over the at-taché case expectantly. General Geng lifted up his sunglasses to see better, revealing mean little snake eyes.

Clench couldn't see what was happening himself, but he could read it in the eyes of the audience, squinted up with suspicion at first, then round with wonder and surprise, then narrow again with calculation and greed.

Sale, Clench thought. *Ka-ching.*

MacBlister fiddled some more, then held up the results for all to see.

The prospective clients were puzzled, Clench could tell. What was the Kalimahanese military supposed to do with sexy underwear?

He leaned toward the interpreter.

"Tell them this is just a demo. The robots can make any damn thing you want. Tell them."

The interpreter looked dubious but relayed the message.

"How do we know that?" the interpreter brought back. "We don't want underwear. Show us something else."

This was the deal, right here.

"Show them the documentation, MacBlister," Clench said. "Lay it all out for them."

MacBlister obligingly reached into his attaché case and brought out a stack of paper. On top of the stack he laid the worn-out composition book. Then he shoved the whole stack across the table toward the Kalimahanese.

Two cringing, nervous men in black horn-rims shuffled forward apologetically. These were the Kalimahanese scientists. They sat down in front of the stack of documentation and began to read through it, conferring occasionally in whispers.

They're like tasters, Clench thought, *checking out the merchandise in a drug deal. Took a whole fuck of a lot longer, though.*

The scientists read slowly through the pile of papers. No one else spoke or moved while they read. General Geng's mirrored sunglasses remained pointed toward Clench and MacBlister.

Stay cool, thought Clench. *Cool head main t'ing.* He slouched sideways in his chair, curling one arm around the back as he tried to ignore the mirror shades and keep his eye on the scientists.

Of course, he only had MacBlister's word for it that everything was there and would work, Clench knew. MacBlister—not the shiniest tool in the toolbox. Maybe, too, Rogell was pulling a fast one. He didn't think so, but you never knew.

And a fuckup would not be well received by the Kalimahanese. He and MacBlister would probably earn an all-expenses-paid trip back to Kalimaha—in the luggage compartment.

Beside him, MacBlister was visibly sweating with terror. Not the most reassuring sight on the planet.

The scientists had come to the multicolored composition book. Suddenly one of them sat up straight. His colleague leaned over; the two of them read on in silence. Every eye in the room was on them.

The two scientists began to babble quietly to one another, then, cringing and smiling, to the general, who listened impassively. Then General Geng leaned over and said something quietly to the translator, something that took a long time to get out.

The translator cleared his throat. "The general thanks you on behalf of Kalimaha for the information you are providing. Our own scientific establishment, while perfectly capable of inventing these things, will benefit from your discoveries. The enemies of Kalimahanese democracy will be driven back. Our country will finally take its rightful place on the world stage."

The general grinned at them, his teeth large and white under the heavy black mustache.

MacBlister's eyes, already wide with fear, grew wider.

"Arthur, you realize they plan to weaponize the bots, don't you?" he whispered, appalled.

Clench shrugged. "I don't give a shit. It's their nickel."

MacBlister stared at him, wild-eyed. Then he suddenly jumped to his feet.

Every head in the room swiveled toward him.

MacBlister looked around the table. He certainly had their attention; even the cringing scientists were looking at him attentively.

This is the right thing to do. I may have fucked up a little, MacBlister thought, as he considered that he had just traded a small bump in his bank account for global destruction down to the molecular level, *but this is my chance to make amends.*

Redemption. Heroism. His moment.

MacBlister took a deep breath and plunged in.

It was the speech of his life. It was true that his only other exercise in public speaking had been a mumbled, apologetic opening speech at a scientific conference, where the bar had been low.

He let the Kalimahanese know that the purpose of science was to probe through the veil of appearances down into the machine room where the truth lived. It had nothing to do with death-dealing and destruction, although revealing the building blocks of life itself necessarily gave you the means to destroy them. But that was not the point. The point was not even to make life better for the average citizen, although that would be the inevitable consequence of scientific discovery. No, the point of science was the process itself, the endless seeking after the underpinnings of reality, decoding the user's manual of the universe. It was wrong, irrelevant, to use this power for destructive purposes, and such use would eventually turn on its wielder with disastrous consequences. He could only hope that, given this power, the Kalimahanese people would come to their senses and use it for good, to live in freedom and democracy. For himself, he could never take part in such a transaction, and so had to regretfully withdraw his cooperation and knowledge. To do otherwise would be a betrayal of science at the most basic level. Thank you.

Spent but proud, MacBlister sat down.

Clench smiled broadly and tried to appear calm. Mentally, he was judging the distance to the closest door. Sunglasses guys were everywhere, and he knew they'd be quick. But maybe he could shove MacBlister in front of them and slow them down some. Or just kill him. If he took out MacBlister himself maybe that would make them happy, or at least distract them. The fucking idiot certainly deserved to die for putting them on the spot like this. Why didn't the obnoxious little fuckhead come up with these scruples before he sold his ass to the operation? Then they could have just killed him and shipped him to the Marianas with Melaleuca.

But Clench needn't have worried. MacBlister's speech, either because he talked too fast, mumbled, and used as much professional jargon as humanly possible, or because the translator's strong sense of self-preservation had kicked in, was being conveyed to the general as a panegyric to the Kalimahanese junta and a passionate defense of science as an instrument of mass death.

The general smiled broadly.

The translator finished speaking, and the general's mirror shades swept over MacBlister. He nodded approvingly. Then his mustache rippled like a blanket with rats under it. The general was speaking.

The translator leaned forward, listening and nodding.

"The general says that he is very grateful for the approval of American Science, and humbly accepts the accolades you have chosen to bestow on our poor country. We appreciate his regret that he cannot be part of our victories, and would also like to offer your scientist a position with the Kalimahanese defense ministry," the translator said.

The general's mustache stirred again.

"He would, of course, be highly compensated."

Well, there had been a misunderstanding, that was plain. MacBlister tried hard not to laugh out loud. That would be rude. But obviously he had been the victim of poor translation. As for the job offer, that was out of the question. He had no intention of relocating to some smelly little shit pile in the third world, especially not now, when a lifetime of scientific work was about to be recognized, or at least paid for. He glanced over at Arthur Murray, expecting to see the same suppressed amusement in Murray's eyes.

But it was not there.

Clench was staring at the translator, alertly, like a pit bull watching a hamster. MacBlister hoped he would read disbelief in his face, if not contemptuous amusement. He did not: Clench was merely wondering if he should ask for a finder's fee.

Finally, Clench decided not to push it. Being allowed to live would have to be enough.

"Okay, deal. I'll throw in MacBlister," Clench said. "You can have him." Clench stood up and stuck out his hand toward the general. The sunglasses guys tracked his moves, rippling and shimmering, but they didn't kill him.

"You can keep him locked up, inventing shit," Clench explained. "Then there's no limit. Everything he thinks up will be yours."

MacBlister was stunned. "Now, wait a minute . . . ," he started to say, half standing.

Two sunglasses guys materialized, one on either side of him. They didn't touch him; he couldn't even tell through the sunglasses if they were actually looking at him. But he sat back down.

"What additional compensation will be necessary for the scientist's participation?" the translator relayed.

"Nada," Clench said. "Zip. He's yours. The first one's free. Think of it as a gesture of friendship between our two countries."

The general stood up and took Clench's hand. He smiled broadly under his mustache.

"This is a wonderful thing, Mr. Murray," the translator said. "The people of Kalimaha thank you."

· · ·

MacBlister grabbed on to Clench's upper arm and leaned over, whispering rapidly into his ear. He seemed upset.

"Murray, you can't do this! It's kidnapping! It's slavery! You can't just sell me like a side of beef!"

Clench smiled at him sunnily, their faces inches apart. MacBlister was surprisingly worked up for someone who had just been awarded a free, all-expenses paid, long-term vacation in Southeast Asia, instead of being dismembered and dumped in the middle of the Pacific.

"You don't have to go," he told the agitated MacBlister. "Stay here. I was going to kill you eventually, anyway. Be easier to get done if you're in the neighborhood."

MacBlister sat back heavily.

"I've heard good things about the coast of Kalimaha along the South China Sea," Clench went on. "Hey, it's not Phuket—not yet. But it's a lot less crowded. Think about it: sun, sand, palm trees. What more could you want? And I'll tell you something. . . ."

"What?" MacBlister asked sullenly.

"You'll be the Man there, the Big Kahuna, Mr. American Scientist. All these discoveries Rogell stole from you, *you'll* finally be getting all the credit."

"That's right, isn't it?" MacBlister said thoughtfully.

"You bet it's right. You'll have the generals eating out of your hand. These guys run half the drug traffic in Southeast Asia, they are, like, rolling in it. You'll get the recognition you deserve, and really outrageous compensation besides. The standard of living what it is there, you'll live like a fucking pasha. Besides, if you try and back out now, they'll be disappointed. You wouldn't want to disappoint them, would you?"

MacBlister looked around at the sunglasses guys planted around the table, arms folded over bulky chests, shimmering with menace. The general caught his eye, nodded, smiled. The translator stared back stone-faced.

"No," MacBlister said. "I guess not."

.   .   .

The two laptops sat on the conference table, tops up, side by side, like alert little animals.

Clench wished he had Trick with him to make sure the wire transfer went okay. But it was pretty simple, so long as you had the passwords and the account numbers. He typed them in slowly, to avoid fuckup, to keep ten million dollars from suddenly appearing in the wrong account, surprising the snot out of a schoolteacher in New Jersey or a small businessman in Nebraska.

A small window swam up on his screen; a bar slowly tracked across it. When the bar reached the far side of the window, everything disappeared. It was just like downloading anything, personnel records, ransom notes, porn.

But with a difference.

"Congratulations, Mr. Murray," the translator grinned. "You are now a very rich man."

Clench watched the general and his entourage march across the runway to a waiting personal aircraft, a small jet. MacBlister, surrounded by sunglasses guys, kept looking back over his shoulder. Clench couldn't make out his features very well, but he knew MacBlister would be having second thoughts, throwing him pleading, disbelieving looks.

Too bad, Clench thought. *He shouldn't have been such a loud-mouthed little asshole. Maybe he'll like it in Kalimaha.*

Clench didn't know a thing about Kalimaha, himself. Until the other night, when Vin had called and told him about the general's interest in Rogell's nanobots, he hadn't even known it existed. Now he had become a multimillionaire, thanks to a country he had never even heard of.

That shit he had told MacBlister about a Kalimahanese tropical paradise he had just made up to keep the scientist calm. Maybe it was even true—could be. (It was not. The southern coast of Kalimaha was taken up by fever swamps and a river delta inhabited by starving farmers and a few scrawny bands of pirates.)

Most likely, the generals will keep his ass chained up in a basement lab inventing death robots, Clench figured. But why not give the guy a happy little send-off? We all live in illusion anyway.

Clench stood at the window in the departure lounge, looking over the empty runways, toward the low, crummy building where he had come into his own.

Across the runway, Clench saw an electric baggage car bumping along, driving too fast, probably at the limit of its speed. There were no bags in the racks it dragged behind it. Several baggage handlers clung to the bouncing carts, stuffed into khaki jumpsuits. All of the baggage handlers wore sunglasses; several of the jumpsuits were still unzipped; one bag monkey was still trying to get his arm through a sleeve.

The baggage car drew up next to the warehouse recently vacated by the Kalimahanese. The handlers jumped off and sauntered into a Quonset hut immediately next to it. The last one was still struggling to get into his jumpsuit.

The CIA. Clench grinned. *Late, as usual.*

Overhead, the private jet of the Kalimahanese contingent was just getting airborne.

Aloha, little MacBlister, Clench thought happily. *Aloha, sunglasses guys. Aloha, freaky little scientists, and Mr. Translator Guy—that was really thinking on your feet. Aloha, scary little general. Ask your hair-dresser about a total makeover; and lose that 'stache, okay?*

Clench hefted the laptop. It felt exactly the same. No replacement, in terms of physical satisfaction, for a gym bag full of currency.

But he knew that virtual dollars had gone whizzing through the tubes and pipes of the Internet to reconstitute as actual money in a secure bank vault somewhere in Switzerland. The numbers of the nameless accounts were stashed in his memory, and on his computer.

Clench walked quickly toward short-term parking, whistling tunelessly but merrily between hygiene-challenged teeth. That had been fun. But there was still a lot of work to be done, people to be paid off, trails to be wiped out, asses to be covered. It would be tricky to see that everyone got satisfied, but it had to happen.

Aloha everybody.

26

Payoff

Clench's office at the Buzzard was small and cramped. Soon he would be moving into more spacious accommodations. In the meantime, though, when somebody knocked on the door he didn't have far to go to let them in.

The door knocker turned out to be Trick Fitzpatrick. He seemed agitated.

"How'd it go with the general?" he asked the second the door closed behind him.

"Smooth as a shaved pussy."

"The money transfer went all right? You remembered the numbers I gave you?"

Clench nodded. "You bet I did. The funds are safe in Switzerland. Had to let the general have MacBlister to play with—it's a long story, don't ask—but other than that, it went slick as snot."

"So, what do I do with Aaron now?"

Aaron? Clench hoped Trick was not going to become a problem.

"Just get rid of the guy," he told Trick.

"Get rid of him? What do you mean? Like get rid of him permanently?"

Clench made a mental note: *Kill Fitzpatrick soon.*

"I think we understand each other," he said.

"Well, how am I going to do that? With my bare hands?"

"If that's what turns you on," Clench said. "Just do it."

Trick was thoughtful. He stared at the corner of Clench's desk and looked depressed.

Another five seconds of this, Clench thought, *and I shoot him here and now.*

"I need a gun," Trick said before Clench's deadline was up.

"Don't we all," Clench said. He opened the tray drawer of the desk and took out an automatic, hulking and black. "This is a gun. You know how to use one of these?"

Trick nodded briskly. "Of course."

"This is the trigger," Clench said. He didn't seem to believe Trick. "You pull it. The gun goes off. But first you have to take off the safety." He clicked a little switch on the side of the gun. "Plus, make sure it's loaded." Clench popped out the magazine, examined it, held it up for Trick to see, then dumped the bullets out on the desk. He tossed the empty magazine to Trick, then scooped up the pile of bullets and held them out.

"What do I do with those?"

"Take 'em. Put 'em in your pocket. You can reload when you leave." Clench sat back and smiled. "Not that I don't trust you or anything. I just don't want you to shoot your foot off."

Once Trick had stowed the shells and the magazine, Clench picked up the gun by the barrel and handed it over.

"There you go," he said. "Should do the trick."

Trick took the gun and looked like he was about to go back to staring blankly again.

"Look, do you need some help?" Clench asked impatiently. *Don't make me help you*, he thought. *You won't like that.*

But Trick seemed to pull himself together.

"No, I can handle it. No problem. Thanks for the weapon."

"Any time." Clench said. "Always glad to be of service."

Trick walked in to Aaron Rogell's little dungeon and put the pistol down on the card table. Then he sat down himself, slumped in his chair, not looking at Rogell.

Rogell eyed the firearm with despair.

"What's that?" he asked Trick.

Trick looked up.

"Gun." He straightened up in his chair.

"What for?"

"You know what it's for."

Rogell did know what it was for.

A sudden, horrible intimacy dropped over them. It was almost erotic.

The gun lay on the card table between them, dull and alien. *Is that real?* Rogell thought. *Yes, it's real all right.*

A quick lunge, he thought, *grab the gun, shoot Trick. Find the key, escape.* It all seemed distant, theoretical.

And then, what if Trick didn't have the key on him?

Starve to death, slowly, chained up in San Bruno.

Shoot yourself with the gun.

Rogell sat there, unmoving, all possibilities cancelling each other out.

"Except that I don't want to," Trick said suddenly.

Rogell looked up from staring at the gun.

"No?"

Trick shook his head.

"No. I never killed anyone."

"What about your partner?" Rogell said, realizing as he said it that it was a very stupid topic to introduce.

"That was an accident," Trick explained. "I didn't mean to kill him."

"What happened?"

Trick made a sour face, remembering. "We were drunk. We had a lot to work out, his turning me in and everything. Drinking seemed to help. We got hammered. I was holding him up, on the curb outside the bar, helping him stand. But who was helping me stand? He fell into the street and the bus ran over his head."

"You didn't push him?"

Trick shook his head. "I couldn't have pushed over a Dixie cup. But nobody believes me."

"The judge believed you, I guess. Or you wouldn't be sitting here."

"Oh, they never charged me with anything. No one saw what happened, but we were clearly shitfaced. The cops just wrote it off as an accidental death. They got it right for a change; that's what it was."

The two of them sat there. So did the gun. Further conversation seemed difficult.

Suddenly Trick lunged forward and swatted the gun off the table. It spun to the floor and went off. They could hear the bullet ricochet and buzz around the little concrete room, and both hunched over and covered their heads, uselessly and much too late.

Finally, when it became obvious that the bullet was not going to lodge in either of them, they straightened up, staring at each other in horror.

"Fuck!" Trick said.

"Holy shit!" Rogell agreed.

"Are you okay?"

"I think so. Look!"

Rogell pointed to the leg of the card table by Trick's right leg. The slug was embedded in the table leg, flattened, a metal bee with a bad sense of direction.

"Man! That was close!"

Trick and Rogell stared at each other across the card table.

"I need a drink," Trick said. He began to shake.

"Get me one, too," Rogell said.

Rogell still felt a little shaky the next morning, but hope rose in him when Trick came in and unlocked his chains from the wall staple.

"What's this? Where are we going?"

"I'm taking you out," Trick said.

"Out? Out where?"

"Just in the backyard, get some sun. You look like you could use it."

"Why are you doing this?"

"So I can say I did."

A board fence, head-high, ran between Trick's house and the house next door. As they were sitting there the neighbor came out, a short-haired man with a thick mustache. He glanced over at them, did a quick double take, and grinned.

"Well, hello!" the neighbor said.

Saved, Rogell thought. He held up his arms so that the chains swung and clanked.

"Call nine one one," he said.

Trick turned around. He didn't seem at all upset at being discovered.

"Oh, hello, Marvin. Haven't seen you in a while."

Marvin came up to the fence and hung on to it as if he were about to start chinning himself.

"So that's what you're into," he said. "I wondered. Can I join you?"

Trick smiled weakly. "Sorry, Marvin. Private party."

Marvin looked disappointed. "Well, maybe I can buy him from you.

When you're finished, I mean." He looked Rogell up and down, avidly. "I love a good slave auction."

"It's a thought," Trick said. Rogell looked at him to see if he was serious. It was impossible to be sure.

"Well, have fun, you two," Marvin said. "Try not to make too much noise." He looked at Rogell appraisingly. "You know, you should probably gag him. I have some ball gags, if you need one."

"Thanks, Marvin, I'm good," Trick said.

With a last, lingering glance at Rogell in chains, Marvin went back in the house.

Well, that was a failure, Rogell thought. No cavalry to the rescue. He looked around at the other neighboring houses, but blinds were drawn, doors and windows shut.

Nobody home.

Rogell had no intention of allowing himself to be put back in the basement. It felt good to be outside, to feel sun and fresh air on his skin, to smell something besides his own stink. Freedom: Just a shot away.

As they were walking back to the house, Rogell made his move, shoulder down like a linebacker diving into the line. He caught Trick a good one just under the shoulder blade.

But Trick turned with the blow, unresisting. Rogell powered past him, fell to his knees—hard—when Trick tripped him, and was propelled by Trick's foot in the small of his back, landing face-down. His chin bounced off the concrete.

Trick put his knee on Rogell's neck.

"I could hear you coming from a mile away. Those chains sound like a runaway freight train, you know? Now, are you going to be good?"

Rogell tried to nod, only succeeding in grinding skin and flesh off the tip of his chin.

"*Uhmkk*," he replied.

"Okay. I'm going to let you up. I don't want any more stupid getaway shit. I told you, I'll let you go when the time comes, not before. Trust me. Have patience."

Rogell was too dispirited to reply. Trick helped him to his feet and pushed him back inside.

When the overhead light came on in the little basement room, Rogell revived a little, just enough to mouth off.

"You're just going to bury me away in your fucking basement? Is that it? Are you going to keep me here forever?"

"Just be patient," Trick said. "When you calm down a little maybe we can play another game or two."

"I'll whip your ass," Rogell said sullenly.

"You'll try," said Trick.

Pablo Clench smiled thinly when Trick came into his office. He raised his eyebrows.

"So?"

"I took him out," Trick said.

"Where is he now?"

"Buried in my basement."

"Let me see the gun."

Pablo Clench took the gun from Trick and examined it. He sniffed the barrel—carefully, from the side. Clench looked up at Trick and waggled his eyebrows. He broke out the magazine and counted the bullets.

"Fired it once?"

Trick shrugged, the experienced killer. "All I needed."

Clench hefted the pistol, polished it with his handkerchief, and handed the pistol and magazine back to Trick.

Trick recoiled.

"I don't want it."

"Take it. You earned it." Clench gave him the big, full-algae smile.

Hesitantly, Trick took back the gun and slid it into his coat pocket.

"I guess I did, didn't I?"

"You sure did."

Clench watched in amused disbelief as Trick sauntered out of the room, only slightly unbalanced, the gun weighing down one side of his raincoat, the magazine the other.

Now you are the proud owner of a murder weapon, Clench thought happily, *with your prints all over it and the death bullet missing from the magazine. A nice little present for the ballistics people.*

What a maroon.

27

Oiling Aphrodite

Aphrodite Anderson was lonely. And broke. Nobody came to see her anymore. Pablo Clench told her that Aaron Rogell had done a book with the company funds, and Jimmy Cacapoulos had just stopped coming by, no explanation offered. In a fit of panic, she had gone off on Carl and told him to get the fuck out of her life. He took her seriously, the stupid loser, and stopped coming, too.

That was smart. Now she had no one to cover her bills, and a condo payment coming up, plus her monthly maintenance fee, plus a grand or two of shopping bills on her American Express. True, she had enough put by to handle any real emergencies. But Aphrodite hated to dip into her capital. She just hated it.

She picked up the phone and called Pablo Clench. Normally, she would have done anything she could to avoid him, but this was different. This was an emergency.

Clench picked up on the third ring.

"Arthur Murray Enterprises," he said. "This is Arthur."

"Pablo, is that you? This is Aphrodite." She wasn't about to get sucked in to one of Pablo's stupid little jokes.

"Speaking. What's up, babe?"

"Pablo, have you seen Aaron Rogell?"

"Why, no, didn't I tell you? Your lover boy took the cookie jar and booked. He's probably somewheres in the Caribbean right now, the Caymans, Martinique."

"I know if Aaron did take that money, it's because you made him," Aphrodite said. "I know Aaron. And I know you. You're squeezing him, just like you squeeze all my boyfriends. But I need him!"

"Everybody needs somebody," Clench said.

"I was counting on Aaron!" Aphrodite moaned. "I have bills to pay!"

"Well, what about your other guys?"

"Jimmy stopped coming by, no reason, no phone call, nothing. And I told Carl to go fuck himself."

"That was smart."

"Pablo, I know you're behind this, I know you are. It's always you." Aphrodite was working herself up. "You can't take everything like that! Who do you think you are? Pablo?"

"Still here."

"Pablo, if you don't tell me where Aaron is, you better give me some money yourself, to cover what Aaron would have given me, if he was here. Because if you don't, I know somebody I can call, somebody I used to date, can get you in a lot of trouble. I know you. I bet you won't want the cops sniffing around right now. Am I right?"

Clench exhaled loudly into the receiver.

"Aphrodite, you are so right," he said. "I can see that I've been selfish, and I'm sorry, I really am. But I'll make it up to you, I swear. I can't come myself, but I tell you what, I'll send the Colley boys over with something for you. How's that?"

.   .   .

Tony Baloot found that tracing Aaron Rogell was a lot more difficult than just tailing him. Rogell had been easy to follow before; Baloot just had to get in line.

But there was no line for Rogell now. The usual Rogell-spotting places—the Lovehole, the porn store—were washouts. Rogell never showed. Baloot wore out the seat of his pants waiting for him to put in an appearance, and smoked so many twisted little black cigars that looked like sticks of beef jerky that even he was sick of them.

This is getting nowhere, Baloot thought. *Time to focus.*

Aphrodite Anderson's condo seemed the likeliest place to pick up Rogell's trail. Out of all of Aaron Rogell's little friends, Aphrodite had always gotten the most play. If he monitored the bugs he left in Aphrodite's place, maybe he could hear something useful. Maybe Rogell was there already, hiding out in the stripper's costume closet. Anyway, the guy had spent most of his away time up there on Russian Hill, doing the dirty. Chances were good to excellent that if he hadn't been kidnapped and was still roaming around loose, he'd come back for another roll or two. Maybe Aphrodite was even in on it.

It was worth a shot, anyway.

But the taps in Aphrodite Anderson's apartment turned out to be a total bust, at least as far as finding Aaron Rogell was concerned. It was interesting and instructive to listen in on Aphrodite's conversations with her various girlfriends—it was amazing, the things women said to each other. But it got him no closer to Rogell. *One more night,* Baloot thought, *then I pack it in.*

Peeping out the spy hole he had drilled in the side of the van (obscured on the outside by the brightly painted logo of Rosa's Flowers and Wreaths, his mom's company), Baloot recognized the shorter of the two men who got out of the car in front of Aphrodite's building right away. It was the bandy-legged little guy from behind the Love-hole, the guy who had been videotaping Rogell on the street.

The taller guy with the beat-up face he didn't recognize, but something about the guy told Baloot he should be glad he hadn't met him yet.

The two men disappeared into the apartment building, and Baloot hurried back to his listening post.

The mikes he had placed by the bathroom door, the living room entry, and the bottom of the phone were pretty good. The pickup zones nearly overlapped, and he could hear what was happening in the apartment so long as people spoke up and stayed in range.

What he heard was hard to visualize, though. The two guys didn't say much.

"Pablo said you'd have something for me," he heard Aphrodite say. "So where is it?" Then she made a strange noise, halfway between a grunt and a sigh. Then nothing.

Footsteps, something—a piece of furniture, maybe—being dragged across the floor, muffled cursing. That was it.

Then he heard Earl ask, "Where's the phone?"

Aphrodite must've just pointed. The next thing he heard was someone punching in a phone number.

There was a long, silent pause after that. Baloot strained to hear, thought he could pick out someone breathing. In the background he was pretty sure he heard a door shut.

More silence. Then, up close to the mike, so close the voice sounded distorted on the cheap shit equipment:

"Well, looky here."

This alarming statement was followed by a thunderous noise that made Baloot rip off the earphones and sit there panting.

Someone had just stepped on his microphone.

Holy shit. He knew he'd better get out of there before the two guys came looking for the listening post. He had parked his ma's van just a bit up the street from Aphrodite's building so he could see the entrance, and was real proud of himself for being able to do that, parking was so hard in that neighborhood.

But guys like the guys he had seen walking into Aphrodite's building looked like they would be familiar with the procedures, and might remember that the florist's van had been parked there when they came in. He had to move his ass, good parking or no good parking.

Just then Baloot heard another crashing sound, near at hand this time, the sound of auto glass smashing and being pushed out of the frame. He twitched aside the curtain that closed off the back of the van just in time to see a long muscular arm reaching in to pop the handle and pull the driver's door open. The larger of the two guys he had seen going in to Aphrodite's climbed into the van.

"Hey," said Billy Colley, "you got any wreaths back there? Like funeral wreaths?"

Tony Baloot came to briefly when the dome light came on and shadowy figures tossed a rolled-up carpet into the van, right next to him.

Baloot squirmed a bit, and found he couldn't move his arms and legs. His cheek was pressed against the floor of the van, which smelled of dead flowers, stagnant water, and motor oil.

He stared at the rug. It seemed weird and lumpy, like a big snake with a pig inside. And long strands of black hair cascaded out of one end.

Baloot shut his eyes as tight as he could. In a few seconds he was out again.

Billy Colley watched in patient silence as Earl drove the van over the Bay Bridge toward Oakland. With two bodies in the back, he knew they were probably heading to that auto junkyard in San Leandro.

But they zoomed on by the San Leandro exit and kept heading south. When they turned east at Hayward and jumped on 580 he couldn't take it anymore.

"Brother, where the hell are we going?"

"Modesto," Earl said.

This made Billy sit up straight.

"Modesto? Why the fuck are we going to Modesto?"

"Just relax, Billy. There's a guy there owes me a little favor. I've been meaning to collect for a while now. This just seems like a good time."

Billy fell asleep before they got to Modesto, but the almighty stink woke him up.

"*Whah*, fuck! What is that smell?" Billy swiped his nose with the back of his wrist as if he were trying to rub it off.

"Turkey guts. Lots of 'em," Earl informed him.

Billy meditated on this, but couldn't get it to add up.

"The hell?"

Earl ignored him. Pulling out his cell phone, he dialed with his thumb.

"Warren?" he said into the phone. "Earl Colley. We're right around the corner, you gonna be there to let us in? Good."

"What was that all about?"

"That was the guy I told you about," Earl said. "I own him. Bought his debt from some guys in Vegas he was into big time."

"What'd you do that for?"

"I just knew he would come in handy some day," Earl said. They pulled up at a gate in a chain-link fence. On the other side the tanks and towers of some kind of refinery smoked and hummed. The stink was fearsome.

A thin, bearded man shuffled out of the shadows and opened the gates. Earl rolled down the window.

"Warren, hey."

Warren nodded silently. He looked a little pale.

"Where do we go?"

"This way," Warren said. "Follow me."

Warren led them through the maze of tanks and outbuildings to a long narrow shed. When he opened the rollup door with some kind of remote the stink that rolled out was strong enough to knock a dozen buzzards off a slaughterhouse fence.

"What the hell is this place?" Billy asked.

"Biodiesel refinery," Earl said. "Turns turkey guts and chicken heads into fuel oil. Ain't that right, Warren?"

Warren just nodded. He didn't seem real happy.

"That's the hopper, there," he told them. "We just loaded her up. Be empty by morning."

A deep, rhythmic grinding and slurping noise filled the shed.

"That's the grinder you're hearing," Warren said. "Turns everything in this hopper to little pieces no bigger than the tip of your little finger."

"Warren, that's just wonderful," Earl said. "Now why don't you give us a little privacy?"

Once Warren slouched off Earl and Billy pulled the Aphrodite-stuffed carpet out of the van and wrestled it up a narrow gangway to the rim of the hopper. A sea of turkey parts stretched out at their feet.

They tipped up the carpet and slid Aphrodite into the turkey guts. She went in headfirst.

"Man, her legs are sticking up," Billy pointed out.

Earl shook his head. "Can't leave her like that."

Scavenging around the catwalk, they found two long poles and managed, with some difficulty, to push Aphrodite down into the mix. Before they had finished, Billy added his dinner to the feedstock.

"It's pretty interesting, this technology," Earl said, as they rested up from their labors. "Turns out you can make oil out of damn near anything. Who knew?"

"What about Tubbo?" Billy nodded toward the flower van. "Lots of oil in that guy."

"Nah." Earl shook his head decisively. "I got other plans for him."

Tony Baloot wondered how long it took to die from being kicked to death. He hoped not long. So far it had been a painful experience, more painful than anything else in his life, more painful than being kicked in the balls—he had passed that threshold a long time ago—more painful even than being thrown down a flight of stairs or having his head slammed in a car door. These had been his previous landmarks of severe pain. The Colley brothers seemed determined to explore new frontiers of violent discomfort. It wouldn't be long now, Baloot thought, before he simply floated up out of his body and drifted away.

"Uhn!" Earl Colley said. "Fuck. Beating the shit out of this guy is hard work."

"He's not talking anymore," Billy Colley said.

"You shouldn't have kicked him in the mouth like that," Earl pointed out. "I wouldn't say anything either, with my teeth all over the carpet."

"Maybe we should stop for a while. Let him recover."

"Let *me* recover." Earl plopped down on the desktop—they had come back to Baloot's office over the flower shop—and contemplated the prone, bloody detective. He reached out a foot and prodded him.

"Hey! You got anything more to say?"

"I think that's all we're going to get out of him," Billy said.

The Colleys had established that Baloot was looking for Aaron Rogell. He hadn't told them who he was working for, at first out of loyalty to Mrs. Rogell, then out of some thought of using the information to negotiate, then finally because he had forgotten, along with most of the other things he had ever known, like his own name.

The Colleys had gone overboard, as usual.

"What should we do with him if he punks out and dies on us? Leave him here? Or take him back to the turkey-guts place?"

"He's not going to die," Earl said. "Are you, buddy?"

Baloot heard this, but was not up to a response. He was concentrating on his breathing now.

"So, who do you think he's working for?" Billy wanted to know. "The cops?"

"Are you kidding? The cops'd never use a sorry-ass piece a shit like him. I think he's working for the robot company. They hired him to find Rogell."

"Probably that dickhead MacBlister. I knew we couldn't trust that guy, but Clench wouldn't listen."

The Colleys were unaware of MacBlister's translation to Kalimaha.

"Maybe. Or maybe the money guys behind the company. Rogell is a valuable property to them."

"Well, this guy is not being much help. Let's just go through his files and see what we can find out."

"Good idea," Earl said, jumping down from the desktop. "No telling what we'll learn."

Tony Baloot's files were not very extensive. It was a simple matter for Earl and Billy to locate the Rogell file and read its meager contents.

"So Rogell's old lady sicced him on us," Billy said in wonderment. "What for?"

"She must want him back," Earl said. He was combing his hair in the mirror over the sink. Kicking the crap out of Baloot had messed up his clothes something awful.

"That piece of shit? She should be glad to get rid of him."

"Well, he's her ride, Billy. All the money, prestige, that house up there on the hill. Anyway, she probably just wants to prove he's dead so she can start probate."

"So what should we do now?"

Earl stared thoughtfully at the blood-covered form on the office floor. Baloot's chest rose and fell, the only movement he was capable of.

"Let's let him come back a bit," Earl said. "Let him get his wind back. Then we can talk to him some more, and maybe now he'll be willing to talk freely. Anyway, I have an idea." He took his brother by the arm and steered him across the room, out of Baloot's hearing, just in case the guy was still conscious.

"Oh, an idea," Billy said. "That's good, an idea. I thought we were in trouble, but now I feel better. An idea."

"He wants to know where Rogell went, right?" pursued Earl, ignoring him. "Well, what if we show him?"

"What do you mean, show him? Like turn up Trick? Clench wouldn't like that."

Earl shook his head impatiently. "Nah, not that. I mean, show him where Rogell was while everybody thought he was working. Sell them the videos."

"What good will that do?"

"Well, it will keep them busy, looking where he isn't anymore. And maybe dampen their enthusiasm for finding him some. The company's not going to be real eager to have this shit come out. And his old lady will maybe lose her enthusiasm for the guy. It'll be like throwing a fat steak to guard dogs. They'll gnaw on this stuff that leads nowhere, and we can go about our business. And, too, we can get paid for all our hard work, filming that shit."

"Yeah, well . . . but wait a minute. Those videos, Aphrodite's on those, and the Lovehole. They could trace 'em back to us. Remember that girl in the wig? The crack whore without the teeth? She can tie that stuff to the Lovehole. That might come a little close to us, if they should talk to her. She might mention our names."

Earl smiled dreamily.

"I already thought of that, brother." Earl looked even more self-satisfied than usual. "By this time tomorrow Aphrodite will be two quarts of motor oil in somebody's crankcase."

"Yeah, but what about that freaky little prostitute? I don't think we can trust her."

"We just have to pay that girl a visit, that's all."

"Man, I don't do crack whores," Billy shivered.

"Not that kind of visit, fuckface. The kind of visit, makes her decide to go see her relatives in Guam. Or else take up free diving, go looking for her missing teeth at the bottom of the ocean."

"Oh," Billy said. He got it now. "*That* kind of visit."

28

Showtime

"Mrs. Rogell?"

At first, Amanda didn't recognize the muffled voice on her cell phone as Tony Baloot. He seemed to be trying to talk with his mouth full.

"Tony? Is this Tony Baloot?"

"It's me, Mrs. Rogell. Look, I have something you should see."

This could only be something bad, she thought. Aaron's dead body. Or not that—would Baloot cart a body around?—but a body part, a finger, a toe, or something else. Maybe kidnappers were sending fingers through the mail?

"Mrs. Rogell, are you still there?"

"I'm here, Tony. What is it?"

Now it was Baloot's turn to fall awkwardly silent.

"It's hard to explain," he said finally. "I'd rather just show it to you. Are you going to be home?"

A finger, for sure. Maybe an ear. "I'll be here," Amanda said. "Would you rather I come down to your office?"

"No," Baloot said decisively. "I'll come there."

Tony Baloot was looking older, Amanda thought as she opened her front door and let him in. His cheeks were sunken, his lips swollen and bruised, his movements stiff and awkward. *This assignment seems to be taking it out of him.*

Baloot had taken a few days off to recover after his session with the Colleys. He had told the doctors at the emergency room he had fallen down the stairs—he had a history there. They didn't seem to believe him. Nothing important was broken, but he pissed blood for a week and sometimes forgot things, like where he was going, who he was, or whether he was driving or eating or taking a shit. Finally, the thought of no money coming in had forced him back to work.

He wasn't looking forward to showing Mrs. Rogell the videos of her husband. Baloot never enjoyed this part—unveiling the incontrovertible evidence of guilt. The out-of-control hurt and anger that his clients displayed were exhausting. He had to admit, though, that this was where he came through, the thing that set him apart from his competition. Baloot was like a big, soft psychic sponge, soaking up the pain and rage that shot out of the wives whose worlds he was ripping apart. He understood what they were going through, he really did. He comforted them. Sometimes he even got laid behind it.

That didn't seem to be a likely outcome this time, though. Mrs. Rogell looked too tough to break down like that. She looked like more of a rager than a weeper. The anger was crackling out of her already, like some sort of electrical equipment malfunction.

Just wait till she sees this stuff, Baloot thought.

"What have you got, Tony?" Amanda asked. "Have you found my husband?"

"Well, I haven't actually found him yet," Baloot said, "but I got on the track of him. I have a theory."

Well, whoop-de-doo, Amanda thought, *a theory.* She realized she was disappointed; even a finger or an earlobe might have been better than a theory.

At least it would have been Aaron.

"I met with some associates of your husband, who they saw him pretty recently," Baloot went on. "They kept a record of who he was seeing, where he was going, what he was doing when he wasn't here, or at work. I thought you should see this." He waved a shiny DVD in the air, like a magician displaying the hidden card.

Amanda Rogell looked at him steadily, her jaw clamped.

"This is a video of my husband?" she asked. Baloot nodded. "Fucking his girlfriend?"

Baloot turned away and slid the DVD into the player. "You'll see," he said, pressing Play.

Amanda saw.

When they had cycled through the videos—including some that Clench hadn't bothered to show to Aaron Rogell, since there was a lot of repetition—Amanda sat silent, her eyes far away. Baloot thought it was better to let her work it out; he didn't disturb her.

She sat there so long, staring into space, that Baloot began to get worried. Suppose she got so angry she blew something out in her brain? he wondered. Had a stroke or something, just sitting there.

Finally, she said, "So what's your theory, Tony?"

"Well, I think he ran away with the woman in the video," Baloot said. This scenario had been suggested to him by the Colley brothers. Privately, he was not real sure that Aphrodite was still alive.

Amanda stared, unreadable.

"Which one?"

"Aphrodite," Baloot explained. "The exotic dancer. I'm not sure, but I don't think she's in town anymore. She doesn't answer her doorbell or her phone."

"And you think they ran away together?"

Baloot nodded.

"I've seen it before, the older guy running off with the younger woman," he said. "Recharging, getting young again. Sometimes they marry them, sometimes they come crawling back."

"And that's what you think has happened to Aaron."

Baloot nodded again.

"Well, I have a theory, too, Tony," Amanda said. "I think maybe Aaron, and that stripper, and the crack whore in the blonde wig all got on the goat and rode off into the sunset together. What do you think? Is that a pretty good theory?"

She was really pissed off, Baloot thought, that's why she was talking so crazy.

"You want me to try and find them?" he asked.

Amanda suddenly jumped out of her chair, walked over to the DVD player, and ejected the disk.

"No, Tony, I don't think so," she said. "I've got another theory. Do you want to hear it?"

"I'd be glad to, I—," Baloot began.

"You're fired," Amanda Rogell said. "Now get out of here."

Baloot was stunned.

"But, Mrs. Rogell!"

"Are you worried about your fee? Send me an invoice."

"The disk . . ." Baloot burbled, "the disk. They want me to pay for it."

"Send me an invoice," she repeated. She hurled the DVD into the fireplace with the lethal velocity of a ninja throwing star. "Just get the fuck out of my house."

Baloot, knowing when something was well and truly over, got the fuck out.

. . .

Amanda hurled herself back in the chair, then almost immediately hurled herself out of it. She stalked over to the liquor cabinet and poured herself a tall scotch, no ice, nothing. She slugged it down, coughed, gasped, and poured another. After a few sips, she turned on her heel and threw the scotch, glass and all, into the fireplace after the DVD. She picked up the bottle, threw the cap away, and drank from the neck, walking around in circles in the middle of the floor.

Everyone, she thought, *has a theory*. Everyone knew just what she was supposed to feel, what she was supposed to do next. Mindy thought she never should have had a kid and left her practice. Aaron thought she should just stay home and look decorative. The police thought she should stop calling them all the time. Everyone had it all figured out.

Everyone but her. But whose life was it, anyway, theirs or hers? Whose fucking life?

And Tony Baloot—it was plain what he thought she should do: Fall apart, take the kid, run home to mother. Or else sit in her living room going through Kleenexes until Aaron decided to come back to her.

Or maybe she should call an expensive divorce lawyer and start proceedings that would strip Aaron to the bone and sell the bones for pet food. She wondered if Mindy could recommend someone.

But none of that was what she wanted to do. She knew that much.

Amanda tripped over the chair, turned completely around, and fell into it, her legs stuck straight out. The scotch bottle was half empty already, though there seemed to be a lot of it on the floor.

What did she want to do? She considered it very carefully.

She wanted to find Aaron. He was still alive, still out there, she knew that. She could feel it. She would know if anything had happened to him.

She wasn't sure what she would do once she found him. Maybe kill him on the spot. Maybe not.

But she was sure about one thing. By disappearing like this, he had taken her life away from her. Their life. And until he came back she was stuck, unable to do anything. She had to find him.

And, obviously, she had to do it herself.

Amanda killed the bottle and tried to get out of the chair. This proved difficult, and after a while she fell back into it.

Just rest a minute, she thought, and passed out.

Hours later, after the sun had gone down, she woke up and dragged around the house, leaving the lights off. She threw up several times, took aspirin, drank a quart bottle of club soda, and went to bed.

Hours after that she crept downstairs with a flashlight and retrieved the DVD from the fireplace.

29

Getting Paid

"Why did you make us come way the fuck over to Oakland?" Pezzuti asked Pablo Clench. Pezzuti had become the unofficial spokesman for the six muscle guys the Colleys had hired. They were a little testy after the Colleys had deferred payment and referred them to Clench.

"Clench will see to that," they were told, so here they were, but not real happy about it.

Pablo Clench lounged back in his chair, swirling the ice in his drink. He was dressed for the beach, or maybe the deck of a yacht, but a little out of place in this dive on the Oakland Riviera, surrounded by goods warehouses, loading cranes, and container yards.

"I'm not about to stand out on the street corner, handing out paper bags of money," Clench told them. "If you want to get paid—in cash— you have to be patient. Take a check, I can write it right now."

"Are you kidding? I don't take a goddamn check, Pablo. You should know that." Pezzuti sounded deeply wounded by the suggestion.

"I do know that," Clench said soothingly. "I was just playing with you. Let's go get your money. I keep some funds at a warehouse over in Alameda."

"The fuck are you saying?" Pezzuti broke in. "We gotta get back in the car and drive some more? What kind of bullshit is this?"

The muscle guys behind him nodded and muttered. Pablo Clench was unmoved.

"Too much cash to carry around with me," he said. "But it's not far. I understand you're feeling a little edgy after all that work. Hey, you guys were great. I couldn't have done it without you." He beamed around at the assembled thugs. "Why don't we have a drink first? Then drive over and get your money."

Somewhat mollified, the group nodded as one.

"Sure, I'll have a beer," Pezzuti said. "Just don't try and fuck with us, Pablo. We do a job for you, we get paid for it."

"You'll get paid, don't worry," Clench said.

Everyone asked for beer except for Jimmy Nixon, who wanted a Dewars. Bob the bartender had to go in the back for a new bottle, and took a long time about it. But soon they all had drinks in their hands.

"To getting paid," Clench said, raising his glass in a toast. "You can't beat it."

"I'll drink to that," Pezzuti said.

Jimmy Nixon rode shotgun in the van on the way over to the warehouse, the window rolled down, looking out at the streets of Alameda.

They were heading out near the old navy base, along the water, following Pablo Clench, who was just ahead of them in his car. Clench drove along pretty fast, tires squealing on the corners. Petey, the driver, had to really jam the piece-of-shit van to keep up. They had blown that last light, squealing brakes and horn honks following them up the street, and had a couple near misses with oncoming traffic in the narrow streets. But all this just seemed to make Clench drive faster.

Good, thought Jimmy Nixon, *the faster we get this done the better. Let's get our fucking money and get out of here.*

Nixon felt shitty, sleepy, a little dizzy, that's why he had the window down. His eyes wouldn't focus properly.

The cool air felt good in his face. *Shouldn't have had that drink on top of not sleeping for a couple days*, he thought. Good thing he didn't finish it, then he'd really be tired.

He looked over his shoulder at the guys in the back. They were all asleep already, heads lolling every which way. As Nixon looked, big Pezzuti threw his head back on the headrest and began to snore loudly.

"Fuckin' guys," Nixon said to Petey. Petey nodded, but didn't say anything. He looked bleary-eyed, too, leaning on the steering wheel as if it was holding him up.

Clench suddenly turned off into a parking lot. Automatically, Petey followed him.

"Where the fuck is he going?" Jimmy Nixon said as the van lurched and swayed out of the turn. "This is a boat ramp. Hey, slow down!" Clench had turned abruptly and shot into a parking space. But Petey kept the van aimed at the water.

"Turn the wheel! Turn the wheel!" Jimmy Nixon screamed at him. In response Petey slumped down in his seat. He was out, his head flopping to one side. His foot came off the gas but it was too late; the van of thugs was already on the slippery downward slope of the launching ramp.

Jimmy Nixon tried to claw Petey off the wheel and get in the driver's seat. It was hard work, and his muscles weren't behaving properly. He was still trying when the cold water of the Oakland estuary came pouring through the passenger-side window.

· · ·

The mug shots of the drowned thugs that had been pulled from the Oakland harbor that morning meant nothing to Aaron Rogell when he saw them on the six o'clock news, but they caught Trick's attention.

"That's Pezzuti," he said, pointing with his chopsticks.

"Who's Pezzuti?"

"One of the muscle guys the brothers hired for security," Trick said. Now that Trick had identified him, the face looked vaguely familiar to Rogell, though it came attached to the memory of Clench's video session, which he had tried hard to erase.

"What about the other dead guys?" he asked.

Trick nodded. "Yeah, I recognize them, too. Pablo is cleaning up." Trick grew thoughtful.

"In other news," the announcer was saying, "an Oakland bartender was found dead behind his bar today, an apparent suicide. Robert Mc-Spivey, bartender at the Kontainer Klub, apparently drank a gin fizz containing large quantities of a powerful barbiturate. . . ."

Trick snapped out of his trance.

"You know he's going to come after us eventually."

"After you," Rogell corrected. "He thinks I'm dead already, which I may as well be."

"What do you think he'd do if he found out you're not?"

"So take my chains off," Rogell said. "I could help you, you know. Together we could surprise him. Trap him."

Trick shook his head. "No, that would be too complicated. I know you. You'd run away, go to the police, something like that. That wouldn't help. I can't have you running around loose. I'd be getting it from both sides."

"I swear." Rogell held up one hand, like a witness being sworn in court. His chains clanked and rattled.

Trick glanced over at him. "Nah."

"Please?"

"Just wait," Trick said. "I'll take care of Pablo. Then we'll both be safe."

30

The Rage of Amanda

Two days after firing Tony Baloot and passing out drunk in her own living room, Amanda began to pull herself together.

The real problem was that Aaron was not there. Until she got him back and had him sitting in front of her, in the flesh—the rotten, guilt-ridden, philandering flesh—Amanda couldn't even imagine what she would do.

So the answer was: Find him.

Okay, but where should she start? She didn't have much to go on— the names Aphrodite Anderson and Jimmy Cacapoulos, the face of an androgynous street prostitute called Chickie, the inside of an adult bookstore.

But one thing was clear. Neither the police nor Baloot really gave a shit about finding Aaron. They had their own agendas, their own theories to prove. Only she really wanted him back. If that was what she wanted.

Her mother looked surprised when she opened her front door to see Amanda on the steps, Delia in her arms. She should have called first, Amanda guessed, and maybe not come over this early. But now that she had made up her mind, she was eager to get started.

"Amanda!" her mother said, clutching her bathrobe around her neck. "What are you doing here? It's six o'clock in the morning! Is everything all right?"

"No, mother, everything is not all right," Amanda said. "May I come in, please?"

"Amanda, dear, of course you can come in."

Her mother fussed around the kitchen, making tea, looking confused. Delia fussed around in her arms, too, a bundle of intense needs.

"Mother, I need you to take Delia for a while," she said once her mother had settled down at the table. "There's something I have to do, and I can't take her with me."

"You know I'm always glad to have Delia," her mother said. "But where are you going? How long will you be gone?"

"I don't really know," Amanda said. "But I have to be able to do whatever needs to be done. I'll be back as soon as I can."

"This is all very mysterious, Amanda," her mother said, taking Delia from her arms. "Is this something to do with Aaron's disappearance?"

"Something," Amanda admitted.

"You're going to go find him yourself, aren't you?"

Amanda shook her head.

"I know you, dear," her mother said. "I know you so well. You're always so impatient with everyone. You always think you can do the job better. But you should let the police handle this. Leave it to the professionals."

The professionals. Amanda thought of Detective Koch and Tony Baloot. "The police are no use, mother. They think Aaron engineered his own disappearance. But I know better. I know Aaron. All the police know is the way things usually happen. But this is different. I know."

"How do you know, Amanda?"

"I just do."

.   .   .

Aphrodite Anderson was still not answering her doorbell, and there were too many adult bookstores in San Francisco to know where to begin looking for someone who knew Aaron.

So Amanda went looking for the little prostitute in the blonde wig.

Amanda started out by cruising Tenderloin sex clubs and porno houses, hoping to spot Chickie outside. She cruised the sex clubs so much that the prostitutes hanging out nearby began to recognize her.

"Come on, honey," one of them challenged her as she walked by the entrance to the Green Neon Lovehole for the tenth time. "You know you want me. I can see it in your eyes. Just go with it. I can show you to yourself."

Amanda shuddered. "No thank you," she said politely. "But maybe you can help me. Do you know someone named Chickie? I heard she works around here."

The prostitute, a hard-faced Asian woman, recoiled.

"You're a cop," she said. "I should have known."

"I'm not a cop. I'm just looking for her, that's all. Have you seen her?"

The hooker shook her head. "She don't come around here any more. Not for weeks. What you want to know for?"

"I just wanted to talk to her," Amanda said. "I think we have someone in common."

The bobbing blonde wig stood out from the monotone crumminess of the Tenderloin as if a searchlight were tracking it. This was Chickie; it had to be. Amanda dove the Jeep into a handicapped parking spot, jumped out, and ran back to the corner where she had seen the blonde ringlets in the crowd.

Past the corner, the crowd thinned out rapidly. Up ahead Amanda saw a frighteningly thin blonde-headed girl drooping along in a scanty dress and stiltlike cork-heeled platform sandals.

"Chickie!" she called out. The girl up ahead stopped and turned around, waiting for Amanda to run up.

"Chickie?" Amanda gasped.

Chickie looked at her doubtfully.

"What're you callin' after me for? I don't know you."

"You know my husband, though," Amanda said.

Chickie laughed. "Is that what it is? I know lots of husbands. You gonna kill me now? You all jealous your husband's gettin his love down here 'stead of at home? Well, let me tell you something, lady, you got lots of company."

"No, it's not that," Amanda said. How to explain? "My husband disappeared. I think he's been kidnapped. I'm just trying to talk to people who saw him recently."

Chickie squinted at her suspiciously.

"Why do you think I know your old man? I don't do kidnapping or shit like that."

"I know you know him," Amanda said. Blushing, she explained about the video. She didn't go into details about the goat or particular sex acts, but fortunately, Chickie seemed to pick up quickly.

"Oh, sure. I remember that. You're talking about Bernie. They told me they were shooting a sex video for a Web site or something." Chickie smiled wistfully. "You know, I really liked Bernie. He was always pretty nice to me. I guess that's not his real name, huh?"

"No," Amanda said.

Chickie wasn't surprised.

"Well, most of my dates don't give me any names, so even a fake one is better than nothing. But Bernie always treated me real, you know? And he paid me good, too."

"He's quite a guy," Amanda said.

"And now you say he's been kidnapped?"

Amanda nodded. "The police think he engineered it himself. But I know him better than that. I think something terrible has happened to him."

Chickie snorted with disgust. "Cops. They couldn't find they own dick with both hands and a road map." She looked Amanda up and down appraisingly.

"Now you gonna go find him yourself, huh? You must really like the guy."

"I guess I do," Amanda said, wondering why. After all, she was probably just going to kill Aaron once she found him.

"Well, I don't know if I can help you much. I haven't seen Bernie since we made that movie. But you seem like a nice lady, and I like Bernie. So if there's anything I can tell you, I will."

"Thank you," Amanda said. "I appreciate it." In her turn, she looked Chickie up and down, noting her bone-exposing thinness. "Do you want to get something to eat? I'll pay for it, of course."

Chickie smiled ear to ear, revealing her toothless gums.

"I sure do. I haven't had anything to eat since breakfast but little weenie dicks!"

Le Bistro Bon Temps was nearby, and Amanda took Chickie there. It was a fairly fancy establishment, patronized by the power elite of the city, and Amanda had often taken clients there. After all, she figured, Chickie was a kind of client.

The waitstaff was deeply outraged by Chickie's presence, but after a certain amount of bustling around and ignoring them, a waiter finally came over.

Amanda ordered lavishly, keeping Chickie's toothlessness in mind and getting plenty of soup and pâtés and vegetable terrines. It was obvious that Chickie hadn't had a decent meal in years, maybe never. Her table manners were surprisingly good, however, even though she ate at supersonic speed.

When the plates were clean, Amanda ordered coffee for them both; once it arrived she got back to business.

"Chickie, this movie you made. How did that happen?"

Chickie, one of her appetites satisfied, grew thoughtful, tapping her lips with the coffee spoon.

"The Colley brothers asked me, one of them, anyway. The short one. I was surprised, you know. I pay them so I can work in front of the Lovehole, but they never paid no attention to me before. I'm too skanky for them."

Amanda couldn't bring herself to protest this frank self-appraisal. But she liked Chickie, somehow.

"What did they say?" Amanda asked.

"They asked me would I like to make a sex movie," Chickie said. "They said I'd get a lot of money up front, more later if the movie did good."

"Did they show you a script or something?" Amanda was pretty cloudy on how such movies got made. But even porno films had scripts, didn't they?

Chickie laughed and shook her head. "Uh-uh. They told me it was like a *Candid Camera* kind of movie, like reality TV, with real johns. They said they would get waivers from the johns afterwards, but they wanted everything to be like real, so they didn't tell anybody before."

"How many guys did you have to do for the movie?"

"Just Bernie." Chickie looked wistful. "It was nice, doing it in a room instead of the backseat of a car or something. The goat was smelly, though. I never did that before. It was nasty."

"I bet. What happened afterwards?"

Chickie shrugged. "They paid me off, but I never heard from the Colleys after that one time. Never got any more money, either. And I never saw Bernie again after that. I thought they scared him off with their waiver shit. But he never came back. I liked Bernie."

"Me too," Amanda said.

"That's right, he's your old man. I was forgetting." Now it was Chickie's turn to stare. "What makes you think he got kidnapped?"

"It's the only explanation," Amanda said. The only one that didn't involve death or deep betrayal, anyway.

"They ask you for money? How much?"

"The kidnappers haven't contacted me yet." This was a flaw in her theory, she knew that. Chickie looked embarrassed and stared at her plate. Evidently, she thought so, too.

"I think they want the business," Amanda said. "I think that's what they're after."

"That's probably it," Chickie said. She dabbed delicately at her chin with her napkin, then put it in her purse in one smooth, card-trick motion. The little purse, the size of a calzone, bulged suspiciously. Amanda noticed that Chickie's silverware had disappeared as well.

"Chickie, will you help me? Will you ask around, talk to people you know? I need to find him."

"Well, I already told you all I know," Chickie said. A whine was beginning to creep into her voice. She seemed distracted, playing with her wineglass.

It will never fit in that purse, honey, Amanda thought.

Chickie kept glancing at the door and shifting in her chair. Amanda could feel her slipping away, as some inner need imposed itself— drugs, probably. The interview seemed to be over.

"Just keep your ears open, that's all I ask," Amanda said. "If you hear anything about . . . Bernie . . . please let me know." She took a business card out of her purse, wrote her cell number on the back, and handed it to Chickie.

Chickie looked at the card as if inspecting it for hidden messages, then crammed it into her purse.

"Okay, if I hear anything. But, you know, guys like the Colleys don't talk to me. I'm just a street ho. I don't hear about anybody's plans and shit."

"Maybe you'll talk to somebody who talked to them."

Chickie looked doubtful. Then she brightened.

"You know what, Amanda, you should talk to the Colleys yourself. Maybe they know what happened to your old man."

"Well . . . but how do I go about meeting them?"

"Oh, they work all over the place. You could try at the Lovehole."

"What am I supposed to do, just walk up to the front desk and ask them if they kidnapped my husband?"

Chickie laughed. "No, that would never work. You know what? What you should do, you should get a job there. So you can spy on them, talk to the other girls, find out what they know."

This had never occurred to Amanda. "Get a job there? You mean as a stripper?"

Chickie nodded. "Why not? You're a good-looking girl, nice long legs. I bet they'd like you." She stared at Amanda appraisingly. "You have to change the way you dress, though. You look like a cop, or maybe a social worker. They won't talk to you like that."

"How should I dress? I mean, I just have no idea."

"You need a makeover, girl. What you should do, call my cousin Rene. She has a salon down on Turk Street. She'll fix you up good."

I bet, Amanda thought.

"Just do what she tells you and you'll be all right."

Chickie had been twisting in her chair like a little girl who needed to go to the bathroom. Now she stood up suddenly.

"Amanda, honey, look, I gotta go now, I'm sorry. It's been nice talking to you." Chickie flashed her gums and half ran out the door of the restaurant, watched with disgust by the waiters.

Amanda paid the bill, left a big tip to make it up to the waitstaff, and left close behind her. Turk Street was just a few blocks away—she'd be able to walk there in five minutes. And finding Rene's salon would be easy enough; most of the other businesses on that part of Turk were either flophouse hotels or liquor stores.

It was time for a makeover anyway.

31

Getting Naked

Amanda had to admit to herself that going into the strip clubs scared her. She wasn't sure why. What was she afraid of, that Aaron would be in the front row, shoving limp twenty-dollar bills into a dancer's G-string? That white slavers would drug her drink and sell her out of the country?

In reality, the most frightening thing about the clubs turned out to be the drink prices.

Her entry into the Lovehole made no impression on the patrons. No one seemed to notice her at all, every eye in the place riveted on the six-foot-tall black woman on stage, down to a white G-string, pink and white pasties on her sizeable tits, and a long, white feather boa that she was running between her legs.

She looks like she's like drying off after a shower, Amanda thought. *Except for the fringy things on her nipples.*

She sat down to watch as the dancer finished up her act, tossing the G-string into the crowd and causing every man in the place—Amanda was the only woman not on stage or in a waitress costume—to rush the stage, waving greenbacks.

In the relative calm between acts, a man a few seats away noticed her, did a double take, then leaned across the intervening seats.

"You must be a lesbo," he told her. "You a lesbo? 'Cause if you are, I'll give you a hundred bucks to do my girlfriend. While I watch. How's that?"

Amanda smiled prettily. "How about I stick a blowtorch up your butt and toast your weiner from the inside? How's that?"

The guy retreated back to his seat, muttering about "fuckin dykes" under his breath. After a few face-saving minutes he got up and changed seats.

Whoa, where did that come from? Amanda thought. *That felt great, to say that.*

Half hoping some other dumbfuck would bother her so she could try it again, she settled in to see the show.

The acts were interesting, not at all what she expected. The girls were younger than she thought they'd be, for one thing, and good-looking. She had imagined tough-faced, hard-bitten babes, like the hooker she had talked to outside, the offscourings of biker bars and drunk tanks. These ladies were not like that at all, most of them. They could be college students.

The dancing—more like prancing and posturing, she thought—ranged across a spectrum from ridiculous to over-the-top sexy. It didn't seem to be the determining factor in a girl's popularity with the crowd. After watching a few acts, Amanda came to the conclusion that the biggest deciding factor was tit size, followed at a distance by height.

I don't fit the profile, Amanda thought, *though I could handle the dancing part. I think.*

A waitress came by and plopped a gin and tonic down in front of her, waiting impatiently to be paid.

"I didn't order this," Amanda said.

"Two-drink minimum," the waitress said. Her eyes rolled over the crowd, looking for likely tippers. Sighing, Amanda paid up.

Amanda's first drink had seemed to have only trace amounts of alcohol in it; the second was even weaker, if that were possible. She checked out another dancer—a pig-tailed blonde in buttless lederhosen and Nazi regalia, carrying a small whip—killed her drink, dropped all her cash on the table for a tip, and left.

Well, there's nothing to be afraid of, she thought. The men were like pigs at a trough; the dancers like Circe: enchantresses in complete control. It had not been at all what she'd expected.

I could do that, Amanda thought. *Strip. I could be an exotic dancer.*

But the Lovehole was up to its ass in exotic dancers, according to the night manager. (Not one of the Colleys, to Amanda's disappointment.)

"But I tell you what," the night manager said to her. He was wearing a sky-blue sports coat, a yellow shirt with a big collar, an ascot, and expensive sunglasses, indoors, at night.

"What?" Amanda asked.

"You should try down the Honeybuzzard," the night manager said. "They're always looking for girls. A lot of turnover. Not like here."

"What's your name, girl?" The big babe behind the desk in the Honeybuzzard's back room wanted to know. Her honey-brown hair was piled on her head like a swirl of soft custard.

"Brandy Valentine," Amanda said. She hoped Mindy wouldn't mind the use of her last name.

The big babe looked up, not pleased.

"Your real name, child, not your stage name. For the paperwork. We got to register all the dancers with the city."

"That *is* my real name," Amanda said. "My stage name too."

The babe behind the desk stared hard at her for a couple seconds, then gave it up.

"Huh," she said, dismissively. "A name like that, I guess you had to become a exotic dancer." She wrote it down.

Shawnessa Bofils, day manager at the Honeybuzzard, looked the skinny white girl up and down. Good legs, good face, too, with that black hair all around it. But a skinny little ass like a boy's, and no tits to speak of. Not your first choice for a stripper. She sighed.

"This your first job as a exotic dancer, honey?" she asked.

Amanda nodded.

"What was your last job?"

"I was a waitress," Amanda said. It was true, in a way; she had worked as a waitress for a while during law school.

"What makes you think you can dance on stage, naked, in front of a bunch of drunk men?"

"I like to dance," Amanda said. She sort of did, too.

"Uh-huh." Shawnessa wrote down "needs the money" on the form. "Well, it all comes down to the audition, baby. If the boss likes you, you got the job."

By the time Jimmy Cacapoulos got down the stairs he was in a bad mood, way cranky and ready for a nap. But he would never let any girl be hired without auditioning her himself.

It wasn't that his standards were set very high; in fact, they were extremely flexible. Basically, anyone with all the arms and legs they were born with, both tits, no large, visible scars, had the job. Dancing ability didn't enter into his decision. Cacapoulos seemed to be mostly concerned that transvestites, androids, or women with four artificial limbs would try to palm themselves off on him. This had never happened, but you couldn't be too careful.

In fact, Cacapoulos rarely rejected anyone. If they were any good they would get good tips. If they didn't, well, no one could live on what Cacapoulos paid as a base salary, not in San Francisco, so that separated the sheep from the goats. And if they got good tips, that meant the clientele was happy. If not, the girls didn't hang around long. Cacapoulos seldom had to fire anyone. Things just ran themselves.

That was the way he liked it.

Cacapoulos sat heavily in a metal folding chair, spilling large parts of himself on either side.

"Let's get it over with," he wheezed to Shawnessa.

The audition took place on the club's main stage, during normal business hours. In fact it was a free performance. The regular girls liked auditions; it gave them a break.

Amanda hadn't expected a live performance so soon. A surge of panic shot through her; her stomach knotted up.

No projectile-vomiting on the customers, she thought.

She forced herself to walk out on the low stage. Loud rap music shook the thin plywood scantlings. The curtains smelled of stale sweat. Throwing back her head, thrusting out a leg in a move vaguely remembered from some Bob Fosse performance, Amanda vogued her way across the stage.

"Shitty dancer," Cacapoulos muttered.

That's for sure, Shawnessa thought.

"She'll get better, once she get some practice in," Shawnessa said.

The lights were in Amanda's eyes and kept her from seeing the audience, which was just as well. A few cheers and catcalls told her that the club wasn't completely empty. In the very back, she made out the striking silhouette of Shawnessa Bofils's inverted ice-cream-cone hairdo. The slumped, shapeless form next to her was probably the boss, though it might have been a bag of kitchen garbage on its way to the Dumpster.

By the time Amanda finished her routine—such as it was—the folding chair was empty. She had gotten two dollars in tips; one of the tippers had surreptiously pinched her tit as he was shoving the bill into her G-string with the other hand.

Oh, well, she thought. She would do better next time.

A bored Shawnessa Bofils waited until Amanda came up to her.

"Start tomorrow, same time," Shawnessa said before Amanda could open her mouth. "Come see me, you get in. I'll give you your stage times, we pick out your music."

"That's it?" Amanda said dazedly. "I'm hired?"

Shawnessa smiled slightly.

"What did you expect, baby girl? Trumpets?"

As Clench was leaving Cacapoulos's office several girls from the club pushed past him on the narrow back stairs, on their way to the dressing room. One of them, a black-haired babe, dragged her eyes over Clench as she went past. It wasn't an invitation exactly, but Clench never needed an invitation. He reached out and grabbed her wrist.

"I know you, don't I?" Clench said to her. "You were one of Jimmy Cacapoulos's girls, back when he owned the Green Neon Lovehole in the Tenderloin."

Amanda smiled uncertainly. "That's right," she said.

Clench was waiting for her to say "let go, you're hurting me," or at least show some sign of fear or discomfort. But the girl's enormous green eyes showed nothing at all. Disappointed, he let her go.

The girl stared up at him, rubbing her forearm. That was something.

"I just started the night shift," she said. "Shawnessa sent me."

"That's right, raw meat," Clench said. "What's your name again?"

She told him.

"You're kidding, right?" Clench said in mock disbelief. "Every third girl here is called Brandy. How am I supposed to pick you out of the crowd with a name like that?"

Brandy just stared back. He liked her big green eyes, and the Louise Brooks hair helmet. But there was something so familiar about her. Where had he seen her before?

"I'll call you 'Slim'," Clench decided. A plan was dimly forming in the recesses of his mind, like the first hour of a cold sore. "It suits your skinny butt. Let me tell you something, Slim. I can help you around here." He paused to see if she was following this. "Or not. It's up to you."

Slim seemed to be tracking. She gave him a big, white smile.

"I need all the help I can get, Mr. Clench."

He could be useful, Amanda thought. Not as a competitive edge in the world of exotic dancing (though, in spite of herself, Amanda felt an urge to show them all she could do it, too). But he seemed to know everyone and be involved with everything. If anyone had heard rumors of the looting of Rogeletek and the kidnapping of Aaron Rogell, it would be Pablo.

There was also the chance that he was involved in some way. She would have to be careful, very circumspect, and not alarm him or stir his suspicions.

Amanda hoped she wouldn't have to actually sleep with him. She shuddered as if she had just eaten a spoonful of vinegar. There was something creepy about Pablo, a sense of something hidden, something you didn't really want to know about.

But it was going to be hard to get close to him without running that risk. Pablo Clench seemed to be a man of limited interests.

32

Great Minds Think Alike

Jimmy Cacapoulos liked the thought of five million dollars. A nice, big, round figure, you could think about what it meant. All those dollar bills stacked up. A lot of fucking money.

But there was no good reason to spread it around too much. Clench was right to get rid of those guys like that, the muscle guys. No one would miss them. Too, it was better if they couldn't shoot off their mouths, like if they went down for some of the petty shit they were always into. The fewer people knew about this the better.

Cacapoulos had some more ideas about that. When Clench got there with the money—well, not the real money, but with the bank account info—they could talk. He knew Pablo would agree with him they shouldn't have to give everything up to guys who weren't smart enough to plan things, to think ahead.

Great minds think alike.

.   .   .

When Pablo Clench finally showed up, he backed through the door holding a big red cooler.

What the fuck? Cacapoulos thought. *Does he have the money in there?*

Clench put the cooler down on the table, looked around, and winked at Cacapoulos.

"Brought you a present, Jimmy," Clench said. "Something even you, with all your experience, have never seen before." He reached into the cooler and took out what looked like a small, square Tupperware container.

"What's in the box?" Cacapoulos eyed the Tupperware container suspiciously.

"Guy's private stash of blow," Pablo Clench said. "He makes it himself. Powerful stuff."

Cacapoulos liked cocaine. Sure, he'd had his problems with it in the past, had done his Coke Enders thing. But he never lost his fondness for the drug.

He pried the top off the container.

"Careful, don't spill it," Clench said. He backed away slightly.

"This shit is all gray," Cacapoulos complained. "It doesn't look like blow. It looks like fucking laundry soap."

"This guy is a scientist, I'm telling you," Clench said. "This is his own private stash he made himself. Supposed to be more powerful than crack."

"More powerful than crack, huh?" Cacapoulos said, putting the top back on. "I better leave it alone then."

"Wise man," Clench said. "I was you, I wouldn't fool with it. Reason I brought it here, I knew you had the willpower to not dip into it. Those other guys . . . it'd be gone before I got out the door."

"Safe with me," Cacapoulos muttered.

"I knew I could trust you," Clench said.

"Pablo, this is what's bothering me," Cacapoulos said. "What about the scientist? What're you gonna do about that guy?"

"Don't worry about him. I had Trick take care of him." Clench grew thoughtful, stroking his chin. "Maybe we should have sold his ass to the Kalimahanese. They like scientists."

Clench briefly considered this transaction, then shook his head.

"Nah. Would'a been too risky. Better the way it turned out. Anyway, the generals are probably maxed out on scientists. One is enough for a small country like Kalimaha."

"So you were never going to let the guy go?"

"No way. He'd go straight to the cops."

Cacapoulos grew thoughtful in turn. He had no objection to taking guys out when it was necessary for business, but the thought of so many bodies piling up made him nervous. Someone would notice and say something, and then what would happen? It could get messy.

"What about the Colleys? You gonna pay 'em?" Cacapoulos, who had used their services many times, had a healthy respect for the Colleys.

"They'll get their share, don't worry."

The word "share" brought Cacapoulos back to the present.

"What about my share? When am I gonna see that?"

Clench smiled broadly. If he hadn't been wedged so tightly in his desk chair, Jimmy Cacapoulos would have recoiled. As it was, he blinked and swallowed.

"Got it right here, Jimmy," Clench said, patting his jacket pocket.

Careful, he might have a gun in there, Cacapoulos thought. He slid open the desk drawer where he kept his own gun, and stuck his hand in, fat fingers feeling around like caterpillars amongst the litter of receipts, chewing-gum wrappers, used toothpicks, rubber bands, and dead ballpoints.

"Let me get a pencil, we can add it up."

Where the fuck was his gun? His questing fingers brushed against the heavy grip.

"Pencil?" Clench said scornfully. "This is the computer age, Jimmy. you don't need a fucking pencil. Look." he pulled a CD in a clear plastic clamshell out of his jacket pocket and smacked it down in front of Cacapoulos.

Cacapoulos relaxed a little. He took his hand out of the desk drawer and picked up the CD.

"What do I do with this?"

"Put it in your computer, Jimmy. You know how, right?"

Cacapoulos knew that much. He slid the disk in, opened it, clicked on the single file folder it contained. The file popped open.

Cacapoulos frowned.

"The fuck is this? Just a bunch of numbers. That doesn't add up to five mil."

"Those are account numbers, Jimmy," Clench explained patiently. "That's the way these Swiss banks work. You don't think I have five million dollars in twenties sitting out in the van? The money is in foreign bank accounts, just waiting for you and me."

Cacapoulos would have liked it if the money had come in big bundles, something he could see and touch, but he recognized that this was a better idea.

"Whose name is on these accounts?"

"No names. Just numbers. It's a business account," Clench explained. "Several business accounts, actually. You and me are the only ones okayed to make withdrawals."

"So how do I get at the accounts?"

"Watch." Clench went behind the desk and reached around Cacapoulos's bulk to get at the keyboard. It was a squeeze, but he managed to open Cacapoulos's browser and call up a Swiss bank Web site. A few more clicks and keystrokes and a new window opened.

"There it is," Clench said. "The first of many."

"How do I get in?" Cacapoulos wanted to know.

Clench clicked back to the CD menu—a little too fast for Jimmy Cacapoulos, who experienced all computer operations as a kind of magic trick. Doves flying out of fucking boxes: How did he do that?

A page opened on the monitor. It contained a few lines of text, letters and numbers jumbled together meaninglessly, a short series of words, like the answers on a TV quiz show—"Daly City," "Helen of Troy," "Bowser"—and the single expletive "fuckwad."

"I had a dog named Bowser," Cacapoulos mused.

"I know, Jimmy, I know," Clench said. "Now these words are the answers to a series of questions that only you can answer. Like passwords. How you get into your accounts."

"Anyone could get into the money with this stuff?" Cacapoulos said, alarmed.

"Just you and me," Clench said. "You trust me, don't you, Jimmy?"

"Sure I do." *In a pig's ass.*

"I were you, I would memorize this, and the account numbers, then trash the file." They both knew he would never do this. "Then you won't have to worry about someone pretending to be you and vacuuming out the accounts."

"Fuckwad, what's that? I don't think I like that."

"That's your final password, Jimmy," Clench said. "Type that in and step into a couple million bucks. I just wanted something I was sure you could remember."

"I'll think of you every time I open my account," Jimmy Cacapoulos said.

Clench slapped him on the back.

"Hey, rich man! I think it's time for a little celebration, don't you?"

"You celebrate," Cacapoulos rumbled. "I got work to do."

"Well, don't work too hard, big guy." Clench straightened up. "I'll leave you to it. But we have a lot to talk about later. I have some ideas about how to shake off the Colleys, I think you'll want to consider them."

"Yeah. Later."

Clench opened the office door, but stopped halfway out.

"Hey, I almost forgot. Okay to leave the cooler here? Like I said, I don't want those other assholes to get their hands on it."

"Don't worry," Jimmy Cacapoulos said. "I'll keep an eye on it.

"Hey, thanks." Clench walked out, closing the door behind him.

So that's what he's up to, Cacapoulos thought. *Setting me up: to-night someone from narcotics comes sniffing around. Clench is black-mailing him, or something, so he forgets how much we're paying him, and he finds the coke in my office. I go to jail, Clench gets all the money. I'm disappointed. I thought he'd come up with something better than that.*

Cacapoulos picked up the Tupperware container. This was going off the premises right away. Maybe even messenger it to Clench's hotel room; that was a thought. Cacapoulos grunted with satisfaction. He waddled over to the cooler to put the box back in, then stopped. Another thought had come to him.

Maybe, before I send this shit back to Clench, I could get a little taste, Cacapoulos thought. *Just a little one. That wouldn't hurt anything. A line or two, just to celebrate.*

Better hurry, though, he thought. Clench was probably calling the narcs right this minute.

Cacapoulos put the container down on his desk and pried off the plastic cover.

Clench stuck his head into Jimmy Cacapoulos's office the next morning, just to see how things had gone. Jimmy wasn't answering his home phone, or his cell. That was good. But Clench wanted to be sure nothing stupid had happened.

The light was still on over Jimmy's desk. The computer screen was black, but the little green light that showed the computer was on burned merrily away. Jimmy Cacapoulos was nowhere in sight. On the desk chair was a puddle of what looked like soapy dishwater, with a dishrag left in it.

Clench could see the Tupperware container on the corner of the desk, its lid off. A hundred-dollar bill loosely rolled into a tube lay on the desktop next to it.

Good thing the light wasn't shining directly on the robot stuff, he thought. *Good thing the Buzzard had great air-conditioning.*

Clench softly closed the office door.

A few minutes later he was back with Alonzo from the kitchen.

"Got something I want you to mop up for me," Clench told him. Alonzo, used to sudden tasks being dumped on him like this, ran up the stairs to Jimmy's office, followed by Clench.

"Door's open, go on in," Clench told him.

Alonzo stepped in and looked around, puzzled.

"Where's Jimmy? I thought you said he was up here."

"He's here, all right." Clench's voice came from outside the door. "Look over on his desk chair."

A pile of damp fabric lay on the chair in the middle of a pool of gray-white frothy liquid. Alonzo bent over and fished something out of the wet, holding it up by thumb and finger.

"The fuck is this? Looks like underwear," he said.

"That's what it is," Clench said out in the hall. "Underwear."

"What happened to Jimmy?" Alonzo said, tossing the damp thong back in the froth pool. "Weren't we supposed to meet him here?" He sneezed mightily.

"Gesundheit. That is Jimmy," Clench said. "What's left of him."

Clench remembered his science. "The human body isn't a good source of materials," Rogell had told him when Clench had quizzed him about feeding robots to people, and what would happen if you did. "It's mostly water."

Alonzo couldn't process this at all.

"You're telling me that Jimmy Cacapoulos is a pile of wet underwear?"

"That's exactly what I'm telling you," Clench said. He stuck his head cautiously around the door frame. "Now clean this shit up for me, okay? I want to use this office and I don't want piles of underwear and spit all over the place."

Alonzo didn't fully understand what was going on, but assumed it was some kind of practical joke or something. He shrugged.

"You got it," he said.

Clench went and waited at the bar until Alonzo had finished cleaning up the mess in Cacapoulos's office.

Finally Alonzo came back, wiping his hands on a paper towel.

"What happened up there? I don't get it."

Clench coughed and put his hand over his mouth. "Don't worry about it," he said. "You don't need to know." He jumped up from his bar stool and clapped Alonzo on the back.

"But I appreciate the help. Why don't you just take the rest of the day off?"

"With pay?"

"You bet."

Alonzo grinned. "Hey, thanks a lot, Mr. Clench."

On the sidewalk outside the Honeybuzzard, Alonzo suddenly went pale.

"I don't feel so good." He looked like a little boy about to puke up a pound of candy corn and birthday cake.

Clench patted him on the shoulder.

"Go home. Get some rest. Big day tomorrow."

Alonzo nodded numbly.

.   .   .

A few minutes later, sitting in a bus shelter on Kearney, Alonzo let out a low moan. The other people waiting for the bus—cleaning women, restaurant help, retirees—looked at him with alarm. When he began to moan rhythmically and appeared to be wrestling with a small animal in his lap, several of the onlookers were concerned enough to get up and wait outside the shelter.

Fortunately, the bus came in a few minutes, and the shelter emptied out. No one looked back. Alonzo made no attempt to board.

As the bus pulled away he began to shriek.

The next person to arrive at the bus shelter, an elderly man on his way to the public library, found only a pool of foam and a piece of damp cloth on the sidewalk in front of the seat.

"People are so disgusting," he muttered, spreading a newspaper over the gray-white froth puddle so he wouldn't have to look at it.

One man's garbage is another man's treasure. A little after nightfall, Jonathan Prince, street name "Chuckles," sat down in the bus kiosk to rest up before pushing his loaded shopping cart the rest of the way down to the freeway underpass where he slept. There was a funny smell in the kiosk, not shit or puke or anything like that, a kind of chemical smell. Chuckles lifted up the newspaper and saw what looked like a big pool of spit with a piece of cloth floating in it. He fished out the cloth and held it up to examine in the glow of a streetlight.

Some kind of lingerie. Not his style. But maybe someone would want it.

He held the damp cloth up to his nostrils and sniffed mightily, but there was no scent of girl on it, only a cold, lonely chemical reek.

Well, shit on it, then. The thong joined the miscellaneous pile of possibly useful items in Chuckles's shopping cart. He gave the overloaded cart a shove and rolled off down Kearney.

"Hey, you seen Chuckles around?" One-Arm, the Vietnam vet, asked Crazy Larry. "He owes me a blow job."

Sitting cross-legged against an expressway pylon, Crazy Larry was rocking back and forth, deep in communication with his inner spirit guides. But he emerged long enough to process the question and answer it.

"Nope, nobody's seen him. All his shit's still there, back under the bridge." Larry poked a long dirty thumb over his shoulder.

"Anything good?" One-Arm wanted to know, but Larry didn't think the question was worth answering. He closed his eyes and increased the pace of his rocking.

It was cool under the freeway overpass, cooler still back in the shadows under the bridge. One-Arm rummaged through Chuckles's shopping cart, throwing the carefully stowed items on top of the pile of wet clothes that was the only thing in sight when he had found the little camp.

"Shit," he muttered. "Ain't nothing worth takin'." A pile of worthless crap. Just another crazy with a shopping cart full of secret treasures. Moodily, he kicked the cart and watched it careen down the steep embankment before pounding into a chain-link fence and turning over.

That was cool, the cart belting down the concrete. That was the highlight of his day.

The weak sun of a San Francisco summer, strained through a thick layer of fog, beat down on the cart and the litter pile that spilled from it.

33

Double the Fun

The Colley brothers were going to be the big problem, Clench thought. Not very smart in some ways, they had a hyperdeveloped sense of self-preservation. It would be hard to come up on them. They were like animals, wild animals. Hard to surprise, hard to kill, always alert to other predators.

How do you kill wild animals? Clench asked himself. *Easy: you trap them.* You put something they want in the trap as bait. They grab it; the hammer comes down.

The question was, what would make the Colley brothers walk into a trap? What did the brothers want?

That's easy again, Clench thought. *There's only two things those guys ever want: money and pussy.*

The money was out. It would take too much to buy those assholes off, and Clench needed it for himself. Keeping the money: That was the whole point of the exercise, after all.

Pussy might work, though, if he could engineer the right introductions. There were lots of candidates. But it would have to be a bitch he could control, with fear or money or both. Someone on his side, to act as a wedge between the brothers, to make them careless, to lead them into Clench's little trap—whatever that turned out to be.

Who, Clench wondered, would make a good piece of meat to bait the trap with?

"Amanda!"

Amanda had stumbled across the tiny hotel room half-asleep and juggled the cell phone to her ear. She was still groggy—the late-night shift she was working at the Honeybuzzard had destroyed her sleep schedule—and the voice at the other end of the phone was hard to understand, curiously distorted. She grunted something into the phone.

"Amanda! This is Chickie. You said call you if I found out anything. Amanda, honey, I'm in trouble. You gotta help me!"

"Chickie!" Slowly Amanda began to track. "Where did you get this number?"

"You wrote it down for me, remember? On the back of your card."

"Oh, right." Had she really done that? Apparently so, because here was Chickie on her phone. "What happened?"

"Happen? The brothers just tried to kill me!"

"Brothers? What brothers?"

"The Colleys. They dragged me in their van and tried to put something over my mouth, like some kind of chemical. I never should have just walked over to them, you know? But I work with them, I wasn't ready for any weird play like that."

Okay, Amanda was fully in the moment now. If the Colleys were trying to kill Chickie, maybe they heard that she was talking about Aaron's disappearance. And maybe that meant something was going on, something to do with Aaron.

"Where are you now? Are you safe?" she asked Chickie.

"I'm over to Rene's, in the storage room," Chickie said. "She let me use her cell to call you. But Amanda, I'm afraid to go out on the street! They meant me something bad, I could tell."

"How did you get away from them?"

"When Billy—that's the big one—try to put the little cloth over my mouth, I poked my thumb in his eye, then I kicked him in the balls. He let me go, I jumped over the seat and went out the back door."

"Look, stay where you are. Tell Rene to look out for a cab. I'll come get you as soon as I can."

"Thank you, Amanda, honey. I love you, baby. Just make sure the cab comes to the back door."

Rene walked her cousin out wrapped in a floor-length bathrobe, with a big towel turban on her head. Chickie jumped in the cab and sunk down in the seat.

"Thank you, baby."

Amanda glanced over at Chickie's swathed and huddled figure. "It's nothing, Chickie. The hard part is going to be figuring out a place to stay that'll be safe for you."

"What about your hotel room? I thought I could stay there."

Amanda had thought of this, too, but saw a problem.

"Chickie, tell me something. And be honest with me."

Chickie tried on being offended. "I *have* been honest with you."

"No you haven't. But this is important: If I put you in my hotel room, how long are you going to stay there?"

Chickie sunk further down in the seat. "Till it's safe to come out, I guess."

"What about if you need something? I mean like drugs. If you go running out into the street, they'll find you in seconds."

"I won't do that," Chickie said, but neither of them believed her.

"Where can I take you?" Not her mom's; that would be too much to put on her mother. Not the South City place; Chickie wouldn't last a day, up there in the big, empty, windy house by herself. *It had been hard enough for me*, Amanda thought.

But South City had other possibilities.

The cab driver was waiting patiently for the two ladies to make up their minds. He was calm and philosophical; the meter was running.

"Take us down to South City," Amanda told him.

The driver pulled away from the curb. "Where in South City?"

Amanda gave him an address just off Grand, as Chickie watched her with big, curious eyes.

"Where we goin'?"

Instead of answering, Amanda pulled out her cell phone and dialed.

"Hello, Tony? This is Amanda Rogell. Yes, I know what I said. But consider yourself un-fired."

Amanda was relieved to have thought of stashing Chickie with Tony Baloot. It was unlikely that the brothers would think of looking for her there.

And Chickie seemed okay with the plan. She had settled right in.

Only Tony Baloot was not happy with the arrangement. For one thing, he thought he might know Chickie's pursuers.

"Two brothers, one short, the other big and tall?" he had asked her.

"That's right."

"Earl and Billy?"

"You know them?" Chickie asked.

"We've met," Tony Baloot said.

His ma, for another thing. She kept asking him about the noises in the storeroom and threatening to bring in an exterminator if he didn't do something about it.

And Chickie coming and going by the fire-escape ladder made a whole fuck of a lot of noise. It was like she was trying to get caught.

When he confronted her with this, Chickie was not real cooperative.

"I can't stay cooped up in that goddamn storeroom all day! The dry flowers make my nose itch. I sneeze like a motherfucker. Besides, I have things to do, places to go to."

Baloot knew about these things. He had seen her hanging around some of the bars and cheaper hotels down toward the airport. And for a known abuser of controlled substances, she seemed to stay pretty happy, which could only mean a steady source of income. He knew she wasn't feeding her habit on the few dollars he had given her from time to time just to shut her up.

Oh well. It'll all go on the bill to Mrs. Rogell.

But it was just a matter of time before word got around that a new whore was hanging around, no teeth, blonde wig. Just a matter of time before the Colleys found out where Chickie was hanging out and come to pay her another visit.

Various parts of Tony Baloot twanged with remembered pain every time he thought of the Colleys. He wasn't eager to see them again.

And if Chickie disappeared and turned up dismembered in a hotel Dumpster or floating in the bay, the other half of the money Mrs. Rogell had promised him would disappear also.

Eventually, to keep his ma quiet he had had to move Chickie to his own grungy little studio apartment down the street from the flower store. That hadn't worked too well, either; before the week was up she had pawned or sold everything of value, including the TV and most of Baloot's tropical shirts.

That was the last straw. Tony Baloot was getting fed up. He thought it might be time he took Chickie back to the store and got a refund. Mrs. Rogell had been pretty generous so far, with a promise of more to come. But Baloot had been very fond of those shirts. They weren't just something you could walk down to the store and replace. Each one had its history.

There were some things even money couldn't get you.

34

Games

The card table wiggled every time Rogell leaned forward to make a move. It was hard to manage his chains, too, without knocking pieces off the chessboard.

"Careful," Trick said. "I can understand why you might want to knock the board over, though, the position you're in. I don't see what else you can do to get out of it."

"If you would just shut up so I can think," Rogell said. His position was critical, he could see that. The wrong move, and Trick would have him boxed in. Mate in four moves. If he moved the bishop to white king five . . .

"Did you hear the doorbell?"

Rogell sat back. "Nice one. You saw that I was about to move, and you had to run a little interference."

"No, really. I thought I heard the front door." Trick got up and stuck his head out of the door into the rest of the basement.

Now Rogell could hear it as well: *ding, dong, ding.* After a short pause someone began hammering vigorously.

"I better go see what this is," Trick said. "You stay here. Don't move the pieces around while I'm gone."

"Don't even worry about it."

Trick slipped out, leaving Rogell to contemplate the board. He never even considered any kind of shortcut to victory; it meant too much to his vanishing self-esteem that he legitimately win a game now and then.

Bishop to king five. That would prevent his knight from crossing over and jeopardizing my queen. . . .

Trick was back in a minute, carrying a large red cooler.

"Messenger service," he explained. "From Pablo. There's a note: 'For all that you do, a little present. Make sure it goes up your nose and not on the floor. Love, Pablo.' How sweet. Do you think it's a bomb?"

Rogell shook his head. "He wouldn't send a bomb by messenger. Too easy to trace."

The red cooler looked horribly familiar. The last time Rogell had seen one like it was in his private laboratory, surrounded by thugs and the ruins of his career.

"Open it."

"You open it." Trick shoved the cooler at him and backed toward the door.

"Relax. Got a knife?"

Nervously, Trick fished out a pocketknife and cut through the packing tape that held the top on.

"You sure this is a good idea?"

Rogell pried the top up. Removing some wadded up newspapers, they saw that the cooler contained a fair amount of dry ice (Clench had looted it from the special-effects cabinet at the Buzzard) and what looked like a small Tupperware container.

Now it was Rogell's turn to be cautious. "Probably not a good idea to open that."

Trick leaned over curiously. "Don't worry, I'll leave it alone. What is it?"

"My firstborn," Rogell said. He smiled wryly. "My first nanorobot assembler horde."

"What would have happened if I'd put that up my nose, the way Pablo suggested?" Trick asked.

"Bad things. Your body heat would activate the bots. They'd take you apart and put you back together. You'd never be the same."

Trick shivered. "Well, there's no way I ever would have honked up something Pablo sent me out of the blue. He is just not trustworthy on any level."

"So while you're sitting here talking about taking care of Pablo, Pablo is trying to take care of you."

"Good thing you were here," Trick said. "Now what do we do with this stuff? I can't just throw it in the trash, can I?"

Rogell shook his head vigorously. "No. But stick it in your refrigerator. It'll be safe enough there. You could just leave it out, it'd be safe at room temperature, too, but you never know what will happen. Safest to just stick it in the fridge."

"I better stick a label on it," Trick said. "I don't want someone to mistake it for a container of sea salt."

35

The Nickel Drops

Billy Colley was frowning.

"You know, Earl," he said, "I've been thinking."

Earl looked up, surprised to be spoken to in a more or less friendly fashion. He waited patiently for Billy's thought process to rumble to a conclusion.

"Those guys we hired," Billy said, after a long interval of silence. "Driving in the water like that. I can't figure out why they would do that."

"What do you care?" Earl said.

"I'm just curious, that's all. Like maybe they were drunk or something. But in the morning? Who gets smashed at ten in the morning?"

"Drunks do."

"But those guys weren't alkies. Fucking Trick is an alkie. I wouldn't a hired them if they were alkies."

Sighing, Earl put down the video mag he was reading. It was time, once again, to explain the obvious to his brother.

"Billy, Clench got to those guys. Don't you see it? I don't know exactly how he did it, but he did. It's got to be."

"You know that?" Billy said. "You know Clench did it, and that doesn't freak you out?"

"I was expecting it. And after all, it's not such a bad deal. It leaves just us and Pablo Clench to split the two million bucks."

(Clench had kept the actual amount of the transaction under wraps, as far as the Colleys were concerned.)

"Don't forget Trick," Billy reminded him.

"Yeah, Trick. But that leaves just three of us to split the two mil."

"Four of us. That leaves four."

"It's what I said, isn't it? But if Clench went away, too, that means a bigger cut for us."

Billy frowned and considered this.

"Yeah, well, he'd do it to us."

"Would do it? You can bet your ass he's doing it to us right now."

"So how do we stop him?"

"I don't know yet," Earl said, picking up his magazine again. "But I got me some ideas."

The Colleys were in the club again, Clench noted. They'd suddenly started hanging around the Buzzard.

Clench knew it was himself they came to see, not the dancers. But he couldn't help but notice that Billy Colley's big head turned every time the new dancer, that Brandy, walked by, working the audience for lap dances.

This is a useful fact, Clench thought.

The next time Brandy passed their table, Billy reached out a big paw and grabbed her by the wrist.

Brandy gave him a big white smile, put her hand behind his neck, and swung herself into his lap.

Nice technique, Clench thought. *She's picking it up fast.*

Billy Colley stuffed some bills into Amanda's thong. The lap dance began. Billy's head got red and seemed to grow larger. *Like the head of his dick,* Clench thought. He wondered if the guy's head would just explode, like a cartoon thermometer on a hot day.

When the dance was over Brandy swung herself off like a kid getting off a carousel, pinched Billy Colley's cheek, and sashayed away. The enormous musclehead turned and watched her cross the room.

When she got to Clench's table, he put a hand on her belly and stopped her.

"What'd he give you?"

Amanda hadn't looked at the bills. She pulled them out and her eyes got wide. Silently, she held them up for Clench to see.

He grinned.

"Two hundred bucks! Not bad for a beginner."

Toward the end of her shift at the Honeybuzzard, most of Amanda was aching. She had watched the other dancers carefully for pointers, but motherhood was poor training for exotic dancing, and the high-heeled shoes they made her dance in were warping her spine, she was sure of it. Oh well, at least she hadn't fallen right off the stage yet.

Aside from the two hundred from the big guy, she had done only okay on tips, not great. Weirdly, this bothered her. Even though taking her clothes off in front of a crowd of businessmen and frat boys was merely a means to an end, and not something she wanted to make a career of, she couldn't help but want to do it well.

Maybe she could think up some gimmick for her act, she thought, like Griselda's black cat skins and witch's hat, or Cement Block Fanny's hard hat. Or Gretchen, with her buttless lederhosen, black leather cap, and riding crop. Or maybe Pablo would let her do a table dance. Table dancers always did much better than the girls on stage. She had better cozy up to Pablo a little.

Getting close to Pablo might serve a dual purpose, Amanda figured. In addition to getting more stage time and maybe a table dance or two, Pablo Clench seemed to be well connected at the Buzzard. He moved in its upper circles. Through him, she might be able to penetrate the inner sanctum and find out what connection there was between the strip joint and her husband's disappearance. He could introduce her to the mysterious Jimmy Cacapoulos, for instance.

She saw Pablo across the room, unloading some budget of shit on a waitress. Finally, the waitress slunk away, and Amanda made her move.

Clench turned around as she approached, as if sensing her. He reached out and took her by the upper arm.

"Hey, Slim," he said, "I was just thinking of you."

"Hi, Pablo." Amanda tried to summon up some sexiness and allure, but frankly, Pablo turned her off. There was something disturbing about him she couldn't put her finger on.

"Pablo, I want to talk to you," she said. "I think it's about time you let me do a table dance."

"No way," Pablo Clench said. "You'll fall off. Look at you: You can barely walk in those things. You want to get up on a table?"

"I can do it. I'm getting better all the time."

It was true. As Amanda got used to being up on stage with her bare butt showing, she began to like it. It was exciting, showing herself like that; powerful, not degrading like she thought it would be. Here it is, boys. What do you think of that? And as she got into it, her tips improved.

But you are not here for tips, Amanda reminded herself. You are here to find Aaron. If that meant cuddling up to the floor boss, then that was where she would start.

She gave him her most devastating smile.

"Can you introduce me to Jimmy Cacapoulos? I'd really like to meet him."

Meet him? Clench thought. *You could wear him.*

"Jimmy's stretched pretty thin right now," he said. "You better not try and talk to him. He might snap."

"Well, when would be a good time?"

Never, Clench thought.

"What do you want to see him for, anyway?" he asked.

"Well, I thought it might be good for my career to meet the big boss," she said. "Since you don't seem like you're going to do anything for me."

"Don't say that, Slim. I'm just waiting for the perfect moment to arrive."

She gave him the smile again, with a little twist. "Just don't wait too long, okay?"

Was she overdoing it? Clench seemed a little distant all of a sudden.

But Pablo Clench was merely lost in thought. A great idea had just come to him.

"Say, Slim," he said. "what are you doing for dinner tonight?"

Clench took them over in his own car, a Porsche Carrera. Amanda looked silently out the window as the Porsche took them out of North Beach and through the Stockton Tunnel.

"Where are we going?" she asked finally.

"Mission District. Almost there," Pablo Clench said. "I want you to meet a couple friends of mine. We're having dinner tonight, talk business."

"Who are these guys? Do I know them?"

"Well, you were getting up close and personal with one of them yesterday. The Colleys. Brothers. Nice guys, you'll like them."

Amanda didn't say anything. She wasn't sure she could have spoken even if she'd wanted to. Her breathing seemed to have stopped. Meeting the Colley brothers was a big step closer to finding out what had happened to Aaron. But it was scary.

She'd had the Colleys pointed out to her by the other girls. The brothers seemed to hang out in the Buzzard a lot. She thought it might take a while to warm up to them.

"What am I supposed to do when we get there?" Amanda asked.

"Just make them like you, that's all," Clench said. "Be nice to them."

"How nice?"

"As nice as you can be."

Amanda tucked her chin down, considering this. From what she had heard of the Colleys, it wouldn't be that easy to be nice to them, even a little.

"Which one?" she asked Clench.

"Both," he told her.

Clench was enjoying himself. The food was good at Bruno's. Brandy Valentine sat next to him, her long, skinny leg pressed up against his. The two Colley brothers sat on the other side of the booth. Billy kept staring at Brandy, sucking his drink through the stirrer. *He looks like a cow hanging its head over a fence*, Clench thought.

Earl looked doubtfully at Brandy.

"I thought this was going to be a business dinner."

"It is," Clench said. "You can say anything you want. Brandy is cool."

Earl seemed less than convinced.

"Well, we all know what this is about. It's about the distribution of proceeds from our recent venture. We're in business together," he explained to Brandy.

"She knows," Clench said.

"We're ready at this end. For the distribution," Earl said. "So we want to know, where is it? When do we get our share? Because, I'll tell you, we're beginning to get a little nervous."

"Nothing to be nervous about," Clench said. "Trick is handling everything. It's not as simple as handing out paper bags of twenties, you know. It takes time to set things up properly. But it's good to go now. Jimmy got his just last night, for example."

"Jimmy, where is Jimmy?" Billy put in. "I didn't see him around today."

"He took his distribution and went to Vegas," Clench said. "I saw him off myself, last night. Probably owns a casino by now."

"We saw that you paid off your people in Oakland," Earl said. "We saw that. That was a good way of handling things, probably. But you understand that wouldn't work with us."

Clench grinned broadly. Earl didn't flinch; he was used to it, but Amanda was glad she only had a limited side view.

"Of course not," Clench said.

Earl Colley threw down his napkin and stood up.

"Gotta piss," he apologized. "Be right back."

Clench smirked as he watched Earl stride toward the restroom at the back of the restaurant. He glanced at his watch.

"Your brother's in a hurry," he said to Billy Colley. "Weak bladder?"

Billy shrugged. What could you say to that?

Clench glanced at his watch again when Earl reappeared.

"That didn't take long. I hope you washed your hands."

. . .

Later Billy quizzed Earl as they walked to their car.

"Where'd you go when you left the table? Was that really to take a piss?"

Earl shot him a "*you've got to be kidding me*" look. "I gave the parking valet twenty bucks to point out Clench's car to me."

"Twenty bucks? Clench's car? What for? You know what he drives."

"I checked out the license plate," Earl said. "I just want to make sure I get the right one when the time comes."

Before Pablo Clench got in the Porsche he threw himself on the asphalt next to it and stuck his head under the chassis. Amanda peered down at him from the passenger seat.

"Pablo! What are you doing?"

Clench got up brushing at his suit.

"Just checking to see if Earl has been around. He's good with his hands, that guy." He whacked at his clothes as if they were on fire. "Man, this jacket is ruined."

He came around the car and slid behind the wheel, reaching under the dashboard and feeling around like a blind man trying to find a light switch. Finally he straightened up.

"Okay, we're good to go."

"What was that all about?" Amanda asked.

"You just can't be too careful," Clench said.

As he was driving Brandy back to the Buzzard, Clench saw it out of the corner of his eye. He couldn't believe it at first, but when he looked back over his shoulder he saw it was really there.

A parking space this close to North Beach. Two blocks from his hotel, three from the Buzzard.

He stood on the brakes and spun the Porsche right around, headed in the other direction. Fortunately the cars behind him were far enough away to take evasive action. He gunned the Porsche back up the hill, braked on a dime, and backed into the space in one smooth motion.

"Wow!" Brandy/Slim/Amanda said, her hand in her hair. "What a car!"

Amanda was apprehensive as she teetered down the steep Russian Hill street toward the lights of North Beach. (High heels were always a bitch in the city.) After drinks and dinner, Pablo Clench might try and take her home. It would be the normal thing to do, after all.

She needn't have worried. Few things in Clench's life could be described as normal, and his sexuality was not one of them. In any case, the concept of "home" was absent from Pablo Clench's mental map. Home was wherever he found himself. He would just as soon fuck Amanda on the hood of his car, or on the sidewalk, as in a bed.

Luckily for Amanda, Pablo had other things on his mind at the moment.

"So what did you think of the Colleys?" he asked Amanda. "Are they cool guys or what?"

"They seemed interesting," Amanda said.

"Really interesting," Clench agreed. "I think Billy likes you. Did you see the way he kept looking at you? I thought he was going to lean over and start licking your arms."

Amanda had noticed. She hugged herself as if the cold were getting to her.

"What do they do for a living?" she asked. "I couldn't really tell, from what you guys were talking about. Are they in the strip club business?"

"Among other things," Clench said. "They're good men to know, if you want things done."

"What kind of things?"

"Difficult things. Things that make money."

Amanda was thoughtful. This seemed like a good opening to get in amongst the brothers.

Pablo Clench was thinking the exact same thing.

"Pablo?"

"That's me."

"Pablo, you know, I have a problem, and I was hoping you could help me with it."

Clench looked at her seriously, trying to keep the shit-eating grin off his face. He loved it when people did all the work for him.

"What kind of problem is that?"

Amanda let her high heels clop out a four-beat pause.

"It's my ex," she said. "He owes me money. A lot of money. And I need it." She looked up at Clench with pleading eyes and a wry smile. "I don't make that much at the Honeybuzzard."

"Well, I could help you there," Clench said. "Give you a few more sets, maybe even that table dance you were asking about."

"Thanks. But I need more money than I can make dancing. I need the money my ex owes me. And I was wondering,"

Here it comes. "About?" he prompted.

"If you know somebody that would help me—convince—my ex to pay up."

"The Colleys are good at that kind of thing," Clench said. "Very convincing."

"I though they might be. And I was thinking that if they could just take him somewhere, and—talk to him, convince him that it's in his best interests to pay me the money he owes me."

"See, that's upping the ante, though," Clench explained. "That's kidnapping."

"I guess it is," Amanda said. She didn't seem bothered by the idea.

"Except that he would be, like, ransoming himself."

"Do you think the Colleys would be up for something like that? Kidnapping?" she asked. "If not, maybe you could recommend somebody else."

"Oh no, the brothers would be okay with that kind of work," Clench said. "They're experienced kidnappers."

Then it hit him.

Holy shit. This girl is the girl from the videos, in some kind of black wig. Not one of the hookers, but the wife. Rogell's wife. The woman with the baby in the backyard. The babe in all those video shorts from the spy cam, cooking, reading, dusting, shoving her tit in the baby's mouth. The woman asleep beneath the sheets in the video that had finally gotten to Mr. Hardass Scientist and made him cough up his little secret.

This was Amanda Rogell.

Thank you, God, Clench thought reverently. *Thank you for doing this for me.*

"Do you think you could ask them?" Amanda asked him. "I can't pay them up front, but they can have a piece of what my ex gives me."

"That should incentivize them," Clench agreed. "But let me put you in touch with them. You can work out the details together."

Amanda Rogell. The Colleys, fucking Amanda Rogell. Amanda Rogell, leading the Colleys into his trap like a judas goat in a G-string. Amanda Rogell and the Colleys, going down together, disappearing from the face of the earth together. This was so sweet. The symmetry of it all made Clench grin. Luckily, there was no one around to see it.

This was great, Clench realized. Slim would get in among the

Colleys and cause trouble. Maybe they would both fall in love with her, go crazy jealous and kill each other. Well, that was too much to hope for. But at a minimum, he would have someone in the enemy camp, and that was always a good thing. He could keep up on their movements and get advance warning of any weird shit in the pipeline.

And the best thing was, he didn't have to do anything to keep it going. As the plan to foist Brandy on the Colleys had taken shape in the reptilian recesses of his brain, Clench had tried to think of where his leverage would be with her. Just keeping her job wasn't enough for what he had in mind. He had planned to investigate her various needs—drugs maybe, a hidden kid somewhere, aged parents— something he could use.

But now he didn't have any use at all for that shit. He knew who she was, and he knew something she would want to know.

Like where her dickhead husband was buried.

Clench smiled happily. He didn't think he would tell her right away.

36

Getting Together

Earl Colley was back in the Buzzard the very next night, sitting at a table in the corner, nursing a 7UP. Pablo Clench went over to him as soon as he had the chance.

"We've been seeing a lot of you guys lately," Clench said. "What're you up to, trying to steal my dancers?"

"We miss you, Pablo," Earl Colley said. "We just want to be around you, that's all."

"Well, if it's the money you're worried about, relax. You'll get it."

"We are worried about the money, Pablo," Earl said. "Really worried. We can't relax. Thinking about that two million bucks in your pocket. Some of that is ours. So when are we going to see it?"

"You'll see it. Soon enough. Meanwhile, just enjoy yourselves. On the house. Drinks, women, just tell me. I got some special blow in, you want a taste of that. Just let me know."

"The only thing you got that I want is my money."

Clench shook his head sadly.

"You know, Earl, you're going to make yourself sick, obsessing like that. It's not good for you. Why don't you take some of the girls out? They'd like that. And you might get lucky, who knows?"

"Fuck that."

"What's the matter, you don't like girls?"

"I like girls," Earl said, "not whores and strippers."

"Well, I'm sorry to hear you say that," Clench said. "I hope that brother of yours isn't as prejudiced as you. That new dancer, what's her name, Brandy, has the eye for him. She keeps looking at him like he's a big fudge sundae with a cherry on top."

Earl snorted. "Bullshit she does. She probably is thinking she should call the animal-control officers and have him picked up."

"You're just jealous," Clench said. "She doesn't look at you that way."

"Pablo, the only things I want to see looking at me are Franklins. I don't need to get laid. You're giving me a pretty good screwing already."

"That girl," Billy Colley said. "At dinner. The one with the black hair? The new dancer at the Buzzard?"

"What about her?" Earl said. He was reading the manual for a new digital video editing program.

"She's beautiful, isn't she? Do you think Clench is fucking her?"

Earl looked up. There was a note in his brother's voice he had never heard before, a sort of pleading tone.

"You got the hots for her," Earl accused.

Billy didn't bother to deny it.

"Clench says she's always looking at you, in the club," Earl admitted. It grieved him to say something positive to his brother. "But that's probably just some of Clench's usual bullshit."

Billy wasn't even listening. He stared out the window, a goofy little smile on his face.

"It's like I've seen her before, you know? Like maybe in another life, or in a dream. I feel like I know her already."

"Jesus, I've never seen you like this," Earl said. He put down the manual and picked up the nearest video cam.

"Could you tell me all that again? All that about Brandy? I think we need a record of this moment."

But Billy wasn't taking direction.

"Brandy," he said. "Do you think her real name's Brandy?"

Earl was disgusted.

"Brandy, Candy, Krystal. Did you ever know a stripper who didn't have a name like that? It's a stage name, Billy."

"Well, what's her real name, then?"

"The fuck should I know? Why don't you ask her?"

This seemed never to have occurred to Billy. His eyes shone thinking about it.

"Yeah," he said, "I'll do that."

Amanda was surprised to find Billy Colley waiting for her outside when she got off her shift at the Honeybuzzard.

"Billy, what are you doing here?"

"Waiting for you to come out."

My first fan, Amanda thought.

"Did you see me dance tonight? I'm getting better, huh?"

"You couldn't get any better," Billy said. "You're the best."

Amanda had been so surprised to see the looming bulk of Billy Colley that she hadn't noticed he was holding a large bouquet of flowers.

Billy held out the bouquet in a hand the size of a Smithfield ham.

"For you."

"For me?" Amanda said, taking them. "How sweet."

Billy swung in beside her as she walked toward the bus stop. It was like being crowded by a big semi on the freeway.

Billy walked with his head down, examining the sidewalk. He didn't say a word until they reached the bus stop on Columbus Avenue. Then he stopped suddenly, as if he had reached the end of his chain. Still looking at the pavement, he rumbled something. It sounded like a dump truck going over a metal bridge.

"I'm sorry," Amanda said. "I couldn't hear you. The traffic's too noisy." There was almost no traffic. She smiled encouragingly.

"Dinner," Billy muttered. "Me. Tonight."

"Billy! I'd love to!"

That was almost too easy, Amanda thought.

Billy Colley took her to a small Italian restaurant in North Beach, a simple family-run place with a dozen tables decoupaged with scenes of the Amalfi coast, Chianti bottles with candles stuck in them, great food in incredible quantities.

Going undercover seemed to involve a lot of free dinners, Amanda thought. *I'd better find Aaron soon, or I'm going to go up a size.*

"Would you like some of this pasta?" Billy asked. All night he had been as deferential as a headwaiter.

"No thanks, Billy." Amanda had meant to just order a salad, but had broken down and gotten the Chicken Marsala. But that was enough.

"Are you sure? You should eat something."

"I have all I can eat, Billy, really."

Though the food was plentiful, conversation was scarce. When Billy wasn't fussing over her, making sure her wineglass was full, passing her the olives, he tended to lapse into a heavy, embarrassed silence. After a very short time, Amanda realized that if she wanted to pump any information out of him she would have to work at it.

"So, Billy," she said brightly, "what do you do when you're not taking dancers to dinner?"

Billy's face, normally as red as if it had just been rubbed with a cheese grater, turned even redder.

"Oh, you know, whatever," he mumbled. "Anything to make a buck."

"Pablo told me you sometimes do contract work, you know, odd jobs for different people."

Billy looked shocked. "Pablo told you that?"

Amanda nodded. "He said you and your brother would help people out with . . . difficulties." She hoped she was getting this across. It was hard to tell how much Billy was following her. The big musclehead kept staring at his plate, sneaking little glances up at her from time to time.

"Yeah, like I said," Billy muttered. "We do a lot of different things."

"I have a difficulty, Billy. I was hoping you could help me out with it."

This was like pouring Miracle-Gro on a half-dead potted plant. Billy sat up a little straighter and for the first time that night looked her right in the face.

"A difficulty? What kind of difficulty?"

Amanda told him the same story she had told Pablo Clench, throwing in a hint of spousal abuse. It worked like a charm; if her imaginary ex had walked into the room right then Billy would have torn his arms and legs off.

"So that's why I need your help," Amanda concluded. "If you could just take him somewhere and reason with him, I'm sure he'd come up with the money."

"We could do that," Billy said. "Me and my brother, we have a lot of experience at convincing people to pay their debts."

"I explained the situation to Pablo," Amanda said. "That's why he referred me to you."

"That was nice of him."

"Yes. But he was worried that what I was suggesting might involve kidnapping, that you might not want to get involved in something so heavy."

Billy waved her concerns away with an enormous hand.

"Don't worry about that. Me and Earl are used to that kind of thing. We can handle it."

"Have you done this kind of thing before? It seems so dangerous." Amanda did her best to look impressed, with just a hint of admiration in the mix.

Billy took it on board like a cactus sucking rainwater after a six-year drought.

"We're used to it. We can handle it. Your ex is nothing compared to what we just went through. That was a rough job. But we're still standing."

"What happened?" Amanda said. It was hard to breathe, and she hoped her voice didn't sound funny. "Was the situation like mine?"

"No, it was a much bigger deal. We took a guy down, and his whole business, and made him give it to us. It was hairy. I never thought we'd pull it off, but Clench said it would pay off big time. So we stuck it out."

"And did it pay off?"

Billy shook his big sconce and seemed a little crestfallen.

"Nah, not yet. But Clench says he has the money, he just has to get it to us. He better."

"What about the guy," Amanda asked. This was the crux. "The guy whose business you took? What did you do about him? Did you let him go?"

"Well, we couldn't do that. But we just handed him off to somebody to take care of."

"And did he?"

Billy shrugged. He had a vague feeling that he was talking too much, and that Earl would be pissed if he knew. But the red wine—a couple bottles so far—and the intoxicating presence of Brandy right across the table were too much for him.

"Who knows? But I don't think we'll see the guy around for a while."

"What kind of business was it? Something worth a lot of money, I bet."

Billy had to stop and think about that one. He shook his head as if to drive away flies.

"You know, I never really figured that one out. Some kind of science stuff, a big laboratory, like in a horror movie. Little robots, Clench said, that make stuff. The guy was worth millions, according to him. I'll believe it when I put the money in the bank." He looked with concern at Brandy's empty glass. "You want some more wine? Some coffee or something?"

Amanda shook her head. She was surprised it didn't fly right off and roll across the floor. Her stomach was twisted around itself like a broomstick dress in storage; she hadn't taken a full breath in ten minutes.

"No, thank you, Billy," she said. "I'm good."

Earl was pissed.

"You told her about Trick? What the fuck is wrong with you?"

"It just slipped out," Billy said sheepishly. "I didn't really tell her anything," he lied. "Just Trick. And it's not like it's his real name or anything. It's not in the goddamn phone book."

"I'm just surprised you didn't tell her all about the scientist job," Earl said. "You're such a fucking idiot. She could be a cop, you know."

"She's not a cop," Billy said with deep certainty.

"So where is the bitch? Why didn't you bring her back?"

Billy seemed hurt.

"It was a first date," he explained.

"A first . . ." Earl could not believe this. "What are you going to do, wait till you marry her to get in her pants?"

"She kissed me good night," Billy said.

Earl's eyes rolled up so hard they hurt. "Billy, she's a stripper. She probably sells it to half the drunks in North Beach, and you just let her go home without fucking her."

"Watch your mouth, Earl," Billy said. "I don't want you talking your trash about Brandy. She is different."

"Different." Earl took a memory card he had just shoplifted out of his raincoat pocket and began to load it into his new digital video cam. "Well, after we kick the shit out of her boyfriend, maybe I can make a porno video of you two. That should be worth something. It'll be like King Kong fucking Fay Wray."

"Earl, I'm warning you," Billy said. His head was as red as a stoplight. "Don't talk shit about Brandy. I mean it."

Earl pointed the digicam in Billy's face.

"Keep talking, okay? I want to get this. Tell me about how she kissed you good night again."

"Fuck you, Earl."

"Did she kiss you on the cheek? Or did you get the lip kiss? She put in any tongue? Tell me about it."

"Keep your fucking camera off of me."

A big hand fish-eyed toward the camera lens, but Earl danced back out of reach.

He got a great shot of his brother stomping out of the room and slamming the door behind him.

At breakfast the next morning, Earl Colley yawned, a big, jaw-cracking gawp.

"Out late last night," he explained to Billy.

Billy wasn't listening. Chin in hand, he was trying to remember exactly what Brandy smelled like, her hair, her perfume, her makeup, the pungent pheromones that swam up from between her sweaty breasts when she got off work. It was hard to conjure up a smell. It required all of Billy's concentration.

"Went back to Clench's car," Earl went on. "Wired a pound of C-4 under the driver's seat. Next time he takes her for a spin: whammo-zammo."

"That's nice," Billy said.

But Clench didn't use his car that week. Having found a parking spot near his hotel, he had no intention of using his car for any trip of less than five miles. Parking was not easy to find in North Beach; Clench had no plans to move the Porsche until next Tuesday when the street cleaners came through.

Billy Colley was sitting on the couch when Earl got in, dressed up as if he were going to a funeral.

"What's up with the suit and tie, Billy?" Earl asked. "You look like a fucking corpse in a casket."

Billy looked at his brother sternly. "Brandy and I are going to dinner," he said.

"A second date? Nice work, bro. The way you are about her, I wondered why you hadn't fucked her yet."

"Watch your fucking mouth," Billy whispered. "She can hear you, she's in the bathroom."

Earl shut up, not because he gave a shit about Brandy, but because the video potential of the scene suddenly occurred to him. His brother and the stripper, like a couple going to the prom. He had to get this.

"Okay, okay, I'll be good," Earl said. "Don't go anywhere. I'll be right back." He hurried out of the room.

Billy Colley had been thinking things over. Maybe it was time to change course, he thought. Time for a new career. Beating the crap out of people to get them to pay their debts wasn't fun anymore; it had become just a job. And his other sidelines—basically, beating the crap out of people, but for different reasons—were no longer doing it for him, either.

And Brandy—what did she think of his occupation? Billy remembered the way she had looked at him when he offered to help her out with her ex. That was something. The memory was like a small, beautiful animal—a butterfly—that he could take out whenever he wanted to and admire.

But leg breaking was nothing to build a long-term relationship on, and that was what Billy had in mind.

There was no future in it.

Over dinner that night, Billy laid out his plans to Brandy. It was a little soon, he knew that. He was worried she would just get up and run out of the restaurant.

But if he managed to work things the way he planned, it had to be now or never.

"To Mexico?" Brandy said. "With you?"

"We don't have to stay in Mexico," Billy explained. "We could keep going. South. To someplace nice, not so dry like Mexico."

Brandy looked down at the table, mouth open just a little. She was thinking it over. A wild hope rose in Billy.

"I have money," he added, to close the deal. "A lot of money. I been putting it away—nothing to spend it on, anyway. And this big job I told you about should pay off soon. American money goes pretty far down there. We should be all set."

Brandy stared at the tablecloth some more. Then a slow smile spread over her face.

"You know, Billy," she said, "I always wanted to go to Costa Rica."

"We could go right there," Billy said. "Fuck Mexico. We'll go to Costa Rica."

"What about your brother? What about Earl?"

"Earl can take care of himself."

"And the money from this job you told me about, this big job. When are you going to get that?"

"Soon."

Soon. Soon was, like, now, Billy thought as he walked Brandy—arm in arm!—back to his place. He was amazed that she had agreed to come back with him. He hoped fucking Earl wasn't home.

Earl. Earl was so smart sometimes he couldn't see what was right in front of his face. He was so busy trying to outsmart Pablo Clench that he forgot that who actually had the money was Trick.

Trick. Trick was supposed to be such a hard-ass, but Billy was sure he could make him listen to reason about the money. Billy, after all, had a lot of experience in convincing people to pay their debts. He was a professional. And maybe Trick took out his fag partner, but he was basically just a homo and a lush. Billy didn't think Trick would hold out on him for very long.

And if he got Trick to give him the money—*all* the money—and that left Clench and Earl with nothing, well, that was just too bad. They could always steal some more somewhere.

But he needed that money now. That money would set him and Brandy up in Mexico, or Costa Rica, or wherever.

Brandy. He looked at her, hanging on his arm, amazed to see that she was still there. He patted her hand to reassure her, and got a big, bright smile in return. It left him nearly speechless, but he managed to mumble something.

"Almost there, babe." Babe! He called her babe! He felt his face getting red. He hoped she didn't get mad or anything.

But she just grinned and hung on.

37

Last Take

Billy was disappointed to find that Earl was still home. He could hear him banging around in the bathroom. This was bad for two reasons: Billy didn't want Earl looking over his shoulder while he tried to talk to Brandy. It made him nervous. Also, Billy had about two gallons of wine and espresso to off-load, and he was getting dancey.

He pounded on the bathroom door.

"Earl! Hurry it up in there!" He heard Earl muttering something with "fuck you's" in it, but that was all right. So long as he knew there was a line.

Brandy was still standing where he left her, in the middle of the living room. Maybe she was scared to move—for the first time Billy realized what a mess their place was, empty bottles and pizza boxes everywhere, socks on the couch, Earl's video cameras piled up on every flat surface.

"Look, my brother's home, we better go in my room where we can talk."

"Talk?" Brandy said with a little smile.

Billy blushed.

"Yeah. We have to make some plans, about Mexico. I have an idea, but I need you to help me make it work."

His room was not as messy as the rest of the place, mostly because he didn't spend much time there. Brandy sat on the edge of the bed while Billy pulled up a chair.

"The thing is," he began, "we need as much money as we can get to make this Mexico thing work. And Clench is holding out on us. I think he wants to keep all the money for himself and just cut us out."

Brandy stared at him, very serious. "Do you want me to help you get the money from Pablo?"

Billy shook his head. "No. We don't need Clench at all. The guy who has the money, who anyway knows where it is and can give us our share, is this guy Trick I told you about. He's the guy took care of the scientist for us. Maybe you met him at the Buzzard—he's a fag, and doesn't get off on girls, but he comes around there sometime to see Clench."

Brandy frowned and thought about this.

"I met him, once. Billy, when you say he took care of the scientist for you, what exactly do you mean?"

"Don't worry about that," Billy reassured her. "He's not such a tough guy. The scientist was all tied up, the way I heard it. Anybody could have taken the guy out. It doesn't prove anything."

Brandy still looked upset. *She's worried*, Billy thought. *Worried about me.*

He reached over and patted her hand. "Look, don't worry. All I need you to do is to go to his place and knock on the door. He might not open the door to me, he sees me standing out there. When he opens the door just talk to him a little. I'll be right there, but out of sight. When he opens the door I'll back him inside."

"Suppose he has a gun?"

"He won't have a gun, he sees you on his doorstep. That's the whole idea."

"Okay. If you think that'll work. Trick, what kind of name is that? Is that his real name?"

Women are funny, Billy thought, *the shit they think of.*

"Nah. His real name's Fitzpatrick. Patrick Fitzpatrick: Trick, get it?"

"I get it."

Out in the apartment, Billy heard the toilet flush, the bathroom door slam. He suddenly remembered his urgent need to piss.

"Look, Brandy," he said, "I'll be right back. Then we can make some more plans, what we do after we get that money from Trick. Okay?"

"Okay." She still looked worried, Billy could see, sick and sad. It made him feel like he wanted to kill fucking Trick for scaring her like that. But he probably would be doing that, anyway—soon.

Billy reached out and patted her hand again. He liked to touch her, even a little bit.

"I'll be right back," he said.

Amanda sat on the bed, stunned and motionless. *So that's that,* she thought. *The last hope gone. Aaron shot in the head by gangsters, buried under a slab of concrete at a building site probably, or else squished up in a car in an auto junkyard. Isn't that how they got rid of bodies, these fucking hoodlums?*

She jumped up and ran to the window. There was a fire escape right outside: Good. While Billy was in the bathroom she could climb down and run away, go to the police, get them all thrown in jail forever. She reached up and unlocked the window, then began to raise the sash.

Tell the police . . . right, she thought. *But tell them what?* She wasn't even sure Billy was telling her the truth about Trick killing Aaron.

Maybe it was just another lie—everyone seemed to be lying like crazy. Maybe Billy killed Aaron himself. Or Earl, or Pablo Clench.

Amanda plopped back on the bed. Maybe she should just go through with Billy's plan, help him get to Trick. She was pretty sure that the visit would end up with Trick dead, and it served him right. She knew only too well that anything could happen between arrest and conviction; she had spent a good part of her career trying to keep people like Trick and Billy out of jail. Suppose Trick walked? How would she feel then? Maybe she should just give him up to Billy and let nature take its course.

Amanda heard the toilet flush, the bathroom door open. She stood up, indecisively. Go or stay?

She expected the bedroom door to open any minute and let Billy Colley's monstrous figure into the room. But nothing happened. Out in the corridor she could hear muttering voices, an occasional swearword. Then the voices got louder, or at least one voice did: Billy's.

"Fuck you, Earl, just fuck you," Billy was yelling. "Just take your goddamn cameras and get the fuck out of my life."

She could hear Earl muttering something in response, but couldn't make out the actual words. Billy roared back, mostly obscenities. The conversation continued; it seemed like it could go on for hours.

Suppose they kill each other? she thought. *What would I tell the cops then? How would I find out what really happened to Aaron? I don't even know where this Trick lives.*

She looked desperately around Billy's barren little room. There was not much in it. A few items of clothing were scattered on the floor. Near the head of the bed a long crowbar was leaning against the wall. Why? Well, if you do the kind of work Billy did, it might come in handy some night.

The only thing that looked information-rich was a small table with a telephone on it, an old-fashioned desk phone, big, black, and hulking.

There was an address book lying next to it.

Amanda went over and picked it up, thumbing through it hurriedly. Even though it was one of those Walgreen's address books with letters in little tabs down the side, the names and addresses were in no particular order. On the plus side, there weren't that many of them.

Trick's phone number was on the second page, with a scribbled street address in San Bruno.

Amanda pulled open the little drawer in the table, looking for a pen or pencil to copy the address. Nothing.

Just then she heard the knob on the bedroom door twist; Billy opened the door a crack, but he was still yelling at his brother.

"Just keep away from me and Brandy, that's all! I see you with that camera again, I'm gonna stuff it up your ass!"

Amanda lifted up her dress and stuffed the address book in the waist of her panty hose, hoping the elastic was strong enough to hold it. She straightened up and saw Billy Colley, standing in the doorway, staring at her with his mouth open.

Billy hadn't noticed the address book. What he had noticed was the line of girl flesh exposed when Amanda had pulled up her dress and hoicked down her panty hose. Billy had seen Brandy plenty of times completely, bare-ass naked at the Buzzard, true, but that was like a performance, like a movie. This spoke to him in an entirely different way.

"Brandy!" he croaked.

With one big step he crossed the room and swept her into his arms.

Twenty-four hours after the scene in Billy Colley's bedroom, the San Francisco homicide squad thought they had an inside track on what had happened. They were a little late, of course, and wouldn't put the pieces together for a few hours. But the evidence was compelling: Earl had recorded the encounter for posterity.

"What is this—a meeting of the video porn club?"

The homicide detective stood in the half-open door to a small office in the Hall of Justice down at Sixth and Bryant. A television monitor hummed bluely at the front of the room. Two detectives and a technician sat in folding chairs in front of the monitor. They stared silently at the detective in the doorway until he came in and sat down.

One of the seated detectives twisted around in his folding chair.

"All right, are we ready? This is the video from the camera recovered at the crime scene. We hope it will tell us something about the homicide at 3555 Green."

"Oh, it will," the technician said.

"You've seen it?" the recently arrived detective asked.

The lead detective shook his head. "Only Wilson has seen it. He says it shows the perp in the act."

"It sure does," Wilson the technician said. He punched up the television, and a video image jumped on the screen, showing an empty room, scantily furnished.

"What are we looking at?"

"Room at 3555 Green, residence of Earl and Billy Colley," the lead detective explained. "The victim, identified as Earl Colley, was found beaten to death, really major head trauma, with a video camera jammed up his ass."

"This video camera?"

The detective nodded.

"Watch."

They watched.

The video continued with a rapid pan at eye level through the empty apartment. Unidentifiable noises could be heard in the background.

"Subjective camera," Wilson said. "You see what the character sees."

The moving camera paused at a doorway, slowly moving around the frame. Then it stopped.

Billy Colley's head and back filled most of the frame. White arms and legs seemed to be growing out of his body; he looked briefly like some sort of Hindu deity. Then the arms pushed him away. A black-haired woman was standing there, looking pissed off.

"Stripper from one of Cacapoulos's clubs, we think," Wilson glossed. "No ID yet."

"Not now, Billy, not now!" the black-haired alleged stripper said.

"Why not now?" Billy wanted to know. His voice was a hoarse whisper.

"We're not alone in the house. Your brother will hear us."

"Fuck my brother. Who cares if he hears?"

There was a snuffling noise off camera, perhaps laughter. Billy Colley's head whipped around; the stripper looked up wide-eyed.

The vid cam backed up, quickly though steadily, tracking back into the other room.

Billy Colley suddenly appeared around the door frame, his face crumpled in rage. He was holding something down at his side. As he stepped forward he raised his arm and the assembled detectives saw that he was holding a crowbar.

The vid cam continued to back up, then stopped abruptly. Billy Colley didn't stop. His enraged face filled the entire screen.

The video blurred through confused images, ending up with a view sideways at carpet level.

"Dropped the vid cam," Wilson explained.

From somewhere out of the shot the watching cops could hear yelling and strange thumping noises, like someone playing softball with a raw frying chicken.

"No, Billy! No, no!"

There was a period of relative quiet during which the only sound was hard, ragged breathing.

Then Billy Colley's wingtips and about six inches of pant leg reappeared. They came close to the lens, disappeared out of frame. Odd sounds could be heard, like something being dragged across the carpet, tearing cloth, more panting.

The video image smeared with movement, then reappeared, right side up now. Billy's angry, sweaty face was close to the lens, his arms fishbowled with distortion. The screen went alternately dark, then light, then dark, then light.

Finally Billy stepped back into the middle of the frame, panting, arms on hips, lips moving.

"What happened to the sound?"

"Microphone must be blocked."

"Blocked? Oh."

"Don't think about it."

"So what's he saying? Anybody read lips?"

"He's saying, I think he's saying, 'Tape that, asshole.'"

"So I guess we know who did this."

"I guess so. Let's pick 'im up."

The cops didn't know it—the test results hadn't come back yet—but it was already too late. Picking up Billy Colley would require a different skill set and retrieval equipment than the homicide detectives routinely brought to a crime scene. Picking up Billy Colley would require a hose, a magnifying glass, and a pair of tweezers.

When Billy picked up the crowbar next to the bed and stormed out of the bedroom, Amanda knew that something bad was going to happen. She didn't want to wait around to find out how it would turn out.

Whether Billy killed Earl or Earl killed Billy, what she wanted to do was to get to Trick. She knew she wouldn't have much time—it seemed like everyone in North Beach wanted to get to Trick. But somehow, she had to find him and get him to cough up the truth about Aaron. She wasn't sure how to do that—maybe warn him about the shit storm about to descend on him? Offer to help him? But why would he trust her? As far as Trick knew, she was one of Clench's little protégés. And Clench seemed to be as much a part of this whole thing as anybody else.

She unlocked the broad window, slid it up, and stepped out onto the fire escape. Peering over the side, she saw she was four stories up. The last section of the fire escape was a metal ladder folded onto the second floor platform. She hoped it wasn't locked.

Slipping off her shoes so they didn't make a racket on the metal rungs, Amanda climbed down the fire escape. The folded ladder was unlocked, if a little rusty, and it let her down with a groan.

The fire escape was at the rear of the building, and had let her down into a narrow alley. At the far end she could see traffic whizzing by, people walking, city street life.

What she needed right now was a nice yellow taxi to take her to San Bruno.

Shoes in hand, she ran in stocking feet up the alley.

When Billy came out of his kill trance the first thing he did was to run back into the bedroom to reassure Brandy. It didn't occur to him that the bloody crowbar he was carrying was not especially reassuring; he had forgotten he was holding it.

He felt sick when he saw the open window.

"Brandy!" He stuck his head out and looked up and down the alley, but there was no one in sight. His voice echoed off the brick walls and lost itself in traffic noise.

"Brandy!"

Maybe she got scared, all the yelling and noise and shit, and hid behind something? Hiding under the bed? Behind the curtains?

Not there. She wasn't in the closet, either.

Brandy was gone.

Billy raced back into the front room and stopped dead when he saw his brother's white buttocks hanging over the back of the couch, with the round glass eye of the video camera staring out between them.

Right, he thought, *you just killed your own goddamn brother. And scared off Brandy, maybe for good.*

Not bothering to sweep off the litter of socks, underwear, and empty cigarette packs, Billy sank down on the sofa. The crowbar dropped from his hand and fell on the carpet.

What the fuck, thought Billy, *do I do now?*

The main thing was to find Brandy, that much was clear. But where would she go? Billy had no idea where she lived. But maybe Clench would know. She worked for him; he had to have her address.

Clench. Pablo Clench had not been on Billy's mind for a while, in spite of Earl's warning that he was out to get them. But now he came up on the screen with a new clarity.

Clench. Clench was the one that got him involved in all this. Clench was trying to hold out on them, hanging on to the cash Billy needed to go to Mexico with.

Maybe Clench had his own ideas about that. He was the one who hired Brandy, after all, the one who introduced them to her. He was maybe fucking her, or trying to, hanging around with her all the time at work and who knew where else?

And Clench was the one that gave Earl his first video camera and put them on the ass of that scientist guy. The whole thing had started right there, with the fucking camera.

Really, it was Clench that was responsible for Earl getting killed. It wasn't his fault that his brother couldn't keep his goddamned camera out of Billy's business. If Clench hadn't given it to him, Earl wouldn't be dead right now.

And now Brandy was on the run, probably heading right back to the

Buzzard. Where else would she go? And to Clench. If Clench wasn't fucking her already, he would sure take advantage of her now, all scared and worried. The motherfucker would comfort her; Billy knew what that meant.

And maybe Clench planned it this way. He was a devious fucker. Maybe this whole thing was a setup, to keep the money and get Brandy too.

Fucking Clench.

Billy stood up suddenly. "Clench!" he bellowed.

Picking up the crowbar from the floor—it stuck to the carpet, pulling it up a bit before it came free—Billy ran out of the apartment, headed for North Beach.

38

Thirteen Forty-two

The Honeybuzzard was slow tonight, Clench thought, just a couple tourists and a party of drunken frat boys watching numbly as a pair of pole dancers went through the motions on stage. Without a lot of sweating bodies filling the seats, the place felt cold—Cacapoulos had liked to set the thermostat as low as he could get away with before people started complaining. Clench saw no reason to upgrade.

Too bad about the Buzzard, Clench thought as he climbed the stairs to Cacapoulos's office for maybe the last time. *It used to be a good place.* He wondered how long it would be before the paychecks started bouncing around like a dump truck load of basketballs, and suppliers started showing up with Louisville Sluggers, looking to get paid. The buffer he had left in the accounts when he had vacuumed them out wouldn't last long—just long enough, he hoped, to see him safely in Mexico.

Clench let himself in with Jimmy Cacapoulos's keys—Jimmy wouldn't be needing them anymore. Soon the place would be boarded up, legal notices nailed to the plywood, fixtures auctioned off. Too bad, but it couldn't be helped. Running the clubs was too much like work, and eventually someone might have asked inconvenient questions, like when was Jimmy coming back from Vegas, or why the signatures on the deed had little cut marks around them. It just wasn't worth the hassle.

Clench sighed. He hated to leave the Cacapoulos empire behind, but it was just too dangerous to fuck with. Someone, he was sure, would take up the slack. The banks would get the buildings, other club owners the facilities and the dancers. New faces would deal the drugs, break the legs, threaten the shop owners. Life went on.

Don't be greedy, he told himself. Ten million is plenty, especially in Mexico. Just get the fuck out before it all unravels.

The Colley brothers were still out there, undealt with, true. The plan to distract them with Brandy/Amanda was maybe a good one, but it was taking too goddamn long. He had to hit the road now, not later; he could feel the whole deal coming apart at the edges, and he wanted to be in position to jump off when it collapsed for good.

Clench had the feeling that the moment was ripe for a little visit to the Colleys; maybe some arson. With blocked exits. And maybe a little target practice from the fire escape outside their apartment. No sense getting too subtle with guys like that.

He planned to pump Brandy/Amanda when she came in tonight, and nail down the brothers' schedule. Brandy had gotten pretty tight with them. If she were, say, to have dinner with them, maybe Clench could meet up with them afterwards for a short discussion. If he waited in their darkened apartment for them to get back, for instance, the discussion might be very short. And if Brandy/Amanda got in the way, well, that was just too bad. She wanted to find her scientist husband so bad, Clench would point her in the right direction.

Then it would be just him, Trick, and the money.

Couldn't really leave old Trick behind, after all he had done to help out. Plus okay, Trick was the only other person who knew the bank account codes, now that Jimmy was lingerie. And it was too dangerous to leave Trick on his own, anyway. The guy wasn't really reliable, drinking like that all the time. There was no telling what he would do.

So they'd go to Mexico together, to start out. American money went pretty far down there. You spread it around and people don't ask a lot a irritating questions, like where it came from. No one gives a shit in Mexico. Get set up somewhere in Baja, Cabo maybe, and after that, who knows? Mexico was a dangerous place. Anything could happen, especially to a drunken gringo with a taste for young men. Clench might not have to take action himself, just let events follow their own, inevitable course.

And if nothing happened on its own, well, there were plenty of good places in Mexico to dump a body.

Things were going well, Pablo Clench thought happily. Almost there now. The airline tickets were in his inside jacket pocket along with the fake passports, one for Arthur Murray—he had grown fond of the name—one for Trick. They would fly first-class (why fuck around?) and by this time tomorrow they would be in Mexico, ready to start over.

He found Cacapoulos's pistol in the desk drawer, took it out, inspected it, and put it in the side pocket of his jacket. Clench hated the way it made the coat hang, pulling it all out of shape on one side. But it wouldn't be for long.

The magazine was loaded with blank rounds of course—Clench had thought that was a sound precaution, just in case Jimmy had ideas of his own. The live rounds he had taken out were in a pay envelope, stuffed in the glove compartment of his Porsche. He could reload before he tooled over to visit the Colleys.

It took a while longer to find the suppressor—fucking Cacapoulos was a slob, and the desk drawers were filled with all sorts of nasty shit— but eventually it went into his other jacket pocket.

Now for the main event.

.   .   .

Pablo Clench loved opening up his bank accounts. It jazzed him to go through the verification process, open up window after window, enter the codes, and get to the numbers—*his* numbers—big, satisfying numbers. It was like a series of theater curtains opening one after the other, finally revealing the scenery, waiting for the actors to walk on, the action to begin.

But this time something was different.

In place of the long string of digits that had transferred over to his account from the Kalimahanese treasury, there was now a single, short entry:

$13.42.

Must be some sort of bank shorthand, Clench thought, *some sort of abbreviated way of representing really large numbers. Fucking scared me for a minute. The thirteen, the forty-two, that must represent the interest on ten million.*

$13.42.

Or not . . .

Maybe it represented thirteen dollars and forty-two cents. And he was fucked.

And Trick was dead.

"You are a dead man!" Clench shouted, rocketing to his feet.

Just then there was a pounding on the door of Cacapoulos's office, as if a dump truck had offloaded a ton of rocks against it. Over the pounding he could hear a deep, bellowing voice:

"Clench!"

Which he recognized without any trouble as Billy Colley's.

Pablo Clench was always alert for people trying to kill him. That was why he was still alive after a lifetime spent irritating people to the point of homicide. When he heard Billy Colley's body whack into the office door like a wrecking ball, he was up and running; by the time the metal door came crashing in he was out of sight.

Jimmy Cacapoulos's office was part of a suite of small rooms, painted black walls, floor, and ceiling, back in the 1960s, that took up the rear of the fourth floor. Clench knew that one rear window opened on the fire escape, and he headed straight for it.

Unfortunately, there were bars across the window. Locked bars, like a hinged gate.

Shit! Clench thought. *Fucking shit. Goddammit!*

He could hear Billy Colley out in Cacapoulos's office, bellowing his name and turning over furniture. It wouldn't be long before he started checking out the other rooms.

Behind him, sounds of breaking glass and cracking plastic as Billy worked over the computer. What was he using, a ball bat? A wrecking bar? Better not wait to find out.

With a feeling of profound gratitude, Clench saw two keys dangling from a key ring, stuck up on a nail about two feet from the windowframe. They were hard to see, black against the black walls. Clench grabbed them and stuck them in the lock on the side of the bars. He could hear Colley, closer now, throwing open doors down the hall.

"Clench! You fucked me, Clench!"

The lock was stiff and rusty, but Clench finally forced it open, swung back the bars, and pried open the window. It made a hell of a lot of noise going up.

"Clench!"

Colley was steps away. Clench dove through the open window and onto the fire escape. A big hand reached out of the window behind him and grabbed the waistband of his trousers. Clench grabbed a piece of the fire escape and tried to pull himself free. The big hand tugged at his trousers. With a surge of panic, Clench pulled free—his trousers shucked off and his shoes dropped down into the alley.

In socks and skivvies, he scampered down the fire escape.

. . .

Billy Colley stood there a second, panting, holding Clench's trousers in his right hand. He was about to toss them away and run downstairs to try and head Clench off. But the jingle of keys in the pocket stopped him.

He knew where Clench would go. To Trick's house, down in San Bruno. Clench didn't have any friends. And that's where the money was. Clench would head for his car, and drive down to San Bruno.

But not if *he* got there first.

Earl's van was way the fuck the other side of Russian Hill, in a parking garage. And the keys were probably in Earl's pocket. It would take too long to get there, and Clench might get away. Bad idea to go back to the apartment now, anyway.

But Billy remembered coming home from the restaurant and seeing Clench and Brandy getting out of the Porsche. It was only a couple blocks away. Maybe it was still there. Or maybe nearby. He was pretty sure he could catch up to Clench before he reached it.

And maybe, after he took care of Clench, he could drive down and talk things over with Trick, the way he had planned with Brandy.

Brandy. Brandy wasn't anywhere around. But Clench would know where she was. He would make him tell, before he crowbarred his head off. Then he would scoop her up and they would go do Trick together.

Billy Colley stuffed his big hand into Clench's trouser pocket and came out with a Porsche-logo key ring. He shoved it in his pocket. Sticking the bloody crowbar into his belt, he clambered out the window and rumbled down the fire escape after Clench.

Pablo Clench was on his belly under a damp clump of rosemary, peeking out the hanging stalks at his own Porsche, parked maybe seventy-five feet away. His feet were freezing in wet socks, and dirt and leaves had gotten all over his striped boxer shorts, but there was one advantage to being in someone's terrace garden overlooking North Beach, hiding beneath a plant.

He was still alive.

He had reached the car in record time—people got out of his way when they saw him coming, for some reason—but he stopped dead by the driver-side door.

The car was locked, of course. And the keys were in his pants pocket.

Clench looked back and saw the enormous form of Billy Colley looming over scurrying pedestrians, a block and a half away. Too close. He thought of rolling under the car, breaking Colley's ankle with the gun when he came up, pistol-whipping him when he went down. But somehow he doubted he could make that plan work. Maybe he could bluff him with the gun? Nah. Even if the bullets in it had been real, he didn't think it would slow the enormous musclehead enough. Nothing short of an RPG would do that.

And then he would get his head beat in by a crowbar, and that would suck.

Clench, crouched down behind the car, waited until a dense crowd of old women with shopping carts got down level with the Porsche, then used them as cover to scramble into the terrace garden and slither under the rosemary.

Billy Colley pounded up the hill, crowbar in hand, ready for action. The Porsche was still there, right where he remembered it. But Clench had disappeared.

"Clench!"

Billy had seen him just a moment ago, from a block away, standing by the car. He couldn't have gone far. Billy looked around wildly, ran up to the next corner and looked up and down the street. There was no one in red-striped undershorts anywhere in sight.

He ran back to the Porsche, swiping wildly at bushes and hanging vegetation that hung over the retaining walls all along the street, on the off chance that Clench was hiding behind them. But it was no use. Clench had gotten away.

Bellowing with rage and frustration, Billy worked over the Porsche with the crowbar, whanging big dents in the fenders and door, taking out a headlight. Then he stopped, exhausted. This was getting him nowhere. Clench was gone, Brandy was gone, his brother was dead, and the money that should be his was down in San Bruno.

San Bruno. Trick. Clench had to be heading there, no matter how he got there. But he had Clench's car. He could be at Trick's when Clench showed up. Then they could have a little party.

Better hurry, though. He could hear sirens down the hill, maybe heading his way. He was attracting way too much attention, yelling and beating up on the Porsche. Time to move.

He dug out Clench's keys, unlocked the Porsche, and hopped in. It was a tight fit—Billy's knees were up around his chin, and his head bumped against the roof. But it wouldn't be for long. He could beat out anything on the road in this ride, and be in San Bruno in five minutes.

He stuck the keys in the ignition.

No, wait a minute, Billy Colley thought, as his big fingers were about to turn the key. Didn't Earl say something about Clench's ride? Billy hadn't been paying close attention. He had been thinking of Brandy, trying to remember exactly how she smelled.

Ah, fuck it, Billy thought. *I'll never remember.*

He twisted the key in the ignition. Just as he heard the starter click over he remembered what his brother had said.

But it was much, much too late.

. . .

The explosion stunned Clench for a minute or two. There had been a rain of fragments following the concussion, Porsche parts and body parts. The crowbar was sticking out of the retaining wall like a dart in a dartboard, inches from his head. His head seemed to have become as large and light as a hot-air balloon, and he couldn't hear a fucking thing.

My car! he thought. *That was my goddamn car!*

39

Getting Packed

Trick looked very smug when he came in with the takeout and a couple bottles of whiskey.

"Pablo will be so mad when he finds out what I've done to the accounts."

"Is making Pablo mad a good idea?" Aaron asked. He didn't think so, personally. He remembered his sessions with Clench in vivid detail.

Trick put down the bag and began taking out cardboard containers with little wire handles. He handed a couple across to Aaron, who eagerly broke them open and began shoveling the contents into his mouth.

"By the time he figures it out, we'll be long gone," Trick said.

It took Aaron quite a while to catch up to this.

"Wait a minute," he said around a mouthful of fish cake. "We?"

"I'm taking you with me. It's the only way, Aaron! I can't just leave you here to die. Besides, Pablo would find you and finish the job. And you might tell him something before he did."

"I might," Aaron agreed. "But Trick, these chains will never make it through airport security."

"I'll take them off, of course. But you have to promise to be good. Look, Aaron, this is our only chance. Clench will figure out any minute that he can't access the accounts anymore. He'll come looking for us. You don't want him to find us, do you?"

Aaron shook his head.

"You wouldn't want him to find out you're still alive, would you?"

Emphatic head shaking.

"All right. So we better get out of here."

"Can I shower first?"

"I think you'd better. You smell like a dead body. But you have to promise me you won't try to get away. You'll only get us both killed. After I get this all squared away, and protect myself, you can come back."

"Come back? Come back from where? Where are you taking us?"

"Costa Rica," Trick said. "You'll like it there. Do you speak Spanish? No? Well, I'm sure you'll pick it up in no time."

Aaron thought about it. There might be numerous opportunities for escape on the way. And even if he got as far as Costa Rica—which didn't seem likely—he could always sneak away and turn himself in at the American embassy.

Or maybe he would just stay in Costa Rica awhile. After all this. He could send for Amanda; it was possible that she would come. And he really needed a vacation.

"Okay," he said to Trick. "I'll be good."

"I'll hold you to that," Trick said, filling a couple of glasses with bourbon. He handed one to Aaron.

"Well, cheers. Here's to Costa Rica."

They ate and drank in silence for a while. Then Trick leaned over and turned on the television. An agitated news reporter with an Australian accent was saying something about the Democratic Republic of Kalimaha.

"Kalimaha? Where is that?" Aaron asked, "I never heard of it."

"That's where Clench sold your robots," Trick told him. "Your buddy MacBlister, too."

"No shit? MacBlister is not my buddy, by the way." This was satisfying news to Rogell, at least the part about MacBlister. He settled in to watch the broadcast.

The television reports were sketchy and mysterious. No one seemed to know exactly what was happening, but apparently large swathes of the Kalimahanese capital of Borborigme had disappeared, replaced by pools of gray spit.

Rogell sat up. This could have something to do with his robots. At least, the gray goo scenario, in which nanorobots got out of control and ate everything, was a common objection to the spread of nanotechnology. Rogell had always poo-pooed the idea.

But what if he had been wrong?

Later reports filled in some of the gaps. Something had happened to the government of Kalimaha, something bad. No one was really sure what, although the consensus was that some sort of secret weapons test had gone horribly wrong.

In any case, a large section of the city, that quarter containing the government buildings, the seat of power, seemed to have disappeared overnight, leaving a gaping hole in the low skyline and a field of froth that looked like a giant spit-loogie.

The Chinese, who shared a border with Kalimaha, had intervened forcefully, sending in troops and specialists in defiance of world outrage. Retired generals were dragged on the air and interviewed, claiming that the rapidity of the Chinese response proved that they had infiltrated the Kalimahanese government.

The mothball military was probably correct, for a change, but world opinion was covertly behind the Chinese presence. Better them than us was the subtext. Somebody had to do it. Mysterious figures in white hazmat suits carrying what looked like flamethrowers could be seen occasionally running across the background of the live reports.

Aaron Rogell watched with a growing feeling of horror.

"MacBlister fucked up," he told Trick. "He forgot to limit the self-replication. That's the only thing this could be."

"Whatever you say, guy," Trick said.

"Government spokesmen are denying reports that a secret laboratory was the source of the explosion," a news reporter was saying.

A quick cut to a harassed-looking spokesperson, one of the few surviving government figures:

"There has been no explosion, none," the spokesperson said. "There is no secret laboratory. And even if there had been an accident, which we deny, the Chinese army is still in violation of all international laws and protocols. We will protest to the United Nations. The Chinese army must withdraw at once. The Kalimahanese National Defense Laboratory, which of course does not exist, must not fall into the hands of international communism. We appeal to the free nations of the world to intervene."

On the other English-language channel, President-for-Life Richard Cheney was holding forth in the George W. Bush Memorial Room, denying any involvement in the catastrophe and threatening the Chinese.

"The people of Kalimaha love freedom," the president-for-life said. "If they want to destroy their own government buildings, though I understand none have been actually destroyed, it is their right and privilege to do so."

Rogell was fascinated by the news.

"You realize what this means, don't you?" he said to Trick.

"Well, it's a good thing about the Chinese, right?" Fitzpatrick said. "We're not all going to become pools of gray robot puke."

"Well, that too," Rogell agreed. He tore himself away from the spectacle of the biohazard suits advancing into the gray botfields, spraying as they went. "But whoever came up with this spray has replicated my discoveries. Has to be. The only way to stop my guys once they get out of hand is with other guys just like them."

"Just in the knick of time, too," Trick said. "But isn't this dangerous? I mean, maybe from eating so many people, so many brain cells, your robots will take on human traits? That could be bad."

Rogell shook his head impatiently. "No. No, humanity isn't catching, like a virus. That's magical thinking, like eating the heart of your enemy." Rogell was close to something here—Pablo Clench had always secretly fantasized about doing exactly that.

"What was that?"

They leaned forward in their chairs, listening. After a moment Aaron switched off the television, chains clanking quietly.

"It sounded like someone pounding on the front door."

They looked at each other. Visitors were probably trouble at this point.

"Clench?"

"Who else?" Trick got up and walked toward the door, causing Aaron to make a noise like a deflating inner tube.

"Trick!" he whispered urgently. "Don't leave me like this! If he finds me here he'll kill me!"

"Calm down. He doesn't know you're here. I'll lock you in. You'll be perfectly safe."

Unless he kills you, Rogell thought. *Then, if Clench doesn't find me and shoot me in the head, I get to starve to death, chained to a concrete wall.* He wondered how long it would take.

"Trick! Take the chains off! At least I'd have a chance!"

But Trick had disappeared.

40

Restless in South City

Tony Baloot had tried to call Mrs. Rogell at the number Chickie gave him, but the lady was never in.

Finally, he had corralled Chickie—making a rare appearance at his studio, no doubt looking for something else to sell—and pushed her into the Buick.

"Come on. We're going downtown. I think you'd better move back in with Mrs. Rogell."

"Whatever you say, Mr. Man."

Chickie didn't seem to care—she was obviously stoned out of her mind on whatever it was. She sat next to him on the ride up to the city rocking back and forth like some kind of machine, singing to herself, and pulling the stitching out of the seatcovers.

Instructed by Chickie, Tony Baloot parked as close as he could to Amanda's hotel, and went over by himself while Chickie hid on the floor of the car.

"Just keep your head down," he told her. "I'll be right back."

But no one answered the buzzer of Amanda's hotel room.

"Now what?"

"Let's try up at the strip club she works at," Chickie suggested. "The Honeybuzzard. Up in North Beach."

Baloot stared at her.

"Mrs. Rogell works at a strip club?"

Chickie nodded happily. "It was my idea. She's looking to find her husband. We think the Colleys kidnapped him."

Baloot had been inclined to give the strip club a look-see. Mrs. Rogell might even really be there. But the mention of the brothers cooled his ardor slightly.

"How about I just drive by and you see if you can see her?"

Now it was Chickie's turn to get upset.

"What? What kind of bullshit is that? Just let me out of the car, I'll go in. I'm not scared."

"You should be. Suppose the Colleys are in there."

That was a thought.

"Well, maybe you can just ask at the door. Get her to come out to you."

But Baloot wasn't put to the test. As they drove up Russian Hill in the general direction of North Beach, Chickie suddenly squealed, "There she is!"

Amanda Rogell was on the other side of the street, standing in the mouth of an alley, carrying her shoes in one hand and trying to flag down a taxi with the other.

Chickie rolled down the window and yelled. "Amanda!" Baloot, trying to be helpful, tooted the Buick's horn. But they were overwhelmed by the traffic noise, and Amanda didn't even look toward them.

As they watched, a Yellow Cab pulled over and Amanda hopped in.

"Follow her!" Chickie commanded.

"What for?"

"Well, then take me back to your place," she said. "I only know I'm not going anywhere unless it's with Amanda."

"Mrs. Rogell."

"Whatever. She is one cool lady."

Tony Baloot thought about it for about five seconds. Then, sighing, he put the Buick in drive and lurched after the cab.

41

Trick or Treat

Catching a cab was easy for a change, and Amanda made good time getting down to San Bruno. Too quick, in fact. She could have used more time to figure out what to do when she got there.

Trick will probably be surprised to see me on his doorstep, she thought, *and more than a little suspicious.* He knew her from the Buzzard, but they hadn't talked much. Amanda couldn't imagine him as part of the kidnapping; he had seemed so nice.

Of course, she hadn't realized that Pablo Clench was part of it either. And Clench hadn't seemed especially nice. This error of judgment on her part disturbed her. Amanda wondered how many other people were involved. Maybe hundreds.

And what was she going to say to Trick? That she knew everything, and he better confess? Not the best approach; she'd end up buried in the same building site as Aaron, and what good would that do?

She had a better idea. She would warn him that the Colley brothers were about to descend on him like a truckload of gibbons with chainsaws. She'd tell him Clench was coming after him, too—that might shake him loose.

No. She had a still better idea. She'd tell him the cops were on the way, to search his house, and that Clench was worried they'd find the body of the scientist. Amanda shuddered as she thought it. It was hard to think, much less say out loud. But Trick would either tell her where he had put Aaron, or, if he still had the body around, try to get rid of it. She would offer to help him then.

Oh boy would she help him.

Amanda had the cab drop her at the end of Trick's street. She walked slowly down the block, reading the house numbers. The houses were small and crammed in, tiny strips of yard between them.

Trick's house, while not large, was still the biggest on the block. She walked up to the door and stood there, unsure of how exactly to play it, what tone to adapt, what narrative to invoke.

Hysterical but helpful messenger, she decided. Slightly off-center, but on your side. Too crazy not to trust.

I can do this, she thought. *For Aaron.*

Amanda began to pound on the door.

After a few minutes of steady beating, she stepped back, panting, and heard a noise overhead, a window sliding open.

She looked up.

"Good. I thought you'd never stop," Trick said. He was leaning out a second-floor window, pointing a large handgun at her. "Who the hell are you?"

"Brandy Valentine, from the Buzzard," Amanda said, still panting. "Trick, I have a message from Pablo. You better let me in."

"I don't think so. You're one of Pablo's little friends, aren't you? So how is Pablo, anyway? Is he standing next to the door where I can't see him, or around the corner of the house? Hiding behind a parked car? That would be cute. Just like Pablo."

"Trick, he's not here, really. He sent me to warn you—the cops're coming here. If you still have, you know, the scientist, you'd better do something about it."

Trick looked thoughtful.

"That's nice of Pablo. Very considerate. I guess I better let you in. Wait right there." He disappeared from the window. In a minute she heard the sound of chains rattling behind the door; then it swung open. Trick was nowhere in sight.

"Step inside," she heard him say. "Shut the door behind you."

She stepped inside. All the lights in the place seemed to be blazing. To the left a pair of large suitcases and a backpack slumped at the foot of a staircase. To her right was the living room. The furniture was arranged in a neat conversation circle, except for one overstuffed armchair, which was facing her.

The armchair moved toward her. She noticed that a large black pistol was sticking around the left side. This was unusual. Most armchairs didn't have them.

"Lock the door behind you," Trick's voice came from behind the armchair. "Put the chains back on."

"Good . . . ," the armchair said when she had locked up. "Now put whatever it is you're holding on the floor and back away from it. Keep your hands where I can see them."

Amanda had forgotten she was holding the address book. She put it on the floor and backed away until a wall stopped her.

Trick stepped cautiously from behind the armchair, keeping the gun trained on her.

"So, how is it that Pablo is suddenly in the loop with the police? How would he know they're coming here?" Trick said.

Amanda was afraid he would ask that.

"He knows someone on the cops," she said. "He got tipped off."

"Well, if it's so urgent, why didn't he just call?"

"Too easy to trace," Amanda lied snappily. "The cops can monitor cell-phone calls."

"Hmm. So Pablo wants me to leave, right away, before the cops get here?"

Amanda nodded. "He wants you to be sure you have the body where no one can find it," she added, her voice shaking.

Trick stared at her oddly.

"Oh, don't worry about that. No one is going to find Aaron's body."

Aaron. Aaron's body. It sounded so—personal. Amanda felt a breakdown coming on but managed to fight it back.

"Well, you'd better be sure. Pablo doesn't want any of this traced back to him."

"I'm sure he doesn't. And when I run out of the house in a stark panic, Pablo will come over and toss my office, looking for the codes, won't he?"

This wasn't going the way she had planned.

"Codes? I don't know what you're talking about."

"Maybe you don't," Trick agreed. "But Pablo does. He wouldn't find them anyway, but that won't stop him from trying."

"I'm just telling you what Pablo said. He didn't tell me about any codes. I left him at the Buzzard, in Jimmy Cacapoulos's office."

"Well, you could be as innocent as you pretend to be," Trick said. "But it doesn't matter. Whether you know it or not, Pablo is right behind you. And that means I do have to get out of here." Trick thought for a moment, his eyes on the ground.

If I were a guy, this is where I'd jump him, Amanda thought.

As if he read her mind, Trick suddenly snapped back to reality and brought the gun to bear.

"But I can't leave you behind. We need to get to the airport, *tout suite*, but I'm sorry, there's no room for you." He took a step forward, raising the gun like a club. It was obvious he meant to pistol-whip her into oblivion.

"Wait!" Amanda said. She put all the urgency she could into it.

Trick waited.

"I just want to help you," Amanda said desperately. "If you have the body here, I can help you get rid of it. Pablo wants me to do that."

"There is no body here, or anywhere else," Trick said. "Yet." He came another step closer.

"No body? What happened to the scientist? Pablo said you took him out."

"I think I better take you downstairs," Trick said, ignoring her. "This will make too much noise. We don't want to upset the neighbors any more than we have already." He gestured with the gun toward the hallway. "You better put your hands up, I guess. Christ, this is such a cliché!"

Amanda thought so, too, but she raised her hands over her head.

"Come on," he said, waving the gun some more. "Let's go downstairs and get this over with."

"Wait!"

"You already said that."

"I have a confession to make," Amanda said. "I'm not really a stripper."

"Don't put yourself down," Trick said. "I've seen you work. You're pretty good. There are some rough spots, naturally. There are always rough spots. But I could give you some pointers."

"Trick, no, you don't understand me," she said. "I don't mean I can't dance. I mean I'm pretending to be a stripper. But I'm really doing something else."

"That's exactly what I'm afraid of."

"No, Trick, listen to me. I'm not working for Pablo."

Trick stared at her. His face fell apart.

"Shit, you're a cop. Figures. I should never have listened to fucking Pablo. I knew this would never work."

"Trick, I'm not a cop," Amanda said.

"No? You're not a cop? And you're not Pablo's little spy? Then what are you, really?"

Amanda took a deep breath. Where to begin?

The sex video? Chickie? Tony Baloot? The police deciding Aaron did it all himself?

She decided to begin at the beginning, with the start-up, the move to South City, Aaron's suspicious absences and ultimate disappearance.

It took a while.

By the time she had finished the gun was drooping in Trick's hand and he seemed permanently marked by astonishment.

"Wow. That's an amazing story," he said weakly.

"So you see, Trick," Amanda summed up. "Maybe we can help each other."

Trick nodded.

"Maybe we can. You know, I have a confession to make, too," he said. "I have your husband chained up in the basement."

42

The Hammer
Comes Down

Rajiv saw the fare waving at him out of the corner of his eye while getting around a delivery van. Without thinking, he swung the cab into
the curb, narrowly missing an old lady with a wheeled cart full of groceries. She shook her fist at him and yelled in Cantonese, which fortunately he had never learned to speak.

But as the fare stepped out from behind a parked car Rajiv saw that
he had no pants on. The loudly striped boxer shorts could not be mis-
taken for street wear, even in San Francisco. Also, he was not wearing
shoes.

But by then it was too late; the fare had jumped in and slammed the
door.

Rajiv sighed. *Make the best of it,* he thought, *keep a sharp eye out for
funny business.*

"Where are you going?" he asked the pantless fare.

The fare grinned, a horrifying spectacle. It was like looking into a
sea cave filled with monsters.

"Not far," the fare said. Rajiv now saw that he was holding a large pistol in his hand. "Right up this alley here should do it."

.   .   .

Clench climbed out of the cab in front of Trick's San Bruno residence and slammed the driver's door behind him. Since he had neglected to put the transmission in park, the impact was enough to break the cab's inertia and send it rolling slowly down the street. San Bruno is much flatter than many parts of the Bay Area, but there was still some incline.

The cab rolled several blocks without incident, picking up speed. But when it reached the main business district and whizzed through a stoplight, it was broadsided by a SamTrans bus.

The one good result of this collision was that it popped the trunk, giving onlookers a nice view of Rajiv, pantless, shoeless, bound and gagged, curled up on top of the spare tire.

The cabbie's pants were a little snug in the crotch, Clench thought, pulling at them. But a big improvement on being bare-assed. That was so noticeable. And he wanted to look his best for the visit he was about to pay on Trick. He knew how important it was to make a good impression in business.

It looked like somebody was home. Lights blazed out of every window. Good. He hated to be late for the party.

Of course, strolling up to the front door and ringing the doorbell was not the best plan. There was no element of surprise in it. Clench sidled over to the front windows and cautiously peered in.

Bingo. Trick was standing right there, a big, fat gun in his hand, talking to someone he couldn't see. It looked like he was having troubles of his own.

A head-high board fence blocked off the rest of the yard from the street. Over on the driveway side there was some sort of gate. Through the space between the boards Clench could see that it was secured by a big chain and padlock.

I could break that, Clench thought. *But why bother?* He couldn't see or smell any big, angry dogs. He hoisted himself up and clambered over the fence.

Piece a cake.

Clench shuffled around the house, occasionally hoisting himself up on a windowsill and peering in. The windows were pretty high off the ground, but he was able to get a footing on the whitewashed concrete blocks cut to look like stone, that made up the foundation.

The house seemed empty, except for Trick and whoever up front. In one room he saw a big computer on a desk surrounded by piles of paper. That looked promising.

But before he made his entrance, he wanted to make sure there was no way for the bugs to get out of the bottle. He let himself into the small garage in back, breaking the window in the rear door without making too much noise, and quickly disabled Trick's car, ripping off the distributor cap and throwing it in a dark corner.

Back at the house, he identified the telephone box and jimmied it off the wall with a thick, rusty screwdriver he had found in the garage.

There. That was better.

Going back to the room with the computer, he used his new friend, the rusty screwdriver, to let himself in.

43

Curb Service

Tailing cars was another thing Tony Baloot was really good at, and he managed to stay on the Yellow Cab all the way to San Bruno. They were still a few blocks behind when they saw Amanda jump out of the cab and walk down the block.

"Catch her!" Chickie squealed. But before Baloot could bring the Buick up, Amanda had gone up to a house and was pounding on the door.

Baloot pulled the Buick to the curb. He was impressed by the ease of parking in this neighborhood.

Chickie rolled down the window and was about to yell when Baloot put his hand on her shoulder.

He had seen a man with a gun leaning out the upstairs window.

"Don't make any noise."

"Why not?" Chickie said, bouncing on the seat with irritation.

Silently, Baloot pointed to the guy in the window. Chickie put her hand over her mouth.

"Tony, we have to warn her!"

"Keep quiet. You'll screw it up, get somebody shot. Wait until the situation resolves itself. Then we'll do something."

"What?"

"Wait."

They saw the door of the house open and Amanda step inside. No screams, no gunshots.

"You think this is doing something, sitting here on our asses waiting for Amanda to get shot?"

"We'll only make things worse, we go barging in. Just be patient. We'll grab her when she comes out."

Chickie didn't say anything, though she looked deeply unhappy. But there was no way Baloot was walking into a house filled with guys with guns and who knew what else. Maybe the brothers Colley with new boots on.

So they waited.

They were still waiting when another cab pulled up and Pablo Clench jumped out. They watched as he climbed the fence and disappeared.

"Who's that guy?" Baloot asked.

"That's Pablo," Chickie said sadly. "He works for Jimmy Cacapoulos too. I think he's, like, the Colleys' boss." She sniffled. "It doesn't look good for Amanda. We better get in there and help her."

In answer Baloot put the Buick in drive and lurched away from the curb.

"Hey!" said Chickie. She was holding on to her wig with one hand. "Where the fuck are you going?"

"Back to South City while I still can," Baloot said. For a soft, indecisive guy, he seemed very determined. "There is no way I'm going to go walking into a house full of gangsters."

"You just let Amanda walk in there by herself," Chickie said reproachfully. "I can't believe you did that."

"You can't believe? I can't believe I let myself get involved in this at all."

Chickie sat back and watched Tony Baloot maneuver the Buick through the traffic on San Bruno's main street, heading back to South San Francisco. There was some kind of accident with a bus and a cab at one of the intersections that took them forever to get around.

After a while, she smiled uncertainly and slid along the seat, closer to Baloot.

"You know, Tony, I know all this has been tough for you," she said. "And I, like, I'm sorry and everything. I really apologize. And I'd like to make it up to you."

Baloot shot her a contemptuous look. "Oh yeah? And how are you going to do that?"

Chickie grinned broadly, toothlessly.

"Pull the car over, honey, and I'll show you."

Later, driving back to San Bruno and Amanda, Chickie leaned against Tony Baloot, smirking.

"I like the way you taste, lover," she said. "I really do. I'm not just sayin' that."

44

Unchain My Heart

Trick's confession rocked Amanda's world.

"Aaron is in your basement? Chained up? Then he's not dead?"

"He was very much alive last time I saw him," Trick said.

"Everybody told me he was dead," she said, staring sideways into the recent past. "I believed them."

"That's what I wanted everybody to think," Trick said. "But I couldn't do it. Kill him, I mean. It's just not part of my skill set."

"What about me?" Amanda asked. "Were you going to kill me?"

"Well, no," Trick admitted. "I wasn't. But there was no point in telling you that. I wanted to get you downstairs, keep you locked up in Aaron's room, while we went to the airport. I thought you would be more compliant if you actually believed I might shoot you."

"What are you going to the airport for?" Amanda asked.

"Why do people usually go to airports?"

"I mean, where are you going? And who is 'we'?" Amanda said. "Are you kidnapping Aaron again?"

"There's no kidnapping involved this time," Trick said. "Aaron is coming along of his own free will. Well, more or less. But he doesn't want to meet up with Pablo any more than I do. You see, Pablo thinks Aaron is dead. He thinks I killed him. He's probably going to be very unhappy with both of us when he finds out it isn't true."

"Trick," Amanda pointed out, "Aaron isn't going to the airport. He's coming home with me."

"Well, I can see why you might think that," Trick said. "But it leaves me in a very awkward position. You see, Pablo Clench thinks he has a lot of money stashed in some bank accounts I set up for him. He's going to be very exercised when he finds out it isn't there anymore."

"You took it?"

"You bet I did. And I want to stay alive long enough to spend it. I would hate to leave you and Aaron here for Pablo to find, but I'll do it if I have to. So please don't try and stop me."

Amanda looked as if she had every intention of doing just that.

"I have this gun, remember," Trick said, alarmed at her expression.

"Why should I be afraid of you?" Amanda asked. "You just told me you weren't a killer."

"I'm not. But I might be a leg-shooter, or a knee-capper. Think about it. Almost any place I shoot you will be really painful and disabling."

"Trick, just let my husband go," Amanda said. "I won't try and stop you. Just leave Aaron with me."

Trick looked thoughtful. "You don't understand, do you? It's not safe for Aaron here. Once Pablo finds out he's still alive, he's bound to want to finish the job. And when he finds out you're not who you pretend to be, it won't be safe for you, either."

"I'll go to the police. What you guys did was not exactly legal, you know. They'll throw Clench's ass in jail."

"Maybe. And maybe they'll be able to protect you long enough for Clench to come to trial. Maybe they'll station a patrolman outside your house. But Jimmy Cacapoulos has a lot of friends. How'd you like to wake up one morning and find the Colley boys in your bedroom?"

I almost did, Amanda thought. "I'm not worried about that," she lied. "The police can protect us."

"Yeah, right. So you can go into the Witness Protection Program and spend the rest of your life working in a convenience store outside Salt Lake City."

"There are worse ways to live," Amanda said with a conviction she did not feel.

"Well, you can console yourself that it won't come to that. Cacapoulos's friends will find you and take you out before the trial. You can count on it."

"Trick, I just want my husband back."

"Well, you can have him after I'm finished with him," Trick said. "But right now I need him." His eyes widened as a thought came to him. "Do you have your passport with you?"

"No. Why?"

"You have to come with us, that's why. To Costa Rica."

"I can't do that," Amanda said. "I have a child here. A house. Family. I don't want to go to Costa Rica. I just want my life back."

"Shit, I thought it was such a good idea," Trick said. "Well, you leave me no choice. I'm just going to have to lock you up and hope Clench doesn't find you, or burn down the house or something. I hate to do it, but I've got to get out of here before he finds out about the money. I've waited too long already." He waved the gun at Amanda. "Come on, let's go."

This wasn't working, Amanda thought. Somewhere along the line she had lost control of the conversation.

"Wait, Trick."

"You keep saying 'wait.'"

"No, wait, what was that noise?"

"That old trick. I expected better from you."

"No, really, listen."

They listened. In the room just off the hallway a floorboard creaked; there was a muffled bumping sound, then nothing.

They looked at each other.

"Do you have a dog?" Amanda whispered.

Trick shook his head. "Not even a goldfish. We better go have a look." He turned to her with a sketchy bow. "After you."

"The hell with that. You go first. You have the gun."

"That's right, I have the gun. That's why you're going to stay in front of me," Trick said. "Sorry, I know it's not very nice of me. But that's the way it is."

45

Pablo Steps In

The problem here, Pablo Clench thought, as he climbed over the windowsill into Trick's home office, *is that I have a real gun with fake bullets. Trick, on the other hand, has a real gun with real bullets.*

Of course, Trick didn't know about the blanks.

Clench slid the window closed and stared into the room, trying to see through the shadows. Outside the door he could hear Trick and a woman arguing about something. That couldn't go on forever. Either they'd work it out or somebody would get shot. Either way worked for Pablo; though, on the whole, he preferred shooting. He would have only one person to deal with then.

As Clench's eyes adjusted he began to make out pieces of furniture and the layout of the room. Not much in it. No good place to hide. The computer was the largest piece of furniture in the room, right in front of him, balanced on a little table.

Like a fucking safe, Clench thought, *with my money in it. Only the combination's been changed.*

Cautiously, Clench worked his way around the computer. A board creaked beneath his foot; shifting his balance, he gave the side of the computer a little hip check, nothing much. But in the silence it sounded like a bass drum. Clench froze. Trick and whoever had stopped arguing outside, probably listening, waiting for the next little giveaway.

As quietly as he could, he crept back behind the computer.

Trick prodded Amanda in the back with the gun.

"Go on, open it," he said.

Amanda turned the knob and pushed the door open, fully expecting to see Pablo Clench standing there with a machine gun.

But the room was empty. Well, it was hard to tell, really, since it was so full of shadows. But it looked empty.

"It's dark," she pointed out.

"The light switch is on the left," Trick whispered. She flicked the lights on, revealing a small room with nothing much in it besides a computer on a small desk, an office chair, and a library table stacked high with documents and notebooks that looked vaguely familiar. There were more notebooks and papers stacked on the floor under and around the table.

"Nobody here."

Trick let out a sigh of relief.

"Well, I didn't think there would be," he lied.

Amanda went over to the table piled high with papers and began leafing through them.

"What's all this? It looks like Aaron's stuff."

"It is," Trick said. "I was supposed to get rid of it, I guess, after Pablo sold the bot formula. But I never got around to it."

"Is it all here?" Amanda asked.

"Most of it. Except for the stuff MacBlister took to sell, of course."

MacBlister. Amanda knew the creepy little lab rat was part of Aaron's disappearance.

"Where is MacBlister now?" she asked.

Trick shrugged. "Aaron thinks he was eaten by robots in Southeast Asia somewhere. I suppose that could be true."

"If Aaron says that, it probably is true."

"I know what you mean," Trick said. "He's quite a guy, your husband. Not a great chess player, though."

Not so great at marriage, either, Amanda thought.

"I'm glad you kept this, Trick," she said. "Aaron's work is the most important thing to him."

After sex, they both thought simultaneously.

"Yes, I kept his little chemical things, too—the bottles? Whatever he has in them. And the early nanobot swarm, too—Pablo sent those over."

"Listen to you," Amanda smiled. "*Nanobot swarm.* You've been talking to Aaron."

"A lot," Trick admitted.

"Were you just going to leave all Aaron's stuff here when you went to Costa Rica?"

"When I *go* to Costa Rica," Trick corrected. "It's way too much to take. But Aaron can get it when he comes back. I'm only going to keep him long enough to protect myself."

Trick put the gun down and picked up a small notebook, a school composition book like the one containing the secret of the nanobots.

"Look at all this work," he marveled. "It's amazing he had time for it."

"Praise Jesus. I thought you'd never put that fucking gun down," someone said—not Amanda.

Pablo Clench suddenly stood up behind the computer table. There was a large black automatic in his hand.

"Hey, Trick, how're tricks?" he said. "Hey, Slim—should I call you Amanda now, or are you sticking with Brandy?"

. . .

Clench was in a bad mood, even for him. Squatting behind the computer desk for what had seemed like hours had put a big strain on his muscles—he was stiff and achey.

And now he was holding down on a pair of assholes with the key to ten million bucks—with a magazine full of blanks.

Oh, well, he thought, *they don't know that. It won't be the first time I bluffed on a shitty hand.*

"So, Trick, first thing you should do," Clench said, "reach over and hand me that gun of yours—by the barrel, please. And slow, or you'll make me nervous."

"We wouldn't want that," Trick muttered. He reached over— slowly—picked up the gun by the barrel, and handed it to Clench, who accepted it graciously and pointed it at them as he stuffed the gun he had been holding into his jacket pocket, and switched Trick's gun to his right hand.

Clench smiled. Both Trick and Amanda looked away.

"So here we all are, together again," Clench said. "I think that's great. I missed you guys, you know? It's just not the same around the club anymore, with everybody gone. And you know something else, Trick? I miss that ten million dollars you stole from me."

"*Ten* million?" Amanda said. "I thought it was *two* million."

"You must have been talking to the Colleys," Clench said. "They can't count to ten, so they settled on two million. But I'm going to have to take the whole thing."

"Have you seen Billy?" Amanda asked.

"Yeah, Billy and I had a talk," Clench said. "He's a hothead, and tends to blow things out of proportion. But he's come down to earth by now, I think. He just has to pull himself together. But enough chitchat." Clench waved the gun in the direction of the computer terminal. "Fire that guy up and give me my access codes. The right ones this time. Then we can all get out of here and go home."

"I am home," Trick pointed out.

"Not yet," Clench said, "But you will be. Now get to work, before I start shooting your toes off."

After a very brief hesitation—he had a close attachment to his toes and other body parts—Trick leaned over and turned on the computer. He looked up at Clench.

"May I sit down?"

"Be my guest." Clench backed over to the other side of the room. He kept the gun trained on Trick.

Amanda shifted her weight slightly, thinking about moving closer to the door. But Clench missed nothing.

"Hey, Slim," he said, "you better get over there and lie on the floor."

Reluctantly, Amanda shuffled over to the far end of the room, but didn't lie down.

Clench didn't insist. He was focused on the computer now. Trick was staring at the screen and rattling the keyboard.

"Come on, fuckhead," Clench urged. "I don't have all night."

"Web site's down," Trick said. "I can't get a connection."

Fuck, Clench thought. *Should of thought of that when I jimmied the phone line.*

"You have a copy for yourself, don't kid me," he told Trick. "I know you're not going to let all that info float around the Web without keeping a backup. Right?"

Trick was silent, staring at his keyboard.

"So give it to me," Clench said.

"Why would I do that?"

"Well," Clench said, "if you don't I'll shoot you in the head. Is that incentive enough for you?"

"If you shoot me in the head you'll never get the money. I'm the only person who knows where it is and how to get it."

Clench gnawed his lip. "Good point. But suppose I start with other body parts. Your knee, for example." He pointed the gun at Trick's kneecap and pulled the trigger.

Nothing happened. Frowning, Clench pulled the trigger again. Still nothing.

"I unloaded it," Trick told a baffled Clench. "A fully loaded gun is just an accident waiting to happen."

"Trick!" Amanda said. "You were bluffing me!"

"Totally," Trick agreed. Then he fell out of the office chair as Clench brought the pistol down on the back of his head.

"Still works," Clench said to no one in particular.

The sound of the door slamming behind Amanda was as loud as a gunshot.

46

The Resurrection
of Aaron Rogell

Find Aaron, Amanda thought, as she stepped out of her shoes and ran from the computer room. *That's first. Second: Kill Clench. Somehow. Or just disable him, not kill him.*

Really fucking disable him.

But first find Aaron. Together they would have a better chance.

Trick had said Aaron was chained up in the basement. The door in the middle of the hall had a basement door look to it. She hoped it wasn't locked.

It wasn't. A flight of stairs led down into the dark. As quietly as she could, Amanda stepped down and eased the door shut behind her. There was no lock on it as far as she could tell.

Slowly, testing every step, she went down the stairs.

It was dark. Totally dark. Amanda stepped across the cold concrete at the foot of the stairs, feeling in front of her in the pitch black until a wall stopped her. Then she felt her way along it.

Her foot struck against something. Reaching down, she felt something cold and smooth. A tarp. Running her hands along it she felt something underneath it, something hard. Not a body, she thought with relief. Not Aaron, chained up and dead.

With some trepidation, she put her hand under the edge of the tarp and felt around. Her hand came up against a bottle. Lots of bottles. A pile of empty bottles that shifted with a soft clinking as she ran her hand over it. She had discovered Trick's stash of empties.

Amanda continued to work her way along the wall, bumping into things occasionally—she stubbed her toe on something hard and metallic, and almost bit her tongue off to keep from crying out—until she found herself back at the stairs.

She kept going—there was nothing else to do. She knew Aaron was down here somewhere, she could feel him, or thought she could. And she knew damn well that Clench was padding around upstairs, looking for her. By this time he may even have reloaded the gun.

The concrete wall she was following seemed to jut out into the main basement. That was hopeful. Then in the middle of the wall her fingers touched a doorknob. Heart in mouth, she turned it.

Locked. The door was locked. She knew Aaron was on the other side. Forgetting to be quiet, she grabbed the doorknob with both hands and rattled the door in its frame. It didn't budge. But it made a hell of a racket.

Oh shit, she thought. *What have I done now?*

Trick's house was as lit up as a soundstage. *Trick's going to hate that electricity bill*, Clench thought as he strode through the brightly lit rooms. He pulled down curtains, flung open doors, looked under beds. Nada. Little Miss Scientist-Stripper-Bitch was nowhere.

Clench hoped Amanda would try for the car in the garage. That would make life simpler. But the back door was still locked. None of the windows was open.

Fuck, Clench thought. He raced for the front door, but all the chains were still in place.

Frozen with indecision, Clench listened. Dead silence; no footsteps, no heavy breathing, nothing.

Slim had vanished.

Then, he heard a rattle down in the basement, like someone tugging on a locked door.

Bingo.

Clench carefully opened the door to the basement. When nothing jumped out at him he reached in and felt around for the switch. The basement suddenly flooded with light.

Warily, he crept down the stairs, wishing he had taken the time to find Trick's ammo and reload the gun. But just maybe the weak-livered faggot had flushed them down the toilet or something, and he'd be wasting his time.

Oh, well, Clench thought, *I'll just have to use my bare hands.*

In fact, he looked forward to it.

At the foot of the stairs he looked around. Nothing much to see: some rusty shit, an old lawnmower, a dead furnace. In one corner there was a big pile of something, a blue plastic tarp over it. Big enough for someone to hide under; better check it out.

Then he saw something better.

A door. A door in an unpainted concrete block wall that stuck out into the main basement.

Quickly, Clench scoped out the rest of the basement. Nothing—no windows, much less another door. He had her trapped.

The door was locked, of course. That was funny.

"Come on, Slim, unlock the door," Clench called out. "You know I'm not going to hurt you. I just want my money."

No answer. He didn't really think there would be, but it was worth a shot. You can never tell how dumb people will be.

Not in the mood for subtlety, Clench kicked the door out of its frame. Then he stepped back, his face screwed up against the horrible fug of alcohol, urine, and funky, dirty human being that came pouring out. It was like stepping into a gorilla house shared by winos.

"Whoa!"

Across the little room, seated in a kitchen chair, staring back at him with wide eyes, was someone who looked like Saddam Hussein when he stepped out of his spider hole. His hair formed a puffy aureole around his head, and a curly silver-black beard hung down, the ends of the mustache wet and sticky from whatever the guy was eating out of a cardboard takeout container.

They stared at each other.

It took Clench quite a while to recognize the guy beneath the filthy clothes and castaway beard.

Holy fuck, he thought. *It's the scientist guy, what's his name?*

Aaron.

He carried that thought with him into oblivion as Amanda stepped around the corner and brought an empty bottle of Early Times down on his head.

Aaron Rogell was really confused now, and thought he was possibly beginning to hallucinate. Something in the food maybe, or maybe just from being locked in a windowless room so long.

Pablo Clench had been replaced in the doorway by his wife, wearing a black wig and holding a broken bottle of Kentucky whiskey by the neck.

Seeing Aaron sitting chained up in a vinyl-covered kitchen chair, covered with hair and smelling like a Dumpster full of week-old drowned dogs, was a complex experience for Amanda. Her first impulse was to rush up to him and embrace him. But the almighty stink wafting off him held her back.

To hell with it. She stepped over the prone Clench and wrapped herself around Aaron.

"Amanda?" Aaron croaked. It would take him a while to come up to speed. "Is that really you?"

"Who else would it be?" *Don't answer that,* she thought.

"Where's Trick?" Aaron asked. "Are the police here?"

"Trick's upstairs," Amanda said. "Clench knocked him out."

"What about the police?"

Amanda shook her head.

"It's complicated," she said. "Aaron, we have to get you out of here. Do you have any idea where the keys to these chains are?"

Aaron was vague.

"Trick has them, I guess. Upstairs somewhere. He never carries them on him."

"Where upstairs?"

"I don't know. I've never been there. Not that I remember, anyway."

Amanda glanced at Pablo Clench. He was sprawled in the doorway, halfway into the room. Blood was dripping off his lacerated scalp and forming a pool on the concrete.

Amanda untangled herself from Aaron and bent over Pablo Clench, feeling his neck for a pulse. He was still alive, anyway. That was a relief. And a disappointment.

Reluctantly, feeling as if she were palpating his interior organs, she went through his pockets, taking out both guns, the silencer, and his wallet. Clench never moved.

Amanda looked desperately around the barren little room for something to tie Clench up with. There was nothing. She stripped off his suit jacket—Clench was limp and unresisting, snoring slightly—and used it to bind his arms together behind his back, putting her foot on the knot and pulling back on the sleeves as hard as she could.

Not very secure, she realized that. But it would have to do.

"Aaron, I'm going to go try and find the keys. If he comes to, yell for me. I'll be right back."

"Do you have to go?" Aaron asked. "Okay, I guess you do, I can see that. But hurry, get these chains off me before he wakes up."

"Don't worry," Amanda said. "Just sit tight." She ran out.

Trick was still unconscious, lying next to the computer where he had fallen. Amanda went through his pockets, found the plane tickets in the inside pocket of his sports coat. No keys.

The computer desk was an old office model that looked as if it weighed half a ton. There were keys in its drawers—lots of keys. It looked as if Trick had kept the keys to every place he'd ever lived in. Amanda took them all.

On the floor, Trick groaned and made swimming motions with his arms and legs. Amanda put her double handful of keys on a corner of the desk, then leaned over and shook him. Was that the wrong thing to do? she wondered. After all, he's been knocked out, not taking a nap.

Trick groaned again. His eyes fluttered open. Suddenly he sat up, clutching his head.

"Trick, are you all right?" Amanda asked. She realized it was a stupid thing to say.

Trick didn't respond.

"Trick, you have to help me. I have Pablo Clench tied up downstairs, but Aaron's still chained up next to him. Which key opens the lock?"

Trick vomited in his lap. That didn't help her much.

"Trick!"

"I need to get some sleep," he muttered, and lay back down.

"Trick, get up! I need you to help me! Trick!"

Trick began to snore loudly.

Just then she heard Aaron shouting down in the basement.

"Amanda! He's awake! He's getting up!"

Oh shit.

"Amanda!" Aaron bellowed. Then there was a confused sequence of sounds, rattling sounds, choking sounds.

That had to be bad. Amanda stood up. When she had come into the room she put the stuff she had taken from Clench's pockets on a corner of the library table next to Aaron's papers. She ran over to them now, then stopped. Which gun was Trick's, the unloaded one, and which one was Pablo's? They both looked the same to her. She picked up the guns in turn and weighed them in her hand. The loaded gun had to be heavier, right?

She heard steps on the stairs, slow, heavy steps, with lots of space between them. Zombie steps. Frankenstein's monster steps.

Out the window, she thought, quick, before he gets here. But that would leave both Aaron and Trick to Pablo's tender mercies, and she couldn't do that.

One gun did seem heavier than the other—or was it just her imagination? She grabbed it up just as Pablo Clench appeared in the doorway.

He was a mess, blood all over one side of his face and running down the front of his shirt. His hair was clotted with blood as well, and sticking straight up, as if the blood were some kind of hair gel. He leaned against the door frame as if he needed both sides to hold him up.

"Hey, Slim," he croaked, smiling crookedly. "Long time no see."

"Stay right there, Pablo," she warned him, raising the gun, holding it with the left hand supporting her right wrist as she had seen policemen do on *Law and Order*. "I *will* shoot."

Clench grinned and kept coming.

Don't close your eyes, Amanda told herself. *Pull the trigger slowly, evenly, don't jerk it.* She aimed at his knee and fired.

Clench didn't seem to notice.

Shit, I must have missed him, she thought. *One good thing about him still walking toward me, though, is that I can hardly miss at this range.*

Sorry, Pablo.

She fired again, this time aiming for the center of Clench's chest.

This time he stopped in his tracks. The smile faded from his face, replaced by a puzzled, surprised look.

Then he grinned again.

"Ow!" he said. "That stings."

Blanks, Amanda thought, *the damn gun must be loaded with blanks.* Still holding the gun out in front of her—it was her only weapon, after all—she began to back away from Pablo, angling toward the door. But Clench moved in quickly. He grabbed her wrists and forced her hands apart, pushing her backwards at the same time.

"You know, I always thought we would end up together," he said.

Amanda, remembering some long-ago self-defense class, tried to knee him in the groin, but he turned his body and took the knee on his thigh. She stomped down, first with her left foot, then her right. But Pablo avoided these moves as well, effortlessly, as if they were dancing.

"It's too bad I have to kill you now," he said.

"Not yet," Amanda said. She turned her face away and fired the gun.

While she and Clench were dancing she had managed to angle the barrel upward, pointing at Clench's face. When the gun went off between them it deafened her, but she was still able to hear Clench howling and cursing. He dropped her wrists and put his hands over his eyes.

"Ahh! My eyes! You fucking bitch, you blinded me!"

Amanda stepped away from him, fumbling with the gun to turn it around and use it as a club.

She needn't have bothered.

Clench, hands still over his eyes, was turning in tight circles in the center of the room. He took his hands down and began to grope around wildly.

"I'm going to fucking kill you, Slim! I'm going to break your fucking neck!"

But before Amanda could get in range to give him a good shot with the gun butt, Chickie's blond, toothless head suddenly materialized behind Clench, floating above him like some kind of street-angel annunciation.

Chickie whacked Clench over the head with a large, painted ceramic statue of a sad bum leaning on a lamppost.

Clench's mouth opened, but no sound came out. He went to his knees, arms at his sides, wavering slightly. Pieces of the shattered bum lay around him in sharp fragments.

Standing behind him was Tony Baloot, holding Chickie around the waist like a ballet partner. He quickly put her down, looking winded.

Chickie wasn't done. Now that she could reach him by herself, she whacked Clench again, right on the back of the head this time, with a large ceramic electric guitar, pale turquoise with green neon strings.

Clench went down hard, face-first into the carpet.

Trick had rejoined the party, wavering slightly. "They were my mom's," he explained to Amanda. "I couldn't bear to get rid of them. I kind of dug the guitar, anyway."

Aaron was a mess. He had spilled cold Thai takeout into his lap, and his neck was still raw and red where Clench had tried to strangle him with the tied-together sleeves of his sports coat.

"He tried to kill me!" Aaron said, still upset. "He pulled his coat off on my neck!"

"Good thing I'm so bad at tying knots," Amanda said.

Trick had hidden the keys to Aaron's chains inside the late-period Elvis bourbon bottle on the mantel—the last of the ornaments from his mother's basement den, emptied long ago. Now he was busy unlocking the leg and wrist manacles that kept Aaron chained to the wall.

"There!" he said as the last manacle clicked open. "Free as a bird!"

Aaron sat in the chair, rubbing his wrists, looking at Trick and Amanda as if he thought they would suddenly pop and vanish like soap bubbles. "Where is Clench now?" he asked.

Pablo Clench was lying conked out on the floor of Trick's study, tied hand and foot with electrical cords. Trick and Amanda, at the mention of Clench's name, looked up at the ceiling, as if Clenchness were dripping through the floorboards, as if they could see his evil aura through the wood and cheap carpet.

"What do we do about Pablo?" Amanda asked. "I mean, we're all implicated, to a degree. Our roles in this won't bear a lot of inspection."

"I'm not," Aaron said. "My role will."

"So long as they can't smell," Trick said. "Come on, we better take you in the backyard and hose you off."

"But what about Clench?" Amanda said.

Trick smiled grimly.

"Don't worry," he said. "I'll take care of Pablo."

Pablo Clench came to with a start and sat upright. His memory was temporarily unavailable; he had no idea where he was or what had happened to him.

A loud banging that could have been coming from inside his skull gradually resolved itself as someone hammering on the other side of the wall. The wall . . . *walls*. There were walls all around him, white walls without windows. They were lit by a single bare lightbulb hanging down from the ceiling on a black electrical cord.

In one wall there was a doorway, filled with boards and pieces of plywood. There was even a door in the doorway, but a horizontal door, nailed over the opening. As Clench watched, the last open space was covered by a piece of plywood. The hammering continued.

Stop the fucking hammering! Clench yelled—or meant to yell: No sound came out of his mouth except for a vague rushing sound, like someone breathing on something before they polished it.

All right, let them hammer. He would deal with the hammering later. There was something else he had to do first, something urgent, if he could only remember what it was.

Kill Slim. That was it. He was going to kill Slim, then Trick. Kill everybody.

Clench tried to stand up. Waves of hot pain sloshed through his head, increasing when he was yanked backwards into the folding chair. It was then that Clench noticed two things:

One, he was attached to the wall, hand and foot, by shiny links of metal chain.

Two, some sort of white powder had spilled all over his legs. *Must of been in my lap, spilled it when I stood up,* he thought.

White shit. The powder looked vaguely familiar, and the spilled container, lying on the floor, its contents spread out on the floor, seemed familiar, too.

The fake blow. Rogell's little robots!

He was chained up in Trick's basement, covered with nanobots.

Clench pounded his legs up and down as if he were running in place, trying to shake the powder off. This was a bad idea: It hurt like fuck, and the white powder flew up in a cloud. He turned his head away as far as he could and tried not to breathe.

So long as I don't get those little fuckers in my lungs I'll be all right, he thought.

The hammering had stopped. Clench almost wished it would start up again; the sudden silence was too intense.

A distant rumbling noise broke through the silence, and Clench felt moving air on his face. He looked up. Directly across the room from him, a grill was set in the concrete block wall. The rumbling, humming sound was coming from the grill, and little metal flaps that had been lying flat a minute ago were now riding on currents of air.

Warm air. And getting warmer by the minute, getting pretty hot.

Trick had turned on the furnace.

47

Home Again

Tony Baloot's '79 Buick may not have looked like much, but it held all of Trick's luggage, Trick himself, Baloot and Chickie, and Aaron and Amanda Rogell.

"Can you make your flight now?" Amanda asked Trick.

"No way," Trick said. "It left hours ago. But there's another flight in a couple hours. Maybe they can put me on that if I whine and make enough of a fuss."

"What will you do?" Aaron asked. "In Costa Rica, I mean."

"Whatever I want," Trick said. He stared at Aaron, unreadable. "Are you sure you won't come? You could probably use a vacation after being cooped up like that."

Embarrassed, Aaron shook his head.

"Thanks, but I want to get back to my work," Aaron said. He glanced guiltily at Amanda. "And my family."

"Bring them along," Trick said. "We can have a blast on ten million dollars."

Chickie turned around and hung over the backseat.

"Woo-hoo! Ten million dollars! Can I come?"

Trick ignored her.

"Trick, what about the house?" Amanda asked. "Are you just going to leave it?"

"It's yours if you want it."

"What would I do with your house?"

Trick shrugged. "Rent it out, burn it down. I don't really care. I'm never coming back."

Tony Baloot pulled into the curb at the airport departures level, hopped out, and made calming motions to the airport cops who immediately began jogging toward him. Together, Aaron and Trick wrestled his luggage out of the trunk.

"Well!" Trick said. "It's been fun. What are you guys going to do now?"

"We'll be okay," Aaron said. "We'll wait till you're in the air to call the cops."

"For all the good they're going to do you." Trick began searching through his pockets, finally finding a bent and dirty business card. Pulling a pen out of his jacket, he scribbled something on the back of the card.

"This is one of my e-mail accounts," he said. "I check it from time to time. If you ever want to get in touch, send me a message."

"Will do." Aaron took the card and put it in his shirt pocket. The three of them stood there silently, staring at each other until Tony Baloot hurried over, followed closely by a gaggle of traffic cops.

"We gotta move," he told them. "They hate me here. They think I'm an unlicensed cab. They're talking big fines and shit."

Trick shook himself.

"Look, I hate good-byes," he said, holding out a hand to each of them in turn. "So don't be strangers, okay? You'll always have a place to stay in Costa Rica."

"We'll take you up on that," Aaron said. "Don't think we won't."

"*Hasta la vista*, guys."

The four of them waved at Trick's back.

None of them said a word until Trick was out of sight, swallowed by the milling airport crowd. Then Amanda turned to Aaron.

"Aaron," she said, in a carefully neutral voice, "we have to talk."

48

Back to Reality

Baloot dropped them at the South City house and smoked off, Chickie on the seat beside him. They seemed eager to leave, but both Amanda and Aaron were sorry to see them go. Neither of them was looking forward to what came next.

Unshaven, filthy, hirsute, Aaron Rogell nevertheless felt worse than he looked. He could barely look up, afraid of accidentally meeting Amanda's eyes.

Amanda meanwhile had jumped off the sofa and was straightening up the room with a threatening briskness.

After a while, hopelessly, Rogell thought he would just get it over with.

"So," he began, "you saw it? The DVD, I mean."

Amanda nodded sharply. There was no need to specify what DVD he was talking about. "I saw it."

"Amanda . . . I'm sorry."

"You son of a bitch," she said levelly, still not looking up from the chair cushion she was plumping for the second or third time. "When I saw those videos I thought I would never be able to trust you again. I thought you'd ruined everything."

"Amanda, I'm sorry, I . . . it was the stress. From the start-up. I don't know what came over me."

"Oh, I think you do. This is your nature. Random fucking, taking chances with your health, my health, the health of your child. This is what you do." She body-slammed the couch cushion into the couch.

Deep down in Aaron's well of misery, a vestigial sense of injustice twitched.

"Well, what about you? From what you tell me, you must have fucked every thug and gangster in the Tenderloin."

Amanda smiled tightly. "Not as much fun as you seem to think."

In fact, she had managed to avoid actually sleeping with any of them, though it was a close call with Billy. Billy wouldn't have been so bad. It would have been like fucking a landmark, a big piece of rock. But not creepy, like Pablo, whose every touch was a kind of molestation.

She knew that, in spite of all his rollicking with goats and strippers and toothless prostitutes, it would devastate Aaron to know that Billy's big hand had touched her naked breast.

Well, let him be devastated. Serve him right.

When it came to sex, she pondered, men seemed stuck in preadolescence.

They were good at killing each other, though.

"Besides, I was doing it for you," she said.

"Huh." This was a proffer, a poker chip of peace. Still smarting from his own criminality, Rogell shoved it away.

"I bet you enjoyed it," he said.

Amanda regarded the couch cushion for a moment before hurling it across the room, where it knocked a framed Matisse print crooked and broke an ornamental porcelain dachshund.

"I could just kill you," she said. There seemed to be a lot of that going around.

"If you just wanted to kill me, why did you come looking for me?"

"Well, the defining moment, for me," Amanda said, "was when I realized I wanted you back more than I wanted to kill you."

Aaron, his one urge to fight back exhausted, hung his head in shame, waiting for the blow to fall.

"And now that I have you back, I'm just going to keep you."

Rogell looked up, unable to process. His mouth hung open, his eyes bugged out. He was not looking his best.

"Amanda! You're not going to divorce me? I thought—"

"Oh, I thought about it, believe me. You rotten son of a bitch. But I love you. Still. After everything. Because you're the father of my child. Because you're my husband. Because I just do."

Amanda came over and sat next to him. She ran her hand along the top of his thigh. Rogell looked at it as if he had never seen a hand before.

"You know, Aaron, that DVD?"

Aaron nodded miserably. "I'm sorry . . . ," he began again.

"That made me so unhappy at first, Aaron," Amanda said. "And so angry. Angry at you. But you know, at the same time . . . I don't know how to put this, exactly."

This was it. The final blow. Rogell trembled.

"But at the same time they made me hot. They were sexy, pornographic. I liked them. I never watched anything like that before. I thought about them a lot. I couldn't stop thinking about them." She paused, looking thoughtful. "Not the goat, though."

"No."

"That was bad," she said. "The poor animal. You understand now that was wrong of you?"

"Yes."

"And the doll—that was just silly. But the other stuff." Amanda's eyes gleamed a little as she replayed Earl's "candid camera" videos in her mind. "I liked it. Aaron, I liked it. It was so—playful. Why didn't we ever do anything like that?"

Aaron gaped. His mouth moved up and down, but only garbled pro-tosounds came out.

"Ab . . . ab . . . ," he said.

Amanda put her hand over his mouth.

"It's not like I forgive you. Asshole. Don't think that. And I'll never forget, not really. But I think we can work something out. Don't you?"

She took her hand away.

"Amanda," said Aaron Rogell. "I—"

"Oh, shut up."

Amanda leaned forward and kissed him.

49

No Fun at All

After months of captivity stress, beatings, chain sores, and Thai takeout every day, Aaron was looking forward to getting back to reality.

But getting back to normal was not as much fun as he thought it would be.

First, the police were not as receptive to his story as he had expected. They seemed politely skeptical, and remained so in spite of Rogell's attempts to convince them. They seemed uninterested in pursuing his leads.

Well, Rogell thought, *they have their pet theory that it was all my fault. People hate to give up their theories.* It was true he had very little proof to back up his story. Not a single participant in the looting of Rogeletek except himself—and Trick, of course, currently unavailable—had survived to testify.

Rogell had to accept not being actively prosecuted as the best outcome under the circumstances.

The physical plant at Rogeletek, meanwhile, was a ruin, the power turned off, the big steel vats filled with a vile protein stew of dead bot embryos, most of the equipment with any resale value stolen, broken glass, papers, and pieces of wallboard strewn over the sodden gray carpet, gang grafitti spray-painted over every blank surface.

His backers were not happy. Not only had the major players withdrawn their promised funds, but a shitstorm of investor lawsuits loomed over the picked skeleton of Rogeletek.

And Vitek, his chief backer, was dead. Someone, thinking he should know the worst, had shown him the goat video.

Meanwhile, Rogell found he had become an international Internet celebrity. Someone—Tony Baloot denied it, but it was hard to think of who else it could have been—had been selling the goat video on eBay, and it—along with most of Rogell's other screen appearances—became a major hit on Xtube. At last count, over two million people had watched him perform with Chickie and her menagerie.

This opened up new career opportunities for him. But it made fundraising difficult.

Whether or not he was the source of Rogell's online fame, Tony Baloot had taken good care of Chickie. In fact, he ended up marrying her. It didn't last, though; a week after the ceremony she took off with his mother's van, a week's receipts from the flower shop, and a barrel of pig noses. The police recovered the van and the pig noses outside Barstow, but the money and Chickie were never seen again.

The molecules formerly known as Aphrodite Anderson had become part of the fuel load in a biodiesel-converted VW Microbus, jamming its way across the desert to Las Vegas. Warren, his credit newly scrubbed, was eager to try his latest system for beating the house at blackjack. This time he was sure it would work.

. . .

Amanda was shocked to find out what had happened to Billy Colley. As she read the newspaper accounts on the Web, she felt tears rolling down her cheeks. She had to close the door and have a good long sob, thinking about him. For a murderous goon with the IQ of grout mold, he had had his good points.

Trick's house had burned to the foundations the day after they had taken Trick to the airport. The fire department blamed the conflagration on a faulty furnace. Efforts to find the owner of record were fruitless.

Luckily no one had been in the house at the time, the firemen reported.

Eventually, the city of San Bruno bulldozed the remains of the house into the foundation and covered it over with dirt so no one would fall into the hole and sue.

Aaron and Amanda Rogell stood on the brown, dead lawn in front of Rogeletek, watching the last very expensive hazmat cleaners drive away. A white van with the simple but effective logo of a nanobot extermination company—a thick, red speed line terminating in a red, stylized fist holding a big hammer—drove by last. The company's name was given in both English and Chinese characters—also big, bold, and red.

"Why not emigrate to China?" Rogell asked sadly. "Everyone else is doing it. That seems to be where all the really important work on nanobots is being done."

"I have a better idea," Amanda said.

"What's that?"

"Let's go to Costa Rica."

"Costa Rica? What's in Costa Rica?"

Amanda felt a little pull of sadness thinking of Billy Colley and his plans. But it would never have worked, even if Billy had survived.

"Trick is in Costa Rica," she pointed out. "Trick, and ten million dollars."

Aaron was doubtful.

"He's not going to be that happy to see us," he said. "He was just saying that to be polite."

"Maybe, maybe not. But I'm sure he'll be happier to see us than to see the U.S. Marshals outside his door. I'm sure he won't mind sharing the ten million dollars with us. He'll probably be glad of the company. You two sort of got along, didn't you?"

Aaron nodded, still doubtful.

"Sort of. I guess I could sell the house—not that we have much equity in it. And I still have the income from the patents. But what would we do in Costa Rica?"

Amanda smiled.

"Do you know what a *finca* is, Aaron?" she asked.

50

Finca Las Cabras

Delia was talking well now, Amanda thought, watching her daughter over the top of her Sunday *New York Times* as the little girl made her way across the patio.

"*¿Mamá, donde es los caramelos?*" Delia asked.

"*Ningún caramelo antes de almorzar,*" Amanda answered. Then, switching to English, "Have you seen your father?"

Trick Fitzpatrick walked in from the garden just then, wiping dirt off his hands. He looked quite the *patrón* in his linen suit and straw panama, Amanda thought.

"*Buen' dias, Señora,*" he said. "I saw Aaron just a minute ago. He said he was going to take the flock up into the pasture today."

The two of them paused and listened. In the distance they could hear the sound of bells—goat bells—which gradually got louder. Finally Aaron appeared, dressed like the farmhands in coarse, white clothes, a big, floppy straw hat on his head. He was leading a flock of Angora goats. Three females, washed, brushed out, belled, and beribboned, followed closely behind Aaron, watching him carefully.

"*Hola,* everybody," he said. "Hey, Deely!"

"Daddy!" She rushed up and hugged his knees.

"Aaron," Amanda asked, "How long do you plan on being gone? We were going to drive into town today. I thought you'd want to come."

Over by the kitchen door three farmhands were standing around, waiting to accompany Aaron on his trek into the hills. One of them was massaging a zucchini with his circled fingers while the other two tried not to look at him. It was painful to watch them trying not to laugh.

When the masseur felt Amanda's eyes on him, he stopped and put the zucchini in his pocket.

"No, go ahead without me," Aaron said. He rarely left the finca any more. "I'll see you this evening when you get back. Trick, don't forget our game!"

"I wouldn't miss it for the world," Trick said.

"Tonight's the night," Aaron said. "Get ready to lose big time."

"In your dreams," Trick said.

51

Something Out There

The climate in San Francisco never heats up much, especially in summer. Global warming may change that, but so far, temperatures above ninety degrees are rare.

They do happen, though, usually during September and October's weeks of Indian summer. But they happen too infrequently for anyone to notice a correlation between super hot days—above 98.6—and the disappearances South of Market, and in South City's industrial park. No one ever notices when street people vanish, of course, but occasionally a highway worker or a dog walker from one of the new condo complexes will disappear into thin air and get onto the news cycle for a while.

The disappearances are happening less often, so maybe the remnant bots are being used up. Some day they'll all be gone.

But, while the official news media have never made the connection between high temperatures and missing persons, the word on the street is more definitive:

Something is out there, people say. Don't fall asleep under a freeway overpass on a hot day, or you may never be seen again.